FOREWORD

It has been five years since *Behaving Badly* was first published in the U.S. Since then I've written three more novels, and so the story of animal behaviourist Miranda Sweet had naturally gone to the back of my mind. I'd come to regard the novel as an old friend, to whom I'd once been very close, but whom I now saw only from time to time, in a bookstore or a library, or flashed up on Amazon. So when I learned that Mira Books had decided to reissue *Behaving Badly* it was a wonderful surprise. My previous novel, *Rescuing Rose,* had been about an agony aunt, or "Dear Abby." I decided that my next heroine would be another agony aunt—but this time one for animals and pets. By then animals had become quite a feature of my novels. I'd always loved writing about animals, because they present an opportunity not just for humour, but also for poignancy, as they're such a touchstone for human feeling. I'd also observed with interest the rise of the animal behaviourist as a popular cultural figure. In the early noughties there were many newspaper and magazine articles about animal behaviourism, and a number of popular TV series devoted to it, too. And all made the same, crucial point: that an animal behaviourist first has to understand the *human* before he or she can begin to work out the pet. So I began my research, talking to animal behaviourists about how they can help curb domineering behaviour in dogs, or inappropriate territory-marking in cats, excessive anxiety in rabbits or feather-plucking in parrots.

But I was also trying to decide the human dimension to the story, and I decided that "behaviour" would be its main theme. So I came up with a heroine, Miranda, an animal behaviourist whose own past behaviour leaves much to be desired: when she was sixteen she was part of an animal rights group that did something bad, and it led to a young man, David, being hurt. I then had Miranda by chance meet David, now a successful photographer. Miranda resolves to confess to David, and to seek his forgiveness; but to her dismay, she realises that she's falling in love with him. Fearing that he'll reject her, she therefore hesitates to tell him the truth.

I then perceived the book as being about courage—moral courage of the kind that Miranda will need to show, and physical courage, too. Miranda's best friend Daisy happily bungee jumps and hang glides and rock climbs, but cannot find the courage to confront her own long-term boyfriend, Nigel, about his failure to commit. Miranda's former fiancé, Alexander, is extremely brave—in the swashbuckling TV dramas he stars in, that is; in real life he shows a dreadful lack of guts. Then there's the TV stuntman Marcus, who comes to Miranda's weekly "puppy parties" with his Jack Russell terrier, Twiglet. Marcus happily throws himself off tall buildings and drives cars across canyons, but can't find the courage to ask Daisy on a date.

My final, and perhaps most important theme, is that of redemption and forgiveness. Will Miranda's mother, bitterly divorced from Miranda's father, be able to forgive him? Will David forgive Miranda once he finds out who she really is? Will Miranda forgive Alexander for his terrible desertion of her? There are frequent references to Shakespeare's *The Tempest,* because that wondrous play is all about forgiveness and teaches us that "the rarer action is in virtue than in vengeance." Miranda seeks to be redeemed, but first needs to be forgiven. She also needs to forgive the grave wrongs that have been done to her. *Behaving Badly* is a romantic comedy with a moral dilemma at its heart. It teems with animals—rabbits and guinea pigs, cats and dogs, parakeets and ponies, not to mention a herd of llamas. Ultimately, though, it's a very human tale, one that I very much hope you'll enjoy.

Isabel Wolff, London, 2011

ISABEL WOLFF
behaving badly

MIRA

ISBN-13: 978-0-7783-1284-0

BEHAVING BADLY

Copyright © 2003 by Isabel Wolff

First published by HarperCollins Publishers

Recycling programs
for this product may
not exist in your area.

For questions and comments about the quality of this book please contact us
at Customer_eCare@Harlequin.ca.

www.Harlequin.com

Printed in U.S.A.

First Printing: July 2006
10 9 8 7 6 5 4 3 2 1

For Greg

Courage is the price that life extracts for granting peace.
—Amelia Earhart

—— CHAPTER 1 ——

'Will you be all right now, Miranda? Miranda…?'

I slowly surfaced from my reverie.

'What?'

'I said will you be all right now?' repeated Clive, my builder. Would I be all right now? I considered the question. I wasn't at all sure that I would. 'It's just that I've got to be in Barnes by five,' he explained, as he began to gather up his emulsion-spattered sheets. 'So if it's all the same with you…' I banished painful thoughts and forced myself to concentrate.

'Oh. Yes. Of course. You want to go.' I glanced round my new workplace—my new workplace and my new home too. In three weeks Clive had transformed six St Michael's Mews from a semi-derelict shell into a smart office with a small living space on the floor above. The estate agent had negotiated a reasonable rent—reasonable by Primrose Hill standards at least—on condition that I refurbish it myself.

'Thanks, Clive,' I said. 'It looks wonderful.'

He pursed his lips judiciously, then pressed a crumpled hanky to his neck. 'Yeah…well, I'm pretty pleased myself. I've checked the electrics,' he added as I reached for my bag, 'and I've been over the roof again and it's sound. Is there anything else needing doing?'

I scribbled out the cheque, sinkingly aware that it represented the last of my savings. 'No. I don't think so. It all looks…great.' I surveyed the newly egg-shelled walls and gleaming skirting boards, and flicked the downlighters on and off. I raised then lowered the green micro blind and tried the drawers in my new desk. I examined the joins in the new wooden flooring and made sure that the security locks on the windows all worked.

'Have you got enough bookshelves?' he asked as he packed away his paintbrushes. I nodded. 'Well then, if you're happy with it all, I'll be off.'

I glanced again at my final checklist. 'Actually there is one last thing—the sign.' I picked up the ceramic plaque I'd had specially made and handed it to him. 'Would you put it up for me?'

'Sure.' We stepped outside, shielding our eyes against the glare of the midsummer sun. 'You can't start your new business without this, can you?' said Clive, affably. He pulled a pencil from behind his right ear and made rapid marks on the walls; then he began to drill, a slender avalanche of pink brick-dust drifting to the cobbled ground.

'Got enough punters?' he enquired as he screwed in the plate.

My stomach did a flick-flack. 'Not quite.'

'Don't worry,' he reassured me. 'You will. There. That's it, then. All done.' He took a step back as we appraised it. 'Perfect Pets', it announced, above a stylized drawing of a dog on a psychiatrist's couch. Beneath, in smaller letters: 'Miranda Sweet BVSc, Animal Behaviourist'.

Clive beeped open the doors of his van. 'I know a few people who could do with your services,' he said as he slung his equipment inside. 'My neighbours for a start. They've got this Labrador. It's lovely, but it's barking mad.' He shook his head. 'Literally. Barking. That's all it does, all day.'

'Poor thing. It's probably being left on its own for too long so what it's doing is calling its humans back.'

'I dunno what it's doing,' he shrugged as he opened the driver's door. 'All I know is it sends me and the wife up the wall. Anyway, give me a bell if you run into any problems Miranda, otherwise...' he got behind the wheel, '...good luck. Take care of yourself,' he added solicitously as he ignited the engine. 'You take care now.'

'Thanks, Clive.' I smiled. 'I'll try.'

Clive swung right out of the Mews onto Regents Park Road, then tooted twice in cheery valediction and was gone. I glanced at my watch—it was ten to four. Daisy would be arriving soon with Herman. She'd been looking after him for nearly a month. She'd been wonderful since 'it'—as I had now come to think of it—happened. Without her, I don't know what I'd have done...

As I wiped the paint splashes off the windows I wondered how Herman would react to being with me again. Apart from the odd visit I'd hardly seen him, so he'd probably be cool and remote. He'd make it quite clear that he felt I'd neglected him, which of course I had. But I hadn't been able to cope. It was the shock. The Never-Saw-It-Coming-in-a-Month-of-Sundays unexpectedness of it all. Not just the end of my relationship but the *way* it happened—the knowledge that I'd got Alexander so wrong. As an animal behaviourist you have to be able to read *people* as well, but with him I'd clearly missed something big.

As I scratched at the glass with my thumbnail I glanced at the other businesses in the Mews. There was the cranial-sacral therapy centre at the far end, and that aromatherapist at number twelve. There was an osteopath two doors down, and a hypnotherapist at number ten. With a chiropractor directly opposite, and a Chinese herbalist at number nine, St Michael's Mews was an oasis of alternative therapeutics and was therefore the perfect location for a business like mine.

I'd discovered it in late April. Alexander and I had been invited to have dinner with Mark, a TV director friend of his, to celebrate the end of *Land Ahoy!*, a lavish period drama—a bit like *Hornblower*—in which Alexander had had his first starring role. And now I thought, with a dragging sensation, of how it would soon be screened. Would I be able to bear watching it? Would I be able to bear watching *him*? No. The thought of it made me feel sick… Anyway, Mark had booked a table at Odettes, in Primrose Hill, and Alexander and I had arrived too early so we'd gone for a walk. As we strolled up the hill, hand in hand, we talked about how *Land Ahoy!* might transform his career, then as we walked back down we discussed my work. And we were speculating about where I might have my new animal behaviour practice, and what I might call it, when we suddenly turned into St Michael's Mews. I was struck by the tranquil atmosphere, and by the fact that it didn't look polished and affluent, like so many London mews do; it looked Bohemian, and slightly unkempt. Then, above the door of number six, I saw a 'To Let' sign. It was as though I'd been hit over the head.

'This would be perfect,' I'd said, as we peered through the cracked windowpane into the dusty interior. 'Don't you think so?'

'Well, it's a good location.'

'And there's that pet shop over the road, and loads of people round here have animals, and the Hill's just a few yards away. This would be the *perfect* place for my new practice,' I reiterated happily.

'Then you should call it Perfect Pets.'

'Okay—I will.'

I hadn't imagined for a minute, as I'd stood there exclaiming over its suitability and writing down the estate agent's number, that it would soon also be my home. I'd only recently moved in with Alexander and we were very happy— in fact, so happy that we'd just got engaged. We'd planned to stay in his flat in Archway for the time being, then buy somewhere together, later on. But, just over a month ago, 'it' happened, and, overnight, everything changed…

I went back inside, inhaling the citrussy aroma of fresh paint, and continued unpacking. I don't have much stuff. I've no furniture because I've never owned my own place; all I have is my clothes, some kitchen things and my books.

From one box I pulled out *The Expression of the Emotions in Man and Animals* by Charles Darwin, and Lorenz's *On Aggression*—a classic text; *Readings in Animal Psychology* by Justin Lyle, and *Why Does My Rabbit…?* by Anne McBride. I unpacked all my thirty or so books on animal behaviour, and all my old veterinary textbooks as well; and as I arranged them on the shelves I thought, yet again, how glad I was that I was no longer a vet. I'd always wanted to be one—from about the age of eight onwards—I never considered anything else. I studied veterinary medicine at Bristol, then practised for five years, but disillusionment soon began to set in. I don't quite know when it started, but it crept into my soul like damp, and I'd realized that living out my childhood dream wasn't going to be quite as fulfilling as I'd thought. It wasn't so much the long hours—I was young enough to cope—it was the constant emotional stress.

Of course it was wonderful to make a sick animal well. To see a cat arrive in a bad way, its family in floods, and to be able to put that cat right. But too often it wasn't like that at all. The way people expected me to produce miracles, the hysterical late-night phone calls—I couldn't sleep. The way some people—especially the rich ones—would complain about the costs. But worst of all, I couldn't stand it when I had to put an animal to sleep. Not so much the very old ones, or the terminal cases—my training had prepared me for that. No, it was when people asked me to put down young, healthy animals—that's what I couldn't take. That's how I got Herman.

I was working in East Ham as a locum, and one morning a permatanned-looking woman of about forty came in with this miniature dachshund—a smooth-haired black and tan male, about a year old. It looked worried, but then dachshunds always do look worried—it's their natural expression—as though there's just been a stock-market crash. But this particular dachshund looked as though the world was about to end, which, in fact, it was. Because when I lifted it onto the table and asked what the problem seemed to be, the woman said that it had just 'savaged' her child and that she wanted it to be put down. I remember looking at her, shocked, and asking what exactly had taken place, and she explained that her five-year-old daughter had been playing with it 'very nicely' when it had suddenly given her a 'nasty nip' on the hand. When I asked her whether the child had needed stitches, she admitted that she hadn't, but said that the 'vicious little bugger' had 'drawn blood'.

'Has he ever done such a thing before?' I enquired, as the dog stood on the table, radiating—appropriately, as it happened—an air of tragedy.

'No,' she conceded. 'It's the first time.'

'And you want me to destroy it?'

'I do. Otherwise it could happen again, couldn't it, and it could be worse next time. I mean, you can't keep a mad dog, can you?' she sniffed. 'Not with kids about. And if it isn't my kid, it could be someone else's, and then I'll end up in court.'

'I do understand your anxiety, but did you see what happened?'

'Well, no. I mean, not as such. I heard Leah scream, then she comes running into the kitchen, crying her little eyes out, saying the dog had bitten her hand. It just turned on her,' she added vehemently—'like *that!*'—she clicked her taloned fingers by way of demonstration. 'It's probably got some bad strain. I never wanted a dog in the first place, but my husband got it off a friend of a friend. He paid four hundred quid for it,' she muttered bitterly. 'And they swore that dachshunds are good with kids.'

'Well, they usually *are* good with children. They're very sweet-natured.'

'Look, I'm not taking no chances, and that's that. It's not biting any child of mine and getting away with it,' she added indignantly.

'But there are rescue homes, I feel it's unfair—'

'But who'd want a dodgy dachshund? My mind's made up,' she said, as she snapped open her handbag. 'You just tell me how much.' And I was just about to go and consult the Principal Vet because I really didn't want to do it, when I noticed that the dog was whining quietly and shaking its head. I lifted up its ear flaps and looked inside. Embedded in its left ear was the broken-off end of a child's knitting needle.

'*Jesus,*' I breathed. Holding the dog firmly, I gingerly removed it, then held it up. 'This is why he bit your daughter.'

The woman stared at it, mutely. 'Oh. Well…as I say, she was playing with the dog, wasn't she? She was just playing. She's only five.'

'But can you imagine how much that must have hurt?'

'He still shouldn't have bitten her though, should he?'

I felt my jaw slacken. 'What *else* was he supposed to do? Write her a solicitor's letter? Ring the RSPCA? He's a *dog*. He did what any dog would do.'

'Yes, but—'

'There *isn't* a but! That's dog behaviour. If we annoy them enough, they'll probably bite. What would you do if someone stabbed *you* in the ear? I imagine you might react!'

'I want it put down,' she insisted, jabbing a bejewelled finger at me. 'It's my dachshund and I want it put down.'

'No,' I said firmly. 'I won't. I refuse to murder your dog,' I added politely. She looked extremely offended at that; and she said in that case she'd take it to another vet's. But I was one step ahead. I calmly pointed out that there was absolutely no need to 'try her luck elsewhere', because I'd be more than happy to keep it myself. She hesitated, then, giving me a look which combined hostility with shame—an unusual mixture—she left. She'd never even told me the dog's name. So I called him Herman. Herman the German. That was four years ago.

The saddest thing of all was Herman's distress at her departure—he whimpered inconsolably after she'd left. He might not have felt quite so upset if I'd been able to apprise him of the awful truth.

'Don't waste your tears,' I told him. 'She didn't deserve you. You're going to be a lot better off with me.' Within a week Herman seemed to think so too, for he seemed grateful for my care and we'd started to bond, and we've been pretty inseparable ever since. But it was saving him from a premature end which got me thinking seriously about changing career. I'd already noticed how, in most cases, it isn't the animal which has the 'problem', it's the *humans*—and I realized how interesting it could be working with that. A week later I went to a lecture given by a vet who'd retrained as a behaviourist, and I decided that that was what I would do too. I'd still be working with animals, just as I'd always wanted, but without the relentless pressure and stress.

I had no serious financial commitments then, so I used my savings to go back to school. I went to Edinburgh for a year—with Herman—to do an MSc in Animal Behaviour, and I had a fascinating time. We didn't study only companion animals, although that's a large part of it, we studied many other species as well. We learned about primate behaviour, about farm animals, and birds, and deer; and there were lectures on marine animals and zoo animals too. I'll never forget the things we learned. That polar bears are always left-handed, for example, and that chickens prefer pop music to rock. That if you chat pleasantly to a cow it will yield more milk, and that when a cat hisses it's imitating a snake; that ants practise a form of agriculture, and that ravens are as clever as chimpanzees.

When I left I came back to London and began running a behaviour clinic three times a week from a vet's practice in Highgate where I'd once worked. I was amazed at how quickly word got round, and I soon had a steady stream of dysfunctional Dobermans and stressed-out Siamese. I began to get good results. I did home visits too, and I set up a website where people could ask for my advice, free of charge. Then, just over a year ago, I got this big break.

I was contacted by a TV researcher who asked me whether I'd be interested in being an expert on a new series called *Animal Crackers*; so I was screen tested, and got the job. They'd been looking for someone young, knowledgeable, female, and tele-genic, which people kindly say I am. Not that I'm glamorous; I'm much too short for a start, I rarely wear make-up, and I keep my fair hair in a boyish crop. But I think I came across well because I felt confident—I knew what I was talking about. I'd do two sections in each programme, in which I'd analyse the problem then return ten days later to see whether my advice had worked. There were some very interesting cases—a police dog that was terrified of thunder, and a cat that went berserk when the TV was on. There was an irritable iguana—it was having romantic problems—and a pony which refused to be caught.

To my surprise, there was quite a buzz about the series. Someone wrote an article about me in the *Mail*, describing me as 'Miss Dolittle', which was just plain silly. I do not talk 'to' animals—I merely think *like* them—and there was a similar piece in *The Times*. But the exposure brought in new clients, so I decided I ought to have my own premises—which is how I found St Michael's Mews…

From outside I heard the crunch of tyres on the cobbles as a car pulled up. There was the soprano beep of central locking, then rapid tapping.

'Mir-an-da! It's only me-ee.' I slid back the chain and opened the door.

'Wow!' Daisy's large brown eyes were shining with enthusiasm. 'What a great place!' I've known Daisy for fifteen years—we shared a flat at Bristol—and what I love about her is that she's always upbeat.

'This looks *so* great!' she repeated as she came inside, cradling Herman over her left shoulder like a baby. 'It's spacious, isn't it? And so light! Your builder's done a fantastic job.'

'He has.'

'And the Mews is gorgeous.'

'It is.'

'It looks rather friendly.'

'It seems to be. The aromatherapist and the osteopath have already introduced themselves, and the others all smile.'

'I've always wanted to live in a mews—lucky you. You'll

feel safe here,' she added, tucking a hank of glossy dark hair behind one ear. I nodded. 'And is that Herman on the plaque?'

'Of course.'

'He's been dying to see you again—haven't you, Herman? Say hello to your mummy, poppet.' Herman gave me a baleful stare.

'Hello, Herman,' I said, as Daisy put him in my arms. 'Have you missed me?' The two tan points above his eyes twitched and pleated into a deep frown, then he emitted a grumbly sigh. 'He's cross with me,' I said as I cuddled him. 'It's all the disruption. He'll come round in a bit. I'm sorry I neglected you, Herman,' I added quietly. 'But, you see… the thing is,' I felt my voice catch, '…things have been a bit tough.'

'Are you okay?' asked Daisy softly. I nodded, but Herman's foxy little face had blurred. 'Now don't worry, Miranda,' I heard Daisy murmur as I sank onto a chair. She unzipped her bag. 'You mustn't worry because even though it's all been horrible and you've had this awful, *awful* shock, I just know you're going to be fine. Isn't she, Herman?' she added brightly, as she pushed a tissue into my hand. I pressed it to my eyes, breathed deeply a few times, then felt my panic subside. On Herman's face was his habitual expression of exaggerated anxiety. It made me suddenly smile.

'Thanks, Daisy.' I blew my nose. 'And thanks for taking care of him,' I added, as I put Herman down and he began to sniff the new floor.

'Oh, he was no trouble at all. He came to work with me most days.' Daisy works for 'The Aid of the Party', an event and wedding planners based in Bloomsbury. 'The clients *loved* him—and when I couldn't look after him I took him round to my mum. She adored having him, and she was really sorry about… Well, she was really sorry.'

'You didn't *tell* her, did you?'

'No. Of course not.'

'Good. What did you say?'

'I just told her that you'd broken up with Alexander, that you were camping here while the work was being done, and that it was a…difficult time.'

'That's fine. You're the only person who knows,' I added quietly, as she put down her bags.

'Don't worry—my lips are sealed. But didn't you even tell *your* mother?' she asked as she sat down. I shook my head. There are so many things—huge things—that I've never told her. I'm too ashamed, so I've bottled them up. 'But why not?' Daisy asked, looking puzzled.

'Well, because she's rather jaundiced about marriage, so I knew what she'd say. I just told her the engagement was off. She mostly seemed relieved that she wouldn't have to see my dad again.'

'But didn't she want to know *why* it had ended?'

'She didn't, actually. But then she's always so busy—you know how it is. What with three teenage girls to look after, not to mention the boys.'

Daisy nodded diplomatically. 'Of course…the boys…'

'Anyway, the fewer people who know, the better I like it.'

'But it's not as though *you* did anything wrong.'

'No, but…'

'But what?'

I stared at a rhombus of sunlight on the wall. 'The whole thing makes me feel somehow…ashamed. The thought that I could have made such a mistake.'

'But you couldn't have *known*. You couldn't have known

that Alexander was like…that,' she said delicately. 'He seemed so, well…' she gave a helpless shrug. '*Perfect*.'

'Yes,' I said quietly. 'He did.'

'So not a whisper from him then?' she asked as she took off her cardigan.

'No,' I said bitterly. 'But as we both know it's over, what's the point?'

'I don't blame you,' she agreed. 'Some things one can get over,' she said carefully. 'But I really *don't* see how you could have got over that. Anyway—today's the summer solstice,' she went on purposefully, 'which is a turning point—and this is a turning point for you too. You're about to start a new, busy, *happy* phase of your life, Miranda, and I know it's going to be *good*. Now, will you give me the guided tour?'

I stood up. 'It won't take long—it's a good job Herman and I are both small.' I'm five foot one and a half (at that height, the half matters) and my frame is slight. People often say I'm 'petite' or 'gamine'. Daisy, on the other hand, is five foot eight and rather curvy. At Bristol we were called Little and Large.

Daisy admired the consulting room with its pale beech flooring, and yes, psychiatrist's couch—in a practical beige—then we went into the tiny galley kitchen at the back.

'Sweet garden,' she remarked, as we looked out of the window into the minuscule courtyard. 'It'll look great when you fill it with pots.' Then we went up the narrow stairs. I carried Herman because dachshunds get back problems. 'I like the skylight over the bed,' she remarked. 'Very romantic. You can lie there and look at the stars.'

'I'm not feeling romantic,' I pointed out matter-of-factly.

'Not now. But you will be. One day.' She squeezed my arm. 'You will get over this, Miranda. You're only thirty-two.'

'I feel fifty-two. It's the stress.' And not simply the stress of Alexander, though I didn't say that to Daisy. As I say, I've always bottled things up.

'Thank God the wedding plans weren't very far advanced,' she breathed as she peered into the wardrobe. That was true. Our engagement was so recent that we hadn't got round to putting in the announcement. All we'd done was chosen the ring. Daisy looked in the tiny en-suite bathroom.

'I must say your builder's done a great job. It's enough to destroy all one's prejudices about them.'

'I know. He did it to budget, and on time. He also did loads of extra things, just to help. He assembled my bed, and the desk; he even installed my computer. He obviously felt sorry for me.'

'Did he know what you'd been…?' Daisy's voice trailed away.

'Well…he was too tactful to comment, but I think he could tell.'

'And how are you…feeling?' she added as she sat on the bed.

I heaved a painful sigh. 'Much better than I was.'

She picked up my bottle of sleeping pills. 'Are you still taking these?' I nodded. 'Well, try not to. And you must eat more, you're much too thin.'

'Mmm.' I'm about seven stone at the moment, though I ought to be eight. Interestingly, my size was one of the things that first attracted Alexander to me because he's six foot one, and well built. He loved the fact that I was so small and boyish—he said it made him feel 'manly'. He loved the fact that I came up to his chin. He liked to pull me into him then tuck me right under. I felt as though I were sheltering beneath a huge rock.

'It was…incredible,' I heard Daisy murmur as we went downstairs. 'And what a let-down,' she added indignantly. I shrugged. Men have let me down all my life. 'Anyway, I've brought you some eggs and bread and some tomatoes, and I'm going to make you *eat*.'

As she opened one of the packing crates and found a bowl and a fork, I wondered, as I often do—I simply can't help it—what Alexander was doing now. Just because it's over doesn't mean I don't miss him; and I knew that he'd be missing me. We'd become great friends apart from anything else; we'd had such an easy, almost effortless, rapport.

I'd met him just over a year ago, not far from here, at the open-air theatre in Regent's Park. I went with Daisy and her boyfriend, Nigel, to see *The Tempest*, a play I love. It was one of those magical summer evenings we sometimes get, with a clear sky, and a sliver of moon; and, as dusk descended, the lamps at the edge of the stage began to glimmer and shine. And when Alexander first appeared, as Ferdinand, a slight *frisson* went through the crowd. He looked just so, well, beautiful, I suppose—he has a beautiful face, with full, curving lips that you want to trace with your fingertip, fine cheekbones, dark hair, and blue eyes. I remember the actress playing Miranda declaring him to be a *thing divine*. And he called her *Admired Miranda! Indeed the top of admiration*, as though she were some rare work of art. And, although I hadn't seen the play for years, so many lines from it still stay in my mind. Ariel singing *Full Fathom Five* so hauntingly, Miranda's ecstatic *O brave new world*; then, finally, the wonderful moment when Prospero is redeemed. For instead of taking revenge on his wicked brother, as he'd vowed, he forgave him, because that was the courageous thing to do.

The rarer action is in virtue than in vengeance, he said simply. That made the hairs on my neck stand up. Then he broke his staff, stepped forward, spread wide his hands and asked for forgiveness himself:

As you from crimes would pardoned be,
Let your indulgence set me free.

We were all so spellbound that there was a silence of about ten seconds before the applause began; then, as it finally died away after at least three curtain calls, Daisy said that she wanted to go and congratulate the director, John, who she knew. So we went down to the stage door, and Daisy and Nigel were chatting to John, and I was standing nearby, clutching my programme slightly self-consciously when, to my surprise, I found myself talking to 'Ferdinand'. Or, to be more precise, he began talking to me. And I couldn't understand why he was bothering, because, being so short, I never assume that anyone's even noticed me let alone that they're interested; so I just said how much I'd enjoyed his performance, which of course I had.

'Thank you,' he said, smiling at me in a way which made my face heat up. 'You'd have been a lovely Ariel,' he added suddenly. 'You're so elfin.'

'Oh.' I felt myself blush again. 'It's a…wonderful play… isn't it?' I murmured, trying to cover my discomfiture.

'And what do you think it's about?' He took a pack of Gitanes out of his pocket, and offered me one. I shook my head. What was the play about? And why did my opinion matter? Again, I felt taken aback.

'Well,' I began carefully as he tapped the cigarette on the side of the box. 'It's about penance and reconciliation, isn't it? It's about the search for forgiveness. It's about the hope we all have that we'll be redeemed.' He nodded slowly at that.

The next thing I knew we were all going for a drink—I remember the delicious scent of his cigarette as we strolled through the park; and although there were quite a lot of us I somehow found myself sitting next to Alexander in the pub.

We talked about the play some more, and he told me that Shakespeare actually invented the name 'Miranda' specifically for *The Tempest*, something I'd never known. I'd always known what it means—'admirable' from the Latin *mirare*, to wonder at—but that piece of information was new. And as Alexander and I sipped our beer, oblivious by now to the rest of the party, he asked me lots of other things about my work and my family and he told me a bit about his; that his parents were both doctors, semi-retired, and that his grandfather, like me, had been a vet. By the time we left, an hour and a half later, I felt as though I'd been talking to Alexander for days. And as he walked me to the tube—I lived in Stockwell then—he asked me for my card.

'He'll never ring,' I told myself sternly as I rattled southwards. 'Forget it. He was just being friendly.' But he did. Two days later he rang to ask me if I'd like to have dinner with him that Sunday, at Joe Allen's, and, to my amazement, things went on from there.

And yes, of course I was physically attracted to Alexander, and yes, flattered by his attention, but the truth is I really *liked* him as well. He was so easy to be with, and so intelligent, and, more importantly, he made me laugh. He was thirty-five, he'd read history at Oxford, then he'd done a postgraduate year at drama school. He'd started out spear-carrying at Stratford, then he'd done ten years in rep, as well as a number of small roles on TV.

'But I've never hit the big time,' he said modestly. 'Unlike some of my contemporaries, like James Purefoy—he's done brilliantly. So has Paul Rhys. They never stop working, while I'm still paddling in the shallows of fame.'

'I'm sure you'll do very well too.'

He shrugged. 'Maybe. Who knows…?'

'All you need is one really good break.'

'That's true. Have you ever been married, Miranda?' he asked suddenly. A small jolt ran the length of my spine.

'Er… No. Not yet. I mean, not ever. I mean, *never.*' He smiled. 'Have you?'

He shook his head. He explained that his last relationship had ended three months before but that he was still 'on good terms' with his ex. And when, heart racing, I asked him why it had ended, he just shrugged and said 'it hadn't worked out'.

By the end of that first date I was stratospheric; I was on Cloud Nine—no, Cloud *Ninety*-Nine—as we strolled down the Strand to the tube. I felt so absurdly happy, I was smiling at strangers; and Alexander said he'd call me again—and he did. As time went on I realized that I simply loved being with him. I loved his warmth, and his sense of fun. And I liked the fact that he was a good talker; there were no strained silences—he always had plenty to say. He wasn't egotistical or 'actorish', though he did have a whimsical side. He could be slightly impetuous—a creature of instinct—he'd suddenly say, or do, surprising things. For example, the first time he told me he loved me was when we were at the dairy counter in Sainsbury's. I'd just reached for a tub of Greek yoghurt when I suddenly heard him say, 'I love you, Miranda. Did you know that?'

'Really?' I looked at him in amazement.

He smiled. 'Yes. Really.' I was thrilled, of course—but what a *strange* place to tell me. 'You're wonderful—you live up to your name.' And when we got engaged, not long afterwards, he had the ring engraved with, *Admired Miranda!* But I don't have it any more…

'And what about the clients?' I heard Daisy ask now, as she broke two brown eggs into the Pyrex bowl. 'You're opening tomorrow, so have you got any bookings?'

'Only two.'

'Why so few?'

'Because I haven't had time to spread the word that I'm in new premises—the practice will take time to build.'

'I see.'

'But I've got a depressed Irish setter coming in the morning—and then this woman called Lily Jago got in touch—'

'Oh *yes*,' Daisy interjected, her eyes widening. 'The editor of *Moi!* magazine. Looks like Naomi Campbell, and often behaves like her too. A friend of mine worked for her once—it took her six months to recover.'

'That's the one. Anyway, she sent me a hysterical e-mail about her shih-tzu—she says it's having a "nervous breakdown"—so I'm going round there on Tuesday afternoon, but that's all I've got in the diary so far.'

'It's a pity animal psychiatry isn't like human psychiatry,' Daisy added as she began whisking the eggs. I nodded. If only it were. Humans go to their shrinks for months, if not years, but with animals it's not the same. They don't come to me week in week out and lie there staring at the ceiling while I evaluate the state of their *id* and their *ego* and then quiz them about their mum. I simply observe them, identify the problem and advise remedial action, which means I usually only see them the once.

'What are you going to charge?' Daisy asked as she lit the hob.

'A hundred pounds per one-and-a-half-hour consultation here, and if I go to them, it'll be a hundred and thirty, to compensate for the travelling time. I'll continue giving free advice by e-mail as that creates goodwill and doesn't take long. And I'm going to have puppy parties,' I added, 'so that should help, but I need lots of new cases to make it all pay. Especially as I'm opening nearly a month late.'

'Well, you needed time to...recover,' Daisy said. That was

true. 'And it'll pick up when the next series of *Animal Crackers* goes out, won't it?'

'With any luck—but that's not for three weeks.'

'Actually, *I* might have a new client for you,' Daisy said as she opened a carton of milk. 'Someone I met the other day at a charity do. Caroline…what was her name? Oh yes, Mulholland. She was complaining about her Weimaraner. Said it was behaving like an "absolute moron". As I didn't know your new number I told her to contact you through your website.'

'Thanks. I hope she does. And how are things with you on the work front?' I asked as I unpacked my plates.

'Oh frantic,' she said gaily as she got out a small saucepan. 'I've got an Abba Tribute hen night in Hammersmith on Wednesday, a Siberian Soiree birthday bash with Cossack dancers on Saturday, and I'm desperately trying to find a couple of contortionists for a Trail to Timbuktu extravaganza in Thames Ditton next month. Plus all the weddings!' she wailed. 'We've got six, and three of them have fallen to me. I've just had to find some biodegradable confetti for this wedding in Holland Park in September,' she went on, as she beat the eggs. 'I managed to track some down on the Net. Dried delphinium petals in five colours, absolutely gorgeous. I've got to enclose a sachet with each invitation—two hundred. Sounds lovely, doesn't it?' she murmured wistfully. 'Two hundred guests…Holland Park…dried delphinium petals…'

'Yes,' I said quietly. 'It does.'

'Sorry, Miranda,' she said, collecting herself. 'That was tactless of me.'

'That's okay.'

'I was actually thinking of myself.'

'I know. Hasn't he said anything?' She shook her head. 'Not even a hint?'

'No,' she said bitterly. 'Not so much as a cough.'

'Well, why don't you propose to him then?'

She stopped beating, her brown eyes widening in amazement. 'Because it's *so* unromantic.'

'So is not being asked.'

'Yes,' she said crossly. 'I *know.*' She picked up the pepper grinder and gave it several vicious twists.

'Don't you ever discuss it with him?' I asked as I sat at the table.

She shook her head. 'I don't want to destabilize things.'

'I see.'

'And I suppose I'm worried I might not get the answer I'm hoping for, so I'd rather keep things nice and smooth. But he does definitely love me,' she added optimistically. 'I say to him, "You do love me, Nigel, don't you?" and he always replies, "Yes, Daisy, of course I do."'

'He should bloody well prove it then. It's been long enough.'

'Mmm. That's just what my mum says. I mean, Alexander didn't hang around, did he?'

I sighed. 'No. It was quite quick.'

It was also, as proposals go, rather unusual; but, as I say, Alexander is an impulsive man. We'd been together nine months and we were very happy; I'd just moved in with him, and it was going well. And we were both in the bathroom one Saturday morning, cleaning our teeth together at the basin, smiling at each other in the mirror, when he suddenly paused in mid-brush, and, still looking at me in the glass, said, 'anda, ill oo arry 'e?'

'What?'

He took the toothbrush out of his mouth, sipped some

water from the glass, then spat neatly into the sink. 'I said, "Miranda, will you do me the inestimable honour of becoming my wife?" I've just decided, this minute, that I want to marry you.'

I looked at him in amazement. *'Why?'*

'Well, because, just standing here with you now, brushing our teeth together like this, suddenly made me realize how happy I am with you, and so, well, I suppose that's why. I'd rather not get down on bended knee if you don't mind, because of my cartilage problem,' he added matter-of-factly. 'But, will you say yes, Miranda? Mm?' A wave of emotion broke over me as I realized he meant it. 'Will you?' he repeated. His swimming-pool blue eyes were staring into me.

'Well…are you sure?' I stuttered. 'I mean…'

'Never been surer of anything,' he said quietly.

'Then…yes,' I said wonderingly. 'I will.' And then, because I was so overwhelmed, I just said, 'Thank you', and burst into tears.

He wrapped his arms round me. 'No. Thank *you*. Don't cry, Miranda. There's no need to cry. I love you. I always will.' I dried my eyes, we exchanged a minty kiss, and that was that.

I'm not being disingenuous when I say I was completely taken aback, because I truly didn't expect to get engaged. Maybe because my parents divorced so long ago—and haven't been that civilized since—I've never had any illusions like that. For me, it was enough just to feel that I was in a happy relationship, to know that I'd been lucky enough to find love. But Daisy's different—she's much more conventional—she wants the church, the meringue, the whole works.

'It's a bit galling having to do all these weddings when Nige won't pop the question,' she said regretfully, fork poised

in mid-air. 'I think he *will* marry me,' she continued judiciously. She often says that. 'But I don't think it's worth
pushing it just now.'

The fact is, Daisy's terrified of pushing it. I know this
because she's been with Nigel for five and a half years and
we've been having the same conversation for three. 'I mustn't
put him under pressure,' she said seriously. 'That's what the
books all say.'

'The books also say that you should be a bit more de-
tached. Don't be there for him so much. Make him miss you.
Be mysterious. Move town if need be. Or even country, God
knows.'

'Oooh—that's a *very* dangerous game.'

'Why?'

'Because,' she said, with an air of spurious authority, 'if I
suddenly withdraw, and act all aloof, then he might think I
don't really *love* him. And that would be disastrous, wouldn't
it?'

I looked at her. 'I'm not sure. I think it might do him
some good to feel a bit less secure.'

'No, I think it'll *all* happen in the fullness of time,' she
added, with a slightly twitchy serenity.

'Hmmm. Well, it's your life.'

But I find it odd that Daisy's so scared of asking Nigel
whether or not he intends to marry her, because in other
ways she's incredibly brave. For example, she spends her
days off bungee-jumping, hang-gliding, abseiling and rock-
climbing—and she did her first solo sky-dive a few weeks
ago.

'It would be catastrophic if I forced him to name the day
and then he booted me,' she said sagely. 'Then what on earth
would I do? I've invested nearly six years of my life in Nigel
and to be quite crude about it I'd like a return. So I don't

want to blow it all at this final—and very delicate—stage by not being quite patient enough.' I nodded, though, as I say, I've heard this line of argument many times before. 'I want to have kids,' Daisy went on calmly, 'and I'm now thirty-three, so if Nigel and I split up—' she gave a little shudder '—it would take me at least two, maybe even three years to get to the same stage with someone else, by which time...' she poured the egg mixture into a frying pan, '...it may well be curtains on the ovary front. And I'd never trap him into marriage,' she added. 'Men resent that. I want him to *want* to marry me.'

'Why shouldn't he want to marry you?' I said hotly.

'Oh, he's just the cautious type.' Too right. Nigel's very cautious; he proceeds as slowly as a three-toed sloth. They move so slowly—it would take them a day to cross a football pitch—that they actually grow mould on their fur. Anyway, when it comes to romance, I'm afraid Nigel's like that. And this dilatoriness is reflected in his hobby—growing bonsai trees. He once won a medal at Chelsea for one of his Japanese maples—he'd been tweaking it for twenty years. To be honest, I've never really been able to see what he and Daisy have in common, but she seems to dote on him. But she has a tiny flat in Tooting and he has a large house in Fulham; and she did once admit after a few too many that, yes, it was the 'security' which partly appealed. Though why a woman who spends her weekends throwing herself out of aeroplanes should be interested in 'security' is way beyond me. But, on the other hand, her father died tragically when she was nine so she's always been looking for someone 'steady' and 'safe'.

And Nigel's certainly that. He's a City solicitor—a partner in Bloomfields. Solidly competent, rather than effortlessly brilliant, he works incredibly hard; and though I'm sure he's very fond of Daisy, I guess he can't see any reason to rush.

He's thirty-nine and has never been married, so what on earth would make him jump now? He hasn't even asked her to live with him yet. Daisy has jokingly suggested it a few times, but she says he never seems keen—I think he doesn't want her messing up his stuff. She's quite untidy and can be rather noisy, though I mean that in the nicest way. It's not that she shouts, or is grossly opinionated, simply that she laughs a lot—she's got this lovely, chortling giggle—and she always has plenty to say. Whereas Nigel just likes his evenings in with his bonsai trees plus a quiet dinner and the odd game of bridge. Don't get me wrong. I like Nigel—he's pleasant and he's generous—but he's also selfish, because he has Daisy entirely on his terms. But if he's what she wants, then that's good enough for me.

'I think it'll be *fine* with Nige,' she said again, not very convincingly, as I ate the omelette.

'I hope so. But I do think you'll have to pin him down at *some* point, Daisy.' *If necessary, by stapling his head to the carpet.*

'Hmm,' she said, anxiously. 'Maybe you're right.'

After she'd gone, Herman went to sleep on his bean-bag, curled up like a burnt cashew nut, while I turned my thoughts back to work. With all the stress and disruption I'd been unable to concentrate on it, but now I forced myself back into professional mode. I turned on the computer, and read my e-mails. There was one from my dad, who lives in California, in Palm Springs, where he manages a golf resort. He just wanted to know how I was. Then I logged on to my website, 'PerfectPets.com', where there were a number of outstanding requests for advice. '*My poodle terrorizes the postman,*' said the first one. '*After his latest efforts to "defend us" (there was actually blood on the letters) we've been told that in future we'll have to collect our mail from the sorting office—can you help?*' '*I think my cat's schizophrenic,*' said the next. '*One minute she's curled up on my lap for a cuddle, purring her head off, then the next second she's biting me—why?'* 'Can you tell me why my *female spaniel insists on cocking her leg?'* enquired a third. There were the usual complaints about dogs jumping up, or chasing their tails; there was a house rabbit which kept attacking its owners' feet. There was a gay guinea pig, a sleep-walking Saluki, and a hamster which had eaten its mate. I sent replies to each one, with suggested reading, and as I was doing this, another e-mail popped in. It was from the woman Daisy had mentioned, Caroline Mulholland.

'Dear Miranda, *I met your friend Daisy at a fundraiser the other day and I happened to mention that I have a young Weimaraner which is being an absolute pain. It bullies our two other, much smaller dogs, and we don't know how to get it to stop. I wondered whether you'd be kind enough to call me, as I'd like to arrange for you to come out.'* There was an out of London phone number which I rang. She picked up, and told me that she lived near St Albans, so we arranged that I'd go there the following day.

In the meantime I had the depressed Irish setter to deal with. So the next morning I tidied the consulting room, then went round the corner—stopping to answer Russell the chiropractor's polite enquiries about how I was settling in—and bought some biscuits and flowers. Then I put Herman in the kitchen—he doesn't mix with the clients—and, at ten-thirty, Fiona and Miles Green turned up. They were about my age, good-looking, well dressed and clearly successful judging from their smart address in Notting Hill Gate. I made them some coffee, then sat behind my desk, observing the dog, which did look rather dismal, while they sat side by side on the couch.

'We're both very busy people,' Fiona explained as she nibbled on a chocolate oliver, 'but you see Sinead's our pride and joy...' Sinead was lying on the rug with her head in her paws,

'...and we felt it was important to get her some psychological support.'

'She does seem rather dejected,' I said, as I took notes. 'Irish setters are normally incredibly lively. So when did this subdued behaviour first start?'

'About three months ago,' Mrs Green replied.

'No, it's not as long as that,' her husband corrected her gently. 'I'd say it was about six weeks actually.'

'No, it wasn't!' she snapped. 'It was three months. Do you think I wouldn't notice something like that—my own dog?' I discreetly wrote down 'child substitute' and 'marital tension'.

'*Our* dog,' he said. Sinead lifted her head and looked at them anxiously.

'It's all right, baby,' said Fiona, leaning forward to stroke her. 'It's *all* right. Mummy and Daddy aren't cross.'

'How old is she?' I asked. 'Two?'

'Just under. We've had her for about a year and a half.'

'And has she had any specific traumas? Did she get in a fight with another dog, for example? Or has she had a near miss with a car?'

'No. Nothing like that,' said Fiona. 'I work at home, so I'm with her all day. All I know is she seems constantly depressed and she just lies in her basket. It's heartbreaking,' she added, her voice suddenly catching.

'I don't wish to be personal, Mr and Mrs Green, but are there any specific stresses in the, well, family dynamics, to which she might be reacting?' This was a rhetorical question. There clearly were.

'Well, no, not...really,' Fiona replied, crossing her arms defensively.

I saw her husband roll his eyes. 'C'mon, Fi,' he said wearily. 'You know there are. And I think it's relevant. I've said so all along.' He looked at me. 'You see—'

'I don't want to discuss it!' she hissed.

'But it might be important,' Miles protested.

'But it's *private*!'

'It's all right, Mrs Green,' I interjected. 'I'm not asking you to tell me anything you don't want to. But I can assure you that I'm bound by a code of confidentiality which means that anything you *do* choose to tell me will go to my grave.'

'Okay then,' she sighed. She opened her bag and got out a tissue; her husband gave her arm an encouraging squeeze. 'We've been trying for a baby for four years,' she explained quietly. 'That's why we got Sinead, actually, to distract us from the stress. This year we've had IVF, but our first two attempts have failed.'

'Well, that would put a strain on any relationship, however happy,' I said. They both nodded. 'And dogs are incredibly sensitive to changes in atmosphere, and I think Sinead is simply picking up on that. So I think that you should try and protect her from emotional stress by having any sensitive discussions when she's out of the room.'

'But it's not just that she's depressed,' said Fiona. 'She's been behaving in a peculiar way. For instance, she's started stealing things.'

'Really?'

'Yes. Very *odd* things—Miles's shirts out of the laundry basket, for example.'

'She might find it comforting if he's out.'

'But she steals old egg-boxes too. And the other day she took five empty plastic flowerpots out of the garden, one by one, and put them in her bed. And she was arranging them so carefully, almost tenderly, as if she *loved* them. It was weird. We didn't know what to think.'

Ah.

I got up and went over to Sinead, pushed her gently onto

her side, and lifted up the feathery fur on her underside. Her tummy was slightly bloated and pink.

'Has she been anywhere near a dog?'

'No.'

'Are you sure?'

'Yes—positive. And when she was last on heat we kept her in.'

'Then she's having a phantom pregnancy. That's why she's so subdued. Females that have never been mated can get very broody. They become listless, and they stay in their beds, which they carefully arrange, because basically they're making a nest. Then they look for objects which they can put in their "nursery" and "mother"—hence the egg-boxes and flowerpots. They even show some of the symptoms of pregnancy, just as she's doing. Look at her nipples.'

Fiona's jaw slackened.

'Good God.'

'If she'd been smooth-haired you would have noticed it, but her long fur covers it up. That's what it is. A phantom pregnancy. I used to see this when I was a vet.'

'I see.'

'So you don't have to worry that she has psychological problems, or any kind of depression—she doesn't. She just wants to be a mum.'

Mrs Green dabbed at her eyes. 'Maybe she's doing it in sympathy with me.'

'We were going to have her spayed actually,' said Miles.

'Can I make a suggestion?' They both nodded. 'Don't. Or, at least not yet. Why don't you let her have puppies?'

'Actually...that's a very good idea,' said Miles slowly. He suddenly smiled. 'We hadn't thought of that.'

'No,' Fiona agreed. She stroked the dog's head. 'We've been so caught up in ourselves.'

'And it's nice for girl dogs to be allowed to have at least one litter,' I pointed out, 'otherwise, well,' I shrugged, 'they can feel a bit sad.'

'Oh,' said Fiona. 'I see. We could have puppies. That would be fun, wouldn't it, darling?' Miles nodded. 'Maybe we won't have a baby, but we'll have some sweet little puppies.'

'Well,' I said, 'that's what I would do if I were you.'

'Well, that's very good advice,' Fiona said as they stood up. 'I feel quite overcome.' She gave me a watery smile. 'Thanks.'

'Not at all.' I felt slightly emotional myself.

CHAPTER 2

Maybe Sinead *was* picking up on Fiona's frustration, I thought, as I prepared to set off for Caroline Mulholland's house half an hour later. Maybe she was even trying to have a baby for her, who knows. I mean, dogs do imitate us, because they love us—they want to do all the things that we do. We sit—they sit. We sing—they howl. We vacate the driver's seat—they jump right in. We get broody—maybe they get broody...? That's the thing about being a behaviourist: you have to work out what's going on with the owners before you can begin to sort out their pet. I checked my appearance in the mirror, retouched the concealer below my eye—I need less now—then ran a brush through my hair and left. Daisy was right about the Mews being friendly, I realized, as Joy, the osteopath, gave me a cheery wave. Caroline Mulholland lived in a village called Little Gateley, five miles from St Albans; I guessed it would take an hour and a quarter if the traffic wasn't too bad.

As I drove through Archway I passed Alexander's road, heart pounding like a tom-tom, my mouth as dry as dust. Masochistically, I glanced down Harberton Road—for the first time since 'it' happened—and felt a wave of distress. But, once I'd got through the queues in Finchley and Barnet,

I was soon coasting down lush country lanes; and as I wound down the window and saw the intense yellow of the rape and the fields of green corn, I relaxed—Daisy was right. This *was* a turning point; the start of a *new* phase in my life and I was determined to make it work out. Fifteen minutes later I came to St Albans, where I soon spotted the village sign. I passed the green with its horse chestnuts, laden with fading pink candles, then just beyond the church I saw gates. 'Little Gateley Manor' was carved on one of the pillars and I turned in.

The house was just as I expected—straight out of *Country Life*. Georgian, painted white, and with a circular drive sweeping up to an imposing, rose-smothered front door. As my wheels crunched over the gravel, I heard a deep throaty barking, saw a silver flash, and the Weimaraner came bounding up. Then a woman appeared, running after it, visibly flustered.

'Oh Trigger! You *naughty* boy! Come *here*! Hello, I'm Caroline,' she said slightly breathlessly as I got out of the car, and the dog jumped up at me. 'I'm *so* grateful to you for coming out.'

I'm normally circumspect when I meet someone new, but I immediately took to her. She was thirtyish, with dark blonde hair scraped back in a ponytail, and she was attractive in a non-glossy way.

'I'm so grateful to you,' she repeated. As we went up the steps I inhaled the scent of the roses. 'I've been at my wits' end. You see, we adore Trigger but he's such a handful, and in particular he's horrid to my two Westies—Tavish and Jock.'

I looked at them, scuttling round her feet in the black and white marble-tiled hallway, casting anxious looks at the bigger dog. 'And they were here first, were they?'

'Yes. I had them before I got married. But then my husband decided that he'd like a proper "man's dog"—' she giggled '—and so I got him Trigger for his birthday, but sometimes I think I made a mistake.'

'He's certainly beautiful,' I said, as I followed her into the large drawing room. 'They're such individual-looking dogs, aren't they?' I gazed at his coat, the colour of pale pewter, and at his unearthly, intense, amber eyes.

'Oh yes,' she agreed. 'They're gorgeous-looking things.'

'But they're also strong-willed and need firm control.'

Caroline laughed. 'Well, that's *precisely* where we've slipped up.' She sank into one of the sofas and Trigger tried to clamber onto her lap. 'Stop it you naughty dog! Get down! Get *down* will you!' One of the Westies then jumped up at her, and Trigger snapped at it viciously. Her hand shot out and she smacked his behind. 'Oh do *stop* it you bad, *bad* boy! Do you see what I mean?' she sighed. 'I wasn't exaggerating, was I? It's hopeless. Anyway, let's have a cup of tea first.'

As she disappeared, all three dogs running after her, slithering on the marble tiles, I glanced around the room. It was gorgeous—twenty-foot ceilings with egg and dart coving, in one corner a baby grand; two apricot-coloured Knole sofas, a scattering of mahogany tables, and an enormous fireplace with a marble surround. There were gleaming oils on the walls, and on the mantelpiece were several photos in silver frames, including one of Caroline on her wedding day. I looked at it, then looked away, glancing into the flower-filled garden. A solitary magpie swooped onto the lawn, chattering loudly. 'One for sorrow,' I said to myself quietly. Then I looked at the photo again...

There was something strangely familiar about Caroline Mulholland's husband, but I couldn't for the life of me think what it was. He looked mid-to-late thirties in the photo, and his hair was receding and already quite grey. But he was certainly handsome—they made a good-looking couple. I found myself wondering what he did. No doubt he was a successful banker, or a captain of industry—perhaps I'd seen him on the news. Yes…that must account for my sense of déjà vu, I thought: I'd seen him in the media somewhere. Caroline reappeared with a tray, then suggested that we had the tea outside so that I could see Trigger 'in action'. But I'd already identified the problem—he was an over-indulged alpha male. He felt he should naturally be number one in the pack. He needed to have his status reduced.

'He's desperate to dominate,' I explained, as we sat on the terrace, watching him with the other two dogs.

Caroline put her tea cup down. 'Is he?'

'Yes. This might sound harsh, but what he needs is to be knocked off his pedestal.'

'Really?' she said. I nodded. 'But how?'

'By you taking far less notice of him. He's a chronic show-off—if he's got your attention he's thrilled. And the more you shout at him, the more he likes it—because then he knows you're focussed on him. You're actually rewarding his "bad" behaviour by reacting to it.'

'I am?'

'Yes—you're inadvertently indulging him.'

'Oh. I see.'

'Every time you shout at him, he actually thinks you're *praising* him, so that's going to make him worse.'

'I *see*,' she said again, thoughtfully.

'I don't like to anthropomorphize animals,' I went on. 'But let's put it this way. If Trigger was human, he'd be driving round in a red BMW—which you'd probably bought him for his birthday—barging people off the road, ogling girls out of the window, then going to some party and getting horribly drunk.'

'How awful,' she said, with mock seriousness. 'Like some silly "It boy".'

'Exactly.'

'He'd embarrass us,' she said, playing along. 'He'd bring disgrace on the family,' she added gravely. 'He'd be getting into fights.'

'I'm afraid he would. He'd be kicked out of school, he'd struggle to hold down a job and—I don't want to alarm you—he might even take drugs.'

'*Really?*' She looked genuinely stricken. 'Well,' she added purposefully, as Trigger bounded joyfully about, barking his head off, 'we've got to nip this in the bud.'

'And we will. I won't be able to "cure" him today,' I pointed out. 'But I can show you how you're accidentally re-inforcing his negative behaviour, then you'll be able to work with him on your own. But you'll need to be committed.'

She looked at me seriously. 'Okay. Tell me what to do.'

I explained that the best punishment for Trigger was not to be yelled at—but to be totally ignored.

'Dogs can't stand it,' I continued. 'It's the worst punishment in the world for them to be denied their human's undivided attention—but that's what you've got to do. And if he behaves really badly—say if he bites one of the other dogs—then he has to have some time out. Because if he's tethered and the other two are free, that'll really take him down a few pegs.'

'I see.' Trigger suddenly snapped at one of the Westies, then pinioned it to the ground.

'Oh you *beast!*' Caroline had rushed up to him and grabbed him by the collar.

'No, don't say anything,' I said. 'Simply tie him up some-where.'

'Tie him up?'

'Yes. I know it sounds unkind, but it's not.'

Caroline disappeared for a moment, then reappeared with Trigger's lead. Then she tethered him to the gatepost, in the shade, with a bowl of water.

'Now, we'll leave him there while we stroll around with the other dogs, off the lead. He won't be able to stand it.'

By the time we untied him five minutes later, Trigger was shaking and trembling. 'Look how his body language has changed,' I said. 'He can't understand why you did that to him. He found it incredibly humiliating. He's upset and sub-dued. Look—he's really grovelling.' He was. He was practi-cally sitting on Caroline's feet, looking up at her imploringly, whimpering softly.

'Wow,' she breathed. 'I see what you mean.'

'If you really want his behaviour to improve, then you've got to make him feel less secure. Basically, he's a bully,' I said, 'and like most bullies he's a coward, so if you're firm you'll put him in his place. He's got to have his desired position as top dog taken away,' I reiterated.

She nodded. 'I just didn't realize all this, because I've never had a difficult dog before.'

'Well, does it make sense to you?'

'*Yes.*' She seemed surprised. 'It does.'

'What you need to do is to carry out a dominance reduc-tion programme, both outside and inside the house.' As we went in again, I reminded her that dogs are pack animals, and need to know their place in the hierarchy otherwise they feel unhappy and confused. 'They're like young children,' I went on. 'Children are happier when they're given firm boundaries—and that's what you've got to do with him. So you mustn't let him sit on the sofa,' I added, 'or get on the bed—otherwise that means he's at your own height. Don't let him go through doors before you, and make him wait until you've eaten before he gets fed. In fact, feed the other dogs first.'

'Really?'

'Yes. Show him that his status is not as high as he'd like to think it is.'

'And how long will it take for him to learn?'

'Well, he's very intelligent, so maybe just a few weeks. But you'll have to stick to it religiously,' I said, as we returned to the drawing room. 'I know you love him, but making him learn how to behave well is actually the kind thing to do. And if he's aggressive to the other dogs, then tether him for a few minutes; he'll gradually make the association and stop.'

'I feel so much better now,' Caroline breathed as she scribbled down notes. 'You've explained it all very well. Now, I must pay you.' As she went in search of her handbag I gazed again at her wedding photo. I hadn't seen her husband on the TV. I'd *met* him. Definitely…There was no question. But where? Suddenly the phone rang, and I heard Caroline pick up.

'Oh, that *is* disappointing,' I heard her say. The hall was so large, her voice echoed. 'Well, don't worry, I quite understand. I don't know who else I'll find at such short notice, but if that's the situation it can't be helped. Thanks for letting me know,' she concluded, regretfully. I heard her footsteps, then she reappeared, looking thoughtful.

'That's a nuisance,' she said. 'We've got the village fete here on Saturday in aid of the PDSA. We're having a dog show as part of it and Trinny and Susannah had agreed to judge it—it includes a fancy dress competition—but Trinny's just phoned to say that they're now filming that day and can't. What a drag,' she groaned as she got out her cheque book and began to write. 'It's going to be very hard to find anyone else and I'm so busy as it is and—' Her pen had stopped and she suddenly looked at me. 'I don't suppose *you'd* do it, would you?'

'Me?'

'Yes.'

'But I'm not a celebrity.'

'Well, Daisy told me that you've been on TV. And as an animal behaviourist you'd have tremendous authority, plus, quite frankly—' she grimaced, '—don't take this the wrong way, but I'm desperate. *Would* you?' she pleaded.

'Well...'

'I just don't have time to ring round with everything else I've go to do, and in any case I *know* you'd be brilliant, Miranda, and it's in such a good cause.' That was true. 'I'd be *so* thrilled if you said yes,' she added.

Why not, I thought. 'What would you need me to do?'

'Judge three of the four different categories. We're going to have the Waggiest Tail, the Dog Most Like Its Owner, the Fancy Dress competition, and finally, Canine Karaoke...' She handed me the cheque.

'Canine Karaoke?'

'Yes, it's a total scream. Literally,' she added with a meaningful grimace.

I smiled. 'All right then. Why not? But can I bring my dachshund?'

'Of course. Oh, thank you *so* much!' She exhaled, smiled broadly, then clapped her left hand to her chest. 'That's *such* a relief. It kicks off at two thirty and we're expecting a big crowd, so if you could come half an hour before that would be great.'

'Okay.' I stood up. 'Well, I'd better get going.' And I'd just picked up my bag when I heard the crunch of wheels on the drive.

'Oh, there's my husband. He said he'd be back early. Do come and meet him.'

As we walked down the steps, a dark blue Jaguar pulled up next to my old Astra, then Caroline's husband got out. Trigger and the two other dogs raced up to him, firing off a volley of excited barks. He bent down to stroke them, then straightened up. And as he did so, then walked towards us, I realized why it was that he'd looked so familiar. I felt as though I'd been pushed off a cliff.

'Hello, darling,' he said to Caroline, kissing her as he glanced obliquely at me.

'James, this is Miranda Sweet.' Now he looked at me directly, with nothing more than polite curiosity, his face a pleasant, inscrutable mask. But in his grey eyes, unmistakably, was a spark of recognition. In that instant, sixteen years fell away.

'Miranda's just worked wonders with Trigger,' I heard Caroline say warmly. 'Now don't blush,' she laughed. 'It's quite true.' My face *was* aflame; but not out of modesty. 'Thanks to Miranda, I now know how to stop his bad behaviour, darling.'

'Really?' he said. 'Well, that's…great.'

'He's got a dominance problem, apparently,' she said with a giggle.

'Has he now?'

'He's got to have his status reduced.'

'I see.'

'We've got to make him feel less secure.'

'Is that so?'

'No more being top dog.'

'Uh-huh.'

'Well...I've got...another appointment to get to,' I lied, my heart banging so loudly I was afraid they could hear it. 'I'd better be on my way.'

'Thank you so much for coming out,' Caroline said, as I fumbled in my bag for my keys. 'So we'll see you on Saturday, then?' I felt my insides twist. 'Miranda's going to judge the dog show for us, James. She's stepped in because Trinny and Susannah from *What Not To Wear* had to cancel. Isn't that nice of her?' Now I bitterly, *bitterly* regretted having agreed to do it.

'Oh...Yes,' he said with a thin smile. 'That's great.'

'About two o'clock, then,' Caroline repeated cheerily, as I got in my car. She waved at me; I gave her a feeble wave back, then, sick to my heart, I drove slowly away.

My hands trembled like winter leaves as they clutched the steering wheel. *Jimmy*. Jimmy *Smith*—not James Mulholland. He'd changed his name. As for his appearance—he was *transformed*. No wonder I hadn't recognized him in the wedding photo. I could have passed him in the street and not known. The mass of blond curls and the light beard he'd had at twenty-one had gone, and he was now clean-shaven, receding, and grey. His frame had filled out, and the frayed jeans and jumpers had become Savile Row suits and striped shirts. Only the voice was the same: the smooth, pleasant voice, and the insolent expression in the pale granite eyes.

As I turned out of the gates, my heart still beating so erratically that I felt dizzy, I recalled Daisy's words: 'This is the start of a *new* phase in your life, and I just know it's going to be *good*.' But how could it be, I thought sourly—how *could* it be—when I'd just been ambushed by my past? And now I was oblivious to the colours of the landscape as I cast my mind back with a deep sense of shame.

It was half my lifetime ago, but it had remained seared on my mind like a brand. I still remembered every detail of that spring morning with photographic clarity, though as the years had gone by, I'd thought of it less. There was nothing I could do about it, and no-one I could tell; so I'd simply suppressed it, and tried to move on. The fact that I'd had to study so hard had helped in blocking out the pain—even so, it had haunted me for years, and still does. And, strangely, I'd been wondering about Jimmy recently, almost obsessively—and now, out of the blue, here he was. Here he was, the epitome, apparently, of affluent respectability. I laughed a bitter little laugh. As I drove through the grey terraces of North London, I wondered what he did. Probably something crooked, I reasoned—how else could he have become so rich? I thought about his wife, and wondered whether he'd ever confessed to her the awful thing that he—no, *we*—had once done.

When I got back to the Mews, Herman was happy to see me—I knew this because his whippety tail was wagging and he wasn't actively looking anxious. His pointy little face was in neutral gear. I took him out for his walk, and as we walked up the hill, stopping for the usual friendly exchanges with other dog-owners—'Ooh, look, a sausage dog!' 'Sweet!' 'Does he speak German?'—I decided what I would do. I'd ring Caroline and tell her that I was sorry, but I wouldn't be able to help with the fete after all. I hated letting her down, not least because I'd liked her, but there was now no way I'd be able to go. And as I unlocked the front door, trying to work out which of my three excuses—mum ill/dog ill/ car problems—would sound most convincing, I saw the light flashing on the answerphone. I pressed 'Play'.

'You have. Three. Messages,' intoned the robotic female voice. 'First message sent. Today at. Four. Forty-five. P.M.'

'Hello, darling!' It was Mum. 'Just ringing for a chat. But don't ring me back as I'll be busy with the boys. I'll try you again later.' Click. *Whirr.* The machine spooled on. 'Hi, Miranda!' My heart sank. 'Caroline here. I just want to thank you again, for helping us out with the dog show—you've saved my bacon. But I also wanted to let you know that I've just told two of my friends that you're doing the judging, and they'd both heard of you, from *Animal Crackers.* So you shouldn't be so modest—you obviously *are* a bit of a celebrity. Anyway, we're all *really* looking forward to seeing you here on Saturday. Bye for now!' Click. *Damn.* 'Hello, Miss Sweet,' said a male voice. 'It's Detective Sergeant Cooper here.' Detective Sergeant? I panicked wildly for a split second, adrenaline flooding my veins, then remembered who he was and calmed down. 'Just to let you know we'll be sending you those forms I mentioned—I do apologize for the delay—you should get them by the end of the week.' Oh. Right. The forms. I'd completely forgotten.

'This is too much,' I muttered to Herman, as I opened the back door and let the early evening sunlight flood the kitchen. 'I've more than enough pain without this.' I sat down, and breathed very deeply to calm myself, but this only gave me a sharp twinge in my rib. Then I went to my computer, waited impatiently while it connected to the Net, and then typed 'James Mulholland' into Google. A whole slew of entries came up.

'Welcome to James Mulholland's Website,' I read. 'James Mulholland has been MP for Billington since May 1997...' Good *God*—he was an MP! I felt as though I'd been struck by lightning. At the top of the page I read, 'Links | Fighting for Billington | Billington Labour Party | News | James Mulholland was born in 1965 and was educated at Walton Comprehensive, Peterborough...'

As I read on my heart was racing—there was a photo of Jimmy, smiling smoothly. 'Click here to find out the latest on James Mulholland.' I clicked again.

'James Mulholland has been MP for Billington since 1997. During the 1997–2001 Parliament he was a member of the Education and Employment Committee and the Social Security Committee. He is now Minister of State for Education (Lifelong Learning).' Christ, he was a Junior Minister! My eyes skimmed down the page. 'Before going into politics, James was a local radio producer and reporter…' So *that's* what he'd done. 'He was educated at Walton Comprehensive, Peterborough and Sussex University…where he gained a First in Biochemistry.' In 'real life', I read, 'James enjoys walking in the Hertfordshire countryside, and relaxing at home with his wife, Caroline, and their three dogs.'

But where did the amazing house come from? He'd been a journalist, not a banker, and MPs aren't loaded. I scrolled through the other entries—mostly promotional guff—then clicked on the *Guardian Unlimited* site. There was an anonymous profile. Entitled 'His Master's Voice', it wasn't exactly flattering.

'Son of an insurance salesman…early years provide little evidence of his later ambition…Walton Comprehensive, Peterborough…Sussex University…1987 joined Radio York… in 1993 he interviewed Jack Straw…so impressed, he invited him to be his parliamentary researcher…quickly rose through the ranks. At 37, Mulholland is on the fast track…good looks, charm, communication skills…"on message"…journey from radical left to centre right. In 1995 Press spokesman to Alan Milburn, then selected to fight the safe seat of Billington in Lancashire…In the summer of 2000 married the Hon. Caroline Horbury, heir to the Horbury property fortune…' *Ah.* '…frequently entertain at their grand country pile…smart townhouse in Billington…elegant apartment in Westminster…he now puts her money where his mouth is…'

So that explained Little Gateley Manor. He hadn't made money—he'd married it. It all made sense. As for the journey 'from radical left to centre right'—that fitted too. I remembered again the Jimmy I'd known, and tried to square it with the suave pillar-of-the-establishment exterior I'd encountered today. I remembered too how charismatic I'd found him, and, ironically, how principled. That's what had drawn me to him—his passionate beliefs. How misguided I was, I thought bitterly. What a dupe. And though I was only sixteen, and he was five years older, I was, at best, culpably naïve. Now I wondered whether he'd ever felt the slightest pang of conscience about the terrible thing that he'd done.

I'd always known that he'd escaped prosecution, because if he'd been arrested he would have named me. I remembered his voice on that awful March morning, as I'd stood in his flat, hyperventilating from exertion—I'd run all the way—and from shock.

'I've just…found out,' I gasped. 'I've just found *out*.' I could feel my face twisting with rage. 'I overheard someone talking about it at the bus stop. How *could* you!!' I croaked, my throat aching. 'How *could* you! You…you…*hypocrite*.' I burst into tears.

He folded his arms, then turned and looked out of the window onto the street below. I could see a muscle in his jaw tense and flex. 'I should keep quiet if I were you,' he said.

I was amazed at his self-possession. 'Keep quiet?' I wept. 'Keep *quiet*?' I was crying so much that my ears hurt. 'No. I *won't* bloody well keep quiet! I'm going to tell *everyone* what you did!'

He turned and faced me. 'No, Miranda. What *you* did. It *was* you after all. Wasn't it?' he said quietly.

'No. It *wasn't*—because I didn't *know*.'

He gave me an indolent smile. 'The police won't care about a detail like that. In any case they've already got your number, Miranda. Haven't they? After your trip to the butchers a few months ago. And then there was your little adventure at the fur coat shop. They won't believe you. Will they?' I felt sick. 'In any case,' he went on smoothly. 'If you name me, I'll tell them that you *did* know. I'll say we did it together. So I really do suggest that it's in both our interests for you to keep your sweet little trap firmly shut. Unless you *want* to go to Holloway, of course.'

It was as though I'd been plunged into a bath of ice water, and I saw, with dreadful clarity, that he was right. So I did keep quiet—for sixteen years—to my shame, and never saw him again. Until today...

I lay on my bed for more than an hour—Herman lying beside me, like a tiny bolster—just staring through the skylight as the hot blue of the evening sky turned pink, then mauve, now deepening to liquid indigo, and a kind of plan began to form in my mind. I *would* go to Little Gateley this Saturday—and I'd find some opportunity to speak to Jimmy alone. I'd quietly confront him and I'd get him to acknowledge me, and to admit—at *last*—that he'd done something terribly wrong. And I'd make him apologize to me, for what he did—because he'd damaged a part of my youth. God knows what other, physical, damage he'd caused, I thought bitterly. I'd never been brave enough to find out. And so, Alexander quite driven from my mind, I went to sleep, dreaming of fire.

CHAPTER 3

The next day I was booked to see Lily Jago and her shih-tzu, Jennifer Aniston. I read the e-mail again. '*Not allowed to take her to work any more...she's clearly having a nervous breakdown... wreaking havoc at home...can't cope... Help!!!!*' It sounded like a pretty straightforward case of separation anxiety. The appointment was at half past four. So I pushed away the negativity which had paralysed me for the previous twenty-four hours and forced myself to work. I spent the morning writing a flyer to send to local vets. I also called the *Camden New Journal* to see whether they might be interested in doing a short piece about me—anything to get the clients rolling in. I wrote my follow-up report to send to the Greens about their Irish setter, then Clare, the producer of *Animal Crackers*, rang. She wanted to arrange the next filming schedule and told me that the new series had just got a good advance preview in *TV Life!*. I went down to the shop and bought it, and there was a photo of the presenter, Kate Laurie, with a Shetland pony, and, inset, a small one of me.

We love our pets, but do we drive them crazy? it asked. *That's what Kate Laurie will be finding out in the new series of* Animal Crackers *with help from our resident 'pet psychiatrist', Miranda Sweet.* It had a five star rating and was described as 'compulsive viewing'. I felt pleased and relieved. I idly flicked through the rest of the magazine and suddenly saw Alexander's face. It loomed out of the 'Hot New Talent' slot on page eight. I caught my breath. He looked heartbreakingly handsome in his eighteenth-century naval uniform. *Alexander Darke in the new swashbuckling drama,* Land Ahoy!, announced the caption. A shard of glass pierced my heart.

Alexander Darke possesses a beguiling blend of old-fashioned charm and courtesy, the piece began. *Unused to being interviewed, he responds to questions with polite enquiries of his own. But he will have to get used to the media spotlight, for, after twelve years of 'treading water more than boards', as he modestly puts it,* Land Ahoy! *is set to make him a star.* It was obvious that the journalist had fancied him. She rhapsodized about his *Byronic looks… like a young Richard Chamberlain,* and his athletic physique. I felt another sharp pang. *This gorgeous Darke horse seems inspired casting as the brave yet unemotional seafaring man,* she gushed. Well, the 'Darke horse' part of it was certainly true. Land Ahoy!'s *female lead is the luscious Tilly Bishop, 25, who recently starred in the hit romantic comedy,* Reality Cheque. I felt sick.

By now it had gone three, so I settled Herman, and walked over the railway bridge to the tube. I got the train to Embankment, then another to Sloane Square, then strolled down the King's Road. Daisy had warned me what to expect about Lily Jago. 'She's a chronic drama queen,' she'd said. I knew that Lily was a fanatical animal lover because she'd recently got into trouble for refusing to employ a Korean girl on the basis that she came from a country where they eat dogs. Lily had been taken to a tribunal, the publishers of *Moi!* had been fined, and it had been splashed all over the press. She'd only kept her job because she'd lifted the magazine's circulation by fifty-six per cent in the previous year.

'Thank *God* you're here!' she breathed as she opened the

front door of her flat in Glebe Place. There were feathers in her hair. 'It's been absolute *hell*!' I went inside, and saw that the avian trail led all the way down the hall to the sitting room. 'Just *look* what the little monster has done!'

The shih-tzu sat on the sofa, amidst the wreckage of two eviscerated cushions, indignation and distress in her bulgy brown eyes.

'I came back ten minutes ago to find this, this…devastation!' Lily wailed. This wasn't really devastation. I've seen houses where the dog has shredded the wallpaper. 'The little *vandal*! I just don't know *what* to do!' I got Lily to calm down, then asked her when the problems had started.

'A month ago,' she replied. 'You see, *Moi!* was taken over,' she explained, as she lit a cheroot with a trembling hand. 'And the new proprietor won't allow animals at work. Not so much as a goldfish!' she added irritably. She tossed back her head and a twin plume of blue smoke streamed from her elegant nose. 'So I now have no option but to leave Jennifer at home. But the point *is* she's not used to it, because for the past two years she's always come in with me. For a while she was even editing her own section.'

'Really?'

'Yes. She had a dogs' beauty problem page. Anyway, she's obviously missing office life, so I suppose *that's* why she's being beastly.'

'I don't think that's it at all.'

'I think she's doing it to get back at me,' said Lily, her eyes narrowing as she drew on the cheroot again. 'For leaving her on her own.'

I sighed. This, sadly, is a common misconception. 'Miss Jago,' I began wearily.

She waved an elegant hand at me. 'Call me Lily.'

'Lily,' I tried again. 'Let me reassure you that dogs are

quite incapable of forming the abstract concept of "revenge".
This is a classic case of separation anxiety. It's not that she's
"missing the office", or "trying to get her own back". It's
simply that being alone gives her terrible stress.'

'Well, she does have a walker who comes to take her out
at lunchtimes, not least so that she can, you know—' Lily
lowered her voice '—*wash her hands.*'

'Hmm. I see. But, apart from that, she's on her own for
what, three or four hours at a stretch?' Lily nodded guiltily.
'Well, that's quite a long time.'

'I've no choice!' I stood up. Lily looked alarmed. 'Christ,
you're not going are you?'

'No. I'm not. I'd like you to show me your leaving routine. I'd like you to pretend that it's the morning, and you're
about to go off to work.'

'You mean, act it out?'

'Yes. The whole works. Putting on your coat, getting your
bag, saying goodbye to Jennifer, and locking the door. Please
make it as realistic as you can and pretend that I'm not here.'

She looked at me sceptically. 'O-kay.'

I followed Lily to the gleaming steel and black granite
kitchen where she filled Jennifer's bowl—it looked like por-
celain—with Dogobix. Then, Jennifer following her, grunt-
ing, down the long, cream-carpeted hallway, Lily picked up
her jacket and bag. Jennifer's body suddenly stiffened with
apprehension.

'O-kay dar-ling,' Lily sang. 'It's time for Mummy to go to
work now.' Jennifer began to whine. 'No, sweetie, *don't* cry,
Mummy's *got* to go to work so that she can buy you all sorts
of *lovely* things. Like that Gucci collar you want—remember?
And that Theo Fennell silver bowl? So I'm just…going *out*…'
Jennifer was racing crazily round Lily's feet, whimpering and
hyperventilating, '…for a *lit-tle* while.' By now Jennifer was

screaming like a banshee as Lily and I backed out through the front door. She turned the key, then bent down and opened the letter-box. 'Bye-bye, my sweet little darling,' she called through it, 'bye-bye, my love,' then she straightened up. She looked at me, and her face suddenly crumpled like an empty crisp packet. 'Oh God—I just can't *bear* it!' She unlocked the door again, scooped Jennifer up in her arms, and kissed her flattened little face several times. 'Be a *good* girl, Jennifer. Be a *good* little girl for Mummy, okay?' Then she put Jennifer down, and left. From inside we could hear outraged howling.

'And this is what you do every morning?' I said to her.

'Yes.'

'Now show me how you come home.'

'Okay.' Lily unlocked the front door, and rushed in, her arms wide open.

'Darling, here I am again—Mummy's *ba-ck*!' Jennifer, though by now clearly confused, responded with an ecstatic grunt. 'Did you miss me, darling?' Lily crooned as she picked her up and cuddled her. '*Did* you? Well I *really* missed you too. I *love* my lickle baby Jennifer, and I don't like leaving her, do I, my darling? No, no, no—I *don't*!'

She put the dog down.

'That's how I do it.'

'Hmm.'

We went back into the sitting room and I explained what she was doing wrong—that she was making such a huge thing of leaving and returning that she was working Jennifer up into a frenzy. 'You've got to be cooler about it all,' I advised her. 'Be quite off-hand. In the mornings, don't go in for these long, drawn-out departures—you make it all so much more traumatic than it has to be, and that gets her in a terrible state.' I advised her to vary her leaving routine, and to leave her on her own at other times, unexpectedly. 'Just pop out without telling her,' I said.

'Without *telling* her?' repeated Lily incredulously.

'Yes. Then come back, as casual as you like. That way she'll get used to you coming and going and she won't panic, which means she won't be destructive. And when you come home in the evenings, be warm to her, of course, but not too delirious—after all, you've only been to work, not round the world. You're making far too much of it all, so you're giving her massive psychological stress.'

'Oh,' said Lily slowly. 'Right.' I glanced at the mantelpiece, which was white with invitations.

'Do you leave her on her own in the evenings—when you go to parties, for example?'

'No, she always comes along.'

'I see.' She got down an invitation and handed it to me. It was for a reception at the French Embassy. In the top left-hand corner, it read, '*Miss Lily Jago and Miss Jennifer Aniston*.'

'Jennifer's extremely popular,' said Lily proudly. 'We go *everywhere* together. They even let her in at The Ivy, which is more than can be said for Geri Halliwell's shih-tzu.'

'So she's never really been left alone at all before now, day or night?'

'No. Never,' Lily replied.

'In that case,' I said, 'I have another suggestion. You could, if you were to follow my advice, gradually get Jennifer more used to being on her own, but given the over-attachment problem that she has—that you both have actually—I think it would take a long time. So a better solution, in my view, would be to get a puppy, to keep her company.'

Lily stared at me as though I were mad. 'A *puppy*?' she echoed. 'You mean, another *dog*?' I nodded. 'Another Jennifer?' I nodded again. She suddenly beamed. 'What a *bril-

liant idea! Would you like that, darling?' she said, lifting the dog onto her lap. She adjusted the diamanté barrette in Jennifer's floor-length blonde hair. 'Would you like a sweet little puppy to play with?' Jennifer grunted. 'A little fwendy-wendy? You *would*? She says yes!' she informed me happily. 'Well, Mummy's going to *find* you one. That's a superb idea,' she said. 'Quite brilliant. I'd *never* have thought of that. You're a genius, Miranda. In fact, you're such a genius I'm going to do a feature on you in *Moi!*'

'Oh!'

'I am,' she said. 'I'm going to send my best feature writer, India Carr, to interview you—have I got your card?—yes, here it is—and I'll hire a top photographer to take some really nice pics. What shall I call it? "Barking Mad"—no— "Miss Behaviour"! Yes!! "Miss Behaviour"! How about that?'

I knew that Lily wouldn't really do an interview with me—she was just being effusive—but when I got back I found that the *Camden New Journal* had phoned to say that yes, they would like to run a piece. I was pleased—some local publicity would be good.

'How long will the article be?' I asked the reporter, Tim, the following morning, as he got his notebook out of his bag. He looked about eighteen but was probably twenty-five.

'About a thousand words—that's nearly a page—I write them up in quite a light-hearted way. The peg is the opening of your practice—"Pet Shrink Comes to Primrose Hill"— and I'll plug *Animal Crackers* as well.'

'Would you also mention my puppy parties?'

He laughed. 'Sure—but what are they? I don't have a dog.'

'They're a kind of canine kindergarten,' I explained. 'They're very important for socializing young dogs so that they don't have behavioural problems in later life.'

'Cool,' he said, as he took the top off his pen. 'Puppy...
parties,' he muttered as he scribbled in his pad. 'Are they by
invitation only?' he asked with a straight face.

'Sort of. I mean, their mums and dads have to book.'

'So it's RSVP then. And is it Bring a Bottle?'

'No,' I said with a smile.

'Dress code?'

'Casual. But collars will be worn.'

'Time and venue?'

'Seven p.m., every Wednesday, here. Fifteen pounds p.p.'

'That's per puppy?'

'Correct. Carriages at nine. They start next week and I've
still got a few empty spaces.'

His pen flew across the page in a longhand/shorthand
hybrid. 'Few...empty...spaces. That's great.' Then he asked
me for some personal background. So I told him, briefly,
about growing up in Brighton, then mentioned my five years
at Bristol and explained why I'd given up being a vet.

'But it wasn't simply the stress,' I went on. 'Being a
vet means that you're usually mending just one bit of the
animal—you're prescribing, or doing surgery, or setting
bones. But as a behaviourist you're working with the *whole*
animal, which I find more interesting, because it means
trying to fathom their minds.'

'And are you Jungian or Freudian?' he asked with a smirk.

I laughed. 'Neither.'

'Seriously though,' he said, 'do animals really need psychiatrists? Isn't it just a bit of a fad for indulgent pet-owners?
Like having aromatherapy for your Persian cat, for example,
or having your dog's kennel feng-shuied?'

'Animal behaviourism is a new area, that's true,' I replied. 'But it isn't a passing fashion—it's here to stay; because
we now know that developing greater insight into animal

psychology means having well-balanced pets. They don't "misbehave" or behave "inappropriately", because they're happy—and they're happy because they're understood.' I then told him the story of how I'd got Herman. 'Did you know that in the West the biggest cause of death in young dogs isn't accidents or illness,' I went on; 'it's euthanasia due to behavioural problems. I find that incredibly sad. Because the fact is that so many of these behavioural problems would be completely preventable if only people knew what made their pets tick.'

'What are the most common problems you see?'

'Aggression, separation distress, fears and phobias, obsessive behaviour, attention-seeking…'

'And what about the animals?'

I laughed. 'Actually you're not that far off, because all too often it isn't the animal's behaviour which has to change, it's the human's, though people don't usually like hearing that.'

'And have you always been "animal crackers"?' he smiled.

I shrugged. 'Well, yes…I suppose I have.'

'Why?'

'Why? Well, I don't really know. I mean, lots of people adore animals, don't they, and find them interesting, so I guess I'm simply one of them.' Tim's mobile phone suddenly rang, and as he stepped outside to take the call I realized that what I'd said wasn't the whole truth. I think the real reason why I became so interested in animals was because it used to distract me from my parents' rows. They argued a lot, so I gradually built up my own little menagerie to take my mind off the stress. I had a stray tortoiseshell called Misty, two rabbits, Ping and Pong, and Pandora, a guinea pig. I had a hamster and then two gerbils which kept having babies which, to my horror, they would sometimes eat. I also had about thirty stick insects, which I used to feed the neighbours' privet to, and a number of baby birds which I'd nudged back to life. I once worked out that, including the humans, there were 207 legs in our house.

Mum and Dad thought I was obsessed, but they let me get on with it. Sometimes they'd try to recruit me to their cause. 'Your mum…' my father would mutter sadly, shaking his head. 'Your *father*…' my mum would fume. But I didn't want to know. At night I'd lie in my bed, stiff as a plank, eyes wide open, listening to them griping downstairs. It was always about one subject—golf—a sport which Dad loved with a burning passion and which Mum loathed—she still does. Dad had taken it up not long after they'd married and, within three years, had become exceptionally good. He was even encouraged to turn professional, but Mum didn't want to know. She said he should stick with accountancy—but he wasn't having it. Eventually, they split up. Then, within a year of their divorce, she met and married Hugh, a landscape architect, and, pretty quickly, had three more kids.

I think that's why I became 'tricky'—because I had a lot of instability then. I didn't smoke or take drugs, like some kids I knew; I didn't pierce my eyebrows or dye my hair. Instead, I became fixated on animal issues. I went vegetarian, almost vegan—it drove Mum mad—and I joined every welfare organization there was. I played truant to go on live-export protests, and I went on anti-hunt demos too. That's how I met Jimmy. I was standing by a fence one freezing December Saturday with a few other protesters as the hunt went by. I didn't like to throw anything, as that's not nice, and you might hurt a horse; so I just stood there, holding up a poster saying 'Ban Hunting *Now*!!' when this handsome man suddenly turned up. He looked like the Angel Gabriel with his thick, curly blond hair and pale beard. And he began chanting, very quietly, 'It's a bloody liberty, not a civil liberty! It's a bloody liberty, not a civil liberty!' And his voice got a little louder, and then he motioned to us all to join in. And so we did.

'It's a bloody liberty! Not a civil liberty! It's a *bloody* liberty! Not a *civil* liberty!' And now he was waving his arms at us, as though he was conducting Beethoven's Ninth.

'IT'S A BLOODY LIBERTY! NOT A CIVIL LIBERTY!! *IT'S A BLOODY LIBERTY! NOT A CIVIL LIBERTY!!!'*

I was sixteen then, and Jimmy was twenty-one. It had taken five minutes for me to fall under his spell...

Tim reappeared, and snapped his phone shut.

'I'm sorry about that. It was my editor. Where were we? Oh yes...' he stared at his notes. 'And are you single or married?' he asked.

'I'm...single.' I prayed that he wouldn't mention Alexander, but there was no reason for him to know.

'And how old are you, if you don't mind my asking?'

'I don't mind at all. I'm thirty-two.'

'And finally, a funny question, which I always ask everyone. What's your deepest, darkest secret?'

'My deepest, darkest secret?'

'Yes. Don't look so shocked. It's not serious.'

'Oh.' He'd thrown me right off balance for a moment. 'Well...' He'd be horrified if I told him the truth. 'I've...got a bit of a soft spot for Barry Manilow,' I managed to say.

'Barry...Manilow,' he muttered. 'That's great.' Then he said he thought he'd got enough material, and if he could just take a quick photo, he'd be off.

'When's the piece going in?' I asked, as he opened his rucksack and pulled out a small camera.

'Tomorrow.'

'That's quick.'

'We had an extra page to fill at the last minute as some advertising was pulled, so I've got to turn this around by two. All our photographers are busy today, so I'm going to take a quick digital snap. If you could just stand by the door, holding the dog, with the plaque just behind you.' We stepped outside. I picked Herman up and smiled at Tim, squinting slightly.

Suddenly he lowered the camera. 'I hope you don't mind my saying this, but you've got a bit of a bruise below your left eye—'

'Have I?' I felt myself stiffen. 'Oh yes.'

'Sorry to mention it, but I just thought you might not want it to show in the picture.'

'Erm, no. No, I don't. My make-up must have come off in the heat,' I added. I went inside and looked in my small hand-mirror. He was right. It was a liverish yellow with a pale mauve outline, as if a black felt-tip had bled on my face. That was careless of me—I must have absent-mindedly rubbed off my concealer. I dabbed on some more Cover-Stick, then pressed on some powder.

'Yes,' he said appraisingly. 'That's fine. Did you have an accident?' he asked.

My heart did a swallow dive. 'No…it was…just one of those…things. I…walked into a lamp post…in the dark. They never look where they're going, do they?'

He laughed. 'Okay, then, hold it. Say cheese! Well, that was my last interview for the *Camden New Journal*,' he announced as he put his camera away. 'I'm going on to pastures new.'

'Really? Where are you off to?'

'The *Independent on Sunday*.'

'That's good. Which bit?'

'The diary. It's a start. But what I really want to get into is political reporting.'

'Well, congratulations—I hope it goes well.'

'Anyway, it was nice to meet you. Here.' He handed me a card. 'You never know, our paths might cross again. Keep in touch—especially if you happen to hear any interesting gossip.'

'Thanks,' I said. 'I will.'

Within two hours of the interview appearing in the paper I had every reason to be grateful to Tim. Not only was it accurate and witty, but I'd already had six enquiries about the puppy parties and three new bookings—a chinchilla, a parakeet, and Joy the osteopath's Bengal cat—which kept me busy for the rest of the week. I phoned Daisy a couple of times but she was busy with clients. But on Friday night she called back.

'Sorry I haven't rung you before, but I've been frantic. So tell me how it's all going?'

'Well, I'm actually quite busy—it's picking up.' I told her about the article in the *Camden New Journal*.

'That sounds good. And what did you think of Lily Jago?'

I giggled at the memory. 'As you said, a complete drama queen.'

'And what about Caroline Mulholland? Did she ring you?'

'Yes, she did. I went out to the house. She was nice.'

'She's as rich as Croesus, apparently—and married to this rather handsome MP.'

'Ye-es,' I said, 'that's right. I met him…briefly. In fact I'm going back there tomorrow—to judge their dog show.'

'Really? How did that come about?'

I explained.

'Oh you'll do it *much* better than Trinny and Susannah,'

she snorted. 'Can you imagine how rude they'd be! "What *does* that Border collie think it's got on?" she said, imitating Trinny. "Makes it look like a scrubber! And that Old English sheepdog looks naff in those pink leggings, doesn't it, Susannah?" "Oh *yes,* Trinny, a complete dog's dinner, and that springer's arse is *far* too big for that skirt." You'll be much more tactful,' Daisy giggled.

'I'll try. But I've never done anything like this before.'

'You'll probably pick up some new clients,' she said. 'It's worth going just for that.'

'That's the main reason why I'm doing it,' I lied. 'Plus the fact that it's in a good cause. So what treats are in store for you this weekend?'

'Well, I've got a blissful day tomorrow. In the morning I'm going Tyrolean traversing.'

'You're going where?'

'Tyrolean traversing. It's a method mountain climbers use for crossing crevasses, but a small group of us are just going to do it above an old stone quarry in Kent.'

'From what height?'

'Oh, only about a hundred feet or so.'

'You're mad.'

'I'm not.'

'You are—you're crazy, Daisy. I've often said it.'

'But apparently it's *really* good fun. Basically, you suspend cables across the gap, with a sort of pulley thing, then you take a running jump off the edge—'

'You do *what*?'

'But then your harness takes the strain and instead of plummeting to the ground you find yourself bouncing along the wire like a puppet on a string. It'll be *fabulous*.'

'Just thinking about it makes me feel sick.'

'And it's supposed to be much more fun than abseiling

because it gives you that *lovely* feeling of falling into empty space.'

'Uhhhh.'

'Then on Saturday night, Nigel's taking me out, *but*—' there was a theatrical pause, '—he won't tell me *where*. He says it's going to be a "very special evening". Very special,' she added happily. 'That's what he said.'

'Hmmm,' I said. 'Do you think it might...mean something?'

'Well, yes, I really think that it *might*. Anyway, enjoy your fete,' she said cheerfully.

'I shall do my best,' I replied.

The next morning I awoke feeling awful, having slept very badly. I'd had this really weird dream. In it, I was in a theatre somewhere—I don't know which one, but it seemed to be quite big—and the curtain had just gone up. And I seemed to be playing Dorothy in *The Wizard of Oz* for some reason, with Herman as Toto, and Daisy as the good witch Glinda, and my mother as Auntie Em. And Alexander was in it too. He was the Lion.

'My goodness, what a fuss you're making. Why you're nothing but a great big coward!'

'You're right. I am a coward. I haven't any courage at all. I even scare myself.'

And then Nigel appeared as the Tin Man.

'Don't you think that the Wizard could help him too?'

'I don't see why not. Why don't you come with us? We're on our way to see the Wizard of Oz to get him a heart, and him a brain, and I'm sure he could give you some courage.'

So we did go to see the Wizard, who, to my amazement, was played by my dad. And then I suddenly realized that it wasn't Alexander playing the Lion any more, it was Jimmy, which confused me. And I was wondering, in the dream, where Alexander had gone, and whether he minded being replaced by Jimmy, because the Lion's a really good part; and I was hoping that the audience wouldn't notice, and I was beginning to feel quite stressed about it all—and that's when I woke up. With my head full of Jimmy. The thought of speaking to him at the fete made me feel sick. To distract myself I spent the morning answering e-mails—I'm constantly amazed at the things people ask.

'*I'm wondering if my cat is obsessive-compulsive as it constantly washes itself,*' said the first. No it's not—that's what cats do. '*How can I get my tarantula to be more friendly?*' asked another. I'm afraid that's just tarantula behaviour—you can't. '*My African Grey parrot keeps telling me to "Fuck off!" Do you think it really means it?*' No.

Sometimes people like to tell me the 'funny' thing their animals do. '*My donkey brays backwards—it goes Haw-Hee.*' '*My horse can count up to ten.*' '*My Persian cat plays the piano—it runs up and down the keyboard.*' '*My mynah bird can sing "Heartbreak Hotel".*' Suddenly another e-mail arrived—from my dad. It contained the usual stuff about the weather in Palm Springs (great), the celebrities he'd seen playing golf (lots), and the Hollywood gossip he'd overheard (scandalous). He said he hoped that my new practice had got off to a good start. Then I got to the final sentence and gasped. '*I also want to tell you that a few days ago I made a decision which will no doubt come as quite a surprise to you—to return to the UK. I've been offered a very challenging job in East Sussex—*' East Sussex!! '*—running a brand new golf club which, as luck, or Fate, would have it, is located very near Alfriston.*' Alfriston? Mum would go *mad*. '*So I'd be grateful if you could break this tragic news to your mother as gently as possible, Miranda.*'

I e-mailed him back. '*I'll try!*'

At half past one I put Herman on the lead, my head still

reeling from the news about my father, then we left for Little Gateley. The journey was easier this time as I knew the way, and I arrived just after two, my stomach in knots. The gates were festooned with bunches of balloons, like aerial bouquets, and there was a poster saying *Summer Fete!* There was no sign of Jimmy's Jaguar—I guessed that he wanted to avoid seeing me. As I parked under a tree I could see frantic activity in the garden, where a number of trestle tables were being set up. Herman and I strolled across the lawn in the sunshine towards the book stalls, home-made-cake stalls and bric-a-brac stalls. There were stalls selling local crafts and toys, a striped marquee marked 'Refreshments', and nearby a brass band was tuning up. There was face-painting, skittles and a tombola, and someone was setting up a slow bicycle race. Strung between the trees were necklaces of bunting—it all looked very festive and gay. Suddenly I saw Caroline coming out of the house followed by Trigger and the two Westies.

'Hi, Miranda, great to see you,' she smiled. 'What a sweet dachshund,' she added admiringly. 'No, Trigger! *Don't* do that to him you rude boy!' She rolled her eyes. 'I'm going to have the brute firmly on the lead today.'

'Any improvement yet?' I asked her, as Trigger leaped about by the flowerbeds, snapping at bees.

'Well, we're working on it. But I don't want to tempt fate. Tempt fete!' she giggled. 'I hope people will be tempted. James is going to be late,' she added. 'He's driving down from Billington after his weekly surgery—he's a politician.'

'Is he?' I said.

'He should be here in about twenty minutes—I do hope he turns up on time. Anyway, that's where the dog show will be,' she indicated a makeshift arena near the tennis court. 'That part will start just after three. Go and get some tea,' she suggested amiably, 'while I man the gates. At least the weather's held,' she said as she looked at the sky. 'It's bliss, isn't it?' she added happily, as she walked away.

'Mm,' I said. 'It is.'

By now people were arriving, many trailing children and dogs. The brass band was playing 'Daisy, Daisy...' and I was just looking at the paperbacks on the book stall when I suddenly heard Jimmy's voice.

'Welcome to the Little Gateley Fete, everyone!' I turned, and saw him standing on a hay bale, in chinos and a blue polo shirt, clutching a megaphone. 'My wife Caroline and I hope that you'll all have a really wonderful time. It's all in a very good cause—the People's Dispensary for Sick Animals. So do please spend as much as you can!' The crowd looked dutifully appreciative and attentive. What a benign figure he cut, I thought. I'd seen him with a megaphone before, of course. He'd looked rather different then as he shouted 'Shame!' at a startled-looking girl on a black pony, the planes of his face twisted with rage. And now, here he was, circulating in friendly fashion, meeting and greeting, patting children and pressing the flesh. He took part in the slow bicycle race and sportingly submitted to having wet sponges thrown at him in the Aunt Sally.

'Come on, folks!' he shouted. 'How often do you get the chance to do *this* to a politician?!' He was in his element— the good-egg country squire, entertaining the locals. And he never once looked over at me. I knew what he was doing, of course. He was letting me know that whatever had happened between us in the past, my presence didn't affect him. I decided not to seek him out yet—I would wait. As the band played the opening chords of 'Scarborough Fair' I heard the church clock chime a quarter past three.

'And now,' Caroline announced with the megaphone, 'we're going to start the highlight of the afternoon—the dog show—in the small arena there at the end of the lawn. I'd like to tell you that we're very lucky in having Miranda Sweet, the animal behaviourist from *Animal Crackers*, adjudicating for us today. So, for anyone who'd like to watch it, the "Waggiest Tail" category will be starting in five minutes.'

'Thanks for the nice intro,' I said, as we walked towards the ring with Herman.

'No,' she said, 'thank *you*. Now, we'll both have cordless mikes so that everyone can hear us.'

There were about ten dogs taking part in this category, their owners all holding up numbered cards. The audience sat on folding chairs or perched on hay bales as the competing dogs were walked round. In the background we could hear the band playing 'Mad Dogs and Englishmen'. Caroline tapped on both mikes, and then spoke.

'Now, it's the quality of the wag that matters, isn't it, Miranda?' she said with mock-seriousness, as a butterfly fluttered past her.

'Yes,' I said. 'It is. That English setter has a lovely sweeping wag, for example—you could polish the floor with it. The retriever's got a nice strong wag too.'

'It has—I can feel the breeze from here!'

'Interestingly, we have two dogs that don't actually *have* tails—the boxer and the corgi—both waggling their behinds there; but it would be unfair to discriminate against the docked breeds.'

'It would. The St Bernard has quite a slow, deliberate wag, doesn't he?' Caroline added. 'I must say that the pug doesn't look as though he's doing much wagging at all.'

'Well, their tails don't actually wag very well, because of the way they curl over their backs. But he certainly looks as though he's trying his best.'

'He does. There's some very enthusiastic wagging there

from the Norfolk terrier and a slightly twitchy wag there from the collie cross. Maybe he's a little nervous,' she suggested with a smile. I saw the owner laugh.

'Okay, everyone,' I announced. 'Please would you walk round the ring just once more?'

'Have you made your decision?' Caroline asked a minute later.

I scribbled in my notebook, then held up my mike. 'I have. In reverse order, the winners of this category are: in third place—number five, the boxer; in second place—the English setter, who's number six. And in first place is number nine, the Norfolk terrier, whose tail really does wag the dog.'

Everyone clapped as I handed the owners their respective rosettes. And now, from out of the corner of my eye, I could see Jimmy, his arms folded, just standing there, watching.

'Now for the next category,' Caroline announced. 'This is always a popular one—the dog most like its owner. So would all the contestants for this class please enter the ring.'

Some of them resembled their canine partners to an astonishing degree. There was a jowly looking man with a bloodhound, a tall, aristocratic-looking woman with a borzoi, and a poodle accompanied by a white-haired woman with a very tight curly perm. Others had resorted to artifice—like the young boy who'd had his face painted white with a black patch over one eye to make him look like his Jack Russell, and the little girl and her yorkie with matching coiffures. Some had clearly entered with a fine sense of irony. There was a bald man with an Afghan, an overweight woman with a whippet, a thin little man with a massive bulldog, and a woman my size with a Great Dane. As they paraded round the arena I found myself thinking that if the competition were about finding a similarity between the human and canine *temperaments* then Jimmy and Trigger would win hands down. By now, Jimmy was standing on the opposite side of the ring. I could sense that he was looking at me. Suddenly I caught his eye, and he looked away and immediately began chatting to the man on his left. He was determined to ignore me. I wouldn't let him. I announced the winners—the first prize went to the aristocratic-looking woman with the borzoi—then it was the Fancy Dress.

'This is always a very popular category,' said Caroline, 'so we have a big field. Would all the competitors please walk their dogs round.' There was a bichon frise dressed as a French onion-seller and the boxer I'd just seen, now in stars and stripes boxer shorts. There was a Rottweiler dressed as an angel, complete with gold halo, and a puli in a Rastafarian hat. There were two Pekes in tutus, a corgi in a headscarf, and a Sheltie in a pink feather boa, which was making it sneeze. There was a wolfhound dressed as Little Red Riding Hood and a Newfoundland wearing fairy wings. Finally, there was a dachshund dressed as a shiny Christmas cracker, its nose just visible through the crimped end. I looked over to where Jimmy had been standing, but he'd gone.

'Are you ready to announce the winners?' Caroline asked me.

'I am. In joint third place are—number seventeen, the regal looking corgi, and the Christmas cracker dachshund, number twelve. In second place is—number eight, the very Gallic-looking bichon frise. But the first prize for the Fancy Dress category goes to—the Angel Rottweiler!' Everyone applauded. This seemed to be a popular choice.

'And finally,' said Caroline, 'we come to "Pup Idol", the canine karaoke competition, the result of which will be decided by you all, in a popular vote. So thanks to Miranda Sweet for being such a great judge.' My duties done, I stepped down. This was my chance to find Jimmy, while the dog show was still going on. 'Now, we've got a selection of songs here,' Caroline went on, 'so may we please have the first of our three talented contestants—Desmond the Dalmatian?' Desmond and his owner stepped up onto the podium and Caroline passed them the mike. Then she pressed the button on the sound system. A familiar song started up.

'*Ebony and ivory…*'

The dog threw back its head.

'Woooow-ow-owwww-oooo…'

'*Live together in perfect harmony…*'

'Ooooo-woowwww-ow-ow-ow…'

'*Side by side on my piano keyboard…oh Lord…*'

'Ow-ow-oooooowwww…'

'*Why don't we-ee?*'

'Oowwoowwwwwwwwwwwww…'

'—That's *rather* good,' I heard someone say as I moved through the crowd.

'—Yes, very nice tone.'

'—Bit of an obvious choice though.'

'—But the diction's clear.'

'—Hmm—you can almost make out the words.'

The song went on for another minute or so, then Caroline faded down the music. Desmond stepped down to a burst of applause and the Christmas cracker dachshund stepped up.

'Now,' said Caroline, as I stood by the rope and scanned the crowd, 'we have Pretzel, who, you may remember, won the event last year. And this year Pretzel has chosen a very challenging classical number, the Queen of the Night's solo from *The Magic Flute!*'

'—That *is* a brave choice,' I heard someone say. 'Notoriously difficult.'

'—Hmm,' acknowledged his friend. 'Let's hope she's got the range for it.'

'—And the breathing of course!'

'—Gosh, *yes.*'

The orchestra swelled to a crescendo, and the dog started to vocalize.

'Yap yap yap yap yap yap yap *yaaap!*

'Yap yap yap yap yap yap yap *yaaap!*

'Yap yap yap yap yap yap yap yap yap yap yap yap yap yap…'

'—Not bad,' said the connoisseur appreciatively.

'—She's hitting those top notes pretty well.'

'—She's not really a coloratura though, let's face it.'

'—Oooh, I wouldn't say that.'

'Yap yap yap yap yap yap yap *yaaap!*'

'—Sounds a bit like Maria Callas, if you ask me.'

'—More like Lesley Garrett.'

'Yap yap yap yap yap yap yap *yaaap!*'

Pretzel's performance was enthusiastically received, then the last contestant, a sheepdog, began to croon along to the strains of 'Danny Boy'.

'Ow wow wow wooooow…'

'—God, isn't that beautiful?'

'Ow wow wow wow wow wow wow *woooooooowww…*'

'—Brings tears to your eyes doesn't it?'

'Ow wow wow wooooow, wow wow wow wow wow *wooooooowwwwwwww…*'

'—Got a tissue anyone?'

'Wow wow ow WOOOOOOOOOOOOOOWWWWWW…'

'—Nice rubato.'

'Wow wow wow wow wow wow wow *woooooooow…*'

'—He could get a recording contract with a voice like that.'

'Wow wow wow wow wow wow wow wow wow woow woow *wooooooooooooooowwwwwwwwwwww!*'

There was a moment's silence, then thunderous applause.

'Now' said Caroline, 'may we please have your votes?' Jimmy was nowhere to be seen. I glanced at my watch—it was a quarter to five and the fete would soon finish. I felt my heart race. Where was he? 'Can we have the votes for Desmond and his cover version of the Paul McCartney?' I heard Caroline ask. There was a few seconds' silence while she counted them. Maybe he'd gone into the house. 'And now a show of hands please for Pretzel and her thrilling rendition of the Mozart...one, two...five...eight, okay...' I looked towards the garden. 'And lastly, your votes for Shep the sheepdog, and "Danny Boy"... Oh, that's a *very* decisive result! So I'm delighted to announce that this year's Little Gateley Pup Idol is Shep the sheepdog. Shall we ask him to sing it again?'

'YEAAHHHH!!!!'

As Shep did his reprise I spotted Jimmy, chatting amiably to the woman running the tombola. 'Thank you *so* much,' I heard him say as I approached. 'We really appreciate it.' I hovered for a moment, knowing that he must have seen me on the periphery of his vision, but he pointedly kept his back turned. Then he moved on to a group of people by the refreshment tent. I could hardly interrupt.

'Yes,' I heard him say. 'It's been a wonderful afternoon, hasn't it? No, we *love* having it here.' I pretended to be engrossed in the bric-a-brac stall. '*So* lucky with the weather, yes. And how old are your lovely kids? Four and two? *Lovely* ages. How sweet.' Now, as he strolled confidently towards the house, stopping every few yards to speak to someone, I discreetly pursued him, my heart racing. It was all very well confronting him, but what would I say? What words could evoke my feelings about the dreadful thing he'd once done? As he headed for the French windows I followed twenty feet behind, feeling like a stalker, the blood drumming in my ears.

I'd go into the house and I'd speak to him. For the first time in sixteen years I'd call out his name.

'Miss Sweet? Excuse me? Miss Sweet?' I turned. An elderly man with a Jack Russell was standing there, smiling at me. I glanced towards the house. Jimmy had gone.

'I just wanted to say how much I like your TV programme.'

'Oh,' I said. 'Thanks very much.'

'I watched them all—and I can't wait for the new series.'

'Well, that's great.' I smiled, then turned to go.

'I just wanted to ask your advice actually.' My heart sank. 'About Skip here.'

'Er, yes. Of course. How can I help?'

'He keeps digging up the garden. It's driving me and my wife up the wall.'

'Tell you what,' I said, fumbling in my bag, and retrieving one of my business cards, 'why don't you e-mail me, and I'll reply.'

'Well it really won't take long for me to explain now, and I just wanted to catch you before the end of the fete. You see we got Skip six months ago, from Battersea actually, and we just *fell* for him the *moment* we saw him…' I stood there, an expression of polite interest superglued to my face while the man went into grinding detail about Skip's excavations of the vegetable patch, the rose-bed, and the herbaceous border. 'We do love him, but ooh, the *damage* he's caused.'

'You need a digging pit,' I said, slightly irritably. 'Terriers are natural diggers. That's what they're bred for, so he'll never stop. But you can make sure that he's fulfilling those natural instincts in a way that doesn't wreck your garden. I suggest you build him a pit, like a sandpit, and fill it with wood chippings, and let him dig to his heart's content in that. You could hide a few of his favourite toys in there to encourage him to use it,' I added, trying to be helpful now.

'Well, thanks very much. That's good advice. A pit,' he repeated, shaking his head. 'I'd never have thought of that.'

'Yes,' I said, nodding. 'A pit.'

I glanced to my left. Everyone was leaving the arena; the fete was almost over. People were packing up. I'd have to be quick.

'Right, well thanks very much,' said the man again.

'My pleasure,' I said. And I was about to walk away when I saw Caroline coming towards me with Trigger, smiling and waving. Blast. I couldn't look for him now.

'It's gone *brilliantly*,' she said. 'I think we've raised over four thousand pounds. Thanks for being such a great judge. Here's a small token of our appreciation,' she handed me a bottle of champagne. 'It's a rather nice one, actually. Vintage—1987. That was a very good year, apparently.'

'Really?' I said faintly. *Not for me.*

'James likes to keep a good cellar.'

'I see. Well, thank you,' I said. I had no intention of drinking it.

'And I do hope you get some new clients out of this.'

'Who knows? I was just glad to help out. It all seems to be winding down now,' I added.

'It does look like it.' People were strolling across the lawn towards the gates. 'Perhaps we'll see you again some time,' she added pleasantly. 'I'll let you know how I get on with this young man's "education",' she grinned, nodding at Trigger. She was *so* natural and nice. I found myself wishing that she wasn't. It made the situation somehow worse.

'Yes. Do let me know. I'd love that.'

I walked towards my car, feeling demoralized. I'd failed in what I set out to do. And I knew I'd never get another chance to confront Jimmy, calmly and quietly, in the way I might have done today. If I wrote to him at the House of Commons, he'd claim he was too busy to see me, or he'd simply ignore me. I knew Jimmy. I knew how his mind worked.

'Okay, Herman,' I sighed. 'Let's go.' I opened the driver's door and was hit by a sudden blast of scalding air. Despite the shade from a huge chestnut, the interior was like a bread oven. We'd just have to wait. As I opened the passenger door I glanced at the house, and suddenly saw Jimmy framed in an upstairs window, standing there, looking down. He hovered for a moment, then disappeared. Disconcerted, I put Herman in the back and got in. The car was still hot, but I just wanted to leave. I'd wound down all the windows and was putting on my seatbelt, struggling with the clasp, when I was aware of a sudden shadow across the dashboard.

'Hello, Miranda.' I looked up at Jimmy. He was blocking out the sun. 'I thought you were ignoring me,' he said. He was doing his best to sound composed, but he was slightly breathless. He'd clearly just run down the stairs.

'You thought *I* was ignoring *you*?' I said, with a serenity which surprised me. 'I had the impression it was the other way round.'

'Oh not at all,' he replied. 'But I've been very busy, what with so many people to talk to and, well, I just wanted to thank you for helping us out.'

'That's fine,' I said coolly. 'Don't mention it.' I looked into his grey eyes, trying to read the expression in them. 'And of course it's in a very good cause. I remember how keen you always were on animal issues,' I added boldly, my heart pounding.

'Hmm,' he said. 'That's right.' He leaned against the neighbouring car and folded his arms. 'And you, Miranda, you were very enthusiastic yourself,' he said pleasantly. 'Quite a fanatic in fact.'

'Oh I wouldn't say that.' Now I understood what his agenda was. He was trying to establish my attitude.

'Do you ever think about those days?' he asked casually. He looked away for a moment, then returned his gaze to me. This was what he really wanted to know.

'Do I ever think about those days?' I repeated slowly. He was hoping that I'd say, 'No. Never. Forgotten all about it.' 'Yes,' I said. 'Actually, I *do*. I've been thinking about them quite a lot lately, as it happens.'

'Really? But it was so long ago.'

'That's true. But at the same time it feels like yesterday in some ways. Doesn't it to you?'

'No.' He'd said it firmly, but I saw a flicker of anxiety. 'But you look *just* the same, Miranda,' he said, trying to steer the conversation back to safer waters.

'You look quite different—I hardly recognized you.'

'Well,' he touched his head and grinned. 'I don't have *quite* so much hair. Anyway, I just wanted to say "hi" and well, thanks. So goodbye then, Miranda. It was nice to see you.' He began walking towards the house.

'Can I ask you a question, Jimmy?' I called.

He stiffened slightly. 'My name's James,' he corrected me.

'Is it? Okay, *James*,' I tried again. 'What I want to know is…' My mouth felt dry as dust. 'Don't you ever feel sorry for what you did?' He stared at me, then blinked a few times. 'Doesn't your conscience ever prick you?'

'I don't know what you mean.'

'Yes you do. There's no point pretending. There really isn't. At least, not with me.'

'Oh. Well…' he put his hands in his pockets then emitted

a weary sigh. 'As I say, it was a *long* time ago. I really think it's best…forgotten.'

'I'm afraid I don't agree.' We stared at each other for a moment and I noticed him discreetly shift his weight.

'Have you ever…mentioned it?' he asked quietly. 'To… anyone?'

'Have I ever mentioned it to anyone?' I repeated. I decided I'd make him wait for my reply. He ran his right hand through his hair and I noticed a dark, spreading stain beneath his arm. 'No,' I said finally. 'I've never told a soul.' I could almost smell his relief.

'I didn't *think* you would have done,' he went on softly. 'And of course that really is the best thing *all* round. I'd forget about it, Miranda. I really would.'

'I've always found that hard to do.'

'Well, I *would*,' he insisted with benign menace. 'Otherwise, well, you could land yourself in a lot of *trouble*. Couldn't you?'

I felt my insides coil. 'Is that a threat?'

'A threat?' He looked mildly scandalized at the suggestion. 'Of course not. It's just…' he shrugged. 'Friendly advice. You've got a nice TV career as an animal expert after all, and I'm a *very* busy man; and you see what happened then—'

'No. Not "what happened",' I interjected hotly. 'What you *did*. To the Whites.'

He shifted his weight again then looked away. 'Well, that was as a result of…' his eyes narrowed as he seemed to grope for the appropriate term, '…youthful indiscretion.'

'Is *that* what you call it?'

He folded his arms again and then stared at the ground. 'Well…maybe we did…misbehave.' *Misbehave?* 'But we were very fired up with our beliefs, weren't we?' he went on smoothly. 'And we were so young.'

'*I* certainly was—I was only sixteen. But it's interesting that you should view it as mere "misbehaviour".' I snorted with mirthless laughter. 'Is that *really* how you see it?'

There was silence for a moment.

'We all make mistakes, Miranda.'

I shook my head. 'Oh it was much, *much* more than that.'

His face suddenly darkened, and the corners of his mouth turned down. 'Anyway, the old git had it coming to him,' he muttered.

'*Why?*' He didn't reply. I stared at him non-comprehendingly. '*Why?*' I repeated. 'What had he *done*? I never *understood.*'

'Oh…plenty of things. *Plenty,*' he repeated, his face suddenly flushing. Then he seemed to collect himself. 'But what a coincidence,' he said smoothly. 'Your meeting my wife like that.'

'Yes,' I agreed. 'It was. But I didn't make the connection immediately as of course you were called "Smith" in those days.'

'Mulholland's my mother's maiden name,' he explained. 'I changed it when I became a journalist to make it a little more…distinctive. It's not a crime, is it?'

'No. *That's* not a crime,' I agreed. 'You must have got a bit of a shock seeing me again.'

He gave me a tight little smile. 'I guess I did. But on the other hand it's a small world, and it did sometimes occur to me that you might pop up. Anyway,' he glanced towards the house, 'I mustn't keep you. And Caroline will be wondering where I am.' He tapped the top of the car to bring the conversation to an end. 'Nice to see you again, Miranda. Goodbye.'

'Goodbye, Jimmy,' I said as I started the engine. His smile vanished.

'James,' he said firmly. 'It's *James*.'

CHAPTER 4

'That's my answer,' I said to Herman, as I drove back with the front windows wide open. 'Not the slightest shred of remorse. He's just worried in case I tell anyone. He's probably been worried about it *all* these years. That's why he decided to speak to me now. He'd clearly been wrestling with it, despite his outward calm, then at the last minute he decided he would. He saw me leaving, hesitated, then made the decision to chance it.' For Jimmy clearly had a lot to lose. And he knew that, even now, sixteen years on, I could let the cat out of the bag. I could go to Scotland Yard and make a statement and he'd be out of Westminster before you could say 'Big Ben'. But what good would be served by doing that, I wondered, as we drove through St Albans. Justice, of course. But who would actually benefit from it? I thought of Jimmy's wife. She seemed a genuine, kind-hearted, nice person, and I had no wish to spoil things for her. She clearly knew nothing about what her husband had done—if he'd told her she would have been appalled. She might well not have married him. I know *I* wouldn't if I'd learned something like that.

Now, as I passed Potter's Bar, I wondered what Caroline did know about Jimmy's past. He'd probably just told her that he'd been a bit of a radical. That would be okay. Having gone on demonstrations in your youth, even taking part in the odd riot, is no bar to public life. Or rather, it's no bar as long as you haven't done anything criminal. But Jimmy *had*. I wondered, as I often had wondered, what would happen to me if I told. This, clearly, was what Jimmy was still banking on. The fact that I'd lose *my* career. It would be even worse now than it would have been before—because of who Jimmy had become. It would be all over the newspapers—I shuddered at the imagined headlines—and that would be curtains for me. Even if there were no prosecution, I'd be tarnished. The TV company would drop me like a shot. Who'd want to watch me on *Animal Crackers*, knowing I'd done something like that? It was one thing to spray graffiti on a fur-coat shop. It was quite another to…I shuddered again as I remembered. Yes… That was quite another thing. There was, of course, one person who would benefit from any disclosure. All I knew was his name. David White.

That night I hardly slept. It was so hot I had the skylight above my bed wide open. I could hear the gibbons shrieking in the zoo, and the occasional roar of a lion—maybe that's why I'd had that dream about *The Wizard of Oz*. Less romantically, I could hear the screaming of car alarms and the dull rumble of traffic from the Marylebone Road. My mind was in turmoil as I alternately dozed and then woke. I'd tried to bury this awful thing in my subconscious all these years, but now I wanted to unburden myself. But to whom? Certainly not to my parents. It's not something I'd ever want them to know.

Now I wondered—as I so often *had* done—about confiding in Daisy, but I didn't want to put our friendship at risk. As my carriage clock chimed three thirty I thought about writing to an agony aunt. Perhaps that nice woman, Beverley McDonald, on the *Daily Post*, with her support dog, Trevor?

I'd seen her on TV a couple of times. She'd sounded sensible and sympathetic. I wondered what advice she'd give. And, as the first birds began to wake and whistle, I composed a letter to her in my mind.

Dear Beverley, I hope you can help me, because I have this dreadful problem. Sixteen years ago I was involved, albeit unwittingly, in something truly awful—something which caused a lot of damage and pain to a totally innocent person, but the thing is… I sighed, then turned over. I just couldn't do it. Even if I used a pseudonym she might, somehow, discover it was from me and feel duty-bound to tell the police. I saw my life, already troubled by my crisis with Alexander, about to be utterly ruined. I wondered if I could talk it out with a counsellor or a therapist; but I didn't have one and, again, what if they *told*? I sat up in bed, as Herman snoozed beside me, sighing intermittently—he even manages to look stressed in his sleep. And as the shreds of pink cloud began to striate the fading navy of the retreating night, I had another, better, idea. There were online therapists and psychiatrists—'Cyber-shrinks'. I threw off the sheet and went downstairs.

I switched on my computer, entered 'online counselling' into Google and came up with about two thousand hits. There were 'Share-Feelings' and 'Help2Cope'. There was a California-based one called 'Blue.com', which claimed to offer a 'cure' for any psychological problem 'within ten minutes'. Sceptical, I clicked to the next. This one was called 'Thought Field Therapy' and claimed to use 'advanced psycho-technologies' to resolve 'any personal issue'. These were listed alphabetically in a sort of tragicomic shopping list, from abuse, affairs and alcoholism through to snoring, transsexuals and stress. Which one of them would I click on? That was easy. 'Guilt.' It had squatted on my life like a dead weight. There were other sites with pictures of the sun rising, of rainbows and of clouds lifting. They all sounded appealing—but how could I choose? Then I stumbled on an Australian website, 'NoWorries.com' for 'people who would like to talk to someone about their problems anonymously, and to do that with total confidence from home'. As I surfed the site I could hear soothing classical music, and there were images of flickering candles and messages in bobbing bottles. Attracted to its simplicity, I logged on.

It said that I could be counselled by e-mail, telephone or face-to-face. I opted for an e-mail session of fifty minutes—the traditional psychiatrist's hour. When did I want it? I could book any time slot, so I clicked on the window marked 'Now'. I used my Hotmail address as it's more anonymous, then began to tap in my credit card number. Hang *on*...I hadn't been thinking straight. My credit card has my *name* on it. Too dangerous. With a heavy heart, I pressed 'Quit'. I went back to bed and lay there, staring through the skylight, trying to work out how I could unburden myself. And I was just wondering whether perhaps the simplest thing wouldn't be to go to the nearest Catholic church and find a priest to confess to, when the phone went.

'Hello?'

'Sorry to ring so early,' said Daisy. She sounded dismal.

'That's okay. I was just getting up. What's the matter?'

'Oh...nothing,' she said, bleakly. 'I'm...' I heard her voice catch, '...fine.'

'You don't sound it. How was last night?'

'Well, to be honest, not quite as "special" as I'd hoped.'

'Where did he take you?'

'The Opera House.'

'But that sounds lovely.'

'Well...yes. It *was*. Seats in the stalls. Champagne before and after. But...'

'He didn't…?'

There was the sound of a suppressed sob. '*No*. Although when I realized it was *The Marriage of Figaro* my hopes were right up. And at the end the singers were knee-deep in confetti, and I was just sitting there thinking…Well, you *know* what I was thinking.'

'Hmm.'

'Then afterwards, Nigel took me to this gorgeous little French restaurant, and I was convinced he was going to do it—at *last*. But we were just chatting in a perfectly normal way and he didn't look at all nervous; and then he had to take an emergency call about this merger he's working on, so he went outside. And at the next table was this couple, and I heard the guy *propose* to his girlfriend.'

'Really?'

'I actually heard him *say* the *words*. She just looked so radiantly happy, and then she started to cry. Then when the waiter realized what had happened he announced it and we all clapped and raised our glasses—and Nigel missed the *whole* thing. So when he came back to the table I told him what had happened; and instead of saying, "How romantic", or "How lovely", or even, "Will *you* marry *me*, Daisy?", he just said, "How extraordinary". Like that. As though it really puzzled him. Then he spent the rest of the evening talking about the opera.'

'Hmm.'

'And as he had to catch a very early flight to Bonn, I came home. I don't think it's *ever* going to *happen!*' she wailed.

'Well there's always his fortieth, isn't there? When's that?'

'Next month.'

'Maybe the prospect of impending middle age will do the trick.'

'But his dad didn't marry until he was forty-*six*.'

'It doesn't follow that Nigel will be the same.'

'Maybe, but I don't want to wait *another* five and a half years to find out. Christ, Miranda, I'll be thirty-nine by then! I'll have jowls and grey hair.'

'Don't be silly.'

'I'll have more lines than the London Underground.'

'You won't.'

'I'll have atomic knickers—and a stoop—and arthritis.'

'Rubbish, Daisy!'

'I'll probably have a Zimmer frame. You'll have to push me up the aisle in a bloody wheelchair!'

'You're being ridiculous now.'

'And I won't be able to have *kids*.'

'You *will*. Honestly, Daisy,' I went on, as her sobs finally subsided. 'You've *got* to get a grip. You've been here with Nigel enough times before, so why are you so especially upset now?'

'Because, well,' she sniffed. 'I've just done something rather…silly.'

'What?' There was silence. 'Daisy, *what* have you done?'

'Come to lunch and you'll see.'

When I rang Daisy's bell at twelve, I expected her to come to the door with red eyes and tear-stained cheeks, but instead she seemed to have recovered some of her natural *élan*.

'Nige phoned me from his hotel,' she said, 'so I'm feeling a bit cheerier than I was. Ooh, what *lovely* flowers. Did you come by car?' she added.

'No. I got the tube.'

'Good, because I've just discovered a bottle of fizz I didn't know I had. I've had it in the freezing compartment for an hour. It should be nicely chilled by now.'

'Great.'

I followed Daisy down the narrow hallway, which was crammed with all sorts of stuff—a large rucksack, two helmets, three kagouls, several coils of rope, a pick-axe and cramponed boots. A pair of racing skis was upended against the wall next to something which looked like a huge kite.

'Sorry about all the junk,' she said. 'I don't have much storage space.'

'What's this thing here?'

'A bit of my hang-glider.'

'Oh. And this netting?'

'It's a sling.'

'A sling?'

'A hammock. For sleeping in when you're halfway up a cliff face.'

'Ah.'

'They're *so* useful, you know. You just knock in a couple of nails, suspend one and climb in. Water for Herman?'

'Yes please.' She went to the sink and turned on the cold tap.

'Okay,' I said, as she put a bowl down for him. 'Tell me.'

'Oh,' she sighed as she straightened up. '*Right*... Well, I'd actually decided, on reflection, that I wasn't going to bother you with it after all; but, okay then, what happened *was*...'

Then I saw it. On a chair. A stiff, expensive-looking carrier bag bearing the legend, 'Bridal Belles'. I stared at it, and then looked at her.

'Oh, Daisy.'

'Well, you see,' she began, 'I was on my way back from the Tyrolean traversing yesterday. And I was driving through Rochester and I saw this lovely wedding-dress shop, and I was feeling *so* happy so I just thought I'd have a *little* look...'

'Show me.'

She opened the bag and pulled out several layers of tissue,

then a long veil, as light as gossamer and spangled with se-
quins. 'Oh, *Daisy.*'

'I *know*,' she shrugged. 'But I was so totally *convinced* that
Nige was going to pop the question last night, and the shop
was having a sale. And I'd just been paid and I was in *such* a
good mood...'

'How much?'

'Ninety-five pounds. But there was twenty per cent off it,'
she added.

'Well, thank *God* you didn't spend any more.' And now
I noticed that Daisy had a very odd expression on her face.
The kind dogs have when they know they're in trouble.
'Okay,' I said. 'What else?'

She sighed, then padded down the hall to her bedroom.
I followed her, she opened the door, and we went in. I
couldn't, at first, see anything out of the ordinary. Then she
shut the door behind us and I heard a sudden swish and a
light thump. I turned. Hanging on the back of the door was
a claret-coloured velvet dress bag, of the kind used for ball
gowns. I felt my jaw go slack.

'I just couldn't *resist*,' Daisy wailed. 'It was in the window.
And it was just so, so *beautiful*. Look!' She pulled the ribbon,
and the velvet bag slithered to the floor, revealing a wedding dress of, admittedly, exquisite loveliness. It was a Fairy
Princess confection of white silk netting, the skirt as lay-
ered as a *millefeuille*, and, above, a fitted satin bodice which
sparkled with tiny, hand-sewn crystals. 'It's just *so* beautiful,'
she sniffed again. 'So I decided to try it on. And I looked so
fantastic in it, Miranda. I really did. And I knew that no other
dress would *ever* do. So I simply *had* to buy it. Can't you understand that?'

'No. How much?' I asked as I stared at it. 'A thousand?'

'Twelve hundred—but marked down from fifteen.'

'Twelve hundred pounds! That would pay your mortgage for three months! Daisy, please don't think me cruel, but I feel I should point out that you are *not* yet engaged.'

'I know that,' she whined. 'But I will be. Quite soon. I mean Nige *is* going to ask me, I'm *sure* about it. So, I do think it'll, you know…come in…handy…' her voice trailed away. 'Do you want to see the shoes?'

'*No!*'

'Don't be cross, Miranda.'

'I'm not cross—I'm *worried*.' She bagged the dress up again. 'You'd better hide it,' I added. 'In case Nigel sees it.'

'Hmm, that's true. Not that he ever comes here that much.'

'Daisy,' I said, as she hung it in the wardrobe. 'Let's talk about this.'

'Okay, but can we have lunch first? I'm starving—and I really need that glass of champagne.' As she opened the freezing compartment I looked at the snaps on her kitchen pinboard. There was one of us at Bristol, in our flat, arms round each other, laughing; and one on a Greek holiday we'd had. There were several of Nigel, looking typically solid, and a few of her mum. There were a number of Daisy in action—beaming, begoggled, into the camera; in free-fall; bungee-jumping, head first, off a bridge; white-water rafting down a raging ravine; at the controls of a glider, thumbs up. On the dresser was a framed studio portrait of her parents—Daisy looks exactly like her dad. He'd been killed, at forty-two, just crossing the road one Sunday morning to get a newspaper. That's her dilemma, I realized, as I gazed at his face. She knows how fragile life is, so she wants to take risks—but at the same time she's insecure, and needs to feel 'safe'.

'Daisy,' I said, as she twisted the cork off the bottle, 'you have *got* to pin Nigel down. The uncertainty is clearly driving you mad. The premature purchase of a wedding dress proves that.' I imagined her going into the shop in her climbing gear and helmet.

'Yes,' she breathed, as she got down two glasses. 'You're right. You're *absolutely* right.'

'You've got to talk to him. It's time.'

'Yes, it's high time,' she sighed. 'I know that.'

'You've been *very* patient, after all.'

She nodded dismally. 'I have. Patient Griselda, that's what I've been. But now I'm feeling a bit "Grisly"—and more than a little "Elda",' she added with a snort of dark laughter. 'So, okay, I *will* definitely ask him.'

'Good,' I said. 'When?'

She looked at me blankly. 'Oh. I don't really know. But… soon.'

I nodded. 'Great.'

She smiled a brave smile, then anxiety pleated her brow. 'But what if I *do* pin him down, and the answer is *no*?' She looked stricken. '*Then* what would I do?'

'What would you do? Well, although it'd be horrible—for a while—I think that, ultimately, you'd be *fine*. And if it doesn't work out, Daisy, maybe it's because it's actually your destiny to meet someone *else*.' She looked at me for a moment while she absorbed this. 'Don't you ever think of that?' I asked. 'That there might be someone out there who won't take the best part of six years to make a commitment to you?'

'No,' she said, shifting slightly. 'I don't. And the reason I don't is because I want to be with *Nigel*.'

'But does Nigel want to be with *you*? That's the awful question you will have to confront, Daisy, if you *do* want more from him than just being his girlfriend; and if it becomes obvious that you're *not* going to get it, then I really think you'll have to be brave and move *on*.'

She looked at me, then looked away. 'I know that's true. Of course I know. And I *will* have to be brave,' she sighed. 'But maybe, on the other hand,' she lifted her glass, 'things with Nige will work out. Anyway, chin chin, Miranda.'

'Chin chin,' I replied. 'And chin *up*.'

'I mean, you were brave,' she went on thoughtfully. 'About Alexander.'

I lowered my glass. 'Brave? You think I'm brave?'

'Yes. When I think what happened to you—or rather, what he *did*,' she corrected herself crossly. 'But, yes, you were incredibly brave—and you're being brave now.'

'I'm not brave at all,' I said quietly. '*Far* from it.' Daisy gave me a puzzled look. We sat on her patio in the warm sunshine, amongst the pots of shocking-pink geraniums, with our smoked-salmon sandwiches and bubbling Bollinger, just chatting. I felt some of my stress ebb away.

'I don't know *what* I'd do without you,' Daisy said, with a large sip of champagne. 'I can't discuss Nigel with anyone else—and especially not my mum because she's already so negative about him. She says he's "behaving badly".'

'Hmm.'

'You're the one person I can really *talk* to about my problems,' she went on, with another sip. 'You're my safety valve. You're the one person I can expose myself to—' she giggled tipsily and waved her glass at me. 'I mean, who I can really open up to without feeling I have to be careful, or that I might regret what I said. With you I don't feel I have to show you only my "good" side, but my ugly side too.'

'You don't have one,' I said as I watched the bees buzzing about in the lavender, their legs fat with pollen.

'I mean my unattractive side. When I'm feeling negative and low, like I was this morning—or desperate. Everyone else thinks I'm always upbeat—Daisy the happy party girl—but I can let my emotional hair down with you.'

'You can.'

'I feel that you'd never think badly of me, whatever I told you.'

I fiddled with the stem of my glass. 'That's right.'

'I know I can tell you *anything* and you won't judge me for it.'

'No,' I said quietly. 'I won't.' A small dragonfly skimmed past, a blur of blue iridescence.

'You're not nearly as open with me,' she observed with another sip of champagne, 'but I don't mind. I never have—I know you've always preferred to keep your own counsel.' I nodded. It was quite true. 'Anyway,' she said brightly. 'How was the fete?'

'Oh…it was…nice. The dog show was fun.'

'And the house?'

'It's fantastic. Like a smaller version of Gosford Park.'

'Well they say she's worth squillions. And what about him? The hubby.'

'The hubby…'

'I've seen photos. He's losing his hair, but he's rather a dish. Tipped for high office, apparently. Did you meet him?'

I stared at the crazy paving. A column of ants was flowing out of a crack in the concrete. 'I did meet him actually… Yes.' *I know I can tell you anything and you won't judge me for it.*

'Apparently he's charming,' I heard Daisy say. 'More champers, darling?' She leaned over with the bottle.

'He *is* charming,' I said. 'He's incredibly charming. He's one of the most charming men that you could meet.' *I feel you'd never think badly of me, whatever I told you.* I looked at her—then made a sudden decision. 'He's also a shit.'

Daisy lowered the bottle. '*Is* he?'

'Oh yes.'

'Well, lots of politicians are,' she shrugged as she batted away a wasp. 'I guess it goes with the territory.'

'It's *much* more than that.'

'How do you know?'

'I just do,' I said bitterly.

'But *how*?' There was silence. 'How do you know that?'

I took a deep breath. 'Because I've met him before.'

'Really?' she said. 'When was that then?'

'Sixteen years ago.'

'When you were living in Brighton?'

I nodded. 'He was a student there.'

'Oh, *I* get it,' she said, her eyes widening. 'He was your boyfriend. Is that it?'

'Sort of. I was infatuated with him—put it that way.'

'Blimey. Small world,' she breathed. 'And he treated you badly?' she asked, with another sip of champagne. 'Bastard!'

I smiled at her retrospective loyalty. 'He treated me *very* badly, Daisy—but not in the way that you think.'

'What did he do then?' she asked, clearly intrigued.

'Well…he did something…very…shocking, and he involved me in it, and it's haunted me ever since.' Daisy was looking at me, spellbound. I stared at the ground.

'Well, whatever it was,' I heard her say, 'remember that you were only sixteen. You were very young.'

I sighed. 'That's true. But even so, the memory still fills me with shame.' I put down my glass. I had a pain between my eyes.

'Anyway, I'm sure it wasn't *that* bad. We all do things we regret,' she went on tactfully. 'Silly things. Unkind things. Don't be too hard on yourself, Miranda.'

There was a knife-like pain in my throat. 'I'm not being hard on myself—it *was* that bad. In fact, it was dreadful. It was absolutely *dreadful.*' I felt my eyes suddenly fill. 'You said I'm brave just now, Daisy, but I'm *not.*' My hands sprang up to my face. 'If I *were* I'd have done something about it years ago, but I never have.' I felt a warm tear slide down my cheek.

'What was it?' I heard her ask gently. 'You can tell me.'

I shook my head. 'You'd despise me if you knew.'

'I wouldn't, Miranda. You're my closest friend.'

'You would—you'd judge me. You wouldn't be able to help it.'

'I promise you I *won't* judge you, Miranda, whatever it was, any more than I know you'd judge me.'

I pressed the heels of my hands to my eyes. 'I've never got over it,' I croaked. 'The knowledge that I hurt someone so much.'

'You *hurt* someone?' I nodded. 'You mean, physically?' I nodded again. 'But who?'

'This…boy,' I replied. 'Well, young man. He was twenty then. His name was David.'

'What was he like?'

I shook my head. 'I don't know.'

'You don't know what he was like?' I shook my head again. 'Why not?'

'Because I've never met him.'

She looked confused. 'You've never *met* him—but you hurt him?'

'Yes.'

'I don't understand. Was it by accident?'

'Sort of. Or rather, *no*—it wasn't. It *wasn't* an accident.' Daisy was staring at me as though I were speaking in tongues. 'It was a *crime,*' I whispered. There was silence, punctuated only by the soft roar of a distant plane.

'A crime?' she repeated softly. I looked away, unable to maintain eye contact.

'It was…' I drew in my breath, '…very *bad*.'

'Was it drugs?' Daisy asked quietly, after a moment. 'Did you give someone drugs?'

'No. I've never got involved with that.'

There was a pause. 'Then…was it like what happened to my dad? Is that what it was, Miranda—a hit and run?'

'A hit and run?' I echoed. '*No*. Although, yes, it *was* like that—in a way—*yes*—except that it didn't involve a car.'

Daisy's bewildered-looking face began to blur as my eyes spilled over again. 'I don't understand,' she said.

Now I took a deep breath, as though I were about to dive underwater.

'Then I'll tell you,' I whispered. 'I *will* tell you. I *need* to tell you. But you must *never* tell anyone else.'

'I absolutely swear not to.'

I glanced next door. 'Can we be overheard?'

'No. My neighbours are all away.'

And so, in a low, cracked voice, I told Daisy what had happened half my lifetime ago.

'Gosh,' she murmured, when I'd finished. There was silence. 'Gosh,' she said quietly again.

'I did say it was shocking, didn't I?'

I heard her inhale. 'Yes.' She breathed out again. 'You did.'

'Do you feel differently about me now?'

She shook her head. 'No, I don't. Because it wasn't your fault. He *is* a shit,' she remarked, as though the thought had just struck her. '*He* did it, Miranda—not you.'

'But I shouldn't have got involved in all that…stuff. I shouldn't have got involved with *him*. I was naïve, at best. But I would have done anything for him—I used to write him these pathetic love letters—loads of them—and he exploited my obsession; and as a result, this guy David got hurt.'

'No wonder it's troubled you for so long,' she said. 'What a huge thing to have to bear.' She laid her hand on my arm for a moment. 'And you never saw Jimmy again?'

'No. Not until last week.'

'Is that why it's all come up again now?'

'Partly—the shock of seeing him again—but actually, Daisy, it's *always* been there. It's *always* haunted me. And recently it's been on my mind a *lot* for some reason—and then, by some strange stroke of synchronicity—or Fate—I met Jimmy again. And now I just can't get it all out of my head.'

'I know what's happened,' Daisy said quietly. 'I think the fact that you were hurt recently has brought it all up—after all, you were a victim too. And that's made you more aware of the hurt *you* once caused.'

'Maybe,' I whispered. 'It's quite possible. All I know is that it's overshadowed a big part of my life. Sometimes I think it would have been better if we'd been caught, and punished, then I could at least have moved on.'

'But if you had been, you might well have gone to *prison*, Miranda.'

'I still could,' I said bleakly. 'So could he.'

'He'd certainly lose his seat. And I don't think he'd ever have been selected if they'd known *that* about him—it's much too serious.'

'I'm sure you're right.'

'And that's why he spoke to you,' she said, more animatedly now. 'He's kept it hidden all these years, then suddenly *you* turn up again. What a nightmare for him, Miranda—he took a huge risk going into politics—and you're his smoking gun. He's probably terrified that you'll try and blackmail him.'

'I think he *did* think that. He said I could get in "a lot

of trouble" if I told anyone, which was obviously a counter-threat. Anyway, there it is,' I whispered. 'My terrible secret. Now you know. I'm *glad* you know,' I added quietly. 'I've been in torment for so long, and there was no-one else I could trust.'

Daisy laid her hand on my arm again. 'I understand certain things about you now,' she said, after a moment. 'I understand why, when we first met, you seemed so guarded. I had to work hard to be friends with you. You seemed, yes... rather secretive, you always have actually. Now I know why.'

'Yes. Because I *did* have a secret. A really dreadful one—and I was terrified that I'd be exposed. I lived in constant fear that one day someone would find out—and that my life would be ruined. It still might be,' I added dismally.

'I just wish you'd told me this before.'

I heaved a painful sigh. 'There have been many, *many* times, over the years, when I *have* wanted to tell you. But you were my one and only close friend, Daisy, and I didn't want to risk that.'

'But I hate to think of you having carried such a big thing alone. It makes me feel sad.' Her sympathy made my eyes fill again. 'And you must have felt...lonely,' she added. 'Not being able to tell anyone.'

'Yes,' I murmured. 'I *did*.'

'Well, I'm very glad that you've told me. But the question is...what now?'

I looked at her blankly. 'I don't really know.'

'Do you want to punish Jimmy? Is that it?'

'No. Although his lack of shame fills me with rage.'

'Then what do you want to *do*?'

I stared at the ground and there was silence for a few seconds while I considered the question. 'I want...to try and make amends.'

'You mean you want to be forgiven?'

My heart did a somersault. 'Yes,' I said. 'I *do*. I want to be forgiven. I want to be…absolved. Sixteen years ago I did something terrible to someone, and I want to put it *right*.'

'But why do you want to try and put it right *now*?'

'Because, instead of fading with each year, it's got worse. It's never left me. I want to get it out of my head—and I don't think I can unless I finally *do* something.'

'And what do you think you could *do*?'

I shook my head. 'I don't know. All I know is, I want to… atone. I'd like to stop feeling guilty. I've been feeling guilty for so *long*.'

'I know what you could do,' Daisy said softly, after a moment. 'But you must have thought of it yourself.' I looked at her, then looked away.

'I have. I've thought of it many times. I've had…' I sighed, 'these fantasies about doing it. But that's all they've been— just fantasies—because I've never been brave enough to carry it out.' I glanced at the sky where a distant plane was sewing a slender white trail across the blue.

'Then be brave *now*,' I heard Daisy say as I gazed upwards. 'Be brave, Miranda.'

'Isn't it too late?' I asked bleakly.

'No. It's never too late.' I looked at her. 'Find him, Miranda.' My heart turned over. 'Find David.'

Find David…

'But what would I *say*?'

'What would you say?' she echoed. 'Well, "sorry", I suppose.'

I laughed a mirthless little laugh. 'I don't think "sorry" would be quite enough. "Hello, David. I'm Miranda. You know that parcel you got sixteen years ago? The one that exploded in your hands? Yes, that's right. That one. You probably remember it quite clearly, actually. Well, the person who delivered it was me!" I'm not sure "sorry" is going to be quite enough,' I repeated, as I felt my eyes fill.

'Well, it might be,' she said. 'It's the least you can say—and the most you can say. It's the only thing *to* say, actually, when you think about it.'

'Hmm,' I croaked. 'That's true.'

'Look for him, Miranda,' she said gently. 'Then maybe you'll be able to put this behind you at last. Isn't that what you really want to do? What you've always wanted to do?'

'Yes,' I whispered, after a moment. 'It is. I *do* want to do it. I've *always* wanted to do it. I've always wanted to find David White. And I *will*.'

— CHAPTER 5 —

By the time I left Daisy's, a couple of hours later, I felt shattered, but relieved. I'd unburdened myself, Daisy hadn't judged me, and she'd given me such good advice. Just the thought of trying to find David made me feel so much better. The thought of taking *action* at last. But where on earth would I look? He could be in Paris, or Peru, or Prestatyn. He could be anywhere in the world. But I knew what my first port of call would be. When I arrived home, I got the number and dialled.

'Welcome to the University of Sussex,' said a recorded voice. 'The switchboard is open from nine o'clock until five thirty, Monday to Friday. If you know the extension number—' I'd have to wait. Then I looked up 'Professor Derek White' on the Net. There was nothing. And so, although I knew it to be a futile exercise, I looked up 'David White' too. There were nearly four million entries. There was a David White selling optical instruments; a David White who bought antiquarian books; a David White offering heating services; and David White, the actor, who starred in *Bewitched*. There were David White power tools and David White furniture, there was even a rap artist called

David White. Maybe 'my' David White had become a scientist, like his father. Maybe he'd completely dropped out.

At nine o'clock the next morning I called the university switchboard again.

'I don't want to be put through to him,' I said carefully. 'But could you tell me if Professor Derek White is still on the staff?'

'Just a moment please…' There was a quick burst of synthesized Vivaldi. 'I can't see that name, no. What department is he in?'

'Erm…I'm not sure. Biology, probably. Or maybe Biochemistry.'

'I'll check for you again. No. There's no one of that name. Do you wish to be put through to anyone else in the Science department?'

I panicked. 'No, thanks.' They might ask me who I was, or why I was calling. I'd have to try a different tack. So I rang directory enquiries again, and tried to find a home number.

'Do you have the address?'

'Yes. I do.' I'd never forgotten it. 'It's forty-four West Drive, Brighton.'

'Please hold… There's no listing for a Professor D. White at that address,' the operator announced.

'Not even ex-directory?'

'There's no listing for that name at that address,' she repeated automatically. 'Would you like another number, caller?'

'No. Thanks.' I replaced the handset with a sigh. This wasn't going to be easy, but then it was a long time ago—they could have moved, or he might have died. He must be well over sixty-five by now, so he'd probably retired. Maybe their neighbours might know where they'd gone, or would

agree to forward a note. With no other leads, I decided to go
down there. I could combine it with a visit to Mum. I looked
in the diary. Wednesday was free. Once I'd done my sleuth-
ing, we could have lunch.

'That would be lovely,' she said when I phoned her. 'The
girls are away—they've finished school now—so we'll have
a nice catch-up on our own. And you can see the boys. You
haven't seen them for a while, have you?'

'No, I haven't. That would be great.'

On Wednesday morning, Herman and I set off for Brighton early. I wanted to arrive before nine in order to maxi-
mize the chance of someone being in when I called. I didn't
need to look at the map as I knew the way there so well.
Through the City, over Blackfriars, then down the A23,
past Hurstpierpoint; then I saw the Brighton sign. I had a pit
in my stomach as I drove through the town centre towards
Queens Park then turned right into West Drive. I'd revis-
ited it in my dreams—and nightmares—so many times. The
house was towards the end, semi-detached, Edwardian, set
back, with a neat front garden protected by a low hedge. As
I went slowly by, I saw no movement, but then it was still
early—a quarter past eight. I turned round at the end, then
parked two doors down, feeling like a private detective on
the trail of some errant spouse. As I sat, waiting and watching, Herman would emit the occasional anguished sigh. At
eight thirty I saw the postman arrive, but by nine there was
still no sign of life. Perhaps they were away—the grass looked
quite long. At nine fifteen, I got out of the car. Breathing
deeply, I opened the gate, then walked up the path—remembering, with a sick feeling, the last time I had done that—and
now, heart pounding, I rang the bell.

Strangely, I hadn't given much thought to what I would

actually say. As I waited I mentally rehearsed it. 'Hello, my name's Miranda. I just want you to know that it was me. In 1987. It was me. I did it. But I didn't mean to. I've just come to say how sorry I am.' There was no answer. I peered through the frosted-glass panel, but could detect no shadows moving inside. I rang again, but still there was complete silence. I'd have to leave a note. I could have asked the postman if they still lived there, I realized, as I returned to the car. And I'd just reached into the glove box and pulled out the writing pad I'd brought with me for this purpose, when I heard a door slam. I looked up. A man was coming out of the neighbouring house with a black cocker spaniel. I got out of the car again and crossed the road.

'Excuse me!' He glanced up, and I smiled at him politely. 'I'm sorry to bother you, but could you tell me if the Whites still live at number forty-four?'

The man looked at me blankly. 'The Whites? The *Whites*?' he said again. 'Goodness me, no. They left years ago. *Years* ago,' he repeated.

'Oh.' I felt crestfallen.

'Mind you, *we've* been here twenty years. Twenty years, we've been here...' He seemed to like saying everything twice.

'So you knew them then?' I ventured.

'The Whites?' I nodded. 'Oh yes. Nice family. *Very* nice family.'

'And when did they move?'

'Ooh, in about, what, '87 or '88? Yes. Must have been. Not long after... Well, they had a spot of bother. Nasty business, that was,' he shook his head. '*Nasty* business.' He looked at me quizzically. 'Why do you want to know?'

'Well, I'm...an old friend of their son, you see.'

'Michael?'

'No,' I said carefully. 'Erm, David actually.' I felt a sudden surge of adrenaline.

'Ah, David. Yes. Good lad. *Good* lad he was.'

'*Was*?' I repeated, my heart racing.

'*Is*. I mean I just remember him as a nice lad. How do you know him then?'

My insides were churning, but I had my lie ready. 'We were at college together.'

'I see. So you're trying to get in touch again. Friends Re-united and all that.'

'Yes,' I said brightly. 'That's right.'

'But don't any of your other college friends have a number for him?'

'Er, no. They've all lost touch.'

'Well, of course he left university early, I seem to remember now.'

'*Did* he?' I felt ill. 'I mean, of course he did.'

'After that nasty business.'

'Er, yes, that's…right. But, um, anyway, I remembered that his parents used to live here,' I stumbled on, 'so I thought maybe there was a chance they still did. I don't suppose you know their present address, do you?'

'I'm afraid I don't.' He clicked his tongue against the roof of his mouth, then shook his head. 'No. I'm afraid I don't.'

'And what about the people who live in the house now?'

'They're on holiday, and, in any case, they've only been there two years. It's changed hands three times since the Whites left. I doubt anyone would have a forwarding address now.'

'Oh,' I said blankly. 'I see. So you have no idea where they went, or how I could get in touch with them again?'

'Not really.' He was making thoughtful little sucking

noises with his teeth. 'My wife might know,' he added, 'but she's visiting her sister. I could ask her when she gets back.'

'Would you? I'd be so grateful.' I scribbled my mobile number down, and next to it, simply, 'Miranda'. 'If your wife does have any information, I'd really appreciate it if you could let me know. I'd, er, really like to see David…again,' I concluded.

'It's been a long time, has it?'

'Yes,' I said. 'It's been a long time.'

By now it was twenty to ten. I wasn't due at Mum's until twelve. I could simply have phoned her to say I was coming early, but there was something I wanted to do first. I wanted to revisit my old haunts—I was in the mood for a trip down memory lane. I drove past the Pavilion, smiling at its absurd splendour, then I parked close to the Palace Pier. The seagulls wheeled and cried as Herman and I walked along the sea front, the waves glinting like beaten metal in the sun. Then we walked through The Lanes. I found East Street, where Jimmy's flat had been, on the corner, above a newsagents. It was a Thai restaurant now. Then I went back to the car, and drove down Kings Road, turned right into Brunswick Place, then parked outside Brighton and Hove High.

As I sat staring at the square, cream-painted, eighteenth-century building, I could hear female voices floating through the open windows, then a bell, then the sudden scraping of chairs. I thought about how much I'd hated it there. Right from the start I'd been earmarked as 'obstreperous' and 'unco-operative', but after the incident with the Whites I changed. Subdued by shock—and terrified I'd be caught—from then on, I kept my head down. I abandoned all my animal rights activity, worked like a slave, and got straight 'A's after that. Now I remembered, on my last day, the headmistress congratulating me as I went up on stage.

'You've been a credit to this school,' she said as I got the valedictory shake of her hand. 'You've also been an example to other, well, *challenging* girls,' she'd added with an indulgent smile. If she'd known the truth she would never have said that. Then I'd gone to Bristol, Mum had moved away, and I'd left Brighton and its dark memories behind.

'Miranda!' Mum exclaimed, as she opened the door to me forty minutes later. 'You're so thin!'

'Am I?' I said absently as she hugged me. 'Yeah, I guess so.'

'I don't have to ask why,' she said as we went down the hall to the kitchen. 'When Hugh ran off I lost nearly two stone. I suppose Alexander did the same, did he?' she went on. 'Just ran off?'

'Well…'

'Men let you down,' she said, shaking her head. I didn't contradict her. 'Animals, however, don't.' That was true. 'You should have phoned me,' she added. 'You must have been feeling distraught.'

'Well, no, not quite. I just feel…' What *did* I feel? '…disappointed. But I'd rather not discuss it, if you don't mind.'

She sighed. 'All right. You know, I don't think you've ever discussed *anything* with me, Miranda. No daughterly confidences. Nothing. It's disappointing.'

I shrugged. 'I'm sorry, Mum. That's just…how I am.'

'I know. Anyway, tell me what you were doing in Brighton?'

'Oh. Erm, work. There was a very…tricky…donkey.'

'What was the problem?'

'It kept…getting…'

'Out?' she anticipated. Mum often anticipates—it's really annoying.

'Ye-es…'

'How dangerous. It could be killed, poor darling, or cause a horrible accident. So what did you advise?'

'I...told them they'd have to get a better...'

'Gate?' I nodded, wearily. 'Well, they could have worked that out for themselves. Still, all money in the bank for you,' she added cheerily as she opened the fridge. 'So Perfect Pets is going well then, is it?' she enquired over her shoulder.

'It's coming along. So where are the girls then?' I have three half-sisters; Gemma, who's twenty, and Annie and Alice, who are twins of eighteen.

'They've gone to see their father. They'll probably spend the whole summer there.'

'Do you mind?'

'No. Not any more. It's very good for their French and I really can't blame them—a grand place like that. In any case,' she shrugged, 'that was the deal, so I can't argue about it.'

'Of course.' Hugh left my mother four years ago. He'd been commissioned to re-landscape the grounds of this small chateau in Burgundy. The owner, Françoise, an attractive young widow, prevailed upon him, successfully, to stay. Mum got the farm on condition that she didn't stop Hugh from seeing the kids. When I say it's a farm, it's really just a large cottage with a barn and a couple of fields. Mum chose to stay there as it suited her, plus the girls liked it, and in any case she was quite resigned about Hugh in many ways. He's ten years younger than her, and heart-stoppingly handsome, so she says she always knew, in her heart, that it wouldn't last.

'I *knew* he'd go off,' she said again today, as I laid the kitchen table. 'I always knew he'd go off, when the girls were older. Of course, it was awful when it happened, but if it hadn't been his French *chatelaine*,' she enunciated disdainfully, 'then it would only have been someone else.'

'Is that why you've always seemed okay about it?' I asked, as she put the vegetarian lasagne in the Aga.

'Partly, but that's not the only reason. The main reason is that if Hugh hadn't left me, I'd never have had the boys, would I?'

'That's true. Can we go and see them?'

'Of course we can. We'll leave Herman inside.'

We stepped through the French windows into the garden and suddenly in the middle distance, through the apple trees, I saw eight pairs of ears prick up. They hung in the air, like furry inverted commas, then slowly swivelled our way.

'San-cho!' Mum called, rattling a bucket of pellets. 'Bas-il! Car-los!' And now they were cantering daintily towards us across the hillocky grass. 'Miranda's come to see us! Isn't that lovely? Come on Pedro! Come on boys! Come and say hello!'

I can understand Mum's passion for llamas. They're so endearing. Just the sight of them makes me smile. They look like nothing else on this earth—or rather they look like all sorts of other things smashed together. With their donkeyish ears, horsey faces, their giraffe necks, and antelope behinds; and their rabbity noses and their big doe eyes with ludicrously long, glamorous lashes, and their luscious camel lips. It's as though the species is the result of a genetic pileup: it's an improbable but somehow elegant mix.

'Dalai Ll-ama!' Mum called. 'Jo-se!!!' They came tripping along, wearing an expression of intense, intelligent inquisitiveness. Llamas like people. They're mad about them, actually. And these ones adore my mum. She often says, when asked about her family, that she has 'four girls and eight boys'.

When Hugh left, I came and looked after my sisters—who seemed spookily unperturbed—while Mum went walking in Peru with a friend. She was in a state when she left, and the trip was meant to be recuperative, but when she returned

I was amazed at the change. She had this funny, secret little smile on her face and she radiated an odd kind of joy. When pressed, she explained, cryptically, that she'd 'fallen in love', but she wouldn't say with whom. So I assumed she must have had a fling with her tour guide, or with someone in the group. But it wasn't that at all.

'I've fallen in love, with…llamas,' she finally announced, with a soppy smile. 'They're just so…*beautiful*. They make you feel happy,' she sighed. 'The way they walk along beside you, humming away—that's what they do, they hum—as if they're *talking* to you, and they're incredibly easy to lead. They're so soft,' she went on rhapsodically. 'And they're so sensitive and clever. It was like an epiphany,' she exclaimed. 'Before I went to Peru I'd never even seen a llama, and now I just want to be with them *all the time*!'

We thought she'd gone mad and that she'd get over it, but the next thing we knew she'd bought two males. Then six months later she bought two more. And then she bought another four—including, recently, Henry, who's a little bit tricky—and she decided to run llama treks. That's what she does now, most weekends. She walks over the South Downs with sixteen people—two per llama—and the 'boys' carry the picnic in their special llama backpacks. It's a very popular day out.

'Hello!' I said as one of them came right up close to me. 'We haven't met before, have we? You must be Henry.' I stroked his piebald fleece, as soft as cashmere. 'Hey,' I giggled. 'Cut that out!' He was kissing me, planting his thick, mobile lips on my right cheek. Now he kissed me again. '*Hey*!' I laughed, dodging his mouth.

'I can't stop him doing that,' said Mum. 'He's very pushy about it. He often chases me round the field demanding kisses, don't you, Henry? I don't mind one or two,' she confided, 'but the constant snogging can be a bit of a drag.'

'Why does he do it? Has he been spoiled?'

'Well, sort of, he had too much human contact when he was a baby. He imprinted on people because he wasn't socialized with other llamas enough. I'm trying to work on it though. Couldn't you feature him on *Animal Crackers*, Miranda? The publicity would be jolly handy as I'm a bit down on the bookings at the moment.'

'Well, I'll ask, but I doubt they'll say yes—my own mum. So you aren't that busy then?'

She shrugged. 'We are at weekends—depending on the weather—but we don't have nearly enough going on in the week. I really feel I ought to develop new things to do with them but I don't really know what.'

'You still do the charity work though?'

'Yes, I take Carlos to Eastbourne hospital every Tuesday morning, and he cheers up the patients. But I need them to make some hard cash. Pedro had an audition for a beer commercial last week, which would have been a nice earner, but I don't think he got it or we'd have had the phone call by now.'

Suddenly my mobile rang and the llamas' ears all rotated like satellite dishes, then they stepped forward, straining to listen.

'Is that Miranda?' asked a vaguely familiar male voice, as Henry gave me another fuzzy kiss.

'Yes?'

'It's Bill McNaught here from West Drive.'

'Hello. Oh stop it, will you! Sorry—not you.'

'Erm…you were asking me about the Whites.'

'That's right.'

'Well, my wife happened to call me a few minutes ago,

and I told her about meeting you. She does have a bit of in-formation about them.'

'Really? That's great.'

'She says that although she doesn't know where they live now, she did hear from a friend of a friend that Derek White had died—this would be about eight years ago now—and that Mrs White had gone to live in Norfolk, near Michael. As for David...'

My pulse quickened. 'Yes?'

'Apparently he became a photographer. Up in London. Now, she didn't know any more than that, but I suppose it narrows it down a bit.'

'It does. He's a photographer? Well that gives me some-thing to go on. Thanks so much for ringing. I'm really grate-ful.'

'What was that about?' Mum asked, as I flipped shut the phone.

'Oh—I'm just trying to find an...old...friend.'

'Who?'

'Oh, this chap called David.'

'David? That doesn't ring any bells. Did I ever meet him?'

'No. You didn't.' *Neither did I.*

'Anyway, let's have lunch.'

We began to walk back to the house. 'Mum, there's some-thing I've got to tell you,' I ventured as she opened the gate.

'What?' She looked at me suspiciously.

I'd been dreading this moment. 'Well...it's about...'

'Your father?' she anticipated. 'It is, isn't it?'

'Actually, yes—it is. I had an e-mail from him last week.'

'Really? And what did he say?' My mother, some twenty years on, is still hostile towards my dad. It's ridiculous.

'That he's leaving Palm Springs.'

'Oh. Is that all?' She sighed with relief. 'And where's he

going? Florida again? Bermuda? Or some other golfers' para-
dise?'

'No. None of those. He's, um, decided to come back here.'

'Here?' She stopped dead in her tracks.

'Yes, here.'

'Here, as in the *UK*?' I nodded. Her face was a mask of
incredulity. *'Why?'*

'For work.'

'Running another silly golf club, I suppose?' she said,
striding towards the house once more.

'Er, yes,' I said. 'That's right.'

'I just hope it's in John O'Groats,' she said crossly.

'Well…it's a bit nearer than that actually…'

She stopped again. 'Where?'

'Erm, about five miles away.'

She looked at me, dumbfounded, her mouth slightly agape.
'You don't, *surely*, mean five miles from *here*?'

'Ye-es. I do mean that.'

'You don't mean that glitzy new one they're building at
Lower Chalvington?' I nodded. Her eyes rolled in her head.
'Oh. *Shit*.'

'Look,' I said, as she stomped off again, muttering exple-
tives. 'Dad just asked me to tell you so that there's no awk-
wardness in case, you know, you bump into each other in the
supermarket or anything.'

'What an awful thought!'

'Well, it *could* happen, Mum—so it's better that you know.'

'This is *all* I need.'

Over lunch she tried to explain her attitude to my dad.

'It's weird,' I said wearily. 'Especially as you're so relaxed
about Hugh. But the fact is Hugh left you for another *woman*.'

'Yes,' she said calmly. 'That's right. Hugh left me for another woman. An attractive, rich—and according to the girls,

perfectly charming—blonde woman, fifteen years my junior. My natural sense of justice means I can't argue with that.'

'But he had three children with you and was married to you. I don't think he should have left you at *all*.'

'Oh I don't know,' she sighed. 'We'd grown apart by then—we hardly talked—and the girls were growing up. But your father abandoned me for a *game*. That's *far* more humiliating! As though he didn't like *being* with me. He played twelve hours a day, seven days a week—we hardly ever *saw* him. There were no family holidays because he was always away playing in some silly golf match. Don't you remember any of this, Miranda?'

'Yes,' I sighed. 'I *do*. I do remember he wasn't around that much. But...'

'Do you know *why* I called you Miranda?' she interrupted.

I groaned, softly. 'You've told me often enough. You called me Miranda because Dad was away *so* much it was a...'

'...*wonder* you were born. Well it *was*!' I nodded wearily. 'It was miraculous, in fact. And it wasn't even as though it was a game I could take the slightest interest in,' she added crossly.

'I see, so if he'd been a tennis player that would have been all right, would it?'

'Well, I wouldn't have hated it as much. But golf's such a *stupid* game,' she muttered as she opened the Aga. 'Whacking a small ball about; ruining the landscape. Just the sight of those over-manicured links makes me spit. Soon there won't be any countryside left—it'll all be fairways and putting greens and driving ranges. Did you know that it's practically possible to circumnavigate the planet without ever actually leaving a golf course?' she added irritably.

'No. I didn't know that actually.'

'Anyway, when's the silly man coming?' I told her. She nearly dropped the lasagne. 'Next *week*?'

★ ★ ★

The first thing I did when I got back to London was to e-mail Dad to tell him that I'd broken the news to Mum. '*She was fine about it,*' I lied. '*Just a little surprised.*' Then I turned to the matter in hand. I grabbed the Yellow Pages and looked up photographers. There were at least four hundred, but only one David White, spelt 'Whyte'. But on the same page I saw a number for the Photographers' Association. I called it.

'There are three David Whites on our register,' the receptionist said. 'Which one do you want?'

'Well, I don't know...' I said, as I nervously doodled on an envelope.

'You don't know?' she repeated. 'Why not?'

I glanced out of the window into the Mews where a strikingly beautiful blonde woman was walking by. I found myself wondering who she was. 'Because I'm...not sure what sort of photography he does, that's why.'

'Is it advertising, editorial, commercial or fashion?' she demanded.

'That's the problem. I haven't a clue. All I know is that he works in London. Or used to.'

'According to our records these three all work in London.'

'And they're all called David White?'

'They are. But one's David M. White, one's D.J. White, and one's just Dave White. Which one do you want?'

My pulse was racing. 'I'm not actually sure. Could you possibly give me all the numbers?'

'Only if you're phoning about work. We don't give out our members' contact details for any other reason.' I heard Herman sigh. 'Is that why you're calling?'

'No. It's a...personal enquiry actually. He's an old friend,' I lied.

'I'm sorry, but in that case I can't help. However,' she went on, 'we do have a website—the-aop.org—and they may have put their details on that.'

I quickly scribbled down the address. 'Thanks.'

I went to the site and found that all three photographers had put their studio numbers and their mobiles alongside their names, and they all had links to their own websites too. I looked at the photos they'd put on them. David M. White was a fashion photographer; D.J. White was a photojournalist; while Dave White did advertising work. I wrote their respective details down. And as I began to dial the first one I mentally rehearsed what I'd say. Obviously I wouldn't just spill the beans over the phone. I'd find out whether they'd ever lived in Brighton. Then, once I'd established that I'd definitely got the right David White, I'd make some excuse to go to his studio, and then…and then…? And then, I'd tell him. But—*how*? I stared out of the window again. How would I begin a conversation like that? I put the receiver down.

'I can't do it, Herman.' He looked stricken. 'It's a big thing. I need more time.' And now, as I put out the folding chairs for the puppy party, I tried to imagine what he might look like. Like his father, perhaps. I remembered the grainy shot of Professor White which had appeared in *The Times* the next day. I went to my desk, found the file at the back of the drawer and took out the cutting. Dated 22nd March, 1987, it was brittle, yellow and frayed. *Letter-Bomb Sent to Scientist* announced the headline. Inset, was a photo of Derek White with the caption, *Animal Rights Target*. I read the piece again. *Derek White, 58, Professor of Biochemistry at Sussex University, was the target of animal rights fanatics yesterday when a letter-bomb was sent to his house in the Queens Park area of Brighton. The device, which was concealed in a video case, rather than the padded*

Jiffy bags usually favoured by animal liberation activists, was de-livered in person in the early hours. Professor White, for whom it was intended, escaped injury, but his twenty-year-old son, David, a student, who opened the parcel in error, suffered serious injuries to his hands. A wave of nausea swept over me. *Professor White has never previously been threatened,* I read on. *His colleagues said the attack had come out of the blue.* And now, as I put the cut-ting back, I remembered what Jimmy had said. He'd said that Derek White had 'had it coming'—but he wouldn't say *why.* I looked at the three telephone numbers again. I'd phone to-morrow afternoon—when I wasn't busy. I wanted to prepare myself emotionally first.

I glanced at my watch. There was half an hour before the puppy party crowd would arrive, so I checked my e-mails. *'My cat has just had kittens,'* said the first one. *'I can't help feel-ing jealous—all the attention she used to give me is now lavished on them. Is it normal to feel like this?' 'I recently got a collie,'* said the next, *'but I'm worried that it regards me as its intellectual inferior.' 'My rabbit refuses to breed,'* complained the third. Suddenly the phone went.

'Miranda? This is Lily Jago. Just to say I'll be coming to the puppy party tonight. I've just seen it on your website.'

'You've got a puppy already?'

'Yes. Another shih-tzu. We collected her yesterday.'

'That was quick.'

'There was just one left in the litter. She's absolutely *exqui-site*—almost twelve weeks. Jennifer and I felt we should get her on the social circuit as soon as possible.'

'Well, the problem is I haven't really got room. You see my maximum number's eight, Lily, and I'm fully booked now.'

'But she's only a *tiny* thing. Honestly, Miranda. She'll hardly take up any room. See you later!'

'Eight *people*,' I said, as the line went dead. Now there was a knock on the door, and the first puppy arrived; a Tibetan terrier called Maisie, with her owner, Phyllis, who's eighty-three. I used to see Phyllis with her old dog, Cassie, when I was a vet in Highgate. When Cassie died last year, Phyllis was heart-broken. I'd advised her to get another dog.

'I can't,' she'd said, tearfully, when I visited her. She gazed at a huge portrait of Cassie over the fireplace. 'I just *can't*.'

'Why not?' I asked. 'Is it because you're worried about having another dog at your age, because I'm sure your daughter would help out if you ever needed her to.'

'No, it's not because of that. It's because of Cassie,' she'd explained.

'What do you mean?'

'Well, it's because Cassie would *know*. She'd *know*, Miranda.' Phyllis's pale blue eyes were shimmering with tears. 'And she'd be terribly up*set*.'

'I don't think she…*would* know,' I'd said. But Phyllis had flatly refused to countenance a canine replacement; then, all of a sudden, she'd changed her mind. She'd phoned me last week to say she'd got another Tibetan terrier and wanted to bring it to the party. I was thrilled…

'Hello, Maisie,' I said now, as I looked at the puppy. 'Aren't you sweet? I'm glad you decided to get another dog, Phyllis. I'm sure Cassie would be happy.'

'Oh she *is* happy,' said Phyllis. Her eyes were shining. 'In fact, she's *very* happy.'

'Really? Er, what do you mean?'

'Well,' she began, in a confidential whisper, 'Maisie isn't really Maisie.'

'Isn't she?'

She shook her head. 'I just call her that in order not to

confuse people. Maisie is actually Cassie,' she explained seriously.

I stared at her. 'Really?'

'Yes. You see,' she said, laying her frail hand on my arm,
'Cassie's come *back*.' She gave me a beatific smile. 'Cassie's
come back—in the body of another *dog*.' She nodded at
Maisie.

'*Ah*.'

'So it's all worked out beautifully,' she concluded happily.

'Well, that's just…great,' I said.

There was another knock at the door, and a rather lively,
good-looking man called Marcus came in with his equally
lively Jack Russell puppy tucked into his jumper; then an
English setter with a woman called Sue. By ten past seven
there were puppies play-biting, ear-chewing, chasing and
paddling in the water bowl, while their 'parents' indulgently
smiled.

'Had all the jabs?' I heard someone enquire above the
Mickey Mouse yapping.

'Oh yes. She didn't cry at all. She's *very* brave.'

'Mine's already house-trained.'

'Really? That's amazing.'

'Well, he's a quick learner. Both ends.'

At a quarter past seven I did the roll call.

'Roxy?' I called out.

'Here.'

'Alfie?'

'Here.'

'Lola?'

'Present, Miss,' her owner giggled.

'Maisie? Yes, you're here. Sooty? Is Sooty here? Oh there
you are, Sooty.' They'd just arrived. 'And Twiglet?'

'Yep.'

'Cosmo?'

'He's here.'

'And finally...Bentley. Oh hi, Lily.' She'd arrived in a cloud of scent, clasping the puppy to her with one bejewelled hand, trailing Jennifer with the other. 'Do take a seat. Now I'd like you all to introduce yourselves, and to say why you've chosen the puppy you have. You go first, Sally, then carry on round the circle.'

'Okay. Hi, everyone,' she began, 'my name's Sally and I work in PR, and my puppy, Roxy, is a Labrador because, well, they're just so adorable, aren't they?'

'Yeah, they're labradorable,' said Marcus. Everyone giggled.

'Next person, please,' I said.

'My name's John and I'm in IT, and I chose Alfie here because I've always liked gun dogs.'

'What's the pointer that?' quipped Marcus again. Oh well. At least he helped break the ice.

'My name's Susan and this is Lola,' said a woman with kohl-rimmed eyes. She looked confused. 'Or is it the other way round? No. I'm definitely Susan and I teach yoga and well, I've always loved English setters because they—'

'Setter good example,' Marcus snorted. He was that slightly irritating thing—a live wire.

'My name's Jane and this is Sooty. And I grew up on a farm, and so I knew I'd just have to have a Border collie one day.'

'I'm Ian, I'm an interior designer, and this is my pug, Bentley.'

'I'm Lily Jago. I edit *Moi!* magazine, and my little puppy's a shih-tzu—'

'Bless you!' said Marcus. There were more giggles. Lily gave him a frigid stare.

'She's a shih. *Tzu*,' she repeated slowly. 'Like her doting aunt here, Jennifer Aniston.'

'Why did you call her that then?' asked Marcus, mystified.

'Can't you see the resemblance?'

'Well, I'm not sure,' he said judiciously. 'The nose is slightly different—' Lily looked offended.

'No. Not the face. It's the *hair*. It's because she's got long silky hair and because she's worth it, aren't you, poppet?' Jennifer grunted. 'And puppy's name is Gwyneth Paltrow, for exactly the same reason.'

'You can't call her *that*,' said Marcus. 'Everyone knows Jennifer Aniston and Gwyneth Paltrow don't get on.'

'That's right,' said Phyllis. 'They fell out over Brad Pitt. Gwyneth Paltrow can't stand Jennifer Lopez either,' she added knowledgeably.

'That's true,' said Jane. 'She's still furious about Ben Affleck apparently. Did you see that piece in *Hello!*?'

'Look, can we please take this puppy party seriously?' I said.

'All right,' said Marcus. 'Anyway, I'm Marcus Longman and I work in the film industry.'

'Oh *really*?' they all said. 'What do you do?'

'Are you a director?' asked Lily.

'No. I do stunt-work.'

'How *fascinating*,' she breathed. 'So you're a stuntman?' He nodded. That made sense, he was very fit and muscular-looking, as though he worked out a lot. 'We must do something on that in *Moi!*—what have you worked on recently? Anything famous?'

'*Land Ahoy!*' I felt sick.

'I've heard that's going to be *splendid*,' said Phyllis.

'It is—it's *brilliant*,' said Lily. My stomach turned over. 'I've seen a preview tape.'

'And why did you choose Twiglet, Marcus?' I persisted, desperate to change the subject.

'Because Jack Russells are intelligent, lively and brave. And because I thought we might be able to do some fun things together.'

'What sort of things?' Lily asked.

'Parachuting, kayaking, a bit of hang-gliding, maybe.'

Lily rolled her huge black eyes. 'But dogs don't *do* those kinds of things.'

'They do. My last Jack Russell used to go surfing—he *loved* it—he had his own wetsuit. He used to go sky-diving with me too. Not solo obviously—we'd be strapped together. But then, sadly, last year, he had his accident.'

'What *happened*?' we all asked, bracing ourselves.

'He twisted his back getting out of bed. In any case he was my girlfriend's dog, and she kept him when she left. But that's why I got Twiglet.'

'Do you still see your old dog?' asked Phyllis. 'I do hope so. He must miss you.'

'I get access visits. It's not too bad.'

'Can we *please* stop barking—I mean, talking,' I said, trying to reassert my authority. 'We've got a *lot* to do.'

A respectful hush fell, punctuated only by a solitary 'yap'.

'Now,' I continued. 'The purpose of these puppy parties is to socialize the puppies right from the start so that they're not fazed by anything in later life. So what we're going to do first is to play Pass the Puppy. I want you to pass your puppy one person to your left, and then I want you all to look in the puppy's ears, just as the vet might do, and feel its paws; have a look in its mouth, and its eyes; generally feel its coat and rub its tummy, which is its most vulnerable part. By the time your puppy has been handled by nine strangers over a period of five weeks it'll be well on its way to becoming a pleasant, responsible and well-adjusted canine citizen. So—pass the puppy please.'

'—Oh isn't it sweet!'

'—No, please don't hold her like that—like this.'

'—Oow—sharp little teeth.'

'—Careful! Don't drop him!'

'—I'm *not* dropping him.'

'—Bye-bye, my little darling. See you soon!'

Then we had a bite inhibition session followed by a general discussion about common behavioural problems and how to avoid them; then I talked about nutrition, and, finally, we had problem-sharing.

'Is anyone having any particular difficulties?' I asked.

'The house-training's not easy,' said Sue with a sigh.

'He won't come when I call,' said John.

'I'm so exhausted from the nights,' said Jane. 'Sooty wakes at least three times.'

'Bentley does that too.'

'I feel so inadequate to the task,' Sue sniffed. There were suddenly tears in her eyes. 'I feel so helpless. The awful responsibility of it all. This tiny little thing who depends on me, and who I love so much,' she sobbed. 'I feel totally—uh-uh— over*whelmed.*'

'You've got post-puppy depression,' said Lily as she handed Sue a tissue. 'I had that with Jennifer. It doesn't last. Maybe you should see your doctor,' she added helpfully.

'It's because it's your first one,' said John. 'Most people feel like that with their first,' he added sympathetically.

'Yes, *I* did,' Phyllis said. 'Don't worry, Sue. I'm sure you'll be a *very* good mother.'

'Yes, don't worry,' they all said. 'You'll be *great.*'

At nine they all began to drift away, with promises of puppy play-dates with each other.

'That was fun,' said Marcus warmly. 'Twiglet loved it, didn't you Twiggers?'

I smiled. Marcus might be a bit annoying but he was very friendly. He was also rather attractive.

'So, who did you stand in for on *Land Ahoy!*?' Lily enquired. 'Was it Alexander Darke? He's rather gorgeous.'

'No. I doubled for Joe Fenton—the guy who plays first mate. I spent most of the shoot being thrown overboard—into the North Sea, unfortunately, rather than the Caribbean. Still, that's what I get paid to do.' He handed me an A5-sized flyer. *You CAN Defend Yourself!* it announced.

'What's this, Marcus?'

'I'm going to be running some short self-defence courses from next month in a church hall near Tottenham Court Road. So if you know anyone who'd be interested in coming along, then maybe you'd help spread the word?'

'Yes. Yes, of course I will.'

'Anyway, I'd better be off.' He tucked Twiglet into the top of his jumper again. 'See you next week.'

'See you,' said Lily. She went to the window and watched him cycle away. 'What a charming man,' she said, as I began to fold up the chairs. 'He's quite good-looking too. Apart from the broken nose. I really *must* do something on stuntmen,' she added as she opened her bag. 'And when can we do *you*, Miranda?'

'Do what?'

'The interview for *Moi!*' She whipped out her diary.

'I didn't think you were serious.'

'Of course I'm serious. I'd write it myself only I haven't got time. What day?'

'Oh. Well…' I was thrilled. 'Any day, really—except Friday, as that's the day I go filming.'

'How about next Tuesday then?'

I glanced at my calendar. 'Tuesday would be great. Could we make it after four though, as I've got my last appointment at two thirty.'

'That's fine.' Lily scribbled it down. 'I'll tell India Carr to come up here at four thirty, then I'll get the photographer to give you a call. Now who shall I get? Let's see…' She bounced the end of her pen against her teeth. 'Johnny van der Veldt? Hmm, I think he's away. Jake Green? Too pricey. Hamish Cassell? No—he's been working for *Vogue*, the treacherous little beast.'

I stopped folding the chairs. 'You want a photographer?'

'Yes, sorry, I was just thinking aloud. Don't worry,' she put her diary away. 'The picture editor will sort it out.' I looked at her. 'We'll be off then—my driver's waiting—and I've got to get this little baby into her bed.' She snapped on Jennifer's diamanté-studded lead, then smiled. 'See you next week.'

'Can I make a suggestion, Lily?' She turned round. 'For a photographer?'

'Yes, okay.'

Adrenaline surged through my veins like fire. 'How about… David White?'

'David White?' she repeated. She blinked twice.

'Ye-es.'

'You mean D.J. White? *That* David White?'

'Erm, yes,' I said uncertainly. 'Him.'

'*This* one?' She'd picked up my copy of the *Guardian G2* section. On the front was a photo of a Pakistani boy—he looked no more than five years old—working at a carpet loom. In the top right-hand corner I read, *Photo: D.J. White*. 'But he's a photojournalist,' said Lily. 'This is the kind of thing he does.'

'Oh. Yes, of course. Oh well—never mind. I don't know

much about photographers, actually,' I said. 'In fact I don't know anything about them at all, but I just happened to have heard his name recently so I thought, you know, why not mention him just in case it was a helpful suggestion and—'

'But it *is!*' Lily exclaimed. 'It's a very helpful suggestion, actually. In fact—it's absolutely *brilliant*. Yes. D.J. White, distinguished photojournalist, doing portraits for a fashion mag. That might give it a bit of an *edge*. Yes, the more I think about it, the more I like it. D.J. White doing the glossies. *Very* edgy. Did I tell you you're a genius, Miranda?' she added casually.

'Er, you did, actually.'

'Good.' She swept out. 'Because you *are*.'

—— CHAPTER 6 ——

But was it the *same* David White? The next morning, heart pounding, I phoned the two other photographers of the same name. Although they sounded slightly suspicious at being contacted, they both told me that, no, they'd never lived in Brighton.

'It *is* him,' I said to Herman as I replaced the handset after the second call. 'It's got to be. He's the right one. The White one,' I quipped frivolously. I felt curiously happy.

'So you engineered the introduction,' said Daisy when she phoned me on her way to work ten minutes later. I could hear her heels snapping on the pavement. 'That was bold.'

'I just decided to go for it, in case he *was* the same one and, as it turns out, he must be.'

'It'll make the whole thing much easier,' she said above the rumble of the traffic. 'The fact that he's got to take your picture first will mean that there'll be a connection between you, which is far less awkward than phoning him up cold. Can you get any more info on him before Tuesday?'

'I've looked at his website and there's no personal stuff. It just says that he was born in 1967—which fits, age-wise; that he trained at the City Poly, and that he worked for Reuters for ten years before going freelance.'

'And how do you feel about meeting him?' *Meeting him.* My stomach did a somersault.

'*Sick.* But I also feel strangely cheerful,' I added. 'Excited, almost.'

'That's because you know you're doing the right thing.'

I wondered what the consequences of doing the right thing might be—they could well be catastrophic—but I couldn't worry about that now. 'And what about Nigel?' I asked. I could hear the shrill beeps of the pelican crossing.

'He came back from Bonn last night. Obviously I didn't want to have any delicate discussions with him then, as he was tired. But I will. Soon,' she said. 'Definitely. I've just got to get him in the right mood.'

'Hmm. Of course.'

'But I'm not going to ask him this weekend as he's decided to have a barbecue while the weather holds—in fact, will you come? That's my main reason for ringing.'

'Yes, okay then.' I saw the postman walk by.

'Anyway, I'd better go. I've got a wedding to organize,' she added dismally. 'The reception's at the Savoy. A hundred for a sit-down. Six bridesmaids. Honeymoon in Galapagos. See you on Saturday night.'

I pulled three envelopes from the brass jaw of the letterbox. There was a council-tax demand and the *Animal Crackers* filming schedule, and finally the form I'd been promised by the police. I quickly filled it in, then posted it. How long was it now? Six weeks. I looked in my hand mirror—the bruising had gone and these days my ribs only ached if I coughed. I'd been very lucky in some ways, I thought—unlike David, who would bear *his* scars for the rest of his life.

I spent the morning with a shy hamster in Hampstead—the little boy was upset because it didn't like being handled—then I went to see a distressed budgie called Tweetie in Crouch

Hill. It had plucked so many feathers from its chest it looked oven-ready.

'Is he trying to commit suicide?' the elderly man asked, visibly upset.

'No, he's just rather unhappy.' Another tiny yellow plume fluttered down.

'But he's got a nice big cage there, and a cuttlefish, and lots of toys.'

'Yes. But there's something he needs much more than any of those things.'

'What's that then?' He looked mystified.

'Another budgie. Budgies should never be kept on their own. In the wild they're flock birds, so they need company.'

'Oh,' he said, mystified. 'I didn't know.'

'So I strongly recommend that you get him a friend as soon as possible and I'll be very surprised if he doesn't cheer up.'

'Right.'

'But please let me know what happens.'

'Yes. I will. I'll get myself down to the pet shop today. Now I must pay you.' He got out his wallet.

'Forget it,' I said. 'I've only been here five minutes and I was in the neighbourhood anyway, and to be honest I could have told you this over the phone, but I was a little…distracted this morning.' In fact, I'm distracted most of the time.

'Oh well.' He smiled. 'Thanks very much. But I'd like to give you something.' He went over to the sideboard, and opened the door.

'No, really,' I protested. 'There's no need.' Then he produced a small, square book.

'I published this myself a few years ago.' He handed it to me. It was called *One-Minute Wisdom*. 'It's just a book of maxims which have helped me through life. I didn't sell that many, to be honest, so now I just give them away.'

'Well, that's very kind of you,' I said. 'Thanks.' I quickly flicked through it—it was full of home-spun wisdom and comforting clichés. *Expect the best, plan for the worst; self-knowledge is the first step towards contentment.* 'It looks very consoling.'

'Yes,' he said. 'That's the idea.'

I went home, glad that I'd been able to help the man, but feeling cross with his pet shop for not giving him the budgie basics. As I parked, I glanced in the mirror behind me and again saw that strikingly pretty blonde girl walking out of the Mews. I'd seen her several times now and I couldn't help wondering who she was. She had a sheet of white-blonde hair, pale skin and enormous blue eyes. In fact, she looked like the Timotei ad. I saw her so often I guessed she must work here, though she never smiled like the others did. I opened the door, and as Herman trotted up to greet me, his brows knitted in consternation as usual, I saw the answerphone flashing. I pressed play.

'Hello, Miranda. Dad here.' Although he uses American expressions, he still sounds *so* English. 'I'll be arriving on Sunday, but just to let you know that I'm going straight down to Sussex. But I'll be coming to town in the next few days on club business so I hope to see you soon.' Then, with a 'whirr', the tape spooled on.

'Hi, Miranda,' said an unknown male voice. Who was this? He was American. Maybe he was a new client. 'This is David White here.' My heart stopped. 'I'm just calling to arrange the shoot for next week. I know you're being interviewed Tuesday at four...' He pronounced it 'Toosday'. 'So I'm hoping to drop by after that. Anyway, here are my contact numbers so please give me a call.' He pronounced it 'gimme'. I pressed play again, then again. By the time I'd listened to the message five times I knew that I'd made a mistake. This wasn't the same David White—it couldn't be. The David White I was looking for was definitely British. I felt disappointed, then suddenly relieved. I phoned the number he'd left and briefly spoke to him—he sounded pleasant, but slightly brusque.

'See you six o'clock then,' he said.

'Hi!' said Daisy, as she opened Nigel's front door on Saturday evening. 'You're the first to arrive.'

'Good—that's why I've come early, so I could talk to you. He was the *wrong* one,' I said quietly. 'He's American. Or maybe Canadian.'

She looked crestfallen. 'Oh. Well, that's the problem, it's quite a common name.'

'Plus the fact that the David White *I'm* looking for might not even *be* a photographer any more. That information is from *years* ago. He could be a pilot now, for all I know, or a personal trainer—or a concert pianist. No, probably not a concert pianist,' I corrected myself bitterly.

Daisy winced. 'Then we'll have to try another approach. Maybe you could get a private detective to find him.'

'It would be expensive and I don't have the cash. Hi, Nigel!' He'd suddenly come upstairs from the basement. He's a bit taller than Daisy with short, fair hair—which is thinning on top—and pale blue eyes. He's attractive, but a bit paunchy, or rather reassuringly 'solid'.

'How nice to see you,' he said.

As I say, I like Nigel. I always have. But I'd like him more if he proposed to my friend. 'Daisy would quite like to know whether or not you're ever going to marry her,' I ventured as he walked towards me. 'After all, she's been with you

five years. Five and a *half* years, actually, which is quite long
enough, and it's getting critical because she'd like to have
kids. So if you *don't* want to share the rest of your life with
her it'd be kind of you to tell her because, sadly, she's too
romantic—and too scared—to ask.'

I didn't really say that; I just said, 'Nice to see you too,
Nigel.' He gave me a fraternal kiss.

We went downstairs into the large basement kitchen, with
its limed wood units and terracotta tiles, and its smart conservatory dining extension in which a variety of bonsai trees
were displayed. As Daisy prepared the Pimm's, I politely admired them. Nigel smiled with an almost paternal pride.

'I must say they *are* doing well,' he said. 'I'm particularly
proud of this Cedar of Lebanon.' I looked at it. It was perfect—with its black-green foliage and graceful low boughs—
and it was about ten inches tall.

I felt sad. '*Multum in parvo*, I suppose,' I said ruefully, remembering a phrase I'd read in *One-Minute Wisdom*.

'Oh, pre*cisely*. That's the appeal. It looks *exactly* like it
would in nature, except that it's been...'

'Stunted,' I said. I couldn't help it.

'Miniaturized.'

'And how old is it?'

He smiled. 'Well, actually, it's not polite to ask the age of
a bonsai tree.'

'*Isn't* it?'

'But, as it's you—thirty-three.'

'Gosh, that's how old *we* are,' Daisy snorted as she sliced a
cucumber.

'I've had it since I was seven.'

'Tell me how you get them to grow like that,' I said.

Nigel pushed his glasses up his nose as he prepared to ex-
patiate upon his favourite subject. 'The key is to keep them

in a state of partial stress. That's why I put them here, in the conservatory, because strong sunlight restricts leaf size.'

'Oh.' I felt sorry for them. 'I see.'

'Bonsai trees grown in bright ultraviolet tend to dwarf better,' Nigel went on enthusiastically, as Daisy went outside to collect some mint. 'It's about controlling their development, you see. By using a variety of techniques—giving them barely enough water, for example—slightly depriving them of what they need—you subtly get the tree to do what *you* want.'

'Uh-huh.'

'The main thing is to avoid luxuriant growth. Now, this Chinese elm has been a particular success...' And as Nigel rhapsodized about 'root-pruning' and 'pinching' and 'correcting design', I thought, he's stunting Daisy too—stopping *her* growing. Keeping *her* in a state of partial stress.

By now the doorbell was ringing as Nigel's friends arrived. He'd invited about fifteen people—some old friends, his neighbours, and a few other lawyers. We stood chatting on the lawn in the pretty walled garden and, as the barbecue began to smoke, and the Pimm's flowed, we all began to relax. One or two of them asked me about *Animal Crackers*, so I told them about the previous day's filming; I'd had to sort out a cat which leaped on its owner's head, claws extended, every time she came home.

'It descended on her like a Fokker,' I said.

'Which is probably what she called it!' someone hooted.

'What it does,' I explained, 'is to sit on top of the hall cupboard, waiting for her, then it pounces. She'd taken to wearing a crash helmet when she walked through the door.'

'And why was it doing it?'

'Boredom—because it was kept inside all day. It was simply trying to fulfil its hunting instinct. That's the thing about so many behavioural problems,' I went on. 'In most cases, the animal doesn't have a behavioural problem at all, it's just being itself in a way which its humans don't like.'

'So what was the answer?'

'A kitty gym with ropes and scratching posts and things to play with—so she's having one built. We'll be filming it again in a couple of weeks to see if it's worked.'

Then the conversation turned to the law. This chap Alan, a criminal barrister, who'd been at school with Nigel, was prosecuting someone for GBH.

'But the interesting thing,' he said, 'was that the offence was actually committed twelve years ago. It was impossible to prove at the time, but now we've got him through DNA. Twelve years,' he repeated wonderingly as he chewed on a chicken leg.

'Gosh,' I said, my heart banging. 'How fascinating. And… is it true that there's…no limit on how long after a crime the perpetrator can be prosecuted?'

'That's right,' he said. 'Of course, it has to be a serious crime for the police to reopen the case.'

'How serious?'

'Well, murder, obviously; attempted murder, arson, or any serious assault.' My stomach turned over. 'But even if the police decide not to prosecute, the victims themselves can pursue their assailant through the civil courts.'

'Really?' I lowered my vegetarian kebab. I'd never thought about that. 'And what would they hope to gain?'

'Financial compensation, or just emotional satisfaction—a sense of closure. That's usually the most important thing.' Now, as the conversation continued, I wondered dismally if David—if I did ever find him—would decide to sue me. Perhaps he would. In which case he'd have to sue Jimmy as well. I was about to open a Pandora's box.

Don't go there, a small voice told me. *Let it lie. Let it lie.*

No, said my conscience. *Tell the truth. Tell the truth and get closure at last. Then you'll be able to restart your life.*

As I resurfaced I realized that the topic of conversation had now changed. Nigel's colleague, Mary, had joined us; a thin, sharp-faced blonde woman about his age. I knew from Daisy that she worked in the same department as him—commercial litigation. I also knew that Mary had liked Nigel, but that it hadn't really been mutual.

'It's Nigel's fortieth soon, isn't it?' she said, as her fork hovered over her plate.

'It is,' said Alan. 'Let's hope he has a party.'

'Yes, let's hope he has a party!' said another of his friends, Jon. 'Let's make *sure* he has one!'

'Let's hope he has a *wedding*,' said someone else. At this there was a collective guffaw. I glanced round for Daisy but she was in the conservatory, just out of earshot.

'A wedding?' Alan exclaimed. '*Nigel*? Come off it, you guys!' Jon was snorting with laughter.

'I know,' Mary concurred with a satisfied smirk. 'I've seen them *all* come and go,' she went on with ostentatious weariness. 'He's *very* naughty like that. I suppose Daisy'll go off too, in the end. I mean, Nigel's a darling, but really…' she shrugged her sloping shoulders, '…who could blame her? Especially after so *long*.'

Right. 'Daisy doesn't want to get married,' I said. 'She's quite happy as she is.'

'How do you know?'

'Because she's my best friend.'

'Oh, *so* sorry,' said Mary with exaggerated contrition. She gave me a hard, false smile. 'I guess it's a bit of a tricky subject.'

'Not in the least,' I replied.

I walked away, my face burning. Daisy was clearly the object of amused pity. And as I watched her coming out of the house with another jug of Pimm's, chatting gaily to everyone, laughing and joking, making Nigel's evening go well, I felt incredibly angry with him. How *mean* of him to keep her dangling, encouraging her just enough to make her stay with him, but never making her feel secure. And how *silly* of her to let him do so, I thought. She's Crazy Daisy in more ways than one. I wondered what would get him to budge. I didn't believe that Daisy really would 'pin him down'; she's still clinging to her hope that he'll get down on one knee. But he clearly isn't going to, because he doesn't have to—plus, I don't believe he wants to share his life. And what if she left him? What would happen then? Probably not very much. Nigel would be out of sorts for a while, but then he'd meet someone else, and do exactly the same thing with her. Now Daisy was pouring Pimm's into his glass, looking at him raptly.

'Say when, Nige,' I heard her say.

Yes, Nige, I thought crossly. Say *when*.

The rest of the weekend passed pleasantly, although I felt like throwing up when I listened to *The Westminster Hour* on Sunday and heard Jimmy. He was talking about some House of Commons report into university funding. I had to turn the radio off. I was busy all day on Monday, then on Tuesday I waited for Lily's star reporter, India Carr, to arrive. I knew she wrote well—I'd read some of her articles—and when she turned up she seemed friendly and nice. First she took notes about the house, then she asked me about my work—about the most difficult case I'd ever had to deal with; then the easiest; the most interesting one; the commonest mistakes people make with their pets. We talked about the growth in animal psychiatry, then she came to the personal stuff. She wanted to know who my favourite designer was.

I laughed. 'I *never* buy designer gear. I wear jeans most days, and the odd vintage jacket if I feel like adding a bit of sophistication, but I'm no clothes horse—or rather Shetland pony!' I quipped.

'You *are* quite tiny,' she said with a smile. 'What size are you?'

'At the moment I think I'm a six. I buy children's clothes sometimes—it's the one advantage of being so small—with kids' stuff there's no VAT.'

'And on the romantic front,' she said. 'You're single. That's right, isn't it?'

'Yes,' I said, shifting slightly. 'I am. Not that it's particularly relevant,' I added with studied casualness.

'Well, I think it *is* relevant.'

'Why?'

'Because you were engaged to Alexander Darke.' Oh *shit*. Her large green eyes were staring into me. 'Weren't you?' she said.

I sighed. 'You've obviously done your homework.'

'Of course I have—that's my job.'

'Well, I'd rather not discuss my private life, if you don't mind.'

'But it's something I have to ask.'

'Why?' I stared at the floor. 'Who's going to be interested?'

'Quite a lot of people, I'd say. Because by the time this article comes out in August, Alexander Darke will be a big name. So it would look odd if I hadn't mentioned your connection with him.' I glanced out of the window. 'So what happened?' she enquired. I felt ill. She checked that the cassette in her tiny tape recorder was still running. 'What happened?' she repeated gently.

I could have stopped the interview, but I needed the publicity. 'It just…'—I sighed—'…didn't…work out.' I picked Herman up, so that India wouldn't see my hands shaking.

'There must be more to it than that?'

'There *isn't*! I mean…there isn't,' I said. 'Really. There's nothing to say.'

'But a friend of Alexander's told me…'—oh *no*—'…that the engagement had ended very abruptly. I just wondered why that was. He said that Alexander never really explained.' I *bet* he didn't. 'He just told them you'd had "second thoughts". He said that they were all quite mystified as you'd seemed so happy. I'm sure the readers would love to know why the relationship came unstuck.'

I realized, reluctantly, that I would have to say *something*. 'Well,' I began, 'I *did* have second thoughts—that's true. Because I'd come to the…very sad…conclusion that it wasn't going to work out between us, long term.'

India gave me a sceptical look. 'Why not?' I did my best to remain calm. If I got upset, she'd sniff a story, and in my present state I might crack.

'I discovered that we were…incompatible. That we had… different values.' Oh God, that sounded so judgemental.

'Was he unfaithful?' she asked. 'Is that what you mean? There *were* rumours about his co-star, Tilly Bishop.'

A spasm of jealousy squeezed my heart. 'No, really, there was no one else involved. By "different values" I simply mean…that we didn't have quite the same attitudes to life. Sometimes these things can take a while to find out,' I went on reasonably, recovering now. 'And it's better not to go ahead if that's the case.'

'So no hard feelings then?'

'No hard feelings,' I lied.

'And do you remain friends with him?'

If I said 'no', she'd only want to know why. 'Yes,' I lied again. 'We remain friends. Alexander's...great. He's a brilliant actor, his career's obviously taking off...and so I...wish him well.'

She seemed satisfied with this, and in any case it was all she was getting. I wasn't going to tell her the truth. And although what he'd done was, as Daisy had often pointed out, 'unforgivable', I didn't want to appear vindictive, or look like a victim. Worse, I knew that if it did ever get out, the ensuing media coverage would link him to me for the rest of my life. I wouldn't be 'Miranda Sweet, animal behaviourist' any more; I'd be 'Miranda Sweet, that poor woman who was treated so badly by TV star, Alexander Darke'. I was determined to protect myself.

'Well, I guess that's it then,' I said, glancing at my watch. 'I'm sure you've got enough material now. In any case the photographer will be here in a moment.'

She switched off the tape recorder and put it in her bag. 'Oh yes, you've got D.J. White. Lily told me she'd booked him. Well, good luck!' she exclaimed as she picked up her pad.

I looked at her. 'What do you mean?'

'I met him once—he's rather hard work.'

'In what way?'

'He's a bit of an awkward sod. He's good-looking, mind you—and brilliant at what he does—but...' she pulled a face. 'He's just...awkward.'

'Oh well,' I shrugged. 'He can be as awkward as he likes. It's not as though I'll be seeing him again.'

As she left, and I cleared away the coffee cups, I felt relieved that it wasn't the right David White. The thought of being photographed by *him* made me feel ill. Suddenly, the phone rang. And I was just explaining to a potential new client how I work and what I charge, when Herman suddenly threw back his head and barked. I turned and saw a dark-haired figure standing in the doorway.

'Oh, hold on please,' I said. 'Hello.' I waved at him to enter. 'So, if you want to make a booking, just let me know.' I replaced the handset. 'I'm sorry about that,' I said. 'You must be David.' He nodded, unsmilingly. India seemed to be right. Oh well. He wasn't that tall, maybe five foot nine or ten, but he was broad shouldered. Macho. Slightly Brando-ish. That's who he reminded me of, I realized—a young Marlon Brando. And as I looked at him, I realized, with a sudden peculiar certainty, that I found him attractive. And now, as he took a step towards me, I noticed a tiny scar on his cheekbone, just below his right eye. And I was just thinking how intriguing it was, and that it looked like a crescent moon, when he suddenly extended his hand. And, as he did so, I saw that the skin on the back of it was mottled and slightly shiny. I felt as though I'd been pushed out of a plane.

'So, you're D.J. White,' I heard myself say. 'You're D.J. White,' I repeated. I suddenly felt as though my throat was crammed with expressions of regret, threatening to choke me.

'D.J. White's my professional name,' he said matter-of-factly. 'To distinguish me from the two other David Whites in the business.'

'I see.' As he put down his bag and began to unzip it, I glanced at his hand again. The skin was stretched looking in places, slightly ridged in others. I glanced at the left. It was the same. 'So you're David White,' I said again. Now, as I looked at him, still feeling as though I was falling from a very high place, I could feel tears prick the backs of my eyes.

You're David White and I hurt your hands sixteen years ago, it was me it was me, I did it but I didn't mean to and I'm so, so sorry and please will you forgive me. I swallowed. 'So you're…David White.'

'Yes.' He looked up at me, puzzlement furrowing his brow. 'That's…right. I think we've established my name now.'

I nodded, blankly, still staring at him, aware of a profound sense of dislocation, as though I was having an out-of-body experience, or, perhaps, an out-of-mind one.

'And you're American?'

'No actually, I'm not.'

'But you sound American,' I said absently, as he took out a camera.

He shook his head. 'I'm as British as you are.' He pronounced it 'Bridish'.

'But you have an American accent. I don't understand.'

'Well,' he sighed, evidently irritated, 'there's a very simple explanation. I grew up in the States.'

'Oh.' *Oh.* I hadn't thought of that. 'Why?'

He looked at me. 'Why what?'

'Why did you grow up there?'

He straightened up, then gave me a penetrating look. 'You're very…curious, if you don't mind my saying so.'

'I'm sorry. But…I just wondered…that's all.' His face expressed a combination of annoyance and bewilderment. 'Why did you live there?' I repeated.

'Why do you want to *know*?'

'Well…' I shrugged. 'I…just…do.'

'O-kay,' he said, putting up his hands, as if in amused surrender. 'My father worked there.'

'Where did he work?'

Now he was staring at me as though I was mad. 'Jesus!'

he said quietly. 'All these *questions*. New Haven, if you must know.'

'Where Yale is?'

'That's right.'

'And what did he do? Did he work at the university?'

'*Look…*' I heard him inhale with barely suppressed irritation. 'We've never met before, but I've come here to take your photograph—not to be interrogated, if you don't mind.'

'I'm…sorry.' I collected myself. 'It's just that I was…surprised. You see, I was expecting you to be American.'

'Well I'm *not* American, okay? Now that I've convinced you of that, I'd like to get on with the shoot.' He pulled out a roll of film and began to feed it into the camera. 'I'll take some of you here—' he glanced round the consulting room as he wound the film on. 'Then a few outside—I thought we could walk up the Hill.' Now, as he held a light meter in front of my face, squinting at the dial, I glanced at his hands again. The skin on the back of them was strangely pale and textured like damask. On his fingers were tiny white lines, like miniature forks of lightning. *I did that to you, David. It was me. It was me.* He noticed me looking. I looked away.

'Would you like a cup of coffee?' I asked, my tone of voice more normal now, as the initial shock began to subside. 'Or would you like something to eat?' *Or maybe I could give you all my money, and my jewellery—in fact everything I own: I'd be pleased to…*

'No thanks,' he said. 'I'm fine.' A sudden silence descended. Then David looked at Herman. 'Nice dog,' he said, suddenly friendlier now. 'What's his name?' I told him.

'Herman the German,' he said.

'*Exactly.*'

He crouched down and stroked Herman's glossy head. 'I

like dachshunds,' he added. 'They always look like something awful's just happened—or is about to.'

'That's why *I* like them too. The way they look so acutely…concerned.' He nodded and now, for the first time, he smiled. 'I'm sorry about the inquisition,' I said, calmer now.

He shrugged. 'That's fine. I guess it's just nerves.' *It is.* 'But don't worry, Miranda…'—what did he *mean*, 'don't worry'?—'…I'm going to make you look great.' *Oh.* And now I noticed how warm his eyes were and how nice his mouth was, and I saw the red-gold lights in his hair. I opened my compact mirror and quickly checked my appearance. The bruising had gone.

'Should I put on any make-up?' I asked. 'I don't usually bother.'

He cocked his head to one side, his eyes skimming over my face as though I were a painting he was appraising. 'No, your skin-tone's even—I think we'll be fine. In any case, I'm shooting black and white so you can get away without it. In colour, everything shows.' He took the camera out of the bag and slung the strap round his neck. Then he pointed it at me, focussed, and pressed the shutter.

I blinked. 'I wasn't ready.'

'You were.'

'But I wasn't smiling.'

'I don't want you to smile. A smile is concealing.'

'Is it?'

'Oh yes. A smile is often a mask. Now, just…' he came in a little closer—I noticed the lemony scent of his aftershave. '…Yees. Nice. Very nice.' He pressed the shutter again. It was so quiet that I barely heard it. 'Now could you sit on the couch there…that's it…with the dog.' He lifted Herman up then moved the two chairs out of shot. 'Now, I want you to face the other way from him, just lean your head this way a bit, and…yes. That's great. Herman, you look at me, okay?' I heard the soft click of the shutter again, then he wound on. He took two more, then another five in quick succession. Then he suddenly stopped.

'I know this is hard,' he said, lowering the camera, 'because I'm pointing a large lens at you, but if you *could* try to relax a little…' *No, I can't. Because it's you. I can't possibly relax.* 'You see, you look slightly tense.'

'Oh.' *I am.*

'Now, look at me, Miranda…'

'This way?'

'Yes, over there, towards the window…that's good.' He pressed the shutter again, then lowered the camera. He was standing there, saying nothing, scrutinizing me. I loathed it. I imagined that he could see my guilt.

'You're very photogenic,' he suddenly remarked as he lifted the camera to his eye again. 'You have neat features, and good cheekbones. No, *don't* smile. I want to see the true you.' *You don't. You don't. Believe me.*

'Don't you use a flash?' I asked, as he clicked away.

'No, I prefer to use natural light. That's nice, yes—towards the window—lift your chin. Good.' Now that he had the camera in his hands he seemed somehow less abrasive, as though it protected him, gave him a barrier. 'We'll have Herman sitting beside you, and I'd like you to look at each other. Yes—hold it—that's great. Now we'll do a few of you standing by the door.'

'I thought you'd be using a digital camera,' I said, as he changed the roll.

'I prefer my old Leica for this kind of work. I know it's not very twenty-first century of me,' he added as he stuck a label on the new cartridge, 'but I'm a bit of a purist, plus I like to print my own film. I don't normally do portraits,' he added. 'In fact,' he went on with a puzzled expression, 'I'm not quite sure why I was asked to do this.' *Because of me—that's why. Because I wanted to meet you.* 'But *Moi!*'s a good magazine, and it's all work.'

'You do news photography, don't you?' I asked.

'Not any more. I was a conflict photographer for Reuters, but I fell out of love with it. I do freelance work now.'

'Photographing what?'

'All sorts of things. Things I'm asked to do—and things I want to do, on issues I think are important. Anyway, we're all done in here—let's go outside.' I put Herman on the lead, still feeling nervous and inhibited, then we strolled up Primrose Hill.

'Where are you from, Miranda?' he asked as we walked up the path. 'If you don't mind me asking *you* a few questions!' He was definitely more relaxed now, in fact, to my surprise, almost friendly.

'I'm from Brighton.'

'That's a coincidence.' *It isn't a coincidence.* 'My family lived there for a while.'

'Really?' I said disingenuously. 'Which bit?'

'Queens Park. West Drive.' *Number 44. The semi-detached house, two doors from the end. I was there the other day, looking for you.* 'Where did you live then?' he enquired.

'Sandown Road.'

'Oh. Not that far away from us then?'

'No,' I murmured nervously. 'Not that far.'

'We never met, did we?' he added. 'At any teenage parties?' My heart turned over at the thought. 'I think if we *had* met I'd have remembered you,' he added thoughtfully.

'No,' I said. 'I don't think we did.'

'That's probably because you're a bit younger than me, plus

I was away at boarding school. My dad worked at the university.' *I know that.*

'Did he?'

'But then, well…he decided to move. To be honest, my memories of Brighton aren't that great.' *That's my fault. I'm sorry. I'm really sorry.* 'I haven't been back for over fifteen years. Nice view,' he murmured. We'd got to the top. There were kids flying kites and joggers jogging and people walking their dogs. 'Let's just have you sitting on one of the benches,' he said. 'This is perfect.' He took some more shots. 'The light's gorgeous now—it's really soft and there's no haze because of the wind.'

I sat there, London's skyline curving before me, from the squat skyscrapers of Docklands to the chimneys of Battersea Power Station; the office windows flashing gold in the evening sun. Now that I'd met him and spoken to him, I knew I'd *have* to tell him. There was no question of that. But *when*?

'Let's have you walking down again with Herman,' I heard him say from my left-hand side. 'Just ignore me and keep going. That's it.'

I walked away from David, feeling slightly self-conscious now, as people looked at me and smiled as he followed me, clicking away, or walked backwards in front of me. I heard the clock strike seven. I knew what to do. I'd ask him back to the house. I'd ask him back to the house and offer him a beer and—

'All done,' I heard him say. He drew level with me again, then we walked down the hill in perfect step, beneath the plane trees, through the gate and into St Michael's Mews. I opened the front door and David rewound the film, quickly labelled it, then put the camera in the bag.

'I took two rolls so there should be some good ones there.'

He hoisted his holdall onto his shoulder. *Say it now. Ask him. Ask him.*

'Would you—' I began. But he was already offering me his hand.

'Well, good to meet you, Miranda. I'll be off. Would I what, sorry?' As I looked at him I suddenly felt as though my chest were being squeezed. 'What were you going to say?'

'I was just going to say, erm…would you…like…a beer or anything?'

'A beer…?'

'Yes. I just thought you might…like one. That's all. As it's the…end of the day. I mean, you don't have to,' I stuttered, 'but…I just thought…you might like one.'

'Well, that would have been great…' He looked confused. 'But actually, I've…got to run.'

'I see. So you've got to run,' I repeated robotically. He nodded slowly, then an awkward silence suddenly descended. *There's something I have to tell you, David. It will change your life.* 'I'm…sorry we got off to such a bad start,' I said.

He nodded again. 'Yes. Me too.'

'It was my fault. You must have thought me very odd.'

'No, no—although, actually, *yes.*' He suddenly laughed. 'I *did* think that. But I know I can be abrasive so I guess I made you feel nervous.' *You did make me feel nervous, but that's not the reason.* 'Anyway,' he glanced at his watch. 'I'll be on my way.' He dug his right hand into his back pocket. 'Why don't I give you my card?' As he handed it to me I noticed the scarring on his hands again, and felt tears prick the backs of my eyes. 'If you need anything, give me a call.' *I do need something. I need to tell you what I did to you and I need you to forgive me.* 'Are you okay?' he asked. He was peering at me. 'Are you okay? You look a bit…upset.'

'Oh. No. No. I'm fine. I'm *fine,*' I repeated. 'It's…'

'Hay fever?' I nodded. 'It's a real nuisance, isn't it?' I nodded again. 'Okay,' he said, as he picked up his bag. 'I guess that's it. It was nice to meet you, Miranda. See you then,' he said as he walked out of the house.

I smiled. 'Yes. See you.' But *how*? How *will* I be able to see him again, I wondered. All I knew was that I had to. He *had* to know who I was.

—— CHAPTER 7 ——

'Just a quick call,' said Dad the following evening, as I prepared for the next puppy party. 'To say I'm installed—more or less.'

'What's the house like?'

'It's not huge, but it's fine, apart from the horrible brown drapes.'

'And what about the club?'

'Well, the course is fabulous, with sea views from the top, and the clubhouse is great. But they've clearly got massive financial problems.'

'Didn't they tell you that beforehand?'

'No. It's come as rather a shock. They just said that they'd need me to do a "bit of a recruitment drive". But I've been looking at the books today and the situation's *terrible*. They've only got a hundred members signed up and they'll need five hundred just to break even. Still,' he added, with an intake of breath, 'I always knew that this would be a big challenge after Palm Springs.'

'Then why did you take the job?'

'I want to retire here, Miranda. I want to lay down my bones.'

'But you're only fifty-eight!'

'I know, but I'd had enough of living in the States. Plus, the awkward fact that I didn't have permanent residency.'

'You should have married some nice American then.'

'I never really wanted to,' he sighed. 'Not that I didn't get offers, what with my oh-so-charming English accent.' Not to mention his good looks. He's still an attractive man, my dad. 'And then, of course, the resort was very nice...' *Nice?* The Hyatt Golf Resort is a *palace*. 'But these luxury hotels feel so faceless after a while. People come and go; you don't get to *know* them—I began to long for the camaraderie that you get in a club. Then I met someone from here and we got chatting, and he mentioned that they were urgently looking for a new General Manager, and I was offered it the following week. When I looked at the map, I realized that the location wasn't exactly *ideal*,' he went on nervously. 'But I'm sure your mother will be perfectly civilized if we meet.'

I'm sure she won't be.

'I'm sure she will be,' I said. There was an odd little silence.

'I've already seen her, actually.'

'What?'

'I've seen her. Your mother. I passed her at lunchtime. She was leading two llamas down the road.'

'And did she see you?'

'No. I would have stopped—I wanted to—but she looked so furious, I thought it best not to risk it.'

'Jose and Pedro must have got out. They go walkabout sometimes. There's always a bit of a crisis when that happens. Or a "llama drama" as Mum likes to say.'

'Pity.'

'No, it's okay—she always gets them back. People phone her up.'

'I said *pretty*.'

'Oh. Well, yes, they are. Llamas are lovely-looking things.'

There was another odd little silence. 'No. Not the llamas,' he said wistfully. 'Your mum.'

Poor Dad, I thought, as I put round the chairs in the consulting room. He's always regretted their divorce: I know this because he told me so a few years ago. He finally wanted to put his side of it to me. He said he'd never seen why it was necessary for them to break up. He said Mum had forced him to choose between his marriage, or his dream of becoming a professional golfer. He'd just carried on playing and hoped she'd calm down, but she didn't. She changed the locks.

Dad did turn professional for a while—he won several of the smaller European tournaments. But he never really hit the big time, so he decided to go into club management instead. He kept in touch with us, of course; but his occasional visits were fraught, as Mum was so unfriendly—she still is. Then, when she married Hugh, Dad went to the States.

He'd call me, whenever he came over, and we'd have dinner. He'd ask me about my studies or my work, or whatever it was at the time; then he'd say, 'And your mother, Miranda? How's your mother, then?' And he'd look rather sad. I felt I could only say the minimum, out of respect for her feelings. I told him about Hugh leaving, obviously, and about the llamas arriving, otherwise, well, I kept Mum...

'Poor Dad,' I said to Herman as I filled the water bowl, ready for the puppies. Herman arranged his features into an expression of exquisite sympathy. Then the phone rang. It was her.

'That's funny—I was just thinking about you.'

'Were you? I just wanted to ask you two very quick things. Number one—what do you think of this idea as a money-spinner?' There was a dramatic pause. 'Llama psychotherapy.'

Llama psychotherapy? 'Well, they'd have to qualify first, Mum—it would be too expensive—and apparently it takes a long time.'

'Don't be facetious, Miranda. What I mean *is*, that I could offer days where stressed-out business people can come and spend time with the llamas. They can groom them and talk to them—you know how sensitive they are—and unload *all* their worries onto them.'

'Hmm, you mean, "beasts of unburden"—that kind of thing?'

'No, I was thinking of something along the lines of "Be Calmer With a Llama".'

'That's quite catchy. Why not give it a go?'

'I think I will. You see the boys really *have* got to earn their keep a bit more,' she went on. 'Especially with the twins going to university in October, what with these wretched top-up fees. Pedro didn't get the beer commercial, by the way. We're all very disappointed.'

'And I'm afraid I can't get Henry on *Animal Crackers*. Although they liked the idea of his kissing addiction, they thought it might look a bit cosy as you're my mum. Can't you get the local paper to do a story about him? The "Llama Charmer"?'

'No, they're always doing me—every time they're desperate they run another "Llama Lady" feature—and it's *national* publicity I need. Oh well,' she sighed. 'But the other thing is that I'd like to know your father's new address.'

'Why? Are you going to see him? That would be great, Mum. I'm sure he'd be delighted.'

'No. I'm not. The only reason I want to know is so that it makes it easier for me to *avoid* him.'

'Oh.'

'So where is he?'

I dug the card Dad had sent me out of the drawer. 'The Old Laundry, Weaver's Lane, Lower Chalvington.'

'God, that's only four miles away.'

'I know. Aren't you even curious about him?' I added, as I heard her scribble it down. 'You haven't seen him since my graduation day, eight years ago—when you were so frosty you gave us all chilblains.'

'No, Miranda,' she said. 'I am not curious. I'm rather *furious*. I mean *why* did he have to come down *here*? It's the last thing one wants, to have one's ex-husband landing practically on the doorstep. I mean, of *all* the golf clubs...'

'...in all the towns in all the world. I know, Mum. Never mind. Anyway, my puppies are arriving. Sorry. Can't chat.' There's only so much father-bashing I can take.

Soon, Sooty the sheepdog was trying to herd all the other puppies; Alfie and Roxy were looking for things to retrieve; Gwyneth Paltrow was looking at her reflection in the water bowl; and Twiglet was jumping off chairs.

'He's absolutely fearless,' said Phyllis to Marcus, admiringly. She seemed to have taken a shine to him. 'He obviously takes after you. I must just ask you,' she added, 'because I'm *so* fascinated by what you do—what's the most *frightening* thing you've ever done?'

'Well...' I looked at him—he must get asked that so often.

'Jumping off a tall building?' she suggested sweetly.

'Not really—so long as it's not more than twenty storeys high.'

'Being set on fire from head to foot?'

He shook his head. 'You wear a flame-proof suit.'

'Riding a motorbike across a yawning *chasm*?' she enquired eagerly.

'That's okay. You just have to get the revs right.'

'Swimming in a tank full of *piranhas*. Naked.'

He shrugged. 'It's fine as long as they've had lunch.'

'What *is* it, then? The scariest, most frightful, *horrifying* thing you've ever done in your entire life?' Her pale blue eyes were shimmering with anticipation.

'Well,' he said. 'You know those big black spiders you get in the bath?' He gave an involuntary shudder. 'I once put one of those outside.'

'You're teasing me,' she giggled, clapping her hand to her mouth.

'No, it's true. I really did. If you don't believe me, you can ring up my ex.'

'Okay, everyone,' I said after I'd done the roll call. 'Welcome again, and let's play Pass the Puppy.'

'I can't help feeling we should be doing this to music,' said Lily as she passed Gwyneth, yapping, to her left.

'—I say, Alfie's grown.'

'—I think Cosmo's second teeth are coming through.'

'—Bentley's widdled on me!'

'—He doesn't *usually* do that.'

'—Where's the kitchen roll?'

We discussed the importance of identi-chipping and poop-scooping, then, finally, we had problem-sharing again.

'And how are things going with Lola, Sue?' I asked her.

'Oh, it's getting *much* better,' she said. 'I mean, I have my good days and my bad days…' Everyone nodded sympathetically. 'But I don't feel *nearly* as stressed.'

'You've got to get them in a routine,' said Phyllis, bouncing Maisie on her lap. '*That's* the key to it.'

'That's right,' everyone murmured as they cradled their puppies. 'You've got to get them in a routine.'

'Okay, so, see you all next week then,' I said.

'Must dash,' said Marcus, as he waved at everyone. He

tucked Twiglet into his jumper. 'Twiggers and I have got a hot date.'

'Oh *that* sounds exciting,' said Phyllis. 'New girlfriend?' Marcus nodded. 'Oh good.' He opened his wallet and showed her a snap. I didn't want to appear nosey, so I didn't look, though I was curious.

'What do you think?' I heard him say.

'Well, she's *very* pretty,' said Phyllis approvingly.

'She is. She's gorgeous. She's a jewellery designer,' he explained as he put the photo back. 'Glass necklaces. They're made out of *tiny* little beads. She strings them herself,' he added proudly.

'Really?'

'She's very successful. She sells them in Liberty's.'

'I *say*. And how did you meet her?'

'In the chemist's by Chalk Farm tube. She was waiting for a prescription and I was buying some Strepsils and we got chatting.'

'*How* romantic.'

'It was. Because it wasn't actually my local chemist, as I live in Camden. But I'd just dropped in there because I had a bit of a scratchy throat—and *there* she was. This *vision*.'

'That's a lovely story,' Phyllis said. 'Anyway, we mustn't keep you, Marcus. Maisie, say bye-bye to Twiglet.' Maisie emitted a cross between a squeak and a yap. Marcus left, then Lily came up to me.

'I had no *idea* you'd been engaged to Alexander Darke,' she whispered, her large brown eyes goggling. I nodded. 'That's absolutely brilliant,' she said. I looked at her blankly. 'I mean, for the piece. It's *fantastic* copy.'

'Oh. Good,' I said dismally.

'And how was the great D.J.?'

'He was…fine.'

'He can be notoriously tricky—the snappy snapper. Was he like that with you?'

'A bit.'

'I've met him a couple of times, but I found him so un-communicative. You'd get more conversation out of a corpse. *I* think it's something to do with what happened to him,' she went on confidentially. 'I'm sure you must have noticed his hands.'

'I, no, not really, I…'

'The poor darling had this *dreadful* experience. Years ago, his father was sent a letter-bomb by the animal rights crazies—not that I disagree with them on *every* issue—but anyway, D.J. opened it instead and *Boom!*'. Her eyes had opened as wide as windows. 'Hence those awful scars. They say he's never been the same.' I felt sick. 'Well, you wouldn't be, would you?' I wished she'd shut *up*. 'They say that's why his marriage didn't last.' I looked at her. 'He was married to this Polish model.'

'Really?'

'Absolutely gorgeous—but she'd had enough after a year. She claimed he hardly ever talked to her. I can well imagine it. Anyway,' she put Gwyneth in her puppy basket, and tugged on Jennifer's lead. 'My driver's waiting, Miranda. Bye!'

That night I hardly slept. Lily's words kept buzzing around my head like trapped bees bouncing against a windowpane: *'never been the same—well you wouldn't be, would you—never been the same—BOOM!'* I eventually fell asleep at about six and was woken by the phone—it was Daisy on her way to work.

'At last I can talk to you,' she said over the dull rumble of the rush hour. 'I've been so frantic—we're doing a Bolly-wood ball and I've been trying to find a couple of elephants. So how's it all going? The search?'

'I've found him,' I said.

'You've *found* him?'

'Yes. That photographer—the one I said wasn't the right one.' I hauled myself into a sitting position. 'Well, it turns out he *is*. The reason why he sounds American is because he grew up in the States.'

'Christ,' she exclaimed. 'You must have got a shock when you realized.'

'I did—about ten million volts.'

'And what was he like?'

'He was a bit…difficult,' I said. 'But then it was a very stressful encounter—not that he would have understood why.' On my bedside table was his business card. I picked it up and turned it over in my hand. 'But I also thought he was…nice.'

'What does he look like?' she said as I heard a bicycle bell tinkling aggressively in the background. I described him to her.

'Gosh, he sounds rather attractive.'

'He…is. Though he's very brooding and watchful—he doesn't exactly put you at your ease.'

'And was it weird, being photographed by him?'

'It was terrifying. I gibbered like a maniac to begin with. But then, somehow, once he was behind the camera, this change came over him and he seemed to relax. As though he was able to talk to me then.'

'How long was he with you?'

I pulled up the blind and my room filled with sunlight. 'About an hour.'

'And was it…obvious…?' she asked tactfully.

'Oh yes. There are scars. You can see. But Christ, Daisy…' I looked out of the window and my vision blurred with sudden tears, 'he could have lost *fingers*—or worse. He could have been blinded. That's always been part of the nightmare for me—not knowing how seriously he'd been hurt. As it is, his hands are okay, but they're just,' my throat was aching, '...scarred. And I *did* that to him,' I wept. 'And it was such a huge shock—actually *seeing it*—seeing the damage *I'd caused*.'

'So you obviously didn't...tell him then.'

I wiped my eyes with the cuff of my nightshirt. 'No. Not yet. But I will. Now that I've met him I can't possibly *not* tell him. So I'm going to call him soon. Very soon. But I've just got to steel myself first. It isn't going to be easy,' I sniffed. 'In fact it's going to be very hard.'

'You sound a bit like me,' she said ruefully, 'with Nigel.'

'So you still haven't spoken to him?'

'No. As I say, I've been busy and so has he. He had his advanced bonsai cultivation on Monday, and I had indoor climbing on Tuesday, then last night I was at the Trail to Timbuktu extravaganza and he was working late because he really wants to get Equity Partnership soon. But I *will* speak to him. Definitely. Any day now...'

'Hmm.'

'But you ring David. In your own time. When you feel absolutely ready, Miranda—you ring him.'

I didn't have to, because, to my great surprise—he phoned me.

I was with a client down in Kingston later that day—a lop-eared house-rabbit.

'What's his name?' I asked his owner, as she passed me a biscuit. She brushed a crumb off her twin-set.

'Bob.'

'Short for Bobtail?'

She looked puzzled. 'No. Robert.'

'Oh, of course.' I opened my pad and began to take notes. 'Bob the bunny,' I scribbled. 'And he's four months old?'

'He is. And most of the time he's a very pleasant and well-mannered young rabbit,' she said approvingly as she sipped her tea. 'But recently he's become *extremely* demanding, haven't you, Bob?' She wagged an admonitory finger at him as he sat next to her on the sofa, washing his face.

'In what way?' I asked as he did his toilette. He licked his forepaws then wiped them several times over his eyes and nose.

'Well, during the day he has the run of the house,' she explained. 'He's litter-trained. But he sleeps in his play-pen at night. And when I come downstairs in the morning I usually feed him before I do anything else, and give him a bit of fuss. But lately I've noticed that if it isn't convenient for me to do that right away because the phone rings, or my little girl needs me, he goes totally *berserk*.' I looked at Bob. He was washing his ears now, carefully pulling them down over his face.

'Berserk?' I repeated. 'How?'

'He throws a *huge* wobbly. He grabs the bars of his cage and shakes them, or he goes over to his pile of toys and throws them about. He's got some wooden bricks and he *hurls* them all *over* the place. It's quite frightening, actually.'

'Hmm, I can imagine.' I visualized a notice outside the house—*Beware of the Rabbit*.

'It's a sort of hysteria,' she observed. 'Sometimes I think it's like he's going through the "terrible twos".'

'Well, you're not far off the mark. He *is* having toddler tantrums—or the lapine equivalent of them—because he's just learning, to his horror, that the world doesn't always go according to his plan. He's shocked to find that he can't have a carrot or a cuddle exactly when he wants it—so he sulks, or he vents his frustration in physical ways. It's what we call "redirected aggression".'

'I *see*.'

And I was just explaining that he'd almost certainly grow out of it, and it was nothing to worry about, when my mobile rang.

'Miranda?'

'Yes?'

'It's David here.' My stomach did a somersault. 'Miranda? Are you there?'

'Ye-es. Yes. Hello.'

'Are you busy at the moment?'

'Well, a bit—I'm with a client.' I glanced at the woman, who was now hunting for her handbag, Bob dangling under her left arm.

'What species?'

'Erm—oryctolagus cuniculus.'

'Wabbit,' he said.

'*Very* good,' I laughed.

'I had one when I was a kid. I used to pride myself on being able to say that.'

There was a moment's silence. 'So…have they come out well?' I asked. 'The photographs?'

'Oh, I don't know. I haven't printed them yet. That's not why I'm ringing.'

'Oh.'

'No, I was just phoning you…'

There was another tiny silence. 'Yes?'

'Well…I was…sorry that I didn't have that beer with you on Tuesday.'

Oh. 'Oh, well, don't worry, David—that's fine.'

'So, I just…wondered if you'd like to come out for a beer with me?'

He's asking me out? My heart did a swallow dive. 'O-kay…'

'In fact, I was wondering if you were free tomorrow,' he went on. 'But I guess you're busy,' he added casually. 'It's such short notice and you probably have plans.'

'No, I'm not doing anything. That would be…nice. Um, where did you have in mind?'

'Well, we could go somewhere near you, or, if you don't mind coming over to Clerkenwell, there's the St John restaurant. They've got a very good menu.'

'Yes, I could come over there. So you mean dinner, then?' I added uncertainly.

'I guess I do mean that. You do eat dinner, I hope?'

'Yes. Yes, I do. Dinner's fine.' *Then, over pudding, I'll tell you the terrible truth about myself…*

'That's great then.'

And you'll loathe me for the rest of your life.

'I'll book the table,' I heard him say, 'and I'll only ring you back if I can't get one, otherwise I'll meet you there at, what, seven thirty? It's at 26 St John Street.'

'I'll find it.'

'Great. See you there.'

The thought of seeing David had an odd effect on me. I felt relieved on one level—filled with terror on another—but at least it distracted me from *Land Ahoy!* I'd been dreading the first episode for weeks, but, as it was, I felt able to watch. That night I lay on my bed, with my tiny portable perched on the chest of drawers, clutching one of Herman's wrinkly paws. As the opening music played, the name 'Alexander Darke' appeared, in a curlicued script, virtually filling the screen. He was playing the ship's commander, Francis Flavell. And now there he was. There was Alexander. I felt my heart-rate increase as the camera panned in for a close-up. He looked so dignified as he strode about the quarterdeck in a gale, barking orders, his face streaming with spray and rain.

'How does she steer, Mr Tree?'

'Holding steady, Sir!'

'Take her to windward, Mr Tree! To windward I say!'

And now the ship was creaking and listing as the sailors pulled on the rigging.

'She's run aground, Sir!'

'Man the decks!'

During the commercial break, Daisy phoned me. 'Are you watching it?' she asked.

'Yes,' I said bleakly.

'Do you feel okay?'

'I feel…strange. I keep thinking, I was going to *marry* that man.'

'Well, I must say I'm glad that you're *not*. Anyway, what do you think?'

'Well, objectively, I think he looks fantastic. There's no doubt about it, Daisy,' I added flatly. 'This is going to make him a star.'

'I hope *not*,' she said. 'Otherwise we'll keep *on* seeing him and I don't *want* to, after what he did. If people only *knew*…' she added crossly. 'Ooh, it's starting again…'

The storm was still raging and one of the mainsails tore in two, like a tissue, then a human figure dropped into the swell.

'Man overboard!' one of the sailors screamed. 'Man overboard! Mr Fenton's gone in!'

'I *know* that chap,' I said to Daisy. 'That guy who just fell in the sea. He's a stuntman. He comes to my puppy parties.'

'Does he?'

'He does self-defence classes too.'

'Really? Well, we must go to them, Miranda. Shall we do that?'

'Okay,' I said absently. 'Why not?'

And now the camera cut to Alexander, who was ripping off his coat and leaping into the sea to save his first mate.

'Look at that!' Daisy shrieked. 'Alexander's jumping in after him. Can you believe it!'

'That's not really Alexander. That's a stuntman too.'

'Well, obviously,' she said. 'I'm not sure I can take this,' she added as there was a close-up of Alexander thrashing about in the water. 'I seriously think I might puke.'

'It's only a drama, Daisy,' I said wearily.

'I know *that*. Anyway, I'm turning him *off*.'

I managed to watch it to the end, and, as the closing credits scrolled down the screen, I remembered how thrilled I'd been when Alexander got the part. He very nearly didn't get it because the producers were worried that he wasn't a big enough name. He had five screen tests—the whole agonizing process took over a month. But the casting director—who'd spotted him in *The Tempest*—insisted that he was the one. And then, at long last, Alexander's agent phoned him to say that he'd got it. I remember shrieking with joy.

I'd felt so relieved for him—it was the big break he'd been waiting for—and I felt terribly proud. I'd often imagined how we would watch *Land Ahoy!* together, on the night it was screened; we'd probably throw a small party, just for close friends. But here I was, watching it with Herman, not having laid eyes on Alexander for nearly two months.

'And you can see the second episode of *Land Ahoy!* at the same time next week,' said the announcer over the final bars of the theme tune. I switched it off.

'No thanks.' Once was enough.

★ ★ ★

The next day I went filming for *Animal Crackers*; I had to
drive out to Oxfordshire to film a pair of aggressive guard
geese—they were vile—one of them nearly broke my arm.
But it was frustrating because there was a tractor in the next
field and every time I tried to do my piece to camera it
would start up. Anyway, Clare, the producer, had a copy of
The Times, and while we were hanging about I read the TV
review. It was captioned *Alexander the Great. Alexander Darke
exuded heroism from every pore*, the reviewer declared. I felt ill.
He was public property now.

We eventually got the geese done, then we all drove to
Bicester to film this goat which was having an identity crisis.
It had convinced itself it was a horse. Finally, at half past six,
I got home with Herman, exhausted, and contemplated the
evening ahead. I left a message for Daisy, telling her that
I was seeing David. Then I opened the wardrobe. What
should I wear? I opted for a simple white dress and a lime
green cashmere cardigan, and put a little mousse in my hair.
I got the tube, because I wanted to have a drink—if not several—the only kind of courage I'd have would be Dutch. I'd
looked up the restaurant. It was near Farringdon. At seven
forty, I pushed on the door.

David was already there, at the bar in smart jeans and
a white tee shirt with a blue linen jacket. He saw me and
waved. We had a glass of champagne—I drank mine pretty
quickly—then we went through to the dining room. It was
refectory style, with white painted walls and simple wooden
tables.

'So here we are,' he said as we were seated.

'Here we are,' I repeated. 'It's nice.' The waiter brought us
the menus.

'They have some quite amazing things here,' David said, as

the waiter poured our mineral water. I glanced at the menu and felt suddenly sick. *Rolled pig's spleen.* I read. *Braised sweetbreads...fried calves' brains...black pudding...roast bone marrow... boiled ox-tail...*

'Seen anything you like?' I heard him ask.

'David—'

'What are chitterlings?' he enquired.

'A pig's small intestines. David—'

'Hmm?' he said, as he continued to peruse the menu.

'There's something I've got to tell you.'

'Yes?' He looked up. 'Is it serious?'

'I'm a vegetarian.'

'Oh. Oh *dear*. I'm so sorry,' he added, pulling a face. 'This is just about the worst place I could have brought you then.'

'It's not your fault. I should have warned you. But I didn't know the restaurant was quite so meat-orientated. It doesn't matter,' I said. 'I mean, I used to be a vet. I've seen plenty of chitterlings and spleens in my time—but they were usually attached to live animals I was doing surgery on.'

'Do you want to leave?'

'No, it's okay. I could just have...' I glanced down the menu. 'The Welsh rarebit.'

'That's not very much.'

'I'll be fine.'

'Well, I won't have anything too ghastly. I'll have the widgeon—that's a duck, isn't it, could you stand watching me eat that?'

'Yes. In any case, I'm not that strict. Usually, going to a restaurant doesn't bother me because there's normally a pasta or rice dish I can have, but here it's nearly all meat.'

'It is—and their speciality's unusual cuts. In fact, it's absolutely *offal*,' he quipped. I smiled. 'Why did you go vegetarian?' he asked as he caught the waiter's eye. 'Was it an animal welfare thing for you?'

I fiddled with the stem of my wineglass. 'Yes. Yes, it was.'

'So you're a veggie with a sausage dog!'

I smiled. The waiter came back and as David spoke to him I glanced again at his damaged hands, resting on the table, and had to fight the sudden urge to cry.

'Is white wine okay for you, Miranda?' I nodded. The waiter returned with a bottle of good Chablis. I had a large sip and began to relax. Then our first course arrived—mozzarella salad for me, and potted shrimp for him—and I noticed that David held his fork in a slightly odd way, as though he couldn't grip it properly. Now he was asking me about my work. And that made the conversation go well because I always have lots of good stories. Then it was my turn to make enquiries about him.

'Did you always want to be a photographer?' I asked, my heart pounding.

'No. I was going to be a doctor, actually.'

'Really? You mean, you read medicine?'

'Yes.'

'Where was that then?'

'At Cambridge.'

'You went to *Cambridge*?' I said. *You went to Cambridge and you had to leave early—because of me.*

'But I went off medicine,' he explained as he put down his knife.

'Oh,' I said, innocently. 'Why?'

'Because, well, I had to leave university halfway through my course.' Now I remembered his neighbour saying that he'd 'left early'. 'I had an…accident,' he said. He nodded at his hands. 'You probably noticed.'

'No, I—'

'So I had to take several months off. And the college were very understanding about it, and they told me I could do the year again. But by the time I was, well, better—if that's the right word—I wasn't sure about medicine any more.'

'Why not?' I asked quietly. I could feel my heart race.

'Well, I just didn't want to be a doctor after that. Maybe because I'd had to spend a lot of time in hospital. Having skin grafts. It takes ages—well, you'd know all about that,' he added.

My breathing suddenly tightened. 'How? How would I know?'

He looked slightly puzzled. 'Well…because of being a vet.'

'Oh…yes…of course.'

'Anyway, that was quite a big…set-back. I had to adjust.'

I felt that I could look at his hands openly, now that he was talking about them. I wanted to take them in mine, and stroke them and make them better.

'I'm so sorry,' I murmured. *I'm so, so sorry.*

'Don't worry,' he said. 'I mean, it's not *your* fault.' *But it is my fault.* 'They're not very pretty,' he went on, 'but at least they work. I hope it doesn't, well…bother you,' he added. *Yes, it does bother me.*

'No, of course not,' I said.

'Anyway, it was ages ago now.'

'Sixteen years.'

He blinked. 'You're good at maths.' I looked at him, shocked. 'You worked that out quickly.'

'Oh…well…you said you were halfway through university, so you must have been about twenty then,' I said, my heart banging, 'and you said on Tuesday that you're thirty-six.'

'Did I?' He looked puzzled. 'I don't remember telling you that.'

'Yes, I think you did…I'm pretty…sure that you did…'
Shut up, Miranda!

'Well, I must have done. Anyway, I took some time off to convalesce. And I went to San Francisco to stay with this friend of mine whose parents had moved there—I told you we lived in the States when I was a kid?' I nodded. 'And this guy's big sister was a photographer on the *San Francisco Examiner*. And I remember how amazing I thought she was. She'd go out and get these incredible photos, and she'd work half the night to develop them—she was so passionate about it—then we'd see them in the paper the next day. And I had time to kill, so she showed me how the camera worked, and she'd let me come into the dark room and watch her develop them, and so, to cut a long story short, I got the bug. So I decided to leave Cambridge…'

'What a pity,' I said. 'You left Cambridge early.'

'Well, there was no point in going back. So I went to the City Poly to study photography, and luckily my hands were healing by then. And I got some financial compensation for my injuries, a sort of insurance payout. So I bought this really good second-hand Leica—the one I used to take your photo the other day. And, luckily, I was fine holding it. The grip on the left hand's not great—there was tendon damage—but it's the right one that matters more. I don't think I could have done it—at least not then—if I'd had problems with the focussing and winding on. Anyway, I got my diploma, then I became an assistant photographer for a couple of years, then I got taken on at Reuters, which was a really good break.'

'So you became a photojournalist?' I said. 'Why didn't you want to be, say, a landscape photographer, or a fashion photographer?'

'Well, I do love taking landscapes actually, and I did wonder about doing that; but the fact is I'd suddenly become more interested in politics. I wasn't before, when I was a teenager, but in my early twenties, I became...' he shrugged, '...more politicized, I guess.' I knew exactly why that was. 'You know, you're so easy to talk to,' he said, with an air of surprise. 'I'm usually a pretty poor conversationalist, but I feel I could talk to you for hours—I'm not sure why. I think it's because you seem to be a very sympathetic person.'

'Do I?'

'Yes. You seem to be very...compassionate. I mean, the way you reacted just now when I told you about my...accident. I found that very touching.' And I was just wondering what on earth to say, when the waiter appeared and took our plates. 'I wasn't sure that you'd agree to come out this evening,' David added. 'I was worried that you thought I was rude.'

'I was worried that you thought I was *mad*.'

'We did get off on the wrong foot, didn't we?' I nodded. Then a silence descended. 'Shall I tell you why I asked you out?' he said suddenly. I looked into his eyes, and noticed that they had amber and green flecks.

'Okay,' I murmured. 'Why did you?'

'Because you looked *so* crestfallen when I couldn't stay for a beer.' He fiddled with his spoon. 'It was really sweet. Your expression. You seemed so...disappointed, if I'm not flattering myself, which I probably am. In fact, you looked quite upset. And I was really touched by that, so I decided that I'd ask *you*.' He suddenly smiled. And as he did so the tiny crescent-moon-shaped scar—which I had almost certainly caused too—disappeared in his laughter lines.

Now, over the main course, the conversation became more personal. And I realized with happiness, and a kind of horror, that he *liked* me—he wouldn't for long. He told me that he was divorced.

'How long were you married?' I asked disingenuously.

'Just over a year.'

'Not long then.'

He shook his head. 'It was a mistake. We didn't have enough in common,' he went on. 'Plus I travelled a hell of a lot, and so did she.'

'What did she do?' I asked innocently.

'She's a model. Lots of photographers date models,' he said. 'We seem to move in the same circles so it's easy to meet, and we both have these high pressure lives. And Katya and I were very attracted to each other, but we made the mistake of getting married when it should only have been a fling.'

'Did you break up with her?'

'No. She left me. She said I didn't treat her well, which is probably true. She said I didn't talk to her enough and that I was selfish—which I guess I am. Photographers often are selfish, because we're so driven.' He poured me some more wine. 'And what about you, Miranda? You're single, aren't you?' I nodded. 'And has there ever been a Mr Miranda?'

'No. Or rather, not…quite.'

'Not quite?'

I fiddled with my wineglass. 'I was engaged for a while.'

'Really? When?'

'It ended in May.'

'Not long ago then. I'm sorry. That must have been very hard.'

'It was. It still is, actually.' I chewed on my lip. 'But I know it's for the best.'

'Why? Was he…?'

'Unfaithful? No.' I absently smoothed my napkin. 'He wasn't.'

'Were you…incompatible then?'

I shook my head. 'We got on incredibly well.'

'So what was the problem—if you don't mind my asking—which you probably do.'

I looked at him. 'He…behaved badly towards me.'

'Was he aggressive?'

'Aggressive?' I smiled. 'Oh no. He just…did something that I couldn't forgive. But I'd rather not talk about it, if you don't mind, because I don't even like thinking about it.'

'Of course. I understand. It's a recent hurt. Maybe that's why I found you a little strained when I first met you on Tuesday.'

No—it's got nothing to do with it. I fiddled with my pudding fork. 'Yes. Maybe.'

'Now,' David said as the waiter appeared again. 'Would you like a dessert?'

'I don't think I could. But I don't suppose they do petits fours with the coffee, do they?'

'I'm not sure. I don't think so. But I tell you what—I've got some Belgian chocolates at home, so if you felt brave enough to come back with me, we could have coffee there. It's only two minutes away and I promise you I'm *not* going to show you my portfolio!' I smiled. Coffee and chocolates? In his flat? Yes. Then maybe I could say what I needed to say. I glanced at the other diners, chatting in low tones. It would certainly be much easier than doing it here. 'Would you like to do that?'

I nodded. David paid the bill, then we walked out into the warm night air. We crossed over St John Street, then turned right into Benjamin Street where there was a row of brown-brick warehouses.

'It's in an old jam factory,' he explained. 'I bought it last year, after I got divorced. I'm on the top floor.' We ascended in the dimly lit lift, then he unlocked his front door. I was expecting to find a vast open space, like an art gallery, with

sugar,' he said. 'Their machetes were bigger than they were. They should be in school, not slaving in the heat.'

'You must have seen terrible things,' I said.

'Yes. I have. Terrible. And at the same time strangely fascinating. The vile things that we humans are capable of doing to one another.'

I felt a wave of shame. 'What was the worst thing?' I said. 'I know it's a crass question, but I can't help wondering.'

'It's okay, I'm often asked that. I'd say the retreat from Basra in 1991. The aftermath of Omagh. And Kosovo was pretty disgusting, as you can imagine—I was there for a year. I still have recurring nightmares from Rwanda. Then last year I went to Israel. And that's what finally did it for me.'

'Why?'

'Because there'd been a suicide bomb in this café in Jerusalem, and I went over there and began taking pictures. And there was this woman, on the other side of the street, just screaming with grief. And I began photographing her, and she suddenly saw me. And she ran right up to me and she hit me. Hard. She really walloped me. And she was right to. And I knew then that it was time to stop. That's the worst of it,' he went on, as he looked out over the city. 'The way the camera distances you and numbs you emotionally. So there can be people lying there with terrible injuries, or even being shot right in front of your eyes—yet your own human sympathy is temporarily suspended. You're just thinking "that's a great shot...there...that one...and *that* one". You're framing and focussing and clicking, because in that moment that's *all* you care about. The picture—not the people. But, later, you're filled with self-disgust.'

'But the pictures are very important.'

'Of course they are. And that's what you're trying to get— an *important* picture. One which transcends its context to become a profound metaphor. But photographers pay a high price for that. Many suffer from depression. A few commit suicide. I'd been doing it for ten years and needed to quit.'

'And that's why you switched to documentary work?'

'Yes. Also, so that I could choose my own subjects—rather than just having to rush to where the dead bodies are.'

'Do you enjoy it more?'

'I do. But it's not as lucrative, so I do some commercial stuff as well to pay the bills. Company reports for example—as long as they're kosher—and recently I've been doing a few magazine shoots. I did a couple of development stories for *Marie Claire*, and then I got that call from Lily Jago.' He shook his head in bewilderment. 'I *still* don't understand why she thought of me to take your pictures.'

'Well...I think...she thought it would give it a bit of an edge. That's what she said actually. That it would make it "edgy".'

'Well, my photos do have a certain look. There's a lot of movement in them, so maybe she just fancied a bit of that. How did you meet her then?' I told him. He laughed. 'I can imagine. She's an animal nut.'

'She said she'd met you once or twice.'

He nodded. 'She's *so* over the top. I find women like that really hard work.'

'So will I look "edgy" then?' I asked.

'You'll look lovely. I'll print them tomorrow.'

'Where?'

'Here. I've got my own dark room. They won't take long.'

'So how do you do it? I've never seen it.'

'Really? Well, first you select the negs you want to develop out of all the shots that you took, and then what you do is—' He suddenly put down his cup. 'Do you want to see it?' he said. 'I could show you.'

'What, now?'

'Yes. I could print your photos while you're here. Would you like that?' he added.

'Well, yes. Yes…I would. But how long will it take?'

'About forty-five minutes. I'll book a cab for eleven fifteen. Is that okay?' I nodded. 'All right then—come with me.' He picked up the tray and we went back in. He phoned the cab company, and as he did so I peeped into his bedroom through the half-open door. He was fairly tidy; the white duvet was pulled neatly up, and there were no clothes lying around. I saw a hockey stick leaning in one corner.

'Okay,' he said 'that's all booked.' He took off his jacket, threw it on a chair, and pushed on a door next to the kitchen. 'It's in here.' As we entered the dark room, an alkaline smell filled my nostrils. 'I love doing this,' he said. 'I love the development process.' There were shiny strips of negatives hanging up, and four or five photos pegged on the line. There were bottles and boxes marked Ilford and Kodak. David topped up one of the trays, then fiddled with what looked like a big microscope. 'This is the enlarger. I've just got to…that's it. Okay. Right. Ready?' He leaned across me, pulled the light cord, and we were suddenly plunged into dark.

'You'll be able to see in a moment,' I heard him say softly. And sure enough, dim outlines now began to loom out of the velvety black, as a faint coral glow filled the room. I looked at David and saw his features materialize. 'That's the safe light we're seeing by,' he explained. 'I've got the three negs I like best in this.' In his hand I could just make out a slim black box, like a CD holder. He flipped it open, took out the first negative, blew on it with a can of compressed air, then he put it in the enlarger, and a small light came on.

'There's a safe filter,' he explained. 'To protect the paper from the light while you're still focussing.' As he did so, I recognized my own projected features, blurred, but becoming clearer now. 'That's it. I'm going to expose it… Okay.' He pulled out the filter and looked at the clock on the shelf in front of us. We both remained silent as the luminous second hand ticked round twenty seconds. Then he turned the enlarger off, removed the paper and slid it into the developing tray. Now he was tipping the tray backwards and forwards, gently rocking it. I could hear the liquid slap against the sides.

'This'll take about three minutes or so.' He put his hands in, and gently moved the paper about by its corners as grey smudges began to appear. 'You're supposed to use tongs,' he said. 'But I like to get my hands in. It's a tactile thing with me. It's not good for your skin but in my case that doesn't really matter.'

There was another silence. 'David.' My heart was banging against my ribs.

'Yes?'

'There's something I want to tell you…'

'Really? What?' I took a deep breath. He glanced sideways at me, then looked down at the tray again, rocking it. 'What is it? You look so serious.'

'Well…at dinner, I said that you'd told me that you were thirty-six. But you didn't tell me that.'

'No. I didn't think I had.'

'That's not how I knew.'

'So how did you know?'

'Because…' I looked at his profile as he tipped the tray this way and that. 'Because…'

'…I look thirty-six, I suppose.'

'No, that's not the reason. It's because…I…' My heart was

pounding. 'I…saw it on your website. It said that you were born in 1967. So…so that's how I knew.'

'Oh!' he laughed. 'I thought you were going to say something absolutely *terrible*! Is that all it is—that you looked at my website?'

'Yes,' I replied. 'Yes, I did.'

'Well,' he laughed again. 'I'm glad. In fact, I feel rather flattered. So is that the end of your "confession" then?'

'Well, I—'

'Oh look,' he said. 'Here you come…' I stared at the paper as it began to darken and pigment. There was the outline of my hair and my jaw, my lips and now my nose. 'I love this part,' he said. 'The way the image fades up, from invisibility, in front of your eyes. It's like turning up the radio and hearing music.' It was one of the photos he'd taken in the house. I certainly did look 'edgy'. Uncomfortable. Distracted. You could see it. In my eyes. You could see the guilt that I'd carried for so long. I felt as though I certainly *had* been—yes—exposed.

'David—'

'You look beautiful,' he said suddenly. 'And your expression's fascinating. You look slightly troubled. As though there's something rather complex going on in your head. Or maybe that's still the aftermath of your break-up,' he added softly. I didn't reply. Then he lifted the photograph, as it now was, out of the developer, and slid it into the adjacent tray. 'This is the stop bath,' he explained, as he gently rocked it again. Then he lifted it out and slid it into the next one. 'And this one's the fix. I'll leave it in here while I develop the second negative.' He repeated the process, talking softly all the time, and now I saw myself emerge again, this time with Herman, walking down Primrose Hill; with kites high in the sky behind us, and, in the foreground, a dog just running out of shot. There was so much movement in the image, as though it was a moment frozen from some ongoing drama. 'You look lovely,' he said. 'You look preoccupied,' he added. 'But that only makes it more interesting.' Suddenly we heard the buzz of his door.

'There's your cab. Damn…he's early.' David rocked this second photo in the fixative, staring at it intently; I was aware of his gentle, regulated breathing as he worked. And I realized that I'd been with him for three and a half hours and hadn't said what I'd wanted to say. I couldn't do it now because the cab was here. So I'd have to see him again. Yes, *that* was it. I'd simply have to see him again, and *then* I'd tell him. I'd tell him, and it would be over…

'I'd like to see you again,' I heard him suddenly say. He was still looking at my photo—as though he was addressing that—not me—as he moved it from side to side. 'I'd like to see you again,' he repeated, still talking to my image. We heard the buzzing of the door again, more urgent now. 'Because, you see,' and now he turned his head and looked at me, 'I think you're rather nice. So would that be okay, Miranda?'

I felt as though I were falling, headlong, down a steep incline. 'Yes,' I whispered. 'It would.'

David smiled, then he suddenly leaned towards me, and for a moment I thought he was going to kiss me. But then he pulled on the cord behind me and a white light flooded everything. He lifted out the photograph.

'Good.'

—— CHAPTER 8 ——

'You went out to *dinner* with him?' whispered Daisy on Sunday afternoon. Her eyes were as big as a bush-baby's. '*Dinner*? As in, a *date*?' We were sitting in the Primrose Patisserie, speaking very softly in order not to be overheard—or rather Daisy was. I was simply nodding, which was as much as I could manage communication-wise, given my delicate emotional state. 'So you had a *date* with him?' she repeated wonderingly. I nodded again. 'But your message just said you were "seeing" him, so I assumed that *you'd* called *him*. But he'd actually asked *you* out?' I nodded. She leaned back in her chair. '*Wow!*' Then she put down her teacup and leaned forward again. 'He *fancies* you,' she mouthed. I shrugged. 'He *does*. Otherwise he wouldn't have done that, would he?' She drew in her breath. 'My *God*. This rather complicates things, doesn't it?' she added, matter-of-factly. I nodded again. 'On the other *hand*,' she mused, her eyes narrowing as she assessed the situation, 'it might actually make it all easier, given that he clearly likes you. So has he called you again yet?' I shook my head. 'But he said he wants to?' I nodded. 'Then I'm sure he will. He just doesn't want to look too keen. *Blimey*,' she breathed. Then she giggled. 'What a turn-up.' She had another sip of Earl Grey. 'So, in those circumstances, I guess you didn't say anything…'

'No,' I murmured, recovering the power of speech now. 'I wanted to. Obviously. In fact, I tried to. But the restaurant was pretty crowded, so clearly I couldn't do it *there*, and then he asked me back to his flat, and…'

'You went back to his *flat*? What happened?'

'Well…it was very nice. We just sat on his roof terrace looking at the lights of London, just chatting, or, rather, he did most of it. He said he's never been a great conversationalist but that, for some reason, he likes talking to me. And I was more than happy to listen—he's interesting—and of course I was preoccupied. But there were a couple of moments when we were sitting there when I might have said it, and I did want to,' I sighed. 'I really *did*…'

'Then why didn't you?' she asked quietly. *Why didn't I?*

'Because…then we went into his dark room while he developed the photos he'd taken of me and, yes, I did almost tell him then. I knew it would be easier there—just whispering it into the darkness, but…'

'But what?'

I stared at her. 'Somehow the words got stuck in my throat. And he'd ordered a cab for me, so I knew I didn't have much time, and the point *is*, Daisy, that it's not the kind of thing I could say quickly, is it? So no, I…*didn't* actually do it, but…'

Daisy gave me a piercing look. 'I know why you didn't,' she said. 'It's obvious. I've just realized. You didn't tell him— because *you* like *him*—don't you?'

I fiddled with the sugar bowl. 'I don't really…know.'

'You do,' she insisted with another giggle. 'I can tell. You can't hide it from me, Miranda. I know you too well.'

'Okay, then. Yes. I *do* like him. Or rather—I'm…*drawn* to him. And so, all right, I admit that I didn't want to blurt it out and spoil a lovely evening—'

'Or the possibility of seeing him *again*…?' I looked at her. 'That's it, isn't it, Miranda? Isn't it?'

I shrugged, drew in a deep breath, then slowly nodded. 'Yes,' I said. 'You're right. That's why I chickened out. Because I knew that if I told him, that would be it.'

Daisy was chewing her bottom lip. 'Oh. Dear. You didn't expect *this* when you went looking for David, did you?'

'No. I didn't.' There was silence for a moment.

'Well, I guess you'll have to bite the bullet at some stage.'

'Hmm. Grasp the nettle.'

'Especially if you're thinking you might…get involved with him.' *Involved with him*. My heart rolled over. 'So maybe next time, then?'

I felt suddenly happy, almost to the point of euphoria. 'Yes. Maybe *next* time. That's right.' *Let there be a next time*. 'Now, what about *you*?' I thought of Daisy's wedding dress, encased in its velvet bag like a butterfly in its cocoon. 'Have you spoken to Nigel?'

'Not…quite.'

'By which, I presume, you mean "No".'

'Well, I had to work all day yesterday on a pitch we're doing for this guy's fiftieth—he wants an Arabian Nights theme with camels and belly-dancers—then Nige had a bridge tournament last night. Then this morning he went into work because he's got a new head of department and he's very keen to impress him because, as I say, he wants to get Equity Partnership, and so…' her voice trailed away. 'But I will,' she said. 'Soon.' An awkward silence descended, in which I was aware of a distant yapping. Daisy looked past me, over my left shoulder.

'There's a man standing outside, gesticulating at you. He's holding the most enormous bunch of flowers. Perhaps he's going to act on impulse.'

I turned round. 'That's Marcus.' I waved and he came in.

'Hello, Miranda.' He was holding a massive bouquet of stargazer lilies, while Twiglet was tucked into his jumper as usual, his paws hooked over the V-neck. 'Twiggers spotted you first and started barking. He just wanted to say "hi" to his teacher.' I stroked Twiglet and got a kiss on the nose, then he suddenly leaped into Daisy's outstretched arms.

'Oh look—Twiglet's made a new friend.'

'This is Daisy,' I said, as she cuddled him. 'Daisy, this is Marcus. Marcus and Twiglet come to the puppy parties. We saw you on *Land Ahoy!*' I went on, as Twiglet gave Daisy a rapid ear wash. Daisy looked up.

'Oh, you're the guy who does the self-defence classes,' she said. 'I remember now. Miranda mentioned it to me.'

'That's right. They're just short courses, aimed at anyone— of any age, sex, ethnic group or religious persuasion—it's all very inclusive.'

'Well *we'd* like to come. Wouldn't we, Miranda?' She was looking at me intently.

I sighed. 'Okay, then. Just to please you.'

'Well in that case—' he reached into his bag, and pulled out one of his flyers, '—let me give you one of these. It's just off Tottenham Court Road.'

'That would be very easy for me to get to from work,' Daisy said. 'I work in Bedford Square.'

'The first one's this Thursday, at seven. It's fifteen pounds a time and we work in pairs, so it'd work well if you two pitched up together.'

'We will,' said Daisy as she handed Twiglet back. 'Put us down for it, will you?' She tucked the flyer into her bag.

'Would you like some tea?' I asked him.

'No thanks. I don't have time. I'm just going to see my girlfriend. She lives in Princess Road.'

'Hence the flowers?' I said. He nodded. 'She'll love them.'

'I hope so. So I'll see you at the next puppy party then.' He gave us a parting smile.

'Christ, he must be *smitten*,' said Daisy. Twiglet had left a few tiny white hairs on her cardigan. 'That's at least forty quid's worth he's holding there. Anyway, I must get going too,' she added as she stood up. 'I said I'd go and see Mum. See you soon, Miranda.' She hugged me. 'And don't *worry*.' I slowly finished my cup of tea and then left. And I was just about to cross the road when two youths came up to me. My heart started to race. I know it's irrational, but I can't help it.

'Excuse me,' one of them said. I braced myself. 'Could you tell us how to get to the tube?' I gave them directions, but felt resentful at being asked, because it happens to me *all* the time. Maybe because I'm small, and don't look threatening—and what I hate most is that it's usually men. Anyway, I went back into the house—smiling at the aromatherapist, who was just locking her front door—then looked at my e-mails. *My sheepdog chases the goldfish round the pond. Is he trying to catch them?* No. He's trying to herd them. *My guinea pig is very aloof.* *My rabbit shakes its head at me the whole time, as if stupefied.* That's canker—he needs to go to the vet. Suddenly, another e-mail popped in. It was from 'DJW'. My heart did a somersault. *Hi Miranda. Just to say I'm in Barcelona for a few days, on a shoot, but I'll be back Friday and wondered if I could book you for Saturday night? David x. P.S. I thought we might do something fun.*

The week passed agonizingly slowly. The first show in the new series of *Animal Crackers* went out on Tuesday—it looked good, though it was odd seeing the case histories that I'd done back in March. The possessive parrot; the demanding gerbil; the passive-aggressive potbellied pig. On Wednesday the puppy party came and went. It was all very friendly, as usual, and at the end Marcus reminded me about his self-defence class the following evening.

'It's in St Luke's Church Hall in Howland Street, off Tottenham Court Road. Wear loose clothing.'

'Fine,' I said. 'I'll be there.'

'Why don't you come along too, Lily?' he added. 'Self-defence is a very useful skill.'

'No, it's okay,' she said airily. 'I don't need it.'

'But being tall is no guarantee that you'll never be picked on.'

'Oh, it's not my height.' She gave him a meaningful smile, then lowered her voice to a whisper. 'It's the fact that I keep a small, but efficient, *axe* in my bag.'

'Okay. Right. Well…anyway,' he tucked Twiglet into his jumper. 'I'd better be off. I'm going to see Natalie.'

'Your girlfriend?' I said.

'That's right,' he said happily.

'What about the flowers? She must have been thrilled.'

'Well, yes…I think she was,' he said thoughtfully. I looked at him. 'The problem is stargazers make her sneeze. Well, there *is* a lot of pollen on them, isn't there? So I've got her some chocolates this time.' He waved a huge box of Bendicks at me.

'Gosh—lucky her.' He obviously had it bad.

'So, see you tomorrow then, Miranda.'

'Yes, see you then.'

But in the event, I didn't go. I was all set to, and was actually rummaging in the drawer for my jogging trousers at five past seven when the phone rang. It was Dad.

'I'm up in town,' he said. 'So I wondered whether I could take you out for a bite to eat?'

'Oh. Erm…'

'I meant to call you earlier, but I was seeing the club's accountant, and then I had to go to a shareholders' meeting. But I thought it would be lovely to see you before I drive back. If you're not busy, that is.'

'Yes. Of course. That would be fine.' Missing one of the self-defence classes wouldn't matter. I called Daisy on her mobile and explained.

'I hope you don't mind,' I said. 'It's just that I haven't seen my dad for ages, what with him being in the States.'

'Oh, don't worry,' she replied. 'That's *far* more important.' I knew she was thinking of her own father. 'I'll tell you what we did, and you can come next week.'

Dad arrived just after eight. His hair was slightly greyer, but he still looked forty-eight, not fifty-eight; his lean, handsome face tanned from Palm Springs. I've inherited his greeny-grey eyes, but sadly none of his height. In that respect, I take after my mum.

'The Mews looks very friendly,' he said as he came in.

'It is. It's a bit like living in a mini-village.' I gave him the guided tour of the house.

'It's quite a Tardis,' he remarked appreciatively. 'Bigger inside than out.'

I showed him the upper floor and as he turned to go downstairs again he accidentally knocked the TV remote off the chest of drawers. Suddenly the television burst into life. There was Alexander with a telescope.

'Into the headland, Mr Tree! As close as you dare!'

'Aye aye, Commander.'

Then there was a close-up of the lead actress, Tilly Bishop, looking adoringly at Alexander. I felt a sudden, uncontrollable urge to stab her.

'Ooh, sorry,' Dad said. He picked up the control, then looked at the screen. 'Oh, isn't that…?' Dad had met Alexander once, on a visit to London, six months ago. With a trembling hand, I hit the 'off' switch.

'Yes it is. But let's go to the pub.' By the time we'd walked down Gloucester Avenue to The Engineer I was feeling slightly calmer. Over the soup, I asked Dad how the golf club was going. He shook his head.

'*Not* well.' A deep frown had pleated his brow.

'Because of the membership problems?'

'Yes—the income from subscription is chronically low. And the point is that this is a commercial club, American style, which is why they gave me the job. It's not like a nice, traditional, non-profit-making club run by some retired brigadier. The shareholders have made a huge investment and will want a return on their money.'

'And if they don't get it?'

'Then I'll be out. I'm on a three-month contract so I've got to get results.'

'Can't you reduce the fees? Be a bit more competitive that way?'

'We can't afford to. It cost eight million to build—the land was very expensive and Nick Faldo designed the course.'

'Then couldn't you do an incentive thing? Like giving people a discount on the joining fee if they sign up now.'

'We already are doing that.'

'Women members?'

'Of course. With access to all areas.'

'Pay and play?' He nodded.

'Yes—they've reluctantly agreed, at a hundred a day.'

'What about advertising?'

'The budget's already way overspent. The meeting was very stressful,' he went on. 'The shareholders made it clear that they expect me to pull a pretty spectacular rabbit out of the hat, but I don't know how. I mean, I ran the resort at

Palm Springs very efficiently but I've never had to make a success of a club from a standing start.'

'And there are a number of them down there already, aren't there?'

'Exactly. So we've got to offer something *new.*'

'Hmm, well, I wish I could help you. When do you open?'

'In mid-August, just before your birthday.'

'And how's it going in other ways? Are you adjusting to life in the UK?'

'A little. At least the weather's decent at the moment.'

'It is. This has been a long fine spell. So what are you missing about Palm Springs?'

'My friends, of course—and valet parking: it took me forty-five minutes to find a space this afternoon.'

'And are you getting to know people yet?'

He shook his head. 'Not really—that'll take months. I just wish your mother would be friendly,' he added. 'I'd find the move here a lot easier.' He was fiddling with his bread roll. 'Actually, I've seen her again.'

'Have you?'

'At the gas station two days ago. I don't know whether or not she spotted me, but I suspect she did as she drove off very fast. But I thought I should make the first friendly overture, so what I did was…' He was looking slightly sheepish.

'What?'

'I called her. I found the number for East Sussex Llama Treks in the local phone book and left a message, asking her to get in touch.'

'And did she?'

'No. So I tried again the next day and found she'd blocked my number. So at least I know where I am. I just wish she'd be a bit more…reasonable.'

'Well...' I sighed. 'You know what she's like. Plus, she's got problems of her own at the moment.'

'Really?'

'With the llamas. She needs a lot more business. They only really come into their own at the weekends because that's when people do the treks. At the moment they're not busy enough during the week and that worries her.'

'I see.'

'So, maybe she'll be a bit more sociable when things pick up.'

'I do hope so,' he sighed. 'I mean, I know I wasn't the world's best husband, Miranda. I know your mother felt neglected.'

'That's because you *did* neglect her, Dad—and me.'

'Yes,' he sighed. 'That's true. I was a young, selfish man. I decided to follow my dream. But you'd think that, after twenty years, she'd give me a break.'

'Hmm. I do know what you mean.'

'Anyway,' he glanced at his watch. 'I'd better get going. It's quite a long drive.'

And I was just waving him off when I heard the phone. It was Daisy, back from the self-defence class.

'It was *fantastic*,' she exclaimed. 'So *empowering*! You really *must* come. It was all about reducing one's "victim potential"; and then assessing the threatening individual and deciding which of three courses of action to take—"Immediate Retreat", "De-Escalation", or "Confrontation". He's a *really* good teacher,' she gushed. 'So you'll be there next week, won't you?'

'Yes.'

'Do you promise me?'

'I do.'

'And have you heard from David again?'

'I have.'

'And?'

'I'm seeing him on Saturday.'

'*Good*. And I've been thinking about it, Miranda—the better you get to know him, the easier it will be to *tell* him, won't it?'

'Maybe.' I wasn't sure about that.

'So what are you going to do this time?'

'I don't know. But he says he wants to do something "fun".'

'Ice skating,' he said, when he called me on Saturday morning. 'How about that? Why don't we go ice skating?'

My heart sank. I'd look inept and inelegant. 'Ice skating? In the summer?'

'Why not? It's better actually because it's not so crowded. And I bet you haven't been for ages, have you?'

'No. The last time was when I was nine.'

'So shall we go? We could go to the Queensway Ice Bowl, then have dinner.'

I chewed on my lower lip. 'O–kay.'

'Great. I'll meet you outside at half-seven.'

When I came out of the tube at twenty-five past, David was already waiting. He was wearing jeans and a pale yellow shirt, and holding a bag. He smiled when he saw me, then kissed me on the cheek; and as he drew me into a hug I noticed his nice lemony scent again. As we went down the stairs I could hear the dull rumble of the bowling alley and the percussive bleeps of the amusement arcade.

'I'll be *useless* at this,' I said, as he bought the tickets.

'We won't do it for long—just an hour. It's a bit tacky here in some ways, but at least the rink's reasonably big. Now, Miss Behaviour—you need skates.'

'What about you?' He smiled, then pulled a black pair out of his bag, along with a green jumper. 'You've got your own ones?'

'I used to play a lot of ice hockey. When we lived in the States.'

'Ah.' I remembered the hockey stick I'd seen in his room. 'So you're hot stuff then.'

'Not bad. It's something I do from time to time and I thought it would be fun to do it with you.' I handed in my shoes at the counter and was given a pair of dark blue skates which looked more like ski-boots and were as hard to get into.

'Let me help you,' David said. I felt my face warm up as he held my right ankle and I held onto his shoulder. 'What small feet you have, Grandmama,' he said as he snapped shut the straps. Then he laced up his own skates, we pulled on our jumpers, and stepped gingerly onto the ice.

'Let me just find my balance,' he said. 'Stay right there.'

'Don't worry, I'm not going anywhere.' As I clung to the handrail with both hands, shivering slightly, David suddenly sped away from me, like mercury, under the coloured lights, and in less than a minute had lapped the rink twice. Then he swished up to me so fast I thought he'd crash into me—then braked with a sharp parallel turn.

'Gosh,' I said. 'You *are* hot stuff.'

'Well I should be—I did it for years. But it's not hard. I'll show you. Come on.' He extended his right hand—he wasn't wearing gloves—and I anxiously reached out my left. I took a small step then skidded, and, with a burning surge of adrenaline, grabbed at the rail with both hands.

'I can't do this,' I said, my heart pounding with the shock. 'I just *can't*. I'm so afraid of falling.' I felt a slight twinge in my rib.

'You won't fall.'

'I *will*.'

'It'll be easier if you give me your hand.' I awkwardly turned myself round to face him. 'Give me your hand,' he repeated gently.

'O-kay.' Now I steadied myself against the rail with my right hand, while David clasped my left. Then he pushed off and I began to inch forward.

'That's *good*. Yes, that's it. We'll just go slowly round like this a few times.'

'Uhhh,' I murmured as three teenagers shot past with a rasp of steel on frost. 'I'm going to be hopeless at this. *Ooh!*' The right skate had suddenly slipped away from me again, but David had caught me under the arms. He laughed as he hung onto me, then lifted me upright.

'I'm sorry.'

'Don't worry. I *won't* let you fall. But don't walk on the ice, Miranda, try to *glide* on it.'

'I can't.'

'Yes you can. Just push forward with each foot—like this.' Now he went in front of me and took both my hands in his, skating backwards while he gently dragged me forwards. 'That's better. Stand a little straighter.'

'I can't. I'll fall down again.'

'You won't. I'm holding you.'

'I *will*,' I said, panicking. 'I'll lose my balance and pull you over too.'

'You're so light you can't. That's it. Now bend your knee, then push to the left, now the right, now the left. That's it—*yes*—good—hey, you're skating!' I laughed with relief and surprise. 'The trick is just to go very slowly at first.' We went round like this for about fifteen minutes or so. I gradually gained confidence, I looked at the other skaters. There were some boys careering around the perimeter, the wings of their jackets flaring, and a middle-aged couple who'd clearly skated for years. In the centre of the rink a small girl pirouetted gracefully, hands clasped above her head; she was clearly practising some routine. And now, as David spun me slowly across the ice in his arms, I became aware of the music. It was Cyndi Lauper.

If you're lost you can look and you will find me. Time after time. If you fall I will catch you, I'll be waiting…

'You're not falling, are you?' said David.

'No,' I smiled. *Or, rather, I am.*

'You won't fall,' he said gently. 'Because I'll hold onto you.'…*Time after time.* He held me closer. *Time after time…* 'You won't fall,' he whispered again, as he spun me slowly off the ice. 'You think I brought you here to show off, don't you?' he added. 'Well, it's not true.'

'Isn't it?' I laughed.

'No. It was an excuse to hold your hand. Okay,' he went on, as I felt my face flush. 'Let's go and get something to eat. Now, was that fun?' he asked as we walked up the steps.

'Yes it was. I really enjoyed it.'

'That's good—so what do you feel like?' We began to stroll down Queensway. 'We could have Moroccan, and smoke a hookah by the looks of it there, or do you fancy that Chinese over the road?' We passed Bayswater underground, the pavement thronging with people, the illuminated blue dome of Whiteley's ahead. 'There's that Malaysian one,' David pointed out, 'or the Maharajah. I know there's a nice Lebanese a bit further down. Or how about that Italian one over there?'

'Yes. Italian. I suddenly fancy a risotto.' The restaurant was pleasant, quiet and smoke-free. 'So tell me about your trip to

Barcelona,' I said as we were seated. 'What were you doing there?'

'Some shots to illustrate a new book about ETA.'

'Oh. And…why did they ask you to do that?'

He shrugged. 'Why not? But as it happens, I'm fascinated by that kind of thing.'

'By what kind of thing—Basque separatism?'

'No. Extremism.' The waiter brought us two glasses of red wine. 'Political extremism of any kind. I'm fascinated by what these people must actually *feel* as they make, or plant, the bombs which they know will maim and kill innocent strangers. Don't you find that interesting?' he added.

'Why should I?' I asked abruptly. David looked at me, slightly surprised. 'What I mean is, I'd rather…turn my mind away from things like that.'

'Well, I don't blame you.' We perused the menu in silence for a moment.

Tell him. Tell him. 'David?'

'I think I'll have the linguini. Yes?'

Say it now. 'There's something I've got to tell you.'

He looked up at me. 'What?' My heart was suddenly beating so erratically that I lifted my hand to my chest. 'Oh God,' he said with a mock grimace. 'You've got some awful "confession" to make again, haven't you? Like last time. I can tell by the look on your face. Okay then. Hit me with it.'

'Well…I…' I looked at him. *I can't do it. I just can't. He'll never see me again.* 'My…ankles are aching.'

He laughed. 'Another *dreadful* admission, Miranda—aching ankles! Well there's only one remedy for that. We'll have to go skating again.' *I'm skating all the time—on very thin ice.* 'There's an open-air rink at Broadgate. We could go there in the winter—if you're still speaking to me, that is.' *No, no—if you're still speaking to me, which I can guarantee you won't be.*

Then he started talking about ice hockey and explaining the rules.

'I'd love to play here, but it's impossible—I get my fix by watching it on cable TV; but when I was a teenager I played a lot. I was in the New Haven Junior Allstars,' he said proudly as our main courses arrived. 'My greatest moment was when we won the New England under-sixteens tournament. It was on my fifteenth birthday. I've never forgotten it,' he said as he picked up his fork. 'March twenty-first, 1982.'

'Your birthday's on March the twenty-first?' I echoed.

'Yes. Why?'

'Nothing...'

'Does that date mean something to you?'

It was the day it happened... 'No. Not really, erm... It's the first day of spring.'

'It is. And when's yours?'

'August seventeenth.'

'Oh, not long. I'll take you out for dinner.' *No you won't. Because by then you'll hate me.* 'You fascinate me, Miranda,' he suddenly said. I felt my face flush. 'I just feel that there's so much going on in your head. I feel there's something—I can't put my finger on it—rather intriguing about you.' *Yes. I am intriguing. That's how we met.* 'I find you...' he narrowed his eyes, '...enigmatic. And yet you're so easy to talk to,' he went on. 'I love talking to you. I probably bore you, going on in the way that I do, but when I'm with you I just can't help it.' I fiddled with the single yellow rose in its tiny vase. 'But I wish I knew more about *you*. About *your* life. What about your friends and your family?' So, as we ate, I told him about my parents' divorce, and Hugh, and my half-sisters, and Daisy, and about my father coming back to the UK. 'And are you close to both your parents?' he asked, as I put down my fork.

'Yes, now I am, reasonably, although I wasn't before. I went through a rather...bad phase when I was younger.' *Don't say any more—just leave it at that!*

'What—you had a misspent youth?' I felt my heart-rate accelerate. 'What sort of things did you do?'

'Oh, I was just a bit...rebellious, I suppose.'

'Any particular reason?'

'I...think it was because my parents weren't *there* for me. My father had moved to the States—I felt very let down by him, to be honest—and my mum had remarried and had no time. But now...' I shrugged. 'I get on with them fine. Not that I ever confide in them.'

'Don't you?'

'No. I never tell them anything personal.'

'Why not?'

'I've just never been in the habit, I suppose. I mean, they don't even know why my engagement ended.'

'*Really?* That's quite a big thing to withhold. But then it's obviously been very painful for you, and some things we just want to bury. It's totally natural.' He glanced out of the window. 'I understand that.' I looked at his face in profile—at his aquiline nose, and his strong, straight chin, and the soft curve of his Adam's apple. 'I completely understand that,' he repeated softly. Then a silence descended. Outside, over David's shoulder, I saw three teenage boys slouch past, hands pushed into pockets.

'We'd been to the theatre,' I said. 'That night. We'd been to the Playhouse to see *The Three Sisters.*'

'It's all right,' David murmured, turning back to me. 'You don't have to tell me.'

'I know I don't,' I replied. 'But I've just realized, sitting here, that I'd actually *like* to tell you.' David looked at me, then lowered his glass. 'After the play we went to this Cuban bar in the Strand and, admittedly, Alexander had had a couple of drinks. But that doesn't excuse what he did. Anyway, we left at about eleven to get back to Herman. And we got the Northern Line back to Archway. Alexander's flat was a ten-minute walk from the tube, and we'd had a nice evening and we were in a good mood. I think we were discussing when exactly in September our wedding would be.' I heard myself breathe in, then exhale. 'And although my memory of it is a bit foggy, I do vaguely recall hearing steps behind us as we walked up Holloway Road. And we'd just turned into Alexander's road, Harberton Road, when suddenly these three men—well, youths really—appeared. And although you'll think this is mad, my immediate thought was that they wanted directions, because people are always asking me for directions—even when I'm abroad and haven't a clue. But I quickly realized that that wasn't what they wanted at all—because by now they were barring our way. And then…then…' I twisted my napkin in my hands. 'Then they started saying, "What have you got for us? What have you got for us?" Like that. Several times. "What have you got?" Then one of them grabbed at my bag. And he was pulling at it, and I was pull-ing back, trying to hang onto it, and screaming. I remember the pain in my shoulder as they yanked on it and the way the strap burned my wrist. And they were calling me a fuck-ing bitch and saying that they'd slit my throat. And I was still struggling, determined that they weren't going to get it, when one of them hit me. Just here.' I touched my left cheek. 'And I fell. I was lying there, crying with the shock, and my bag had gone, and so had they. Or rather, two of them had.' I stopped. David's face was a mask. 'The third one was still there. He was trying to get my engagement ring off, but I'd clenched my fist hard. He was trying to prise open my fin-gers—I thought he'd break them—I still remember his rasping breath in my ear. Then I felt this terrible pain in my side, and a soft crunch, and I couldn't breathe—it was agony. Then I felt the ring being removed. Then I heard running footsteps, and, not long after, a police siren.' My throat ached. 'Sorry.' The yellow rose had blurred. 'Sorry.' There was silence.

'And where was Alexander?' David asked gently.

I felt a wave of shame. 'Well…that's just it.' And now my eyes spilled over.

'He wasn't there?' I didn't reply. 'He ran away?' I nodded. David laid his hand on mine, and a tear fell onto it with a quiet splash. He reached into his pocket and handed me a hanky. There was a pause. 'And when did you see him next?'

'At the hospital. The ambulance had taken me to the Whittington. And I was lying on this trolley in casualty, and it hurt to breathe because of my rib, and the back of my head was very painful because I'd cracked it on the kerb when I fell. And they'd given me this strong painkiller, which was making me feel sick. Then, the curtain parted and there was Alexander. I'll never forget the look on his face. He was shocked, of course—not least because my face was a mess. But at the same time I could see that he felt ashamed, but was trying not to show it.'

'*Jesus*. What did he *say*?'

'Nothing at first. Then he said, "Oh, Miranda", like that. Then he tried to hold my hand, but I wouldn't let him. I just looked at him, then looked away. And in that moment we both knew that it was over.'

'Did he try to explain himself?'

'He said that he'd shouted at me to run, that he'd thought I was running with him.'

'Do you remember hearing him shout?'

'No. But then there was a lot of confusion. Maybe he did, I don't know…'

'But in any case…' David murmured, shaking his head. 'He should have made *sure*.'

'Yes,' I croaked. 'He should have made sure.' I pressed the hanky to my eyes. 'But he didn't. He just…ran off. It was that animal instinct—fight or flight; and Alexander flew. I realized within a few seconds that he'd gone. And do you know what I kept thinking? I kept thinking how *amazing* it was that he'd been able to run so fast, because he had a serious cartilage problem. Anyway,' I sniffed, '*that* is why I ended my engagement.'

'What a terrible story,' said David. He reached for my hand again, and held it in both his. 'Not least because you're so small. But you put up a real fight. You were brave.'

'I wasn't brave,' I said. 'Just *angry*. And the irony is that I didn't want them to get the engagement ring—because it meant so much to me. Even though Alexander had already gone. His name means "Defender",' I added. '"Defender of men". I thought about that quite a bit too.'

'So has he…apologized to you?'

'No. Because that would be to admit what he did. That's why I'm so profoundly hurt. Because if he'd only said that he was sorry and acknowledged how badly he'd let me down then I'd have been able to forgive him. I wouldn't respect him, but I could let it go. But he just made excuses, trying to make out that it was some sort of awful mix-up and that he thought I was okay, and that maybe he'd got confused in the heat of the moment because he'd had a couple of drinks.'

'So what did he tell the cops?'

I smiled bitterly. 'He gave them a statement in the hospital. And at first he told them the same story—that he thought I was with him. Then he said that when he'd realized I wasn't, he'd decided to run to his flat to raise the alarm. But the point is…'

'That he had a mobile phone?'

I nodded. 'He did ring the police, but by then someone had already dialled nine-nine-nine.'

'And how do you feel about him now?'

I sighed, then shook my head. 'All sorts of things. Anger, mostly, but I also have this dragging sense of sadness and disappointment.' I tapped my sternum. 'Right here. It sort of pulls me down. Because I'd thought Alexander was wonderful. There was nothing about him that I didn't like. But then I was suddenly made to see him in an *entirely* new light.'

'Weren't there any signs beforehand?'

'There were, though I didn't attach enough importance to them at the time—that was my mistake. The main clue was that he was impulsive—he'd suddenly do things on a whim. I'd found it rather endearing—until then. He wasn't a...*solid* sort of man, I suppose. But he was such good fun, and he was in love with me, and I imagined that I was in love with him. I was certainly very happy to be with him. I haven't had that many relationships, you see.' David looked into my eyes. 'Hardly any, actually.'

'Why not?'

I shrugged. 'I don't...know,' I lied. 'I've just...avoided them for...various reasons. For most of my adult life, I've been on my own. So being with Alexander was a big thing for me.'

'And do you have any contact with him now?'

'None. I don't want to see him again. And he doesn't want to see me either, because he feels too ashamed. So the next day Daisy went and collected Herman, and my things, from his flat. And I haven't laid eyes on him since that night.'

'So he didn't argue about the relationship ending.'

'No, although he was clearly shocked that it happened so fast. I think he thought we'd talk about it, but to me it was crystal clear. The big, strong man, who said he loved me, had abandoned me to be mugged. He did write to me afterwards, to say that he was sorry that I—what was it?—oh yes, "felt the way I did". As though I'd left him for some other, far more trivial, reason. But he didn't say that he was sorry. But, tellingly, he asked me not to mention the "incident in Archway", as he delicately put it, because he was obviously worried that I'd spill the beans. Anyway, I've obliged him on that front. Only Daisy knows—and now you do too—but I know you're not going to tell anybody.'

David shook his head. 'No. I'm not. In any case, you haven't told me his second name so I don't even know who he is. All I'd say is that you don't have to protect him, Miranda.'

'I'm not protecting him—I'm protecting myself.'

'But *why?*'

'Because the whole thing makes me feel so ashamed. The humiliation of it. Can't you see? As though I wasn't worth defending.'

He looked at me. 'I'd have defended you. To the death,' he added with a melodramatic smile. 'Seriously, Miranda, I would. I'd have protected you.'

I half-smiled. 'I believe you, actually.'

'To be honest, *most* men would. I think what he did was very…unusual.'

'Yes,' I murmured. 'That's what makes it even worse.'

'How long were you in hospital?'

'Just one night. At least my injuries weren't grievous; a broken rib, some bad facial bruising and a nasty bump to the head. Anyway it's all healed now.'

'And psychologically? That's so much harder to get over than the physical damage.' I knew that he was speaking from experience.

'I could hardly sleep for the first month. I had bad dreams and flashbacks—I still do. And I'm very tense on the street. I can't *stand* it if anyone comes up to me, or even walks too close to me. I have to fight the urge to scream at them.'

'Well, no one's going to be doing that tonight, because I'm going to take you home.'

'Really?'

'Yes, I've got my car.'

We left the restaurant and crossed over Queensway into Moscow Road, where David had parked his black Saab.

'I imagine it's made you distrustful of men,' David said as he started the engine.

'I already was distrustful of them.'

'Why?'

'Because the ones I've been close to—from my dad onwards—have either let me down, or betrayed me in some way.' Now, I remembered my dream about *The Wizard of Oz*, with Alexander and Jimmy both playing the cowardly lion.

'It's sad that you feel like that,' David said quietly, as we drove down Sussex Gardens.

'I can't help it.'

'And have the muggers been caught?'

'No. They found my bag in a dustbin the next day. All they'd taken was the credit card, the purse, and the phone. And the engagement ring, of course. The police contact me from time to time, but nothing's happened yet. No ID parades or anything like that, not that I'd ever want to set eyes on them again—even in the dock. I just want to forget.'

'You must *hate* them,' he said quietly, as we waited to turn right into Marylebone Road. I heard the hypnotic tick-tock of his indicator, like a metronome.

'I'm not very fond of them, no.'

'That kind of physical attack is very hard to get over,' he said, as we moved off again. 'I know that because I've been through it too. You see, what happened with my hands...' I glanced at his left one as he changed gear, '...wasn't an accident.'

My stomach began to churn. 'Wasn't it?' I heard myself say. We passed the Planetarium then turned left into the park.

'No. I told you it was, because that's what I tell people—because I don't like talking about it. But it wasn't an accident at all.'

'No?' I said faintly.

'It was a letter-bomb. It had been sent to my father by an animal rights group, but I opened it...' *Because it was your birthday.* '...because it was my birthday.' I felt tears prick the backs of my eyes. 'Usually I was careful to read the envelopes first as Dad and I shared the same initial—his name was Derek—' *Yes, I know it was.* '—but I was expecting a few things in the post that day. And I was the first to come down, and there was this parcel on the mat. So I unwrapped it, and inside was a video. And I remember thinking that it was odd that someone had sent me a video, as we didn't actually have a video player then; I also remember thinking that it had a slightly strange smell. But I had no reason to be suspicious, so I opened it. There was this thudding sound—not a "bang", interestingly, but a "thud"—and a bright blue-white flash—like oxyacetylene—and a flame, then I couldn't see. Then everyone came running, my parents and my brother, and then the pain began to kick in and I was hyperventilating, and there was quite a lot of blood, obviously, and this awful caustic smell...'

'Oh David.'

'Then the ambulance came. They sedated me, rushed me

to Brighton Hospital, and I was in the burns unit for about a month. Then the long haul with the skin grafts began.'

'Oh David. I can't bear it.' My throat ached. 'It's just so awful. I'm so sorry. It's so *awful*.' He reached his left hand out and placed it on mine for a moment.

'It's okay, Miranda, you don't have to feel so upset about it.' *I do. I do.* 'It was a long time ago. And at least my eyes were okay—thank God. I just got a bit of shrapnel in my face—all I've got is this tiny scar, here—' he touched his cheek, '—you must have noticed it. Anyway—to cut a long story short, I know what it feels like to be physically assaulted by a stranger, so I can sympathize.'

'Yes, but what you went through was a thousand times worse. Mine was just a common or garden mugging, David; it wasn't nice, but I can get over it. But you—you…' I stared out of the window again, my eyes brimming now with unshed tears. 'You could have been killed.' *I could have killed you.*

'The device wasn't big enough—though I don't know whether *they* knew that, as the police said it wasn't a particularly competent job. But yes, I could have been, I suppose; or my dad could have been, because of course it was intended for him. But, you know, *that* was weird in itself, because he wasn't involved in animal experiments at all. I mean, he had a pet rat in his lab, Rupert, which he'd actually saved from vivisection. But most of his research was plant-based. That's why he was never able to understand it. To his dying day it totally mystified him. He always assumed that they'd targeted him out of ignorance.'

Why did Jimmy do it, I wondered again. *Why?*

'And no one was ever caught,' I murmured.

'No, they weren't. How do you know that?'

'No, I—I don't know that—I was just asking you. No-one was ever caught—*were* they?'

'No. There were no witnesses. The device was delivered very early, you see. No one knows exactly what time.' *Five a.m.* 'The milkman said he thought he'd seen a slim figure cycling away.'

'Really?'

'But it turned out to be the paper girl.'

'Oh.'

'The investigation went on for several months. But all the hard-core animal rights extremists were in the clear because they had alibis. That's what's been so hard, I think. I got over the physical injuries a long time ago—I was young—I healed. But the psychological effect has never left me—partly because I never had anyone to blame. This totally unknown person turned my whole life upside down that morning—they detonated it. Literally. And to this day I have no idea who that person was, or what it was that motivated them.' A silence descended, punctuated only by the hum of the engine.

'And would you want to know? I mean, if it were possible to find out? Would you want to know who they were?'

'Well, that's not very likely as it was so long ago.'

'But if you could, somehow, discover who it was—would you want to find out?'

'Yes. I would. Of course I would. I'd like to come face to face with that person.'

I felt my sternum tighten, as though a large screw was being turned in my chest. 'And then what?' I whispered. 'What would you do?'

'What would I do?' he repeated blankly. 'I really don't know.'

'Do you think you'd be able to forgive them?'

'*Forgive* them? Do you think you could forgive the men who mugged you?'

'Well, if they said that they were truly sorry for what they did and gave me back my things—not that that's a very *likely* scenario—then yes, I probably could. If someone's genuinely contrite, you *have* to forgive them—don't you? Don't you?' I persisted. 'Tell me.'

'These are difficult questions, Miranda. I don't know.'

'But I want to know whether you, personally, could forgive the person who…who put that bomb through the door?' I watched his face strobing in the streetlights as I waited for an answer.

'No,' he said. My heart stopped. 'I couldn't. Or at least, I don't *think* I could. Some things can never be forgiven. Why should they be? I've photographed too many unforgivable things, Miranda, to feel that.' He was turning right now, into the Mews. 'Anyway, I'm glad I've told you about it. I wanted to tell you last week but I thought it was a bit heavy for a first date. I was worried that it might horrify you,' he added. *It does horrify me. It does, it does…* 'Anyway, here we are.' He'd stopped right outside the house. Shall I see you to your door?' he asked.

I smiled. 'It's all right, David. I don't think we can get any closer.'

He took my hand, then leaned forward. 'Well, actually. I think we can.' And now he took my face in his hands, and pulled me towards him, then I felt his lips on mine, pressing gently at first, then slightly harder, and I felt myself kissing him back.

'You're lovely, Miranda,' he murmured. *Would you be saying that if you knew who I was?* 'You're lovely. You intrigue me.'

I panicked. *You can't do this until he knows.* I undid my seat belt and opened my door. 'I—'

David saw my expression. 'I know,' he said gently. 'It's too soon, Miranda—isn't it?'

'Yes,' I replied quietly. 'I think it's too soon.'

CHAPTER 9

'He *kissed* you!' Daisy almost shouted on Monday.

'Please, shhhh, Daisy,' I hissed. We were in the Heals café where we'd met for a quick lunch. It was crowded, but we'd managed to get a corner table.

'He kissed you,' she repeated, in an awe-struck whisper. '*Blimey.* Anything else?'

'No.'

'You mean it was just a kiss?'

'Yes. A goodnight kiss. That's all it was.'

'Where?'

'In his car.'

'*No.* Cheek or lips?'

'Oh. Lips, since you ask.' I felt my insides suffuse with warmth at the memory.

'Blimey,' she said again. '*Then* what?'

'Then I thanked him for a lovely evening, opened the door and got out.'

'Didn't you ask him in?'

'No—I didn't feel it was right.'

'Why not?'

'Because I was in turmoil after the conversation we'd just had. But I'll be seeing him again.'

'When?'

'On Friday. He phoned me last night and asked me to keep it free.'

'I bet he wanted to do more than kiss you,' Daisy added knowingly as she sipped her coffee.

'Yes. I think he did. In fact, I know he did—although it's much too soon. I mean, I've only met him three times, Daisy. And in any case, he thinks I'm holding back because I'm still getting over Alexander.'

'Aren't you?'

'Well, yes—and no. I'm not heartbroken about Alexander, I'm just angry and disappointed. I told David what happened.'

'Good. I bet he was horrified.'

'He was, rather.'

'So you're getting closer to him?'

'I am.'

'Things with your photographer are *developing* then,' she giggled. 'You're *clicking* with him?' I rolled my eyes. 'And did you flirt with him?'

'No. I find it impossible.' I lowered my voice to a barely audible whisper. 'I mean, how *do* you flirt with someone whom you once caused GBH?'

'Hmm. That would be rather...inhibiting.'

'It *is*. But I think that's partly why he likes me, because he thinks I'm so "mysterious". But I'm not. I'm just sitting there in an agony of apprehension. But, ironically, *that's* why he's attracted to me. Because he finds me, what was it? "Intriguing."'

Daisy shook her head. 'He's attracted to you because he's attracted to you, Miranda. Anyway, back to the matter in hand. How to tell him... How *are* you going to tell him?'

I groaned quietly. 'I don't *know*. The more I see him, the

more I *want* to tell him—and yet, at the same time, the *less* I want to, in case he never sees me again. And he actually talked about it this time, Daisy. About what happened. So I asked him whether he could ever forgive the person who'd done it, and he replied that he didn't think that he *could*.'

'But if he knew it was you—he might.'

'I don't know. I can't assume that. It's such a *big* thing. But I need him to forgive me because I'm…'

'Falling in love with him?'

I stared at her. 'Maybe. Yes, maybe I am. I find him very… attractive.'

'Then wait until he's fallen in love with *you*.'

I sipped my cappuccino, momentarily tempted; then I put down my cup. 'I can't. It would be dishonest.'

'Yes,' she sighed. 'You're right. Of course you are. He'd feel that you'd deceived him. Well—you have a moral di-lemma on your hands.' A silence descended, then the waitress brought the bill.

'Do you know what else David said?' I went on as I reached for my bag. 'That his father's work didn't even in-volve animal experiments. I don't know *why* Jimmy did it. I just don't *understand*. And I really need to.'

'Then ask him,' she said simply. 'Write to him at the House of Commons.'

'But the letter would get read by his press officer.'

'Then send it to his home.'

'His wife might see it.'

'Then just ask to see him at work, and speak to him in private.'

'I know what would happen if I did. He'd refuse to see me, and, if I insisted, then he'd accuse me of trying to black-mail him. He's got powerful friends, Daisy. He could go to the press and say that I was harassing him—he'd totally discredit me. He'd tell them that I used to be infatuated with him—which is true. He'd tell them that I wrote him these pathetic letters saying that I'd do anything for him.'

'But you were only sixteen then, Miranda!'

'So what? The tabloids won't care. But the point is that I don't *want* to see Jimmy again, Daisy. This is about *my* conscience—not his. Not that he seems to have one—the lucky bastard. It must make his life rather easy.'

'You're very hard on yourself, Miranda,' Daisy said suddenly. She glanced left and right to make sure we couldn't be overheard. 'I mean, it's not as though *you* made that bomb—is it?' she whispered. 'You didn't even know there *was* one. You genuinely thought it was a video.'

'That's what Jimmy said. He said that it was a video about neurological experiments on vervet monkeys, to prick Professor White's conscience—and I had no reason to doubt that's what it was.'

'I can understand you feeling awful at being involved,' Daisy went on, 'but you weren't responsible for what happened so I don't see why you feel *quite* so guilt-racked.'

'For the simple reason that I didn't speak *out*. I knew, absolutely, that I should tell *someone*—my parents, a teacher, or the police; but, in order to protect myself, I kept quiet—and *that's* why I feel so bad. And my silence must have made it far worse for David because he never got closure on what happened to him. He still hasn't. That's obvious.' We handed the waitress our credit cards.

'But why did Jimmy think he could get away with it?' Daisy whispered.

'Because he knew he was above suspicion.'

'Why?'

'Because he'd publicly condemned violence so many times. He'd written articles in the local paper saying it was wrong,

and attacking the ALF, so everyone thought him principled
and brave. That's what he used to say to me too. He said that
better treatment of animals would only come about through
a hearts and minds campaign.'

'So he'd put himself above board?'

'Yes. But I *wasn't* above board, because of my history. And
I was terrified that the police would come looking for me—I
kept waiting for the knock on the door. But they didn't
come—perhaps because they knew I'd never done anything
violent. In any case, there were enough genuine extremists
round there to keep them busy—not that it ever led to an
arrest.'

'What if you went to one of the newspapers about Jimmy?'

'Then I'd automatically be shopping myself. I want to tell
David first, and see how he reacts. And if *he* decides to go to
lawyers then I can't stop him. But it has to be *his* choice.'

'You are brave,' Daisy said as we stood up. 'This could
have terrible consequences for you.'

'Yes,' I said quietly. 'I know. But I also know that I simply
have to tell David. And I do want to—and equally I *don't*
want to. It's like having one foot on the brake and the other
on the accelerator. It's psychological stalemate.'

'Well, I'm sure you'll find a way.' *But when?* 'Anyway,'
Daisy went on, 'can we just have a look downstairs before I
fly back to the office? I've got to try and find a present for
Nigel's fortieth.' We went down the wooden spiral staircase
to the ground floor. 'Maybe I'll get him a really nice rug. He
is going to have a party, by the way,' she added as we flipped
through the pile of kelims. 'You know that old friend of his
you met at the barbecue? Alan? The barrister? He phoned me
on Friday to discuss Nigel's birthday. So I just said that I'd
be taking Nigel out to dinner somewhere, but he said that
he thought Nigel really ought to have a proper party—a *sur-*

prise party—and that he'd arrange it with that other friend of theirs, Jon. So I said that was fine and Alan phoned me this morning to say they've booked the venue.'

'Where?'

'At the zoo.'

'The zoo?'

'Yes, you can have parties there, apparently. I've never been to one myself,' she went on, as we looked at the glassware. 'It's going to be on the day itself—August the second. They were very lucky that it was available at such short notice.'

'Are you going to arrange it?'

She shook her head. 'The zoo do it all, which is great as I haven't got time. All I'm doing is sending the invites—I sneaked the addresses from Nigel's Filofax. I'm asking about seventy people.'

'I hope you don't have to ask that colleague of his, Mary. I thought she was rather unpleasant at the barbecue,' I added, though I wasn't going to tell Daisy why.

'I'm afraid I will have to ask her,' Daisy replied. 'She works quite closely with him, and she seems to have the ear of their new head of department, so Nigel likes to keep in with her—but I agree, she's a bit of a cow. You can invite David, if you like,' she added, as we looked at the standard lamps.

'Can I?'

'Of course. Nigel won't mind, and it'll be nicer for you as I'll be pretty busy, and anyway, I'd like to *meet* him. I know so much about him. In fact—Christ, Miranda—just think: *I* know things about David that he doesn't even know *himself.*'

'I will ask him, then,' I said. 'Thanks. After all, if it wasn't for you, Daisy, I wouldn't have met him.'

'Is that right?'

'Yes, because you recommended me to Caroline—' Trigger was the trigger, I suddenly realized, '—which is how I met Jimmy again. And then you encouraged me to look for David.'

'And you found him!'

'Yes.' My heart turned over. 'I did. Anyway, I'm glad Nigel's having a party—it would be a shame not to.'

'And obviously, I'm not going to bring up the marriage issue before then,' Daisy went on, with surprising calm. 'Because, well, it would spoil his birthday, wouldn't it, if we were having a crisis.'

'It's up to you.'

'And what's another two weeks, when you think about it?'

'Hmm.' We finished browsing and made our way outside.

'That's where the self-defence classes are, by the way,' she said, as the traffic roared past. 'Over there, in Howland Street. You will come this week, won't you?'

'Yes, sure.'

'Marcus is a great teacher. And although you're not very likely to be mugged again, I think it's good to have these techniques up your sleeve. Anyway, I'd better dash. I've got an underwater theme party to organize and I've got to find some mermaids' tails for the waitresses.'

'And I have to attend to a nymphomaniac cat.'

Animal Crackers has been getting huge ratings—seven million—which is great for business. By Wednesday afternoon I'd taken six new bookings. If I have seven a week, I'm fine. With eight I'm in profit. Nine and I'm laughing. My money worries have begun to subside. Unlike my mother's.

'The cash-flow's *dire*,' she said, when she called for a chat at six. 'So I've decided I'm definitely going to do the Llama Psychotherapy during the week. I'm going to call it "Llama

Karma". I've already put it on my website and I've had some leaflets printed up. I put some in the post to you yesterday.'

'How much will you charge?'

'A hundred for the day, to include lunch. The local radio people are interviewing me about it but what I really need is *national* publicity. Do you know anyone on one of the broad-sheets?'

'I'm afraid I don't. I'm not in that loop. Oh, I do know a young guy on the *Independent on Sunday*,' I suddenly remembered. 'He's on the diary, but he'd tell you who you could contact for some feature coverage.'

'Are you *sure* you can't get me on *Animal Crackers*?' she asked plaintively.

'You *know* I can't, Mum. I don't want to annoy them by even asking again, to be honest.'

'Well, if there's *anyone* you know who's really stressed—anyone at all—then tell them to call me and they can come and spend the day with the boys.'

Ten minutes later, Dad phoned—it's funny how he and Mum often phone within minutes of each other. Perhaps they're more in tune than they realize.

Dad sounded depressed. 'I've had the chairman giving me an ear-bashing about the cost of paving the parking lot, and hiring green-keeping staff, and we've only had five new members this week. Plus the golf pro has resigned because he thinks the club isn't going to work out. *Plus* I sent your mother a friendly card, and she returned it, unopened.'

'Oh dear.'

'I just don't under*stand*. You said she was "fine" about me coming down here. But she clearly isn't. I can't even get her to acknowledge me, let alone be civil. She pretends not to know me. It's absurd.'

'Then why don't you just turn up at the house?'

'Jesus, no! She'd probably call the police. I didn't exactly expect her to hang up a "Welcome" sign for me; but I didn't think she'd be so openly hostile either.'

'Well, she's not the most forgiving person in the world.'

'Tell me about it. You know, Miranda, maybe I've made a big mistake in coming back,' he went on. 'I mean, I've been here less than a month and already I'm so wound up. I'm just so *stressed*,' he added wearily. *Ah…*

By seven, the puppy party crowd had arrived. Lily had come in brandishing two bottles of champagne to celebrate the fact that *Moi!* had won Magazine of the Year the night before.

'Let's have a *proper* party!' she said. 'You don't mind do you, teach'?'

'No,' I said. 'That's fine by me.' I nipped round the corner and bought some crisps and olives. Then we all sat there sipping Laurent-Perrier, playing Pass the Puppy.

'Couldn't we go outside with them?' Lily suddenly asked.

'Yes,' Phyllis agreed, with another large swig. Her papery cheeks were quite pink. 'Couldn't we go outside?'

'Yes, Miranda, please, please, please—can't we go outside?' they chorused.

'Okay,' I said. 'Why *not*? There's plenty of light left, and we could do some basic disobedience.'

'Shouldn't that be "obedience"?' said Sue.

My head was swimming slightly as I reached for Herman's lead. 'Yes. Obedience. That's what I said.' As we left the Mews, the chiropractor grinned at us as he got into his car.

'It's the puppy posse!' Lily called out.

'Now, *do* tell me more about your film stunts,' Phyllis asked Marcus as they strolled along in front of me. He'd gallantly offered her his arm.

'No, Phyllis,' he protested. 'It's *too* boring talking about work.'

'But *your* work isn't boring at all. Please tell us,' she insisted.

'Yes, do, Marcus,' said Lily. 'Anyway, I need to know because I might do an article about you.'

'What do you enjoy most?' Phyllis asked, as a small boy stopped to stroke the puppies. 'Horse-riding stunts?'

'No, horses aren't really my thing. My favourites are aerial stunts—parachuting, flying, sky-diving, hang-gliding—anything like that. I like stair falls, and motorbike skids; and I do enjoy a good car crash.' I noticed that the little boy was giving Marcus odd looks. 'I also quite enjoy being blown up when I get the chance,' he added. 'Air rams are brilliant for that.'

'What are *air rams*?' asked Phyllis, enthralled, as we walked on.

'They're nitrogen-powered footplates. You just step onto them and they blow you *right* into the air. We used them in *Private Ryan*—we got some fabulous explosions.'

Phyllis was sighing with happiness.

'What's your best stunt *ever*?' Lily asked, as we passed The Queens pub.

'Do I have to tell you?' he groaned.

'Yes, you do,' she commanded.

'Okay,' he sighed. 'But only as you're asking. It was a high level fight I once did.'

'How high?' asked Phyllis.

'Well, you know that statue of Christ outside Rio de Janeiro.'

'Jesus!' Lily exclaimed.

'Yes—that one. I had to climb up into the head via a small hole and cling to the crown of thorns. Then I walked out

along an arm, two and a half thousand feet above the city and
had to fight this other stuntman.'

Phyllis had clapped her hand to her chest in an ecstasy of
terror. I was worried that she was going to collapse.

'Did you have a safety harness?' Lily asked, her eyes goggling.

'No.'

'Did you fall?' Phyllis asked. 'Is that how you broke your
nose?'

'If I'd fallen two and a half thousand feet, Phyllis, I can
assure you I'd have broken a *lot* more than my nose. No, I
was lifted off by helicopter, on the end of a rope, and they
dropped me on Copacabana beach.'

'Were you always a daredevil?' Phyllis asked as we crossed
Primrose Hill Road.

'No, I was a bit of a squit really. I was very anxious and
got picked on all the time. *That's* how my nose got broken—
in the playground. Maybe that's why I went into this business—to conquer my fears.'

'And how's your new young lady?' Phyllis asked with a
tipsy smirk.

'Oh she's…fine,' he replied. 'She's absolutely fine.'

'She must have been thrilled with the chocolates,' I said.

'Well, she was,' he replied. 'Except…well, unfortunately,
chocolate gives Natalie migraines.'

'Really? Oh dear.'

'Yeah.' He shrugged. 'I didn't know that. It's quite a serious problem for her actually, she really suffers with them
but—hey—there she is!' Coming towards us, on our side of
the road, was a slender blonde of exquisite prettiness. It was
her—the Timotei ad. The girl I'd seen in the Mews. So *she*
was Marcus's new flame.

'She's *very* pretty,' Phyllis said admiringly.

'Yes, she's gorgeous,' Marcus whispered back. He waved at Natalie who suddenly stopped dead in her tracks, then crossed to the other side of the road. Then she got out her mobile phone, and dialled. Suddenly Marcus's mobile trilled out.

'Hi, Nats!' he said. 'How are you? Good. Yes, I'm fine—apart from a slight sniffle. And where are you going? To the chemist? Piriton? For your hay fever? Oh, I see. Well we're just going onto the Hill with the puppies.'

'Why's she *doing* that?' Phyllis whispered to Lily. Lily shrugged her slim shoulders.

'Haven't a clue. Maybe it's her way of playing hard to get.'

'Okay,' said Marcus. 'See you later, then.' He snapped shut his phone, and waved at Natalie, who gave him a little wave back—then she carried on down Regents Park Road.

'What was *that* about?' Lily enquired.

'Oh, well, unfortunately, Natalie's allergic to dogs. And when she saw all the puppies she just knew it would bring her out in bumps.'

'Oh dear,' I said.

'Yes, it can be quite bad actually—so she was just playing it safe. With cats it's even worse. She has a very nasty reaction.'

'But isn't that a bit of a problem?' Phyllis asked. She nodded at Twiglet.

'Oh not...really,' he said, shifting slightly. 'No, no, I wouldn't say that's a problem.'

'I've seen her in the Mews,' I said, as we turned in at the gate. 'Quite often actually. I assumed she worked there. I didn't realize she was your girlfriend.'

'Well, she has aromatherapy once a week to de-stress her, and she goes to the homeopath for her allergies, and to the chiropractor for her lower back pain. She has a cranial massage once a fortnight for her migraines, and she uses Chinese herbal remedies to improve her yin and yang. That's how I knew about you,' he said. 'Because she saw your plaque on the wall when you first opened up.'

'I see.' We'd caught up with the rest of the group. 'Anyway, everyone, we're going to do some sit and stay. So take the puppies off the lead and plonk them down in a row, here, next to Herman. Then, using hand signals, like this— make them wait to the count of five; then fling open your arms, and they'll come. If they do it properly, reward them with lots of praise and a liver treat—I've got the bag here— but *don't* reward them until they've done it.'

'—Stay, Bentley.'

'—Stay, Lola.'

'—Staaaaay, Sooty.'

'—Maisie, sta-a-a-a-ay!'

'—Stay there, Gwyneth darling, don't move an *inch*.'

'—*STAAAAAYYYYYYY!!!!!!!!*'

'—Not an *inch*, Gwyneth—do you hear me?'

The puppies all looked stupefied to start with, but then they got the hang of it.

'—Oh darling, *well* done, that was just *so* brilliant—you little *genius*!'

'—Good *girl*, Roxy!'

'—*Good* boy, Cosmo!'

'Well done, Twiggers. Give me five.' Suddenly Marcus's mobile trilled out. 'Hi, Nats!' he said happily. We all looked up. Natalie was standing on the other side of Regents Park Road, her curtain of white-blonde hair lifting slightly in the breeze. 'Oh,' Marcus said. 'Oh.' He looked crestfallen. 'Well, it's only a little sniffle. Honestly, it's nothing. I shouldn't have mentioned it. It's just a bit of a summer cold. No, no, no, I'm sure I'm not infectious. Streptococcal? I very much doubt it.

Virus? *No…* Of *course* I'm sure. Okay,' he sighed. 'If that's how you feel. All right then. All right. I'll ring you later.' He snapped the phone shut, then smiled ruefully.

'I take it your date's off,' Lily said, as we watched Natalie drift away.

'Yes,' he said. 'She's decided that she doesn't want to see me after all in case she catches my cold. She's *very* sensitive, you see.'

'She's the delicate type then,' said Phyllis.

'Yes,' he said, 'she's *very* delicate.'

'Fragile.'

'Yes,' he agreed, with a slightly idiotic smile. 'She's fragile.'

'So I don't suppose she's very sporty, is she?' Phyllis asked.

He smiled indulgently. 'Oh no, she's not sporty at *all.*'

'She's not the outdoors type.'

'Far from it.'

'So she's rather different from you, then?' Phyllis persisted.

'Yes. But then it's opposites that attract. Isn't it?'

'Yes,' she replied. '*Some*times.' An odd silence descended.

'And…does she go to the self-defence classes?' I asked him.

He shook his head. 'I've tried to persuade her, but she says it's too rough. And it *is* quite rough; we do a lot of mock-attacks and throws and falls—it's very physical, obviously. Are you coming tomorrow, by the way?'

'I certainly am.' I glanced at my watch. It was nine. 'Okay, everyone, the light's going, so I think we'll call it a day. See you all next week at the same time, and I'll see you tomorrow evening, Marcus.'

'See you then,' he said with a smile. But when I got back there was a message on the answerphone from David, asking if he could bring our date forward to Thursday as he had to fly to Stockholm on Friday to do a couple of shoots.

'But I'd love to see you,' he said when I phoned back. 'Es-

pecially as I'm travelling quite a bit at the moment. I thought
we could go to the Photographers' Gallery—a friend of mine
is having an opening there. And we could maybe see a film
afterwards, or go for a Chinese, whatever you like. How does
that sound? Are you free tomorrow?' I thought about the
self-defence classes with a slight pang.

'Ye-es,' I said. 'I am.'

'I'm *really* sorry to let you down again,' I said to Daisy a
few minutes later. 'But you see, David's going to Sweden on
Friday morning and he'll be away for five days, so I just...'

'Don't worry,' she said. 'That's *fine*. I'll phone Marcus tomorrow morning and tell him you're not coming after all,
but it's going to be *really* good this week. He's going to teach
us the elbow jab and the wrist grab. Then we're going to
learn how to disable a single unarmed assailant. Marcus is
going to be in a fully padded body-suit, built to withstand
heavy blows. I'm going to find out how it actually feels to *hit*
someone!'

'Crikey.'

'Have you written down Nigel's birthday party, by the
way?'

'Yes, I have. August the second.'

'And don't forget—he knows *nothing* about it.'

'Don't worry. My lips are sealed.'

The next morning my mother's 'Llama Karma' leaflet arrived in the post. On the front of it was a photo of Carlos and
Jose, looking concerned and compassionate. I remembered
my idea. I picked up the phone and dialled Dad.

'Can you ever take a day off?' I asked him.

'Well, it's a bit tricky at the moment because we're so busy
in the run-up to the opening.'

'But could you take at least, say, a morning off? Or even just a couple of hours.'

'I suppose I could. Why are you asking?'

'I'll explain in a moment, but do you definitely want to see Mum?'

I heard him sigh. 'Yes, I do. I feel that if I could only *talk* to her, then I might be able to neutralize her hostility and her attitude towards me might change. I just want to feel we can be…civil,' he went on. 'But I don't know how to achieve it.'

'Well, I think I *do*.' I told him about the Llama Karma days. 'Why don't you sign up?'

'But how? She's blocked my phone calls. And if I made the booking by letter, she'd recognize the writing—and she'd see my name on the cheque.'

'Hmm. That's true.' I stared out of the window.

'I could always pay her cash,' he went on. 'But then it would be very easy for her to refuse. She'd take one look at me and shut the door.'

'*I* know how to do it,' I said. '*I'll* send her the cheque and pretend that you're a friend of mine. I'll say that I owe you a hundred quid, so I'm paying for your llama therapy. She's hard up at the moment so she'll cash it immediately, which means she'll be obliged to honour the booking.'

'But won't she want to know who I *am*?'

'Yes—but I'll give her a pseudonym.'

'Such as?' I glanced at my bookshelf. Charles Darwin… Konrad Lorenz.

'Lawrence Darwin,' I said.

'Is he one of *the* Darwins?' Mum asked, as she took down the details half an hour later.

'Um, I think so.'

'How *interesting*. And how do you know him?'

'He's a friend of…'

'Daisy's?' Mum anticipated.

'Yes.'

'Well, of course, Daisy knows so many people,' she said. 'What with all those parties she does. But why are *you* paying?'

'Because…we went to a…'

'Ball?' she anticipated.

'Ye-es.'

'I'm *so* glad you're getting back on the social scene, darling. And he paid for your ticket, did he?'

'That's right—so I've told him I'll pay for this.'

'Well, that's *very* nice of you. And what does he do?'

Ah. 'He's an…act—'

'Not another *actor*,' she interjected. 'I do hope not.'

'No. Actuary. For a large in—'

'—surance firm?'

'Ye-es.'

'Well, no wonder he's stressed. All that number-crunching must be exhausting.'

'That's right. He's *really* stressed. He's just changed jobs, and the people aren't very friendly, plus he has to work incredibly long hours and there are billions at stake if he gets his sums wrong, and he's wondering whether it's all worth it—in fact he's close to—'

'A nervous breakdown?'

I was going to say 'packing it in'. 'Yes. A nervous breakdown. That's right.'

My mother was making sympathetic 'tut-tut' noises. 'Well, don't worry—*I'll* look after him. We'll feed and groom the llamas, then I'll leave him on his own with them, one on one. I think I'll put him with Sancho,' she went on. 'Sancho's *very* understanding. Then Lawrence can take him for a walk and talk to him about all his problems. I guarantee that things will look *very* different by the end of the day.'

Oh I do hope so. 'That sounds…great.'

'When does he want to come down?'

'He'd like to come a week today, if that fits in with you.'

'Thursday the thirty-first,' she echoed. 'I'm putting it in the diary now. *Thanks*, Miranda. My first client!'

The rest of the day passed pleasantly. *Animal Crackers* phoned to say our ratings had jumped by ten per cent since the last series. Then I got a call from PetWise, the insurers who were sponsoring the 'Pet Slimmer of the Year' competition, reminding me that I'd agreed to judge the final in three weeks' time. In the afternoon I had an appointment with a pair of ferrets which refused to stop fighting, then at six fifteen I settled Herman on his beanbag, and got the Northern Line to Leicester Square.

The Photographers' Gallery was in Great Newport Street. As I entered the narrow, tunnel-shaped space there was a powerful aroma of alcohol mingled with smoke. I surveyed the dense crowd, but couldn't see David. But then, with a jolt, I noticed Caroline Mulholland, standing with her back to me a few feet away, talking to a woman in a green raincoat. What if Jimmy was here? With a rising sense of panic, I scanned the sea of faces but couldn't see him. Then David emerged out of the crowd.

'Hi there!' He kissed me, and the touch of his cheek on mine made me feel almost weak with desire. 'I'm really glad you could make it. Let's get you a drink.'

'Whose exhibition is this?' I asked, as we pushed our way through the throng.

'It's Arnie Noble's—an old friend of mine. He used to be a photojournalist too—with the Sygma agency. I'll introduce you.' To my relief he led me to the back of the gallery, away from where Caroline was standing. If she saw me, I might

well find myself in the grotesque position of having to introduce David to Jimmy. The thought of it made me feel faint.

'David and I have been in many of the same hellholes,'
Arnie explained as he shook my hand. He was a sandy-haired
man of forty-five or so. His freckled face, though handsome,
was lived in and lined.

'That's right,' said David as he handed me a glass of champagne. 'We've dodged the same bullets.'

'We have,' said Arnie with a guffaw. 'We've also fought
to get the best picture and sometimes the best women,' he
laughed, slapping David's back.

'Don't listen to him,' David said with a smile.

I looked at the walls. They were covered with landscapes.
'But these aren't news photographs.'

Arnie shook his head. 'Like David, I gave that up. I do
landscapes now. It's more peaceful. And war is a young man's
game.' As someone else came up to Arnie to congratulate
him, David drew me away, gently propelling me through
the dense crowd towards the perimeter, his hand round my
waist.

'These are so *good*,' he said. We'd stopped in front of a
photograph of a canyon in Arizona. 'I've never seen Arnie's
landscapes before. The composition's fantastic.'

'They're very dramatic,' I said. As David looked at the picture I discreetly glanced into the crowd to make sure Caroline was nowhere near us.

'They are dramatic—they're not idealized at all. There's so
much darkness in them,' David added admiringly. I looked at
the stark leafless trees, and the boiling grey clouds with their
fiery underlighting.

'They have an ominous atmosphere.'

'They do. That mountain range looks like a sleeping
dragon. And look at the way the wind's sweeping through

the grass in the foreground here.' He took me by the hand. 'Let's look at the rest.' I would have been happy to leave the gallery as soon as possible, but David was still enthusing about Arnie's pictures as we made our way round the walls. 'Brooding...' I heard him say, as I discreetly glanced over my shoulder to see if I could spot Jimmy. 'Threatening...black and white is perfect...but as far from Ansel Adams as you can get...the landscape not so much majestic, as menacing...the sense of impending violence...legacy of twenty years spent in war zones...it inevitably informs his vision.'

Suddenly, David's mobile phone trilled and he flipped it open.

'Oh hi! Yes, hang on. I've just got to take this call,' he said. 'I won't be long.' As he made his way to the front of the gallery, I decided to stay where I was. As I stared at the photos, I could make out snatches of ambient chatter.

'—Fabulous contrast!'

'—Have you seen Don McCullin's landscapes?'

'—Isn't that the Quantocks?'

'—Over there, in Issey Miyake.'

'—Looks more like *Dorset* than Somerset.'

'Miranda?'

I turned. Caroline was standing beside me, smiling broadly. To my surprise, she looked slightly tight. 'I *thought* it was you, Miranda.' Her blue eyes were shining and her colour was high. 'How *are* you?'

'Oh, hi, I'm fine. Thanks.' I glanced anxiously over her shoulder but there was no sign of her husband.

'It's *so* nice to *see* you,' she said, emphasizing random words in the way people do when they've had a few too many. 'And how do you know *Arnie*?' she enquired, as she held out her glass to a passing waiter.

'I don't. I only met him tonight. I'm here with a…friend of his,' I explained. 'A fellow photographer.'

'*Ditto*. I'm here with a friend *too*.' She nodded in the direction of the woman in the green raincoat. 'That's Arnie's agent, Jessica. We're *old* pals, and she asked me *along*, and, as James has got a rather *dull* dinner to go to tonight, I thought it would be *fun*.' A wave of relief swept over me. Jimmy wasn't here. I felt my heart-rate suddenly slow. 'You know,' she suddenly said with a confidential giggle, 'I think I've had *too* much *champagne*. The waiters have been *very* attentive, unfortunately, and it's *fatal* on an empty stomach, *isn't* it?' I nodded sympathetically. 'And there are *no* canapés. Not so much as a *crisp*. Oh well,' she shrugged, with another sip. 'You worked *wonders* with Trigger by the way,' she added warmly. 'I was at my wits' *end* that day, but the blighter's *almost* a reformed *character* now.'

'Really?' I smiled. 'Well, that's great.'

'He's not behaving *nearly* as badly. Your friend Daisy did me a *huge* favour, recommending you,' she went on. 'But I didn't…realize…' She seemed to hesitate.

'Realize what?'

'Well, what a…*coincidence* it all was.'

I stared at her, electrified. 'What do you mean?'

'Well,' she giggled again. 'What I mean *is*—your knowing *James*.' I felt as though I'd been punched in the solar plexus.

'I, erm, don't know him, actually.'

'But you *used* to?' I looked at her. 'Didn't you? He *told* me.' I felt as though an ice cube had been dropped down my neck. 'I saw him talking to you after the *fete*, you see, so of *course* I *asked* him, as any wife *would*…'

'Oh, well,' I said, recovering, 'I did…know him, yes, that's right, but it was…a long time ago.'

'Don't *worry*,' she said, placing her hand on my forearm in a gesture of solidarity. 'I *completely* understand.'

'Understand what?' I was still smiling in order to cover my discomfiture.

'Well, *why* he didn't *tell* me at first.' And now, suddenly, I felt as hot as a flame. 'It's so *typical* of James,' she went on. 'His consider*ation* for other people's *feelings*.'

'I'm *sorry*?'

'Well, because he didn't want to *embarrass* you. But there's no *need* for you to be embarrassed, Miranda. When I think of all the *huge* crushes *I* had when *I* was a teenager.' I felt my palms go damp. 'And I *know* that James was *very* dishy when he was younger—those blond *curls*!' she exclaimed with a laugh. 'I've seen the photos, Miranda—I'm quite sure he was *irresistible*.'

'I…hardly knew him,' I shrugged. 'It was a very…casual acquaintanceship.'

'Oh! But that's not what *he* said! *He* said you were in-fatuated with him. But don't *worry*,' she went on, with tipsy, though clearly genuine, sincerity. 'I *just* wanted to tell you that it's *okay*. I'm *not* the jealous type. I'm *very* happily mar-ried, and I *wouldn't* like you to think, if you *ever* met us again *together*, that it was in any way…' she groped for the appro-priate expression, '…*awkward*.' Alcohol had made her tact-less and crass. 'I'm very *happy* to be friends with James's old flames,' she concluded warmly. She laid her left hand on my arm again. 'I just wanted to *tell* you that.'

'Thank you,' I managed to say.

'I must *say*, though, I think you were very *brave*,' she went on, with another sip of champagne.

'I'm sorry?'

'Well,' she said, her eyes widening. 'He told me about the *things* you used to get up to.' I stared at her, my heart banging against my ribcage. 'When you were in *Brighton*. He said you were quite…*naughty*,' she grinned. 'Mind *you*, I think spraying graffiti on a fur shop's rather *heroic*, actually. Good for *you*, Miranda! I wish *I'd* had the *guts* to do that kind of thing, but my father would've cut me *off* like a *shot*!'

'Caroline—' I said.

'Oh, there you are, Miranda!' It was David. 'Sorry about that.' He peered at me. 'Are you all right? You look rather flushed. I guess it *is* a bit claustrophobic in here. We'll go and eat now. He suddenly noticed Caroline. 'Hi, I'm David White,' he said, extending his hand. I saw her glance at his scars, then she looked back at his face.

'I'm Caroline Mulholland,' she replied with a smile. '*Very* nice to meet you. Anyway, it was *lovely* to see you, Miranda. I *really* hope we meet again.' I gave her a faint smile.

'Shall we go then?' David asked.

I nodded. 'Goodbye, Caroline,' I managed to say.

'Who was that?' David enquired as we left the gallery. *It's the wife of the man who's responsible for your disfigurement.* 'The name "Mulholland" rings bells with me for some reason,' he added, as we turned right.

'Oh, she's just a client of mine.'

'Isn't there a politician called Mulholland?'

'Yes, I…think there is. But she had a very difficult…Weimaraner, you see.'

'What was the problem?'

'It was a total bastard.'

'It was *what*?'

'I mean…to her other dogs. It was very…domineering, and basically it needed to have its status reduced.'

'Did it work?'

'Apparently it did. She was just telling me about it.'

As we crossed Charing Cross Road, I worked out *why*

Jimmy had told Caroline what he had. Yes, she *had* seen us talking at the house, and yes, she must have wondered—especially as she'd had no idea we'd ever met. But what Jimmy had done wasn't just to cover himself against her spousal suspicions. He had launched a pre-emptive strike. By telling her that I'd been 'infatuated' with him, and that I'd been 'naughty'—he'd effectively discredited me, in case I blabbed. His pretence that he'd been protecting me from embarrassment by not telling her that he had once known me, filled me with rage.

'Do you like Chinese?' I heard David say as we walked down Cranbourn Street.

'Yes, I do.'

'Because there's a good one I know in Lisle Street.' It was dusk by now and I saw a cloud of starlings zig-zag across the darkening sky. As we turned into Leicester Square we heard music. On the east side was a funfair, with an old-fashioned carousel and a white-knuckle ride. We looked up at its huge Meccano arms, spinning and oscillating with their shrieking human cargo, heads thrown back, hair flying.

'EEEEEEEEEEEEEE!!!!!!!!!' we heard above the music.

'AAAAAAAAAAAHHHH!!!!!!'

'CONFESS YOUR SINS AND BE *SAVED!!*' Standing a few feet away was a man in a bomber jacket clutching a powerful microphone. A small crowd had gathered in a semi-circle and were listening to him in a desultory way. 'CONFESS YOUR SINS AND BE SAVED!!' he boomed. 'FOR DOES IT NOT SAY IN EZEKIEL, CHAPTER EIGHTEEN, VERSE THIRTY, "REPENT AND TURN AWAY FROM ALL YOUR TRANSGRESSIONS. LET INIQUITY BE YOUR *RUIN!!*"'

'Come on,' said David. He grabbed my hand. 'We can do without the fire and brimstone.'

'FOR GOD *REJOICES* IN THOSE WHO REPENT,' the man roared. 'FOR, AS IT IS WRITTEN IN LUKE, CHAPTER FIFTEEN, VERSE SEVEN, "I TELL YOU THERE SHALL BE MORE JOY IN HEAVEN OVER *ONE* SINNER WHO REPENTS THAN OVER *NINETY-NINE* RIGHTEOUS PERSONS WHO NEED *NO* RE-PENTANCE"!!'

'Still, it's a free country, I suppose,' David muttered.

'SO I SAY TO YOU AGAIN, MY BROTHERS AND SISTERS, CONFESS YOUR SINS AND *REPENT!!*'

I *must* confess to David, I thought bitterly, as we walked through Leicester Place. There was no longer any excuse for me not to have done so. At the beginning I could reasonably argue that I didn't know him well enough; but we'd met four times now, so that was no longer the case. I *would* tell him. This evening. I would finally do it.

'Here we are,' he said. We'd stopped outside a restaurant called the Feng Shing. 'They do good lobster noodles here. Is seafood out of the question for you?'

'No. I eat it occasionally.' We were shown to a table at the back.

'I'm starving,' David said. 'Fried squid?' I nodded. 'Scallops in black bean sauce?'

'Fine by me.'

'Do you mind if I have chicken?'

'No—as you said, it's a free country.'

'And we'll have some stir-fried vegetables with bamboo shoots.' He waved at the waiter and placed the order. 'And we'd like some mixed starters, some crispy seaweed, and a couple of Tsinhao beers?' I nodded. 'Great,' he said. 'You're easy to please.' He suddenly smiled at me, and I noticed his tiny scar disappear. 'It's *so* nice to see you again—Miss Behaviour.' *If you knew precisely how I'd misbehaved, you wouldn't say that.* He snapped open his chopsticks, then smiled again. 'I think I'm getting used to you.'

'Are you?' I smiled back. 'So what have you been up to?'

'I went to Glasgow for a couple of days to take some pictures for Action on Addiction, then I've been in the dark room quite a bit; I've got so many films to catch up on before I go to Stockholm.'

'And what will you be doing there?'

'A shoot to illustrate a piece about Ethiopian asylum seekers for *Newsweek.*'

'Ethiopians in Stockholm? That's somehow hard to imagine.'

'Well, it's a global village now. Then I've got to take some photos of the Nobel Foundation. And what about you?'

I told him about the puppy party, and about my mother's llama psychotherapy—that made him laugh—and about my ruse to get her to talk to my dad.

'So she has no idea that it's him?'

'No. She thinks it's "Lawrence Darwin", a supposed friend of mine, so she's going to get a bit of a shock. But if I have to practise a minor deception to get her to be civilized to my dad, then so be it.' The waiter arrived with our drinks.

'Do you think your dad still likes your mum?' David asked, as we sipped our beer.

'I think he does. I'm sure that's why he went to live in the States when she remarried. He couldn't take it.'

'But he never married again?'

I shook my head. 'He had girlfriends. They were always rather glamorous and very keen to impress me. There was Sheryl, I remember—she gave me a silver bracelet—I've still got it. Then there was Nancy, a tennis coach. I liked her a lot. She took me to Seaworld at San Diego one weekend when Dad was working—she seemed to be nuts about him.

But none of them ever became a permanent fixture, so I suspect he was still holding a candle for my mother.'

'How do you think she'll react when he turns up?'

'She'll be livid. It may make the situation worse, but I thought it was worth a try. I mean, you're friends with your ex-wife, aren't you?'

'Yes. Inasmuch as we're able to talk from time to time, and there are no hard feelings. Just because she decided she didn't want to be my wife any more doesn't mean I have to hate her for the rest of my life.'

'So you forgive her?'

'For leaving me? Yes. I made her unhappy so why should she stay?'

'But you said that you couldn't forgive the person who… hurt you?'

'I said I didn't *think* I could. But it's entirely academic as I don't know that person—or people—and how can you forgive someone you've never *met*? And as I'm extremely unlikely ever to do so, the question is irrelevant. I'm never going to find out who did it,' he said. 'I accepted that a long time ago and moved on. It's very sweet of you to be so concerned about it, Miranda, but I actually got over it years ago.'

'David,' I said faintly. 'There's something I want to tell you.'

He looked at me and smiled. 'Here we go again. Confession time.' I stared at him. 'You don't really want to eat any seafood—is that it?'

I shook my head. 'You wanted something completely vegetarian instead?'

'No, no. It's something *serious*, actually…I…'

Suddenly the waiter appeared with our starters but he'd forgotten the seaweed, so that had to be rectified before our conversation could continue, and by that time the moment was lost.

'David,' I tried again, as I fiddled with my chopsticks.

'Before you tell me whatever it is you want to say, can *I* say something serious to *you*?'

'Okay.'

'I wondered whether you'd come away with me in a fortnight's time.' My heart did a swallow dive. 'I know we haven't known each other that long yet.' He was fiddling with his glass. 'But I thought it would be...nice.'

I looked at him. 'Where?'

'West Sussex. I've got to take photos of Petworth and Arundel for the English Tourist Board. They've booked me into this gorgeous hotel and I just thought it would be fun if you were there too. They allow small dogs—' he went on before I could answer, '—so there'd be no problem with Herman. And you could come along with me while I work or you could just stay in the hotel and read. I don't want to put any pressure on you,' he added, without looking at me. 'But I'm travelling quite a bit at the moment, so I thought that if you felt like coming along that weekend, it would give us a bit of time together. But you don't have to say now. You could see how you feel.' He was fiddling with his chopstick rest. 'You could even make up your mind on the day.'

'I'd love to come,' I said.

He looked at me. 'Really?' His face was suffused with surprise.

'Yes. I can't think of anything nicer.'

He smiled. 'Well, that's good. In fact, that's...great.' He reached across the table for my left hand and stroked it.

'But would it be okay if we had separate rooms? I'd just feel more...comfortable with that.'

He nodded slowly.

'I understand. That's fine. I guess you're still getting over Alexander.' *In some ways, but that's not the real reason.* 'So, tell me,' he added quietly. 'What was the "serious" thing you wanted to say?'

'Oh...' I clutched my napkin. 'Well...'

'Come on. What's on your mind this time?'

'Well, it's just that...' I took a deep breath, then felt my courage trickle away, like sand through an hourglass. 'I...I... wondered whether you'd like to come to a birthday party with me on Saturday?'

'Is that *all*?' he laughed.

'That's all.'

'You are funny. Well, thanks.' He reached across and kissed me. 'I would.'

—— CHAPTER 10 ——

'He's asked you to go away for the *weekend*,' gasped Daisy the following day. I was in Stroud, filming a cat that had adopted two orphaned rabbits which its owner had found in a hedge. We filmed the cat suckling them as peacefully as if she'd given birth to them. I'd then done a piece to camera on other examples of inter-species adoption—a sheepdog which had nursed four piglets, the lioness which had 'mothered' a baby gazelle, the Alsatian which had suckled two fox cubs, and the donkey which had adopted a lamb. Then, while the crew were packing up, I'd called Daisy.

'A weekend away?' she reiterated as I sat in the parked car with Herman. 'Gosh. Things *are* hotting up. So when's that happening?'

'The weekend after Nigel's party. David's in Stockholm this week, then he comes back for three days, then he goes to Paris for a few days. But the idea is that we'll drive down to Petworth on Friday the eighth.'

'So you're going away with David?'

I felt myself smile. 'I'm going away with David. That's right.'

'And did something *happen* last night—to prompt this?' she enquired with a giggle.

'No. He saw me into a cab, then went home.'

'Poor bloke,' she breathed. 'He clearly fancies you to bits—he must be gagging for it.'

'I think he is,' I said ruefully. 'But he's not pushing it. He's nice. In any case he had to catch an early plane this morning.'

'But don't you want to…take things further?'

I stared through the windscreen. 'Yes, actually, I *do*. I'm so attracted to him.'

'Then why *don't* you?'

'Because I can't possibly get *involved* with him, unless he knows who I really *am*.'

'Hmm.'

'It wouldn't be right, Daisy. I've given it a lot of thought.'

'I understand. But it does rather put the brakes on things.'

'Well, it's a huge complication, so yes. But at least the whole thing with Alexander buys me time.'

'Maybe you could tell him when you go away for that weekend.'

I felt my entrails twist with anxiety. 'That's what I've decided to do. I'll have known him for six weeks by then. I can't delay it any longer. No more prevarication. Anyway, how was the class?'

'It was *wonderful*,' she replied. 'We did a number of assault scenarios. Did you know that if someone grabs you from behind you shouldn't step forward to try and escape them; you should step backwards, and jab them hard with your elbows, or drive your heel into their shin. We practised that on Marcus. He was all padded up and he "attacked" us and we had to defend ourselves. It was huge fun.'

'I hope you didn't hurt him.'

'Oh, no. Marcus is indestructible, Miranda. He's such a *solid* person. The things he's survived! We were asking him about his work in the pub afterwards.'

'I just hope you never have to use what he's taught you for real.'

'I hope so too—but simply knowing *how* to defend myself makes me feel more confident. Do you promise you'll come next week?'

'I solemnly promise. And what are you doing this week-end? Are you seeing Nigel?'

'I'm not…sure,' she said vaguely. 'He's working all day tomorrow, then I've got to be at one of my parties in the evening. I'll probably have to stay there till at least ten, so I'll probably just go home and crash.'

'What's happening on Sunday? Maybe we could meet for tea?'

'Sorry, but I won't be around.'

'You'll be with Nigel, of course. Don't worry. You need to spend some time with him as you've both been so busy lately.'

'Oh no, it's not that. I'm going microlighting.'

'Microlighting?'

'Yes. I've never done it before. It's basically a big kite with a motorbike engine. Apparently it brings back the romance of the early days of aviation as you go phut, phut, phut around the sky. And recently I…got offered the opportunity to try it, so I thought, why not give it a go? I mean, life's so *short*, Miranda,' she went on expansively. 'I feel you should take every chance you get. And what are you doing this weekend?' she went on quickly.

'Well, not very much. I've got a couple of clients on Saturday, then I'm looking forward to a relaxing Sunday.'

But this wasn't to be.

It started quietly enough. I had breakfast at Primrose Patisserie, and was sitting outside in the sunshine, reading the paper, when I saw Natalie float down the road. She looked as fragile and delicate as her glass jewellery. That seemed to be why Marcus liked her so much. Now she stopped, pulled up a chair at the next table, and ordered a cup of cranberry tea. I gave her a brief smile of semi-recognition but she seemed not to know me. Suddenly her mobile trilled out.

'Oh hi, Marcus,' she said. No doubt he was coming to meet her. 'How's Bedfordshire?' No—he wasn't. 'Oh good. Excellent conditions? No, I don't mind at all...I *know* I could have come. But I didn't *want* to. It sounds *horribly* danger-ous...This evening? Okay. But don't book *anywhere* where they allow smoking. You *know* I can't stand it...Well, I can't...I don't *care* if it's a tall order, Marcus, I'm *not* having people smoking within fifty feet of me. I'm *very* asthmatic... Yes, I *have* told you that...Well, that's *their* problem, isn't it?' And I was just wondering what Marcus was doing in Bed-fordshire that was so 'horribly dangerous', when my phone rang. I'd diverted my calls.

'Is that Miranda Sweet?'

'Yes.'

'My name's Keith Bigley, and I'm calling from Oxford about my rescue cat, Ali.'

'What's the problem?'

'Well, basically, we think he's insane. My wife and I are quite worried about him actually, and we saw you on that *Animal Crackers*, and we know it's the weekend and every-thing, but we wondered if you'd come out.' So much for my relaxing Sunday, I thought ruefully. Still, the money would be handy. I paid for my breakfast and left.

Keith had said that the cat 'kept playing with water'. It had a 'fatal attraction' to it, he claimed. I had an inkling why this might be, but I had to see it to be certain. So I put Herman in the car, and set off.

'Thank God you're here,' said Keith, as he opened the door an hour and a half later. 'This cat is really freaking us out.' We shut Herman in the dining room, then I followed Keith through to the kitchen, where his wife was washing up. Standing on the draining board, trying to dip its head under the stream of water, was a large ginger and white cat.

'We've only had it four days,' he explained. 'We got it from the local rescue centre. But it's got this *thing* about water. I was having a bath last night and it tried to get in with me. It tries to get into the loo as well. We're worried that if we forget to put the lid down one day, it might drown.' Suddenly the cat jumped off the draining board, ran into the garden, and leaped into the pond with a huge splash.

'You see,' said Keith's wife. She shrugged. '*Weird*. We don't like to leave the house, in case it gets into difficulties while we're out.'

'So you're on lifeguard duty?'

She nodded. 'We've ordered a pond cover,' she explained, 'but it won't arrive for a week. Maybe we should get it some water-wings,' she mused, as her husband and I went outside.

'What's *wrong* with it?' her husband asked, as we stood by the pond watching it doing a vigorous breaststroke amongst the lily pads. 'Is it crazy? Maybe it's got a brain tumour or something?'

'There's nothing wrong with it at all,' I replied.

'But what sort of cat goes for a swim?'

'A Turkish Van,' I replied.

'A what?'

'It's a Turkish Van,' I explained, as it hauled itself out of the pond and shook itself. 'They come from South-East Turkey, near Lake Van, and they have this unusual fascination with water. I thought that's probably what it was when you phoned me, but I needed to see it to be sure. I think it's a cross breed…' I looked at it, as it lay on the grass, purring like a tractor and licking the water off its fur. 'But it's got most of the Van characteristics—the high ears, the ginger and white colouring, and the long, broad body.'

'I thought he was a big fella.'

'They are. They can reach three feet in length—and they're very clever. You can teach them tricks and take them for walks, like a dog. How long had it been in the rescue centre?'

'Only five days. Someone had dumped it there. The staff didn't seem to know what it was. They just described it as a tortoiseshell.'

'Well, that's because it's not a pure-breed—it's got these brown patches on its tummy. And if it had been kept in an ordinary pen, they wouldn't have seen it in action, so they wouldn't have known what it was. It must have been thrilled to come here and have a good splash.'

'So what should we do?'

'Nothing,' I said. 'Don't cover the pond—except in winter, because of ice. Don't keep fish, for obvious reasons. Oh, and don't let it go swimming on a full stomach in case it gets cramp.'

He looked at me. 'Oh. Right. Is that it, then?'

I nodded. 'That's it. You don't have an insane cat—just an unusual one,' I added as we went inside.

'Maybe we should take it to the beach,' his wife said.

As I was driving back, David called me from his hotel in Stockholm. He talked about the shoot, then I told him about my client.

'They're known as swimming cats,' I explained. 'They're very rare. I've never seen one before.'

'How bizarre. And are there any dogs that climb trees?'

'Not to my knowledge, though Staffordshire bull terriers practically do, because they love sticks so much.'

'So you've been having an interesting day?'

'I have. And now I'm going to have a quiet evening, and catch up with my paperwork, maybe watch a bit of TV, and…'

'Think about me?' he said with a laugh.

'Yes. Think about you. I *do* think about you, David.'

'Nice things?'

'*Very* nice things.' *And things which you could never guess at.*

'Now, before I go, have you got anything serious to confess?' he asked in a mock-serious tone. 'You usually do.'

'No. I haven't, David.' *At least, not today.*

'Well, there's something *I'd* like to confess to *you*.'

'What?'

'That… I miss you. Do you think I've got separation anxiety?'

I smiled. 'It sounds like you might have.'

'Then you're the perfect person to cure me of it. In fact, you're the only person who can. I hope I'll always know you,' he added. My heart turned over.

'*I* hope you will too,' I replied.

Animal Crackers aired again on Tuesday, and the following morning I got a call from a researcher at London F.M. asking me to take part in a phone-in on animal behaviour.

'We're calling it "Pets Behaving Madly",' he said. 'It's on tomorrow night, seven until eight. I'm sorry it's such short notice.'

I agreed to do it, though I felt bad at having to miss the self-defence class yet again, but I knew the show would generate work. I phoned Daisy, but she didn't sound too upset, in fact she sounded slightly distracted; but then she clearly had a lot on her mind. I asked her about the microlighting and she said it was 'blissful'.

'It was *so* romantic,' she said. 'You just buzz about in the sky, with the earth beneath you. It's so liberating—I felt *free*.'

'How high up did you go?'

'Not that high. Only a thousand feet or so.'

'It sounds terrifying.'

'No—they're safe, because if the engine cuts out you just glide. The landing was a *little* bit hairy,' she went on. 'You have to head straight for the ground, nose down, then pull up at the very last minute. Apparently, the trick is to get the thing down without burying it.'

'You weren't flying *solo*, were you, Daisy?'

'Oh. No. I wasn't.'

'You had an experienced instructor with you, I hope?'

'Er, yes. Yes, I did. He says he'll help me get my licence—you only need to clock up twenty-five hours. Anyway, how was *Animal Crackers*?' she went on quickly. 'I meant to watch you, but I forgot.'

'Oh. That's okay. It was fine.'

'I thought *Animal Crackers* was *great*,' said Dad, when he phoned me later that day for his weekly chat. 'The way you handled that hyperactive tortoise.'

'He *was* rather temperamental.'

'And those aggressive rabbits. Starsky and Hutch.'

'Stropski and Bitch, more like. Those bunnies really were *very* bad-tempered. Speaking of which, are you ready for your rendezvous with Mum tomorrow?'

'As ready as I'll ever be. I'll go armed with some flowers, and I'll just *talk* to her, Miranda. I haven't talked to her properly for years. Have you got any tips?'

'Yes. Take an extravagant interest in the llamas. Just tell

her how beautiful, sensitive and intelligent they are, etcetera, etcetera, and she'll be eating out of your hand.'

On Thursday morning I braced myself for a furious phone call from my mother—but, to my surprise, I didn't hear a thing. Then I had a couple of appointments to go to and didn't get back until five. I thought she might have left an angry message on my answerphone, but there was nothing. There was still no message when I left for London F.M. I tried calling Dad from the taxi, but his phone was switched off. Maybe he'd actually survived the whole day. Or maybe Mum had murdered him and was busy disposing of the body.

'Thanks for coming in,' said the producer, Wesley, when he met me at reception at a quarter to seven. 'The show's an hour long,' he explained as he signed me in. 'And we'll be filtering the calls, which we'd like to be a mixture of behavioural problems, plus any pet stories which the listeners want to share. We'd like to keep it informative but light-hearted,' he added as he called the lift.

'I'll do my best.'

In the studio, the presenter, Minty Malone, greeted me warmly, then I put on my headphones, the studio manager took level, and at three minutes past seven, the phone-in began.

'Now...' said Minty as she leaned into the microphone. 'Is your borzoi unbalanced? Is your iguana introverted? Are your tropical fish psychologically fragile? If so, then do call us this evening, because our subject tonight is pets—and their peculiarities. And our special guest is animal behaviourist, Miranda Sweet, from TV's *Animal Crackers*. Miranda, a warm welcome to the show.'

Minty spent a couple of minutes chatting to me, then she took the first question.

'On Line One is Pam from Penge, and Pam wants to know why her cat sleeps so much.'

'That's right,' said Pam. 'It does—it sleeps all the time. And it's only five, so it's not old age. What I want to know *is*, has it got urban stress—or is it being a lazy little git?'

'Neither,' I replied. 'It's simply behaving like the predator it is. The reason cats—like lions—sleep so much—up to sixteen hours a day, is because they're conserving energy in order to have maximum strength for the hunt.'

'Oh, right,' said Pam. 'I won't worry then. Thanks.'

'Thanks for calling in, Pam,' said Minty. 'And now we have Patrick, who's got a question about his sheepdog, Murphy, who's car crazy. Will you tell us what he does, Patrick?'

'Well, he's a *super* dog, but he's very excitable,' Patrick replied. 'He really is. Very excitable. *Very* excitable.' Patrick sounded pretty excitable himself. 'He likes to sit in the back with his head *right* out the window.'

'That's *not* a good idea,' I interrupted. 'I wouldn't let him do that.'

'But the *really* annoying thing is the way he keeps saying, "Are we there yet? Are we there yet?" All the way. It drives me round the bloody twist, I can tell you.' Minty was making circling gestures by her temple.

'Well…that…would be annoying,' I said.

'And now we have Mrs Edith Witherspoon on Line Three, who's concerned about her bulldog, Archie.'

'Oh, that's right,' said Mrs Witherspoon. 'I really am *most* concerned. He behaves in a very…' she hesitated. 'Unsavoury way.' Minty's eyes had widened but I knew what was coming.

'So what exactly is the problem?' I said.

'Well…he's fine when I'm on my own. But if I have my

friends round for tea—or it's my turn to host the Women's Institute—he behaves *so* badly. I put him out, but then he barks to be let in. So I relent. But if I then *ignore* him and *dare* to talk to my friends he…he…oh dear…I can hardly *bear* to tell you.'

'Is it inappropriate mounting, Mrs Witherspoon?'

'Oh no, no. It's *worse*.'

'Does he drag his bottom along the carpet? Is that it?'

'No, no, no. It's, just that, he, well, he…' By now her voice was a barely audible whisper.

'Yes…?'

'*Plays* with himself.'

'Oh dear.'

'He's fine if I pay him attention,' she went on. 'If I have him on my lap, feeding him bits of cake, telling him how *gorgeous* he is, then he behaves. But if I start chatting to my friends, then he backs himself into a corner and starts…'

'I can imagine,' I interjected. 'How disgusting. It's attention-seeking of the very worst kind. No wonder you want to put a stop to it—it must be extremely embarrassing for you, Mrs Witherspoon.'

'Oh, that's not my main concern.'

'Isn't it?'

'No.'

'Then what is?'

'Well—I'm worried that he'll go *blind*!'

There were calls about kleptomaniac ferrets, and love-sick lizards. There was a Labrador which hogged the TV.

'Every time we put it on, she sits *bang* in front of it, her nose glued to the screen,' said Kevin on Line Two. 'She's doing it right now…' In the background we could hear the theme tune of *Eastenders*, and shouts of 'Get *out* of the way, Goldie! *Move*, will you! *Move!!!*' '…No one can see a *thing*.'

'Then I suggest you simply put the TV somewhere higher up so that you can all watch in comfort. Maybe you could mount it on a wall bracket.'

'Oh right,' he said. 'That's a good idea.' He laughed. 'I hadn't actually thought of that. Yeah, we'll give it a try.'

'Do you know much about mynah birds, Miranda?' Minty asked. 'Because on Line Three we have our former agony aunt, Rose Costelloe.' Oh. Rose Costelloe. I'd heard of her. 'Rose has a major problem with her mynah—isn't that right, Rose?'

'It is. You see, I've got five-month-old twins, and they cry a lot at the moment. But that's not the problem. The problem is that my mynah bird, Rudolph, has learned to imitate them.'

'How ghastly,' I said.

'It is—but the real killer is that he only ever does it when they're *asleep*.'

'You must be exhausted,' said Minty with a sympathetic giggle.

'I *am*. If it isn't the babies screaming the house down, it's Rudy. So I just wondered if Miranda might have any ideas?'

'Gosh, this is a difficult one. Perhaps you could play him lullabies all day, and maybe he'll learn to imitate *those* instead.'

'Okay, I'll give it a try.'

Then people began phoning in with stories about the funny things their pets do.

'—My Siamese can do handstands.'

'—My rabbit can do back-flips.'

'—My cockatiel *adores* Picasso.'

'—My Festive Amazon parrot can sing Neapolitan love songs.'

'My guinea pig likes *classical* music,' said Bill from Totter-

idge on Line Four. 'So I put Classic F.M. on for her. A nice
bit of Vivaldi—that's what she likes.'

'Vivaldi?' said Anita from Stoke Newington, sniffily. '*My*
guinea pig likes Mozart.'

'My guinea pig likes Schoenberg,' said Malcolm from
Weybridge. 'The *late* stuff.'

'Well, *my* guinea pig likes Harrison Birtwistle,' said Roger
from Hanwell on Line Five. 'He's been to the Festival Hall.'

'Just time for *one* more call,' said Minty as she surveyed
the flashing lights on her desk. And the subject is…oh, here's
something a bit different—llamas. I didn't actually know that
people kept llamas as pets.'

'Oh they do,' said my mother on Line One. 'And I just
thought your listeners might like to know the therapeu-
tic benefits of spending time with these *lovely* creatures. I
run llama treks in Sussex every weekend—you'll find them
at Llamatreks.com—but I also offer llama psychotherapy
days during the week. So if any of your listeners are feeling stressed or depressed they *might* like to consider "Llama
Karma"—it's the land equivalent of swimming with dol-
phins.' I pushed a note across the table. *It's my mother—sorry.*

'Well, that sounds great,' Minty said.

'Oh it is. Llamas work wonders on the human psyche,'
she went on, unstoppably, as I rolled my eyes. 'For example, I had one client today who arrived feeling extremely
stressed and exhausted, and all I can say is, he seemed a *different* person by the end of the day.' *Ah.*

'Well, thank you for that,' said Minty.

'The phone number is 01473 289340.'

'Thank you.'

'That's 01473 289340. And do leave a message on the answerphone if I'm not there.'

'*Thank* you,' Minty repeated with polite emphasis. 'And

that concludes tonight's phone-in. So thanks for all your calls, and many thanks to Miranda Sweet for joining us; and you can contact her direct via her website, PerfectPets.com.

'Thanks, Mum,' I said irritably on the mobile, as I went home in the taxi. 'Nice one.'

'Well, you sprang a surprise on *me* today, Miranda, so I thought I'd spring one on you. And, as I say, I need national publicity at the moment.'

'How did you know I was on air?'

'Because a friend of mine rang me and told me it had just started.'

'Fair enough—so how did it go with Dad?'

'How did it go with your father?' she echoed. I heard her draw the air through her teeth, and braced myself. 'Well, actually, it was...*fine*. I was *very* annoyed with you to begin with, naturally, but then I realized I'd banked the cheque, so I wasn't in a position to turn him away. And as it turned out he was quite...' she made a funny little singing noise as she groped for the appropriate term. '*Interesting*.'

'So what did you do with him?'

'I just treated him like any client. He groomed the llamas and fed them—he was *very* taken with them, I must say. And he and Sancho got on rather well, so, yes, as it turned out, it was really quite...reasonable.'

'And how long did he stay?'

'Until half past three, then he had to go back to work. I went and had a look at the club, actually.'

'You did *what*?'

'I went and had a look at the golf club.'

I felt my jaw slacken. 'But you *hate* golf, Mum. You *loathe* it. You always have. You said that it's "not so much a sport, as an insult to lawns".'

'Did I...?'

'You said that they should all be converted to public parks.'

'Oh, well...'

'You have a tee shirt which reads "I Hate Golf".'

'Hmm. That's true. But I'm allowed to change my mind. I actually think your father's golf club has tremendous potential, so I *really* hope it works out.'

'How the hell did you manage to charm Mum like that?' I asked Dad, ten minutes later.

'It was quite easy,' he replied. 'She was quite nasty to begin with—the *look* on her face when she opened the door! But she knew she couldn't get out of it, so she took me to the barn, and I did as you advised and lavished praise on the llamas. They *are* sweet things, I must say. So I groomed them, and talked to her about them, and then, I don't know, she just began to calm down and we...talked—about all *sorts* of things. I finally apologized to her for not being a great husband—and that seemed to cut *some* ice—and I just asked if we couldn't be friends. Then I told her about my difficulties at the club and how worried I am, and well...'

'What?'

'She was surprisingly sympathetic.'

'I know. She said she even went to see it.'

'She did. We had a very interesting conversation about the club, actually. *Very* interesting.'

And before I could ask him what he meant, I heard a 'Call Waiting' beep in my ear—it was Daisy—so Dad said he'd call me another time.

'Tonight's self-defence class was the *best* yet!' Daisy gushed. 'I had to throw Marcus—and I managed it. He was *so* impressed,' she added with a laugh. 'We also learned how to do a shin kick and a really lethal heel stamp. That's another thing you can do, if someone grabs you from behind, you just stamp on their foot, really hard.'

'Sounds like a laugh a minute.'

'Oh it was.' I told Daisy about the strange conversation I'd just had with my parents. 'But you must be pleased,' she said.

'I suppose I am—but I'm also *confused*. Why on earth would my mother want to go and see my Dad's *golf club*?'

'I don't know. Do you think she…'

'What?'

'Well, fancied him again?'

'Unlikely.'

'But she must have been in love with him once. And she's single again now, and she hadn't seen him for years, and your dad's a good-looking man. So maybe a little *flicker* of something was rekindled…'

'I don't believe it. Why would she suddenly feel like that, having done nothing but bitch about him for the past two decades? I really *don't* get it, Daisy.'

'Well, I wouldn't complain. You've effected a degree of parental harmony you never thought possible.'

'That does seem to be the case. Anyway, how's everything else going?' I asked. 'Are you ready for Nigel's party?'

'I suppose so. I'm just going through the RSVP's. Are you bringing David?'

My heart did a bungee jump. 'Yes. I am.'

'Good. I'll put him down on the list. There'll be about fifty of us. Alan and Jon want everyone to be there by seven thirty, latest, so Nigel doesn't spot us all going in.'

'Which bit of the zoo do we make for?'

'They haven't told me that. They just said to tell everyone to follow the signs. Then Nigel and I will turn up in a taxi just after eight, by which time the signs will have gone. We'll be shown where to go by the security guy, who's pretending to be a keeper.'

'So it's an elaborate subterfuge.'

'It is.'

'And what does Nigel *think* he's doing on Saturday.'

'He thinks we're going to a firework concert at Kenwood, followed by dinner in Hampstead. He's in for a bit of a shock.'

On Saturday evening, David came to the Mews at a quarter to seven, to pick me up. He kissed me, and the interest between us crackled like static.

'Hi. Can I kiss you again?' he asked. I nodded. I felt his arms go round my waist and his lips press against mine. 'What a nice way to start the evening,' he murmured as he rocked me from side to side. I could smell the cologne on his neck. 'So we're going to the zoo, are we?'

'We are. But I've just got to wrap Nigel's present, could you...put your finger...there.' I bit off a piece of Sellotape. 'And here...that's it.' Then I got out the card. 'Do you want to sign it too?'

'I've never met the guy, but why not?' He scribbled his signature, next to mine. *Miranda and David.* Seeing our names linked like that, made me feel suddenly, unaccountably happy, as though I had just been given good news.

'This is nice,' David said as we strolled down the road, hand in hand. As we crossed over the canal and entered Regent's Park, I saw a poster for the Open Air Theatre. I thought of Alexander, and realized for the first time that, despite my anger, I felt strangely grateful for what he'd done. For if he hadn't abandoned me that night, I wouldn't be here, now, with David—and I'd wanted to find David for half of my life.

'What are you thinking?'

'Oh, just how glad I am that I've met you.'

He squeezed my hand. 'I'm very glad too. It was Fate, I guess.' *No, it wasn't, it wasn't.* 'I feel we were meant to meet.' *We were.* 'Anyway, tell me who'll be there tonight?' I gave him the background about Nigel and Daisy.

'Five and a half years? That's quite a while.'

'It is. Daisy's dying to get married. She's fed up with waiting.'

'But does she love him?'

'I think she does.'

'You only think so?'

'Well, she's been with him a long time, and she's very used to him.'

'Is that real love?'

'Well, many people get married for less. And I can understand her not wanting to start all over again with someone new, after so long. She'd like to settle down. And Nigel's a bit stodgy, but he's basically *fine…*'

'And do *you* like him?'

'I do, but—'

'But what?'

'He's very selfish. He exploits the fact that she's never forced him to make a commitment because she's afraid of bringing things to the crunch.'

We crossed over to the Inner Circle, and saw smartly dressed people drifting in knots towards the zoo's side entrance, Albert Gate.

'Just follow the signs round to your right,' a member of staff instructed us as he ticked off our names. And sure enough there were large notices, with balloons tied to them, saying *Nigel's 40th—This Way.* We passed a cage with several huge, blue, hyacinth macaws, then the gibbon enclosure, and the Diana monkeys. Near the main entrance, now locked for the evening, we saw the last sign. A large arrow, with a yellow balloon tied to it, was pointing towards the Reptile House.

I let out a snort of surprise. 'It's in the *Reptile House?!*'

'Poor guy,' said David with a laugh. 'Is this Daisy's way of punishing him?'

'No—she had nothing to do with it; it was all arranged by Nigel's friends, Alan and Jon.'

'I see—so it's a blokey joke, then.'

'I guess so.'

The other guests were all grinning at the choice of venue as they went in. I recognized Nigel's mother, and his brother, and some of the people who'd been at the barbecue, including his sharp-faced colleague, Mary, whom I ignored.

Alan, the criminal barrister, greeted us. 'Please make your way *right* to the back of the room there, and stand behind the central display.'

We passed the illuminated tanks, peering briefly at the Chinese alligators and the turtles and the puff-adders and rattlesnakes; then we huddled together by the giant monitor lizard, whispering like conspirators.

'—He's going to be *so* surprised.'

'—Do you think they feed the snakes live animals?'

'—Don't you think he'll be cross?'

'—I'm sure I'm going to get the giggles.'

'—I know *I* would be.'

'—I saw a black mamba once.'

'Nigel will be here in five minutes,' Alan said. 'But instead of jumping out at him, and shouting "Surprise!", I'd like us all to drift out, casually, in twos and threes, as if it's all perfectly normal. It'll confuse the hell out of him.' Suddenly his mobile phone rang. 'Are they? Okay. I'll tell them. They're coming, everyone, so could you all please keep *very* quiet.'

We smiled at each other in the semi-darkness as the tension built. I looked at the giant monitor, swaggering slowly across its pen, its elbows out, its forked tongue flicking lazily. Then we heard steps, then the creak of the door.

'Daisy, I just don't *get* it,' I heard Nigel say. His voice echoed across the stone floor. 'Why couldn't we come here tomorrow? We'll be late for the concert.'

'It's only a *little* detour,' I heard her reply. 'I just wanted to see the, um…blunt-nosed viper. And look, there's a poisonous tree frog, Nige. Ooh, and look at this green mamba, it says here it should be "treated with caution".'

'I'm sure that's right. But the concert is starting *now*.'

'Oh, it won't matter if we're a bit late.'

'But I don't want to miss the Beethoven.'

Now, from our hiding place, I saw Alan step forward with his wife, Jane, then a few seconds later, Nigel's younger brother, Jack. We heard their footsteps tapping across the floor.

'Have you seen this spitting cobra, Nigel?' I heard Daisy ask. 'And there's a *really* nice tortoise over here.'

'*Alan*…?' I heard Nigel suddenly say. 'What the—?' He emitted an odd noise, like a cross between a laugh and a hiccup. 'And *Jane*! What the hell are *you* two doing here?'

'We just came to wish you a Happy Birthday, Nigel,' Alan replied.

'Jack!' I heard Nigel exclaim now. 'What are *you*—? Christine? *Jon*?' And now we were all drifting out from our hiding places in twos and threes. 'Edward? Mary! *Mum*?'

'Happy Birthday, darling,' said Nigel's mother.

'*Miranda*? What the—?' Nigel's expression was one of total stupefaction.

'Happy Birthday,' I smiled. 'This is David.'

'Happy Birthday, Nigel.'

'HAPPY *BIRTHDAY!*' we all said.

Nigel looked at Daisy, then rolled his eyes, then laughed again and shook his head. 'So *that's* why we're not going to Kenwood,' he grinned. Daisy nodded. 'Well—what can I say? Good *Lord!*'

'Well, it's not every day that you turn forty, Nigel,' said Alan. 'So the general view was that you ought to celebrate it.'

'It's like *This Is Your Life!*'

And now aproned waiters came through the doors, bearing trays of champagne and plates of canapés, and the party began. Nigel's face was still a mask of shocked amusement as he greeted his guests. 'I can't *believe* it,' he said, over and over. 'I just can't believe it.' Soon the building was echoing with conversation and laughter.

'—Have you seen that anaconda—it must be twenty foot long.'

'—And the rest!'

'—Weren't you at school with Nige?'

'—There's a snake over there which produces enough venom to kill fifty thousand mice.'

'—That's right.'

'—Wow! How many humans is *that?*'

Then we all went outside and stood in the low, slanting sunshine, by the scarlet ibis enclosure, listening to the distant whoops of the gibbons and the hoots and shrieks of the chimpanzees. Alan was explaining the choice of venue to Nigel.

'We actually wanted the Lion Terrace, but it was already booked for another party. Plus, it wouldn't have been possible to hide everyone there, so that's why we went for the Reptile House.'

'I'm glad *that's* the reason,' Nigel laughed, with a large sip of champagne. 'I was worried! And how long have you been planning this?'

'Just under three weeks. Daisy drew up the list.' Daisy smiled.

'Well, it's…amazing,' said Nigel, surveying the throng. 'It's just…amazing,' he repeated wonderingly. He ran his hand through his thinning hair. 'What a *tremendous* surprise.' He finished his champagne, and then took a fresh glass. Indeed, the drink was really flowing, I noticed, as I introduced Daisy to David.

'It's *so* nice to meet you,' she said. 'I've heard such a lot about you.' *Much more than you'd like.* 'All nice things, of course!'

David smiled. 'It's good to meet you too, Daisy. I've brought my tiny camera with me,' he said. 'Would you like me to go round and take a few shots?'

'You don't have to do that,' she said. 'You're off duty.'

'I don't mind at all.'

'Well, that would be wonderful,' she said. 'But let me take one of you and Miranda first.' David handed her the camera, then slid his arm around my waist. I leaned into him. 'You look perfect together,' Daisy called out. 'And another one.' David gave my cheek an extravagant kiss.

'That's lovely!' Daisy giggled. Then she handed the camera back. 'He's *very* attractive,' she whispered, as David wandered into the crowd. 'Plus he's obviously *nuts* about you.'

'Do you really think so?'

'God, yes. You can see it. The way he looks at you. So hang *on* to him, Miranda.'

'I will—if I *can.' God knows, I want to.*

As I followed David, I passed Mary.

'Oh yes, the *eternal* bachelor,' I heard her say wearily. 'But very sweet. Oh, no, *I* was *never* interested in him.' I smiled to myself. 'Goodness me—*no*. Not my type.'

I watched David snapping away. He was so inconspicuous that no one realized that he was even doing it. He moved amongst the throng, casually framing and firing, then moving on without being noticed. His shots were slanting, oblique. The detachment probably suited him, psychologically, I realized. It was as though he needed to filter people through his viewfinder first.

'I just wanted to get them done while the light holds,' he said, as I caught up with him.

'Shall I get you another glass of champagne?'

'Yes please.'

As I made my way over to the nearest waiter, I heard Nigel's fellow bonsai-fanciers admiring the eucalyptus tree.

'—It would look great if it was ten inches tall, wouldn't it?'

'—Mm. But eucalypts are *very* tricky.'

'—But they're so rewarding.'

'—You have to keep them cold to discourage new growth.'

As I took a glass of champagne for David, I noticed Nigel downing his in two gulps. He doesn't usually drink much, so I guessed it was the emotion of the occasion. At the same time, I thought Daisy look strained.

'It's a great party,' I whispered. 'Are you enjoying it?'

'Oh…yes. It's quite a success.' In the distance we could hear the gentle strains of a string quartet. 'That must be the other party,' she said. 'We could have had music, but we decided against it.'

'And what are you doing tomorrow?'

'Erm…I'm going microlighting.'

'Again?'

'Yes. You see, I loved it last week. I just…*loved* it.'

'But don't you want to do something with Nigel?'

She shrugged. 'Well, I *would* have done. But he's got to work. You know how it is with Nige.' I glanced at him. 'He never stops. Especially at the moment.'

'At least he's having a good time tonight.'

'That's true—but he's drinking too much.'

I looked at him. He did look slightly red in the face. 'Well…if he can't get a bit pissed on his fortieth, when can he, Daisy…?'

'I'm going to keep quiet about the M question by the way,' she murmured.

'*Are* you?'

'Yes.'

'Why?'

She shrugged. 'I…don't know. I've just decided—*que sera, sera.*'

Suddenly, David reappeared. 'I think I've got everyone, Daisy. I'll e-mail them to Miranda and she can send them on to you. Are we allowed to wander round the zoo, by the way?'

'I don't think we can go very far. Alan said they want us to stay in this area because they don't want us unsettling the animals. Oh, I've just got to have a word with the waiter—will you excuse me?'

So David and I went for a short walk. And we were just looking at the sloth bears on Bear Mountain when we heard rapid footsteps behind us.

'Where's the *bloody* exit?' demanded a familiar voice. I turned and there was Lily, looking elegant but indignant. 'How the *hell* do you get *out* of here?'

'Lily?'

'Miranda!'

'Hi. You're not at this party, are you?'

'No. I've just been to the one at the Lion Terrace—Nancy de Nobriga's bash—and I got lost trying to find my way out.'

'Were the lions fun?'

'No—they were asleep—lazy buggers—but we did spot the missing lynx.' Now she suddenly noticed David and did a double take. 'D.J. White? Good God!'

'Hello, Lily.'

'What are *you* doing here?'

'Well, I'm here with…' He nodded at me, and Lily's elegantly plucked eyebrows rose half an inch up her high, domed forehead.

'I *see*,' she said with an insinuating smirk. 'So you're… "walking out together", are you?'

'You could say that,' David smiled.

'Well *you're* a sly one, Miranda,' Lily snorted. 'I had *no* idea. So did you know each other before…?'

'No,' I replied. 'We didn't.'

'We met through you, actually,' David said.

'You *did*?'

'Yes.' My pulse started to race. 'Because if you hadn't commissioned me to take Miranda's photograph, I would never have met her.'

'Of course. I remember that now,' said Lily.

I felt goose-bumps suddenly stipple my arms.

'I don't know why you thought of *me* to do that particular job,' David went on. 'But I'm very glad you did.'

'Oh, but it wasn't *my* idea!' Lily exclaimed.

'What do you mean?'

'It was Miranda's.'

I felt as though I'd fallen down a mineshaft.

'*Miranda's?*' David repeated. He looked at me, dumb-founded.

'Yes,' said Lily. '*She* suggested you—didn't you, Miranda?—

and I must say it was a *brilliant* idea. Anyway, I can't stand here gossiping. I've got two other parties to get to, and my driver's waiting, so could you please tell me how to get *out*?' David pointed her in the right direction, then she blew us a kiss and was gone.

'You *asked* Lily to commission me?' David said. His brow was corrugated in puzzlement.

'Yes,' I said quietly. 'That's right.'

'But *why*? You didn't know anything about me, Miranda.' *Oh yes I did.* 'I don't understand.'

'Because…I saw that photo you did…the one on the front of the *Guardian G2*.' The lines on David's forehead began to clear. 'And…I thought it was…so good. And I was with Lily at the time and she was wondering who to get to take the pictures—and so,' I shrugged, 'I suggested *you*.'

David was shaking his head in bewilderment. Then he smiled. 'So you actually *wanted* to meet me?'

Oh yes. 'Yes. I did.'

'Because you liked my work?'

'That's…right.'

'So you *engineered* it all?' I nodded. He smiled, and then laughed. 'Well, you *are* a dark horse. But why didn't you tell me before?'

I looked away. 'I don't really know.'

'Well…I feel…quite flattered. So you specifically wanted *me* to take your photograph?'

I nodded. 'And…Lily thought it was a good idea, and so she called you, and you came to my house that day and took my picture.'

David held his breath for a moment, then exhaled with a sudden burst of laughter. 'You are *funny*, Miss Behaviour.' He had clearly believed me. My anxiety flooded away. 'Is *that* why you asked me to stay for a beer that evening?'

No, that's not the reason. 'Yes,' I replied quietly. 'That's right.'

'You are an *intriguing* woman, Miranda Sweet.' *Yes, I am. I'm intriguing. It makes me feel awful.* 'There are times when I just don't know what to make of you,' he said. 'I— Oh, what's happening now?'

Alan had clapped his hands. 'Ladies and gentlemen! Can I have your attention please...*please*, everyone?' The babble of voices dipped to silence, then, out of the gathering darkness, a waitress stepped forward, bearing a huge, flaming cake.

'*Happy Birthday to you,*' Alan sang.

'*Happy Birthday to you,*' we all joined in.

'*Happy Birthday dear Nig-el.*'

'*Happy Birthday TO YOU!!!*'

Everyone applauded as Nigel walked, or rather staggered, over to the cake and blew on it noisily.

'—Careful Nige!'

'—Do it in one!'

'—Someone stand by with a fire-blanket!'

'—Oh good man!' We all clapped.

'—Speech!'

'—*Speeeeeech!*'

'Come on, Nigel. Give us a few words.'

Nigel heaved a tipsy sigh, then ran his left hand through his hair.

'Well...' he began. Even in the semi-dark you could see that his face was quite red. 'What c'n I say? What c'n I *say?* 'Cept that I'm 'slutely 'ver*whelmed.*'

'And over the limit!' Jon called out.

'Yes,' Nigel giggled. He adjusted his glasses which were slightly awry. 'Prob'ly am. But then it's been...*quite* an evening. And...well,' he was blinking slowly, in the way people do when they've overdone it. 'I'd just like...t'thank...Alan 'n' Jon 'n' D'sy…f'ranging t'all. Quite 'mazing. And I'd like t'thank all 'f *you*…f'r'elping me cel'brate. I had no *'dea*…be spending the evening like this,' he went on. 'No *'dea 't'all*. I thought…'s going to a concert wi' D'sy f'lowed by…*dinner*. 'N to be honest…' He seemed to hesitate. His eyes raked the crowd. 'To be honest, *I'd* planned…L'il s'prise for *her*. D'sy— where *are* you?' He peered at us all now, as though he was having trouble focussing.

'She's over there, you moron!' said Jon.

'Oh. Y's. Thanks. *There* y'are.' He looked at Daisy, standing next to me, then heaved another drunken sigh. 'I wanted t'give you something, you see. Here.' He jabbed his left hand into his pocket, missing it twice; but at the third try he pulled out a small red box. 'I just wondered, D'sy, whether…' Nigel was swaying slightly now. 'Whether…y'd do me…honour… ver' *great* honour…'coming…*wife*?'

'*What*?' she whispered.

Nigel took a couple of steps towards her, then opened the box. He did it slightly too forcefully, and suddenly something gold and sparkling flew into the air, then fell to the ground with a quiet 'chink'.

'Oh buggeration.'

Nigel dropped to one knee, groped for it with his left hand, then held it up to Daisy between thumb and forefinger, like a dainty titbit. It was a large sapphire, flanked by two baguette diamonds. Daisy gazed at it as though transfixed.

'…'d you do me…honour…*wife*?' Nigel mumbled again.

'You want me to *marry* you?' she said softly, as though she had never entertained the idea. She looked genuinely amazed—and at the same time, slightly appalled. I saw her glance at the assembled guests. We were all motionless. Then she looked at Nigel again.

'Y's,' Nigel replied. 'I *do*.'

'Oh, *God*,' said Daisy quietly. Nigel grabbed her hand—more to steady himself than anything else, it seemed to me—and pushed the ring onto her finger. Then someone started clapping, and someone else joined in, and now, suddenly, we were all applauding.

'He's *done* it!' Alan exclaimed, as Nigel got clumsily to his feet and brushed the dust off his knees. 'He's actually, finally done it! Let's raise our glasses, everyone—not just to Nigel's fortieth—but to his engagement to Daisy! I give you Nigel and Daisy.'

'*Nigel and Daisy!*'

I looked at her face. It was streaming with tears.

—— CHAPTER 11 ——

'I guess it was the shock,' I said to Daisy when she phoned me the next morning.

'Yes,' she croaked. 'It was the shock.'

'You didn't expect it, did you?'

'You can say *that* again! The weird thing is that I'd decided to wait a bit longer before confronting him about it—I told you. I was somehow…less bothered than I had been before.'

'But that's *why* it happened. When we want something very intensely, then we often don't get it, and it's only when we let up that we *do*.'

'How *ironic*,' she said quietly.

'Sorry?'

'The timing.'

'What do you mean?'

There was a funny little silence. 'I mean…the moment I become more relaxed about it, he finally *proposes*.' She sounded slightly exasperated, irritated almost.

'But it's *wonderful*,' I said. There was another odd silence. 'Isn't it?'

'Yes,' she said faintly. 'I guess.'

'You do feel happy? Don't you?' I heard her inhale.

'I think so. Or rather, yes, of *course* I do. I mean—Christ—

I've finally got what I *want*; or what I… But…at the same time…' Her voice trailed away. 'I don't…*know*. I don't know *what* I feel,' she added dismally.

'That's because your emotions are very mixed up. It's not surprising—getting engaged is a major thing.'

'No, it's not just that.'

'Then it must be the anti-climax.'

'It's not.'

'Then what's the problem? You should be delirious with joy.'

'I *know* I should be.'

'But why aren't you?'

I heard her draw in her breath. 'Because…' she began. 'Because…' There was a pregnant pause which seemed to hum and throb. 'Because…'

'Of the way he did it?' I suggested. There was a tiny pause. 'Is that the reason?'

'*Ye-es*,' she replied.

'Because he was drunk?'

'That's…right. Because he was drunk. *That's* why I'm feeling like this. Because it was so…disappointing. He proposed to me, drunk as a lord, in front of all those *people*. It should have been a private, intimate thing.'

'Well, the fact that he had the ring with him suggests that he was going to do it in the restaurant, which *would* have been private and intimate, but that events overtook him.'

'Yes,' she sighed. 'That's what he said.'

'That's probably *why* he got drunk,' I went on. 'The stress of it all.'

'No doubt. He threw up twice on the way home. So if I sound a bit flat it's because…my proposal wasn't quite as romantic as I'd hoped.'

'Well, at least he's done it, Daisy. And that's the main thing, because Nigel's the one you want.'

'I guess so,' she said flatly. 'I mean…yes. Yes… Of course he is.'

'And the ring's *lovely*.'

'It is.'

'And you'll be able to wear the dress.'

This seemed to buoy her momentarily. 'Yes. I'll be able to wear the dress. Although…Nigel's talking about a December wedding. Before he went into the office this morning he looked in his diary and suggested the twentieth of December.'

'Never mind, you can wear a wrap, or a gold pashmina, or have a matching jacket made.'

'That's not what I mean.'

'Then what's the problem, Daisy? I don't understand.'

'Well, don't you think December's a little bit…soon?'

'It's nerves,' I said to David later that day, as we did a postmortem on the party. We'd gone to my local vegetarian restaurant, Manna, for lunch. 'For the past three years Daisy's been gagging for Nigel to propose—as though her whole happiness depended on it—and now he's finally done it, she seems upset. It's the size of the commitment,' I said as I speared the last of my pumpkin gnocchi. 'It's suddenly hit her. She'll be absolutely *fine* in a few days.'

'But didn't you notice, Miranda?'

'Notice what?'

'What she said when Nigel asked her?'

'What she said when Nigel asked her?' I echoed. 'Well, I don't remember her saying anything.'

He put down his fork. '*Precisely*.'

'What do you mean?'

'What I mean *is*—she didn't actually say "yes".'

I looked at him. 'Didn't she?'

He shook his head. 'Nope.'

I cast my mind back. '*Oh*. You're *right*…I guess that was shock. Plus, it must have been hard for her to observe the usual formalities in that situation.'

David shrugged. 'Maybe.'

'*Plus* she was embarrassed because he was drunk. I've never ever *seen* Nigel drunk before.'

'So what are they doing today?' he asked, as the waiter cleared our plates.

'Daisy's gone microlighting.'

'With Nigel?'

'You must be joking. He'd never do anything like that. He's gone into the office.'

'That's a pretty strange way for a newly engaged couple to spend Sunday.'

'I know—but it's normal for them. Their interests have always…diverged.'

'I've e-mailed you the photos for you to send Daisy, by the way. There are some good ones there.'

'Thanks. She'll be pleased.'

'It was *funny* seeing Lily, wasn't it?' David went on with a grin, as I called for the bill. He shook his head. 'I can't get over that. I kept thinking about it last night, when I got home. So *that's* why you were so odd with me when we first met. Because you'd wanted to meet me all along…' *I've wanted to meet you for sixteen years.*

'Yes,' I said carefully. 'That's right. If I'd known how lovely you are, David, I'd have wanted to meet you even more. It was just that I…really liked that photo of yours in the *Guardian*. So, I suggested you to Lily.'

'I'm very glad that you did. Otherwise we wouldn't be

sitting here now, would we?' I felt his bare foot caress my ankle.

'I don't suppose we would.'

'And we wouldn't be going away next weekend.'

'That's true.'

'It'll be wonderful,' he said as we pushed back our chairs. 'One of my nicer commissions.'

'I'm looking forward to it,' I said, as he took my hand. I was also dreading it. Because David would learn the truth at last. I knew this couldn't go on any longer. My heart began to race. By this time next week, he'd know...

'I'd better go,' he said as we stepped outside into the sunshine.

'What time's your Eurostar?'

'Three thirty. I've got forty-five minutes to get to Waterloo and check in.' He kissed me, and a cloud of butterflies took flight in my stomach. 'I'll call you when I arrive. See you, Miss Behaviour.' He set off towards the tube, then turned and waved.

'See you,' I said.

As I walked up Regents Park Road I saw Natalie sitting outside the café next to the Mews, talking on her mobile. So she wasn't with Marcus this afternoon. For some reason, this made me feel glad. Not that Marcus's love life was any of my concern, but she was *such* a drip. She probably didn't even kiss him in case she got germs.

'And he brought me some *strawberries*, Mummy,' I heard her say in her soft, but somehow penetrating voice. 'Yes... *terrible* rash. I know. Absolutely *clueless*...Tonight. He wanted to pick me up at eight, but I *insisted* on seven...I told him that I *have* to be in bed by ten otherwise I just don't *function* well. Yes, I think it *could* be M.E.' I mentally renamed her Gnatalie because she whined so much. Poor Marcus, I thought, as I turned into the Mews.

When I got back into the house I downloaded David's photos and printed them off to give to Daisy. The first two were the ones she'd taken of David and me. I was struck by how happy we looked. We looked like a proper couple. If I kept quiet, we could probably become one. No one was *making* me tell him the truth.

'It's so tempting *not* to,' I confided in Herman. He turned his worried little face to me, eyebrows twitching. 'But I couldn't live with myself.' Herman climbed onto his beanbag with an air of tragic resignation.

As I waited for the photos to print, I opened the main section of the *Sunday Telegraph*. In the diary section on the back was a photo of Alexander, captioned *Hollywood Ahoy!* I skimmed through it, my stomach churning.

Before the credits had even rolled on the first episode of Land Ahoy!, *Alexander Darke had caught the attention of Tinseltown's top casting agents. Next month he flies to Los Angeles for screen tests…Reese Witherspoon is said to be keen to work with him on her new film…Darke says he's more than happy to be swapping Archway for Beverly Hills.*

'Good luck to him,' Daisy said later. She'd turned up at six, unexpectedly, explaining that her microlighting friend lived locally and had dropped her off at Chalk Farm. 'I just thought it would be nice to pop in for a few minutes,' she explained with a rather tense smile, which I put down to post-engagement stress. 'As I was so near.' She glanced at the paper again, then tossed it to one side. 'Good luck to Alexander,' she repeated disdainfully. 'Hollywood can keep him. Anyway, you don't care.'

'No, I don't. Or at least—not much. I don't suppose I'll

ever see him again. That's weird, isn't it?' I went on. 'You
can be engaged one day, and strangers the next… Anyway,
how was the microlighting?' A look of rapture, combined,
oddly, with a kind of regret, passed across Daisy's face.

'Oh, it was…wonderful,' she said, almost sadly. 'It's one of
the best things I've *ever* done. It gives you such a *high*, Miranda—no irony intended. A feeling of euphoria. There you
are, a thousand feet up, with the fields and hills curving away
beneath you, chatting away to your co-pilot. It's *so* exciting,
and it's also quite…intimate, in a funny sort of way.'

'What do you talk about?'

'Ooh, all *sorts* of things,' she replied. 'Life. Love. The Uni-
verse. Abseiling. Rock-climbing,' she went on dreamily.
'Hang-gliding. Sky-diving. Paragliding,' she sighed. 'Scuba-
diving…' She seemed suddenly to collect herself. 'All…sorts
of things.'

'And who is it you do this with?'

'Oh…' A red flush had stained her throat. 'This, erm…
chap. His name's…Mar-*tin*. And he's just bought a half share
in a microlight, and his girlfriend's not interested, so…he
asked me if I'd like to go again as it's more fun with two.
And as Nigel was working all day, *again*, I said yes.' I suddenly noticed her left hand.

'Christ! You haven't lost your engagement ring, have you?'

'What? Oh. No. *No.* I didn't put it on this morning. I, um,
didn't want to lose it. And in any case, it's a bit big,' she said.
'I need to have it sized.'

'And how are you feeling?'

'I'm fine,' she replied absently.

'Has last night sunk in now?'

'Yes it has,' she sighed. 'I'm…fine,' she insisted. 'I'm…
engaged,' she went on, slightly bleakly. 'I'm finally…*engaged*,
Miranda.'

'Well, thank God you *are*. And it's better that he finally did it off his own bat like that, without you having to bludgeon him into it.'

There was silence, except for the hum of my hard drive. 'It's funny, isn't it?' Daisy said quietly. 'I was so terrified of bringing things to a head, but now I've got the answer I've always wanted, I'm not quite sure how I *feel*.' I registered that there were short white hairs on her navy jumper. 'I wonder *why* he's done it?' she mused. She gazed out of the window.

'*Why*? Because he loves you, that's why.'

'Do you really think so?'

'I do. Nigel's not a *very* demonstrative person...' I went on.

'You can say that again.'

'But I'm sure he's sincere.' Daisy shrugged. 'And it'll be fun organizing your own wedding at last. I mean, how many have you organized for other women?'

'I don't know—fifty or sixty—maybe more.'

'Well, now it's *your* turn.'

At this she brightened for a moment. 'Yes. Yes. It's my turn.'

'And are you going to put the announcement in the paper?'

This seemed to alarm her. 'Oh. Erm...probably not for a bit, no. I mean, there's no *hurry*, is there?'

'And are you going to have an engagement party?'

'I'm not really...sure. In fact, Miranda—'

'Yes?' Suddenly the phone rang. It was a prospective client. We had a brief chat.

'Sorry about that, Daisy. Where were we? Oh yes, and have you decided which church you'd like?'

'Oh. No. No, I haven't.' This surprised me. I would have thought that anyone capable of buying a wedding dress without a proposal would have planned every other aspect of the hypothetical Big Day.

'Wherever it is, you'll have to book it soon if you want a Saturday. On the other hand, maybe it won't be a problem in December.'

'December?' she repeated. 'I do think that's a bit early. I mean, I'd like to get used to being engaged, before I actually…take the plunge. Till death us do part and all that,' she added anxiously.

'And I guess you'll be moving in with him soon?'

'Oh. Yes. I hadn't thought of that…' The idea seemed to dismay her. 'Moving *in* with him? I'm not sure… Oh God, Miranda…'

'That's why you're like this, Daisy. Because however much you've wanted it emotionally, you know, rationally, that marriage entails a loss of freedom. Hence your ambivalent feelings. Here—' I handed her the sheaf of photos from the night before. She quickly flicked through them, frowning slightly.

'You look *so* happy with David,' she said wistfully. 'You look happier than I do with Nigel.'

'Oh, I don't think that's true.' As she finished with each photo I glanced at it again and I saw that Daisy did look tense and preoccupied, as though something was troubling her. Her smile didn't quite reach her eyes.

'Miranda—' she said.

'Yes?'

'Miranda…' She was staring at me with an intensity which took me aback.

'What is it, Daisy?'

'Well, I just wanted to ask you something, actually, I, er…'

Suddenly the phone rang again. It was David to say he'd got to Paris. 'I'm sorry about that, Daisy, what were you going to say?'

'Well, I just wondered...' She stared at me again. 'I just wondered...'

'Is there something the matter? If there is, you can tell me, Daisy—you know that.'

She seemed to hesitate, then shook her head. 'No. Nothing's the matter.' She heaved a painful sigh. 'I just wondered when you're going to tell David, that's all.'

'Oh.' *She made it sound so wonderfully simple.* 'This weekend. Definitely. I've decided. But I thought I'd told you that.'

'You did. But which day? Saturday, or Sunday?' What an odd question.

'On Sunday,' I replied. 'He's working on Saturday, so Sunday will be easier.'

She nodded. 'Well *I* think he'll be fine. Now that I've actually met him, and seen you with him, I don't think you have to worry. The apprehension of something difficult is always much worse than the thing itself, isn't it?'

'That's true.'

'It's like a difficult test that you've got to pass. So how will you broach it?' she added.

'I'll just sit him down after breakfast, and quietly tell him the whole story.'

'And will you tell him that it was Jimmy?'

'I don't know. I'm hoping to avoid it.'

'But David will want to *know*. And he'll have the right to know, Miranda.'

'I suppose so. But it would make me look vindictive—plus, I don't want to hurt Caroline—and in any case this isn't actually *about* Jimmy—it's about me. My aim is simply to get it off *my* chest. The bigger problem I have is that David will want to know *why* Jimmy did it—and I won't be able to tell him—because I have absolutely *no* idea.'

★ ★ ★

'Welcome to *Question Time*,' said David Dimbleby on Thursday. 'Which this week comes to you, live, from the West Yorkshire Playhouse, Leeds. And our distinguished panellists this week are; the Shadow Secretary of State for Health, Liam Fox, the Independent MP, Martin Bell; the Bishop of London, Richard Charteris; the comedienne, Jenny Eclair; and finally, the Minister of State for Education, James Mulholland, MP. A warm welcome to you all.' A floor manager in headphones held her hands aloft in a mock-clap and we produced a round of obedient applause.

'And our first question is from Mrs Kay Spring, a retired biology teacher.' I saw the microphone arm swing over our heads until it came to rest above Mrs Spring in the row behind.

'Does the panel believe that the Government has badly misjudged public opinion on GM food?' she asked.

'Does the panel believe that the Government has badly misjudged public opinion on GM food,' Dimbleby repeated. He peered over his half-moon glasses at Liam Fox. 'Dr Fox? Will you please give us your views on this.'

As Liam Fox began to hold forth, I stared at Jimmy, sitting on the right-hand side of the desk, hands clasped firmly in front, immaculate in his bespoke suit and yellow silk tie. From time to time he made the odd note, or took a sip of water, or narrowed his eyes in judicious fashion as he gave consideration to Fox's views. I knew that he hadn't spotted me, as I'd made certain to sit behind someone tall. As I glanced at the question card in my trembling hands, I mentally thanked Daisy for ringing her friend, Jo, a researcher, and making sure I got on the show.

'Extreme caution needed…' I heard Liam Fox say. 'Scientific jury still out… Potential hazards yet to be identified…' I saw Jimmy shake his head. Then we clapped Liam Fox and it was the turn of the Bishop, who expressed his disquiet at the idea of 'Frankenstein foods' and 'corporate greed'—as indeed did all the panellists, with minor variations. Then it was Jimmy's turn.

'James,' said David Dimbleby. 'You studied science at university, didn't you?' Jimmy nodded. 'In fact, my notes tell me you got a first-class degree.' Jimmy modestly blushed. 'So what's your view on this?'

'My view is that there is still not one shred of evidence to support the idea that genetically modified foods are harmful,' he began confidently. 'Indeed, opponents of GM, living in the rich West, choose to overlook the many benefits to the developing world that GM presents. Rice implanted with a gene enabling it to be grown in salt water; potatoes given a gene to make them resistant to blight; wheat implanted with a gene to prevent river blindness...' *His Master's Voice*, I remembered from the *Guardian* profile as Jimmy loyally spouted the Government's line. He spoke with passion and moral indignation—as though he believed what he was saying—and maybe he did. But I knew that if the official line had been *hostile* to GM, he would have denounced it with equal zeal.

Jimmy got a respectful round of applause, which prompted in him a slightly sorrowful half-smile, as though it had pained him to have to apprise the dimwits in the audience of these simple, but incontrovertible, facts.

My mouth began to feel dry as the panellists took the next question—should the Congestion Charge be extended to other cities? Then there were questions on prisons, on asylum and crime. There was a question about civil liberties in the face of the terror threat. Then, heart pounding, I knew it was me.

'And our final question is from Miranda Sweet, an animal behaviourist. Where are you, Miranda?' David Dimbleby enquired as he peered into the audience. 'Oh there you are, behind that very tall gentleman in the blue jumper.' I saw the sound engineer coming towards me with the microphone and was aware, behind him, of Jimmy running a nervous finger under his collar. I took a deep breath.

'And your question is about live exports?' Dimbleby began as he glanced at his script. I was aware of the camera closing in on me.

'No,' I said. 'It's not. It *was* going to be, but I'd like to ask another question, if you don't mind.' Dimbleby was frowning, but I wasn't going to be deflected.

'Well, okay, go ahead.'

'I'd like to ask James Mulholland why, in March 1987, as a recent science graduate, he sent a letter-bomb to Derek White, Professor of Biochemistry at Sussex University, causing grievous bodily harm to the Professor's son, David?'

A gasp rippled round the studio, like a Mexican wave. The other panellists were all staring at Jimmy, dumbfounded. Jimmy had gone deathly white.

'Well, this is rather irregular,' said Dimbleby. 'But as we have three minutes left perhaps you *could* try to answer the question, James.'

'Yes, answer the question,' said Jenny Eclair.

'Yes,' said the Bishop. 'We'd all like to know why you did such a terrible thing—if indeed you did do it.'

'Oh, he did!' I called out. 'There's no doubt about that.'

'Then how did he ever become an MP?' someone enquired from three rows in front of me.

'—Yes—how did he become an MP?'

'—What a shocking thing to do!' I heard someone behind me say.

'—Absolutely dreadful!'

'—You wouldn't think it to look at him, would you?'

'—No, he looks so *nice*.'

'Quiet please,' said Dimbleby. 'Please let James answer the question.'

'Well…' Jimmy began. I could see beads of sweat spangling his brow. 'Well, I, er…deny *absolutely* Miss Sweet's outrageous accusation.'

'There's no point denying it!' I yelled. 'Because I'm willing to swear an affidavit that you did it—because I was there at the time—as I'm quite sure you remember, Jimmy.'

'My name is *James*,' he said. 'And this is an entirely uncorroborated allegation. I shall sue you for libel, Miranda!'

'Go on then—you won't win!'

'But we want to know if it's *true*,' said Liam Fox, as he stared at Jimmy.

'We certainly do,' insisted Martin Bell. 'What you did—if true—was a dreadful crime.'

'You can say that again!' I yelled. 'He's got away with it for sixteen years, but he's not going to get away with it *now*. So come on, Jimmy, just answer the question and tell us all why you did it.' In the background I was aware of a bell ringing.

'And I'm afraid that bell brings us to the end of this week's edition of *Question Time*,' said David Dimbleby smoothly. Oddly, the bell was still ringing. Except that it wasn't a bell, I now realized—it was a phone. Why on earth didn't someone pick it up? 'So do join us again at the same time next week, when the programme comes from Swansea. Until then, goodbye.'

The phone was *still* ringing—I couldn't stand it. I reached out my left hand, my head swimming as I surfaced now from my dream. I felt disturbed by it, but also curiously happy. If only I could expose Jimmy like that in real life.

'Hello,' I croaked into the mouthpiece, my mouth as dry as sandpaper.

'Is that Miss Sweet?'

'Yes.'

'Detective Sergeant Cooper here from CID. I'm sorry to ring you so early.' I looked at the clock—it was eight thirty. 'But there's been a development with your case.'

I pushed off the duvet. 'What's happened? Have you caught them?'

'I'm afraid not. But I believe we've found your engagement ring.'

'*Really?*' I swung my legs out of bed. 'Where?'

'In a pawnbroker's in Kilburn.'

'And are you sure it's mine?'

'Quite sure. It's a solitaire diamond, with an eighteen-carat gold band. And inside is the inscription, *Admired Miranda!*'

'Oh yes,' I breathed. 'That's my ring.'

'I'm sure you'll be very pleased to have it back,' he said. 'You can come and collect it whenever you want. Would you like to call in today?'

I released the blind, then stared out of the window. 'No.'

'How about tomorrow, then?'

'No. Not tomorrow either. In fact, I won't be coming at all.'

'I'm sorry?'

'I don't want the ring back.'

'You don't want it back?'

'That's right.'

'Are you quite sure?'

'I am.'

'But it's very valuable, Miss Sweet.'

Not to me. 'I daresay.'

'Well, what should be done with it then?'

'I'd like you to send it to my former fiancé, Alexander Darke. I'll write you a letter authorizing you to do this and confirming his name and address, which I believe you already have from the statement he gave you.'

'Well, all right, Miss Sweet. If you're *sure*.'

'I am sure. But thank you for letting me know.'

I had no wish to see the ring again, with its bitter associations. Alexander could have the inscription erased and sell it—or he could give it to someone else. *Admired Miranda!* I thought bitterly. I'd been anything but admirable. As David was about to find out.

The next two days passed slowly. I had a number of calls from David in between shoots, then on Wednesday was the fifth and final puppy party. I'll miss the group, I thought, as I put round the chairs—they're one of the nicest I've ever had. I left the front door ajar, as I usually do, so that they could just come straight in without knocking, when the phone rang. It was Mum, sounding happier than usual.

'Darling, I'm so thrilled about Daisy's engagement, and I just wanted you to pass on a message to her. I thought she might like to have a llama trek *hen party*—don't you think that would be fun? I've just thought of it.'

'It does sound quite novel.'

'It would be free, of course—I'll do the picnic—all she'd have to provide is the champagne. But I'm thinking about developing it as a commercial idea so will you ask her if she'd like to do a test drive?'

'Okay.'

'Maybe I could get something in *Brides* magazine,' she mused. 'Or even *Harpers and Queen*. By the way, what's the name of that chap you mentioned, at the *Independent on Sunday*?'

'Tim...hang on.' I groped for his card in my desk drawer. 'Tim Charlton. He's working on the diary but he'll point you in the right direction for feature coverage.' I heard her scribble it down.

'And the *other* thing I thought of, on the wedding front, is that Daisy might want to borrow Carlos for the big day. He'd make the most *perfect* usher. Tell her he'll stand outside the church before the service and after, with a garland of flowers round his neck, looking very sweet and nuptial. What do you think of that?'

'Well, it could look lovely, especially as he's white, but—' I felt a sudden breeze on the back of my legs as the door was pushed open, '—Daisy's probably getting married in December, Mum.' I turned and saw Marcus standing there with Twiglet, and waved at them. 'Yes, that's right. So if it's wet, Carlos might end up looking less than pristine. But I'll tell her you suggested it, okay? Anyway, I can't chat now, my puppy party's starting...Yes, all right...hmm...I'll speak to you soon.'

'Sorry about that,' I said to Marcus. He was looking at me in a slightly odd way. 'Are you okay?' I said to him.

'Er, yes. I'm...fine. I'm er...sorry...I didn't mean to eavesdrop just now, but it was difficult not to overhear. Did I...did I hear you say that, erm...Daisy's getting married?'

'Yes. She's just got engaged.'

He nodded slowly, as though he found the news disconcerting, somehow. 'Oh. She didn't tell me that.'

'Well, she didn't know last Thursday,' I explained. 'It only happened on Saturday so she wouldn't have had a chance to mention it yet.'

'On Saturday?' he repeated.

'Yes.' His face expressed a mixture of puzzlement and disappointment. 'So she got engaged on Saturday?'

'Hmm. Saturday night.'

'To, er, Nigel?'

'That's…right. She obviously mentioned him to you.'

'Yes…she did.'

'Anyway, I'm sure she'll tell you herself at the self-defence class. Speaking of which, I won't be coming along again tomorrow, if you don't mind. I'm sorry, but I feel it's a bit silly for me to do the last one when I haven't done the first three. Perhaps you'll do another course,' I went on as I put down the water bowl.

'Yes,' he said absently. 'Maybe. I mean, probably.'

'I'll come to the next one, then. Daisy says the classes are wonderful.'

'Really?' he said.

'Oh yes—she's absolutely adored them.'

This seemed to cheer him momentarily. 'Well…just let me know.'

Then Lily swept in, and Sue and Lola, and by ten past seven we were passing the puppies as usual.

'—It's not quite so easy now, is it?'

'—No, they've *really* grown.'

'—Bentley's doubled in size.'

'—And Roxy's quite a little porker—aren't you, darling?'

'—Don't worry—it's just puppy fat.'

'You've been a wonderful group,' I said at the end. 'I'll miss seeing you here on Wednesday evenings.'

'Well, *we'll* miss coming,' said Phyllis. 'I know Maisie will be very sad, but she's got to go to big school now, haven't you, Maisie?'

'Yes, they've all got to go to *big* school,' everyone said.

'That's right. But we'll have Puppy Olympics on Primrose Hill for them after Christmas, so we'll all catch up again then. But please do knock on the door, any time you're round here.'

'See you, Marcus,' I said as he put Twiglet's lead on. 'Well, I probably *will* see you, won't I?'

He looked at me non-comprehendingly. 'Will you?'

'Yes. Because of your…girlfriend. I'm sure I'll bump into you again round here.'

'Oh. Yes…' he said vaguely. 'That's right.'

Later that night I phoned Daisy and gave her my mother's message about the llama hen party.

'Marcus was a bit strange this evening,' I added.

'In what…way?'

'Well, he overheard me talking to Mum about your wedding, and he was quite…funny about it actually.'

There was an odd little silence. '*Was* he?' she whispered.

'I do like him, but I thought that was odd.'

'Miranda…?'

'Yes.'

'Miranda? I know you're very distracted at the moment, but do you remember when we were talking in my garden about a month ago?'

'Yes.'

'Well, there was something you said to me then which I've been thinking about recently; I've been thinking about it quite a *lot* actually; I just can't get it out of my head…Oh, sorry, Nigel's just arriving. Can't talk. I'll ring you tomorrow.'

But she didn't. She didn't call me after the self-defence class either. And then Friday came and I still hadn't heard. I left a message for her, then packed my weekend bag, my stomach churning and lurching like a tumble-dryer. David was to pick me up at six. By ten past I was beginning to feel slightly anxious. At six fifteen, he phoned.

'This is a real *drag*,' he said. My heart sank and I braced myself. The weekend was cancelled. 'But I can't get my car to start. I've got the horrible feeling it's something electrical. We couldn't go in yours, could we?'

I laughed. 'Of course we can.'

'Great, I'll be with you by seven.'

He turned up at ten past, grinning broadly, and enveloped me in a huge hug. 'Mir-an-da,' he said, drawing out the vowels. 'I love that name. Mir-an-da.' He kissed me, then rocked me in his arms. 'I'm so glad you're coming. We're going to have a great weekend.' *Yes—except for the last bit.* He peered at me. 'Hey, don't look so sad.'

'I'm not sad, David.' *I'm just terribly worried.*

He picked up my bag. 'Come on.'

We headed south, David driving, through Vauxhall, Battersea and Putney, then down the A3. Then we saw the signs to Petworth and Pulborough.

'We'll be there just in time for dinner.'

'And what's the hotel like?' I asked as we saw a sign to Amberley.

'Well…it's a bit old-fashioned.'

'That's okay.' I had visions of a Lutyens-style country house, with mullioned windows and faded chintz. 'I like old-fashioned things.'

'Good, because it's *very* old-fashioned, actually.'

'Is it?'

'Hmm. Extremely.'

'What do you mean?'

'Well—look.'

I stared. Ahead of us now were two crenellated towers flanking a huge portcullis. 'It's a castle?'

'It is. Amberley Castle. It's really a fortified manor—but the battlements are huge.'

Now we were turning in. 'It's amazing.'

'They still lower the portcullis every night.'

'And how old is it?'

'Nine hundred years.' An enormous, striped lawn swept up to the main entrance. On the right was a lake on which, in the deepening dusk, we could make out a pair of black swans.

We parked, took Herman for a short walk, then went through the circular courtyard into the hotel reception, where there were two suits of armour and a display of lethal-looking pikes.

'You're in Arundel, Mr White,' said the concierge, handing him the key, 'and Miss Sweet is next door in Amberley. What time would you like dinner?'

David looked at me. I shrugged. 'In half an hour?'

'Nine thirty? Very good.'

We followed the concierge up the wide wooden staircase, at the top of which were a pair of brass cannons. The bedroom doors were like church doors, and, as the concierge pushed mine open, I felt my eyes widen. Inside was a huge, mahogany four-poster bed, canopied and curtained in maroon velvet.

David let out a low whistle. '*Very* nice,' he said as he put down my bag. He peered into the bathroom. 'Hey, you've got a Jacuzzi here. The lap of luxury,' he added. 'Not that you deserve anything less.'

David's room, next door, was similar, with a huge bed with barley-twist posts, but furnished in duck-egg blue. 'I'm going to have a quick bath—as this is a clean weekend,' he announced. 'I'll knock on your door in twenty minutes.'

As I unpacked my bag, I felt relieved that I'd brought my smartest things. I ran a brush through my hair, put on my white linen dress, with a lilac cashmere cardigan, then tipped a little *Femme* onto my wrists.

At nine twenty-five David knocked on the door. His hair was still wet and he looked gorgeous in his green linen suit and white tee shirt, and he smelt of bubble bath.

'*Very* nice,' he said appreciatively as he stepped inside. He glanced at the table by the window. 'Hey—you've got a chess set. Shall we play after dinner?'

'Okay.'

We went across the landing to the restaurant in the Queens Room. 'The receptionist must have been a bit surprised by us,' he whispered, as we were shown to our table by the huge stone fireplace. An attractive couple arrive together, but sleep in separate rooms. I shouldn't think that happens very often.'

'I don't suppose many of the other guests would believe it,' I whispered as I glanced at the barrelled ceiling.

'Shall we ask them?'

'No.'

'Champagne, Miss Behaviour?'

'That would be wonderful.' As I studied the menu, I flinched. 'David, is your client really picking up the bill for this?' I said softly.

'I'm sorry,' he replied. 'My hearing's not great this evening. I think I've still got water in my ears.'

'I just hope this isn't all on your tab?'

'I didn't catch that.'

'Please will you let me get dinner?'

'I haven't a clue *what* you're saying. It's hopeless.'

'It's lovely here,' I said. 'Thank you for bringing me.'

'Thanks for coming,' he said. 'You didn't have to.'

'I wanted to.'

'Did you?'

I smiled. 'Oh yes.'

After dinner, feeling replete and slightly tipsy, we walked round the grounds with Herman. The moon was so bright that we could see our shadows.

'This is bliss,' I said, as we gazed at the ruined battlements silhouetted against the navy sky. We walked down to the lake, watching the moonlight glinting on the water. Then we returned to my room, and played chess.

'I'll play white,' said David.

'Of course.'

'Are you any good at this?' he asked as he moved his pawn forward two squares.

'No. You'll beat me in about five moves. Strategic thinking has never been my strong point.'

'Hmm, I see what you mean. I really wouldn't get your knight out quite yet, Miranda.'

'No? Okay, then I'll do…this…'

'Yeah… Much better. Hmm…' he said a few moves later. 'You're better than you said you were. But can we finish this tomorrow…?' He stood up. 'Because I must get to bed—I have to be up early.'

'Can I come with you?'

'To bed?' he smiled.

I felt my face heat up. 'No. No, I…'

'Of course you can. In fact, I wish you would.'

'I meant—can I come with you to *work*. Tomorrow morning?'

'If you want, but I'll be leaving at five.'

'That's okay.'

'Really? Well, that would be great. Maybe you could even help me.'

'Of course I will.'

He bent down and kissed me, then he held his face, for a

moment, against mine. I was so attracted to him, I had to resist the urge to to pull him to me. 'Sleep well, Miss Behaviour.'

'I'll try.'

Just before five, David knocked on my door. He was standing there in a white bathrobe with a cup of tea in his hand.

'If you do want to come, I'm setting off in ten minutes.'

'Fine,' I whispered. I brushed my teeth, pulled on my clothes, and put Herman on the lead. Then we loaded David's equipment into the car and sped towards Petworth. Soon we were driving past the walls of the estate.

'They're letting me in a side entrance at five fifteen,' he said.

'And what are you taking?'

'They want one really great shot of the house and park. But it's got to be absolutely top notch as it's for an advertising campaign for the English Tourist Board.'

'How did you get this commission? I didn't think you did landscapes.'

'I don't normally, although I've always loved taking them when I have time. But they originally asked Arnie, and, as he was going to be away, he kindly recommended me. It's all work,' he added. 'It's interesting, plus it's quite well paid, so I was more than happy to say "yes".' We parked by the east gate as the first light began to crack the obsidian of the sky; then we walked through the grounds in the dissolving dark. Ahead of us now was the lake, fringed by willows and thinly shrouded in mist. David skirted it, checking angles, holding his hands up to make an impromptu viewfinder; then he set up the tripod, close to the island.

'This is the spot,' he said as he screwed on the camera. It was large and square.

'Aren't you using your Leica?'

'No, I'm using a Hasselblad for this. You get a bigger negative which gives greater detail and tonal quality. Could you pass me the Polaroid in the bag there? In the middle compartment.'

'This thing?' I held it up.

'That's the one.' I handed it to him, happy to be helpful and involved. 'That's fine,' he said. He slid it onto the back of the camera. 'And have you got a second hand on your watch?'

'I have.'

'Then time this for me, okay?' I heard the deep click of the shutter. Then he slid out the Polaroid and handed it to me. 'Stick that under your armpit, will you?'

'Why?'

'To warm it up—it'll develop quicker. Then peel it off in exactly...two minutes.' I glanced at my watch. 'It's alkali,' he warned, 'so be careful not to burn your hands.'

I did exactly as David asked, then handed it to him. 'Hmm,' he murmured appreciatively, as he appraised it. 'Yes... That'll do it.' He glanced at the sky, then squinted through his light meter. 'We'll start shooting in about ten minutes or so, as magic hour starts.'

'Magic hour?'

'The hour starting just after sunrise, or just before sunset, when the light is at its best. You don't want the sun to be high—you want it to be low and slanting, as that gives depth and texture, and the colours are warm and soft.' As David watched the sky, occasionally reading his meter, or trying out different lenses, I saw how passionate he was about his work, and how focussed, to the exclusion of almost everything else.

'You love this, don't you?' I said quietly.

'Yes,' he replied, without looking at me. 'I do. It's what

I live for. I'm glad you're here to share it,' he added, as he peered into the viewfinder again.

'I'm glad I am too.' And I was. I loved watching him work. I loved the intensity of it. I felt infected by his passion. I found it…yes, romantic. Decidedly. Sexy, even. And now, as the sky began to turn from moonstone to a luminous turquoise, I saw David stiffen with anticipation as the optimum moment approached. As we waited for the light to be perfect, I felt like Bronze Age man waiting for the sun to rise through the arch at Stonehenge. We sat immobile on the springy turf, listening to the geese on the lake, and the trilling of coots. Then we spotted a herd of deer coming over the hill.

'This is it,' David whispered. The light was pale gold by now, and the air so pellucid it seemed to sparkle. 'If I can get them in shot too, this is *it*.' He held up his right hand. 'Keep *very* still,' he mouthed. 'They're coming our way.' And sure enough, they came within fifty yards of us, bending their heads to the water to drink. Suddenly a twig cracked under my foot, and the largest stag lifted its head and looked directly at us for about five seconds. I heard the soft click of the shutter, then again, then again. Then the stag moved slowly away.

David circled his left thumb and index finger. 'Perfect,' he whispered. 'Bloody *perfect*.'

'Thanks for not barking,' I said to Herman.

David spent the next half hour shooting from the same vantage point, sometimes moving the camera forwards or backwards a little; then he set up nearer the house. As he finished a roll, he'd hand it to me; I'd seal and label it, then tuck it into a bag in the special pocket of his holdall. By a quarter past eight, he thought he was done.

'That's…it,' he said. 'What a fantastic morning.' He tucked

the last finished roll into his bag. 'I know there are at least four or five really great shots there. We'll go back to the hotel for breakfast, then I'll do Arundel late this afternoon.'

I thought the early start would have exhausted David, and that, like me, he'd flop. Instead, he seemed energized, and, as we drove back, he talked non-stop about his work—he was on a high.

'The exhilaration you feel when you know everything's combined to produce a great picture,' he said as we approached Amberley. 'There's nothing like it. Edward Weston, an American photographer, calls the art of photography "the climax of emotion", because it's about finding that split second when the light and what you see in the viewfinder and your own artistic instinct all come together to capture one moment in time, one unrepeatable moment, for eternity. That's the essence of photography. And that's the rush I got when that stag looked straight into the lens this morning.'

We had breakfast back at the hotel, then, exhausted, went to our rooms and slept for two hours. I love this, I thought, as I drifted off. I love being with David. Please, please, don't let this stop.

At lunchtime we walked into Amberley and looked at the village church, then wandered round the graveyard for a few minutes, reading the stones. *In memory of Sarah Hunt… Sacred to the memory of Richard Freeman…* And now a particular inscription caught my eye. *In loving memory of William Galpin, departed this life 10th May 1873, also of his beloved wife Alice, died 19th October 1875. United in life for forty-five years, now together to the end of time.* And I was suddenly struck by this morbid—yet strangely comforting—thought, that I'd like to be buried with David. And yet I'd known him for only six weeks.

We went back to the hotel and finished our game of chess,

then, at half past four we went to Arundel. David set up just below the castle.

'I'm using a wide angle lens,' he explained, 'in order to compensate for the slightly giddying perspective. The light's quite nice now,' he added, narrowing his eyes as he looked at the sky. 'There's this lovely pinky-gold quality to it. Can you see?'

'Yes, I can. So have we hit magic hour yet?'

'Almost.' He peered into the viewfinder. 'I'm going to take my time. I want to get it just…right.' He looked at the sky again, then bent his head to the camera once more.

'Okay, here we go.' Suddenly, a flock of crows took flight, and I heard the click of the shutter.

'Yes,' I heard him say as he clicked again. 'Yes…*yes*. God, that was fantastic,' he exclaimed softly. 'The uprush of the birds, all that movement, against the solidity of the stone, and that glossy black against the gold.' He took a whole roll from the same spot, then he unscrewed the camera and we walked down the hill to find another vantage point. I handed him the Polaroid again.

'You're a very good assistant.'

'I enjoy it.'

'Why?'

'It's interesting. And you make me see things I wouldn't have seen before. Like what colour the light is, for example—or the shape of the clouds, or which way the wind's blowing.'

'But there's a lot of hanging about with photography,' he said as he peered into the viewfinder. 'Don't you find that boring?'

'No, I don't. Because I'm hanging around with you.'

He didn't look at me, but I saw him smile.

By now it was seven thirty, and David was satisfied that he'd got enough shots.

'I've taken four rolls, from three different spots. So we'll go back now. What time do you want to eat?'

'I don't know? Eight thirty? I'd like to have a quick bath first.'

'Sure.'

When we got back I filled the Jacuzzi, climbed in, poured in a tiny amount of bubble bath, then pressed the button to start the whirlpool. It was slightly complicated as it was an electronic panel, with icons to illustrate the various functions, but eventually I found the right one. And I was just leaning back into the jets of water, letting them massage my shoulder blades, when I heard my mobile.

'Damn.' I turned off the taps, then padded across the floor and flipped the phone open.

'Miranda!' It was my mother. 'It's about the llamas.'

'I've told Daisy about the hen-party idea, Mum. She's just having a think about it—she'll let you know in a few days.'

'No, I wasn't ringing about that. I just wanted to tell you that I think I might have cracked the boys' problems long term: there's something which, if it takes off, should keep them gainfully employed during the week.'

'And what is it?'

She told me. I rolled my eyes. 'It sounds absolutely *nuts*. Honestly, Mum. Whoever *heard* of such a thing? Llama hen parties are one thing, but that's just ridiculous!'

'No, I think it's a *wonderful* idea. And so, I may say, does your father, and—ooh, what's that funny noise in the background?' she suddenly asked.

'Oh, it's just the Jacuzzi.'

'But you haven't *got* a Jacuzzi.'

'I know, but I'm staying in a hotel.'

'Are you? Where?'

'In Amberley.'

'What? Amberley Castle? How lovely, darling, but why didn't you *tell* me—you could have come over. It's not far.'

'Oh, I, er…' I didn't want to explain. 'I had to see a client, and so you see—' I glanced at the bathroom. 'Oh…*fuck*…'

'Miranda? *Miranda*?'

A tide of glistening white froth was advancing across the floor. I dashed into the bathroom, and, as the Jacuzzi jets roared away, the bubbles kept rising, pouring extravagantly over the edge of the bath, like the foam in an over-filled glass of champagne. I groped desperately for the switch, but it was submerged, and, when I finally located it, I couldn't see which bit of it to press. And still there was the noise of the jets, and the bubbles were cascading over the side, covering the floor, and moving out of the bathroom now and over the bedroom carpet like a tsunami.

'Oh *shit*!' Panic-struck, I pressed the switch again and again, but still the jets were roaring away, whipping up the mass of white foam. I grabbed a towel, wrapped it round me and knocked on David's door. After a moment he appeared in his bathrobe.

'What's up?'

'The Jacuzzi,' I panted. 'I can't turn it off.'

He came into the bathroom. 'Oh bloody *hell*. Where's the switch?'

'There! On that side,' I said.

He groped with it for a few seconds, as I tried, vainly, to repel the progress of the bubbles across the bedroom.

'I can't see how to do it—it's not like the one on my bath and—oh shit, this is awful—*ah!*' Suddenly there was silence. I clapped my hand to my chest in an ecstasy of relief.

'Thank *God*!'

'Christ!' he said, as he surveyed the mass of glistening froth. 'What a *mess*...'

'I only put in a tiny bit of bubble bath,' I said sheepishly.

'That's all it takes. Did you leave it unsupervised?'

'My mum called. I'm sorry. I feel *so* embarrassed.'

'Never mind.' He grabbed the other bath towel and began to swab the floor with it, while I reached into the bath and pulled out the plug.

'I'm sorry,' I said again. 'I do normally know how to behave in hotels.'

He looked at me and smiled, and I felt suddenly self-conscious in my bath towel. 'It's because the switch is electronic, not mechanical, so it was tricky to turn off, but my God...' He surveyed the white swamp. 'What a *mess*...' And now, suddenly, he began to laugh, and I did too, as we soaked up the foam with the spare towels and bathmat, and wrung them into the sink. We were both laughing, our shoulders shaking, and then we suddenly looked at each other and stopped laughing, and David's hand reached out for my face. He drew me to him, and now his mouth was on mine, and I felt his hardness through his robe, then he tugged at my towel and it fell to the floor. I untied the belt of his bathrobe, pushing it off his shoulders, and now we were half-walking, half-falling onto the bed in a tangle of wet, foamy limbs, and then he was naked beside me, stroking my face and my breasts and kissing me and calling my name, over and over.

'Oh Miranda,' he groaned. 'Miranda.' And now as he raised himself over me, I saw the flat, smooth scars on his thighs, from where I knew they must have taken the skin to repair his hands. I'd told myself that I would not do this until David knew—until he *knew*—but there was no way that I could stop. And now he was pouring himself into me, his open eyes locked onto mine as he came with a great, shuddering spasm.

'Miranda. Mir-an-da,' he groaned.

— CHAPTER 12 —

On Sunday, I awoke with David's right arm encircling me like the hoop of a barrel. As I gazed towards the window, where a splinter of light had pierced a gap in the curtains, I felt elated—and, at the same time, dismayed. For I had done precisely what I said I wouldn't do. But today David would know who I was. Terrified, now, I watched his sleeping face, listening to his gentle, regulated breathing. Then I saw his eyelids flicker, and open.

'Miranda Sweet,' he smiled. He drew me further to him, wrapping his arms around me so tightly I could hardly breathe. 'You *are* sweet,' he murmured as he gazed at me. 'And I *think* I'm in love with you. I'm not *absolutely* certain,' he added as he stroked my face. 'But I'm ninety-nine per cent sure I am.'

'Only ninety-nine per cent?' I said. He nodded. 'But I'm one hundred and twenty per cent sure I'm in love with you.'

'That's impossible.'

'Love doesn't obey mathematical imperatives.'

'That's true.' He dropped his hand from my face to my left breast, then his expression changed. 'That's funny,' he said quietly.

'What?'

'Your heart. It's racing. You're not anxious, are you?' *Yes, I am. I'm very, very anxious.*

'No…it's just the effect you have on me.'

He drew my right hand to his chest. 'Feel mine.' His pulse was slow and steady and strong. 'I feel unassailable,' he said as he stretched luxuriously, then clasped his hands behind his head. 'I feel that, just for today, nothing in the world can get to me. I'll remember this day for a very long time.' *You will. You will. You'll remember it forever.* My heart still pounding, I slipped out of bed.

I put on my bathrobe and pushed open the casement window. In the courtyard below, the square, topiarized yews were casting long, lozenge-shaped shadows in the morning light. Two white peacocks strolled across the lawn; while a flock of turtledoves warmed themselves in a patch of sunlight on the neighbouring roof.

'What are you doing?' David demanded softly. 'Come back, Miranda. Come back here. I want to make love to you again.'

I let the robe fall to the floor…

Afterwards, we had a bath together, then, while he was shaving, I got dressed and took Herman out.

'It's today,' I whispered to him bleakly, as we crossed the dry moat and walked towards the lake. 'It's *today*.' Herman looked up at me with an expression of unmitigated solicitude. When we went back inside, David was standing by the reception desk, studying a leaflet.

'What would you like to do?' he asked as we went upstairs. 'We could, according to this, go to Goodwood, Parham House, or, and I quote, "to the delightful coastal towns of Chichester, Worthing, and…*Brighton*". Brighton,' he echoed with a wry smile, as I opened my door. 'I haven't been to Brighton for fifteen years. I never wanted to go back,' he said, as I put Herman on his blanket, 'after what happened; but actually, I think I *would* like to go. Now that I've met you, and knowing you have a connection with the place too, somehow I think I could cope. Let's go to Brighton this morning,' he said, as we went into the dining room for breakfast. 'I've got this inexplicable urge to see it again. Is that okay with you?'

No. No. It isn't. I gave him a weak smile. 'Yes...' I said. 'That would be fine.'

After breakfast we climbed onto the ruined battlements, and looked at the South Downs rolling away beneath us to the far horizon. Then we went upstairs to get our things. And I had just put my clothes in my bag, and was sitting on my bed waiting for David to come in—*David, there's something I have to tell you*—when my phone rang. It was Daisy.

'Are you okay?' I asked.

'I'm...all right.' She didn't sound it.

'What's the matter?'

'It's just that...well, I was going to go microlighting again today, but my friend's just cancelled and so, well, I can't help feeling rather...disappointed.'

'Oh dear. And when did you arrange that?'

'Last week.'

'Did he say why he had to cancel?'

'No. He just said that it wasn't convenient, after all.'

'I'm sorry, Daisy. But in any case you really ought to be spending your free time with Nigel.'

'Oh, I am,' she replied. 'He's decided not to work today, so we're going out to lunch with a few of his crowd—including that awful baggage, Mary.'

'She is rather awful. You have my sympathies. Her bite is worse than her bark.'

'That's true. Anyway, what's the hotel like?'

'Heaven. It's a ruined castle.'

'A ruined castle,' she repeated achingly. '*How* romantic.'
There was such profound longing in her voice. 'And have
you told David yet?'

I felt my pulse quicken. 'No. I'm going to do it today. I
don't want to do it here, though, and spoil the memory of
this lovely place. But he wants to go to Brighton for lunch,
so I'll find a quiet place there, and then I'll tell him.'

'Well…I'll be thinking of you—good luck. But don't
worry, Miranda. He's obviously very attached to you—I'm
sure he'll be fine.'

Suddenly, David was standing in the doorway. 'Tell me
what?' he enquired, as I put the phone back in my bag. My
heart looped the loop. 'How irresistible you find me?'

I nodded. 'I do. I do find you irresistible. I find you…'
I suddenly rushed up to him and flung my arms round his
neck. 'I find you *so* nice, David, and *so* gorgeous, and I'm *so*
glad I found you.' *And I've got this awful, awful thing I have to
tell you. And it might ruin everything.* I felt tears spring to my
eyes.

'Hey,' he said soothingly. 'You're not crying, are you?' He
looked at me. 'There's no need for tears.' *Oh, there is. There is.*
'Or, don't tell me, you're crying with happiness?'

'Yes,' I sniffed. 'I am.' *Happiness, and also acute anxiety.*

He handed me a hanky. 'Don't cry. There, Miranda.
Please, *don't*. Now,' he added, after a moment, 'let's drive
straight there, and have a walk along the sea front. Then we
could find somewhere nice for lunch—maybe Beachy Head?'
I nodded. 'I'll drive, shall I?' *Why not just tell him now? This
second. Get it over with, at last.*

'David, I—'

Suddenly his mobile rang. 'Oh, hi, Mum.' He went back

to his room and talked to his mother for a few minutes, then he reappeared with his bags.

'Sorry about that—we usually have a chat on Sunday mornings. She says she'd love to meet you.' *She won't, she won't. Not when she knows.*

As we drove through the Sussex villages, down curving lanes fringed alternately with beech and then bracken, I kept trying to imagine how David would react. Brighton was only fifteen miles away, so in less than an hour I'd know. And now we had come to its fringes and were driving through Hove, along the Promenade, past the hotels. I gazed out to sea at the white sails dotting the glinting water, and at the sunbathers on the shingled beach.

'You know what I want to do, don't you?' I heard David say. I looked at him. 'Before we have lunch?'

'No. What's that?'

'I'd like to show you where I used to live.' A sudden jolt ran down my spine. 'Let's see if I can find my way to the house.' We drove past the ruined West Pier, then the Palace Pier and then, at Marine Parade, he turned left. And now we were negotiating the backstreets of Brighton, with their colourful Regency villas painted in pale pink and green and blue, and we were climbing now, rising high above the city. 'Egremont Place,' he said. 'I think that's the one I want.'

'Yes, it is,' I said, before I could stop myself. I felt David's slightly curious glance pass over me.

'You're right,' he said. 'And here's the memorial arch. Gosh, I remember this.' We passed under it and now we were in West Drive, with Queen's Park below us on our right; the shrieks of children playing on the swings rising to our ears, and the soft 'thwock' of tennis balls. David drove slowly to the end, and I saw his hands tighten on the wheel as he drew to a halt opposite his old house.

'Christ, Miranda,' he breathed. My heart was banging. 'I suddenly feel rather…strange. This is quite…emotional for me, actually, this little trip down memory lane.' *And for me. And for me.* He shook his head, and I saw the muscles around his eyes tighten. He turned and looked at me. 'Oh, you look upset too.' He put his hand on mine. 'It's sweet of you, Miranda, but it was sixteen years ago and I've long since got over it. It's just…' he shrugged, '…seeing it again. Actually *being* here. It's bringing back the memories—that's all. We were quite happy here, until, well…' he heaved a painful sigh. 'Until…that. It was a good place to live. Our neighbours were nice,' he added, suddenly. 'The McNaughts. I wonder whether they still live here.' I felt sick. 'I'd love to see them again. In fact…' *No! No! No! Please DON'T!* His hand was on the car door. 'I'll just ring the bell. You don't mind, do you?' *YES! I DO!!!*

'No, of course not,' I heard myself say.

'You can come with me, if you like.'

'No!' David looked at me strangely. 'I mean…no,' I repeated. 'I…don't want to.'

'Why not?'

'Well…because if they *don't* live there any more, and there are two of us standing on the doorstep, the present owners might feel a bit intimidated.'

David nodded. 'That's true. Okay, you stay here. I'll just knock, and if they are still living there I'll give you a wave and you can come and say hi.'

Please, dear God—let them be out.

I watched David cross the road, my heart beating like a kettle drum. I saw him look at the front of number forty-four for a moment, then he opened the gate of number forty-six, walked up the short path, and rang the bell. *Let them be out. Please, please, let them be out.* Then I saw him ring it again.

And now a third time. My heart-rate began to subside. Now David was looking at the upstairs window, then he rang once more, turned and came back to the car.

'They're obviously not there.' *Thank you, God.* 'Or they're away. Are you okay, Miranda?'

'Of course.'

'You look a bit…agitated.'

I am. 'No, I'm not.'

'Do you want me to drive past your old house? It's not far from here, is it?'

'No. It's in Sandown Road, but I'm not really bothered.'

'Okay then, we won't.'

We went down to the sea front and strolled through The Lanes, then crossed over to the Pier with its gaudy entertainments.

'We used to love this,' David said, as we walked through the amusement arcade. 'Michael and I used to hang out here when we were kids. I remember there was a girl I used to meet here. I was crazy about her,' he confided with a laugh. 'She was a French language student, Chantalle. I lost my virginity to her in 1982. And who did you lose yours to?' *Jimmy. Jimmy. In March, 1987.* 'Oh, I'm sorry, Miranda. I've embarrassed you. Ignore that utterly ungentlemanly question.' He took off his linen jacket. 'It's hot, isn't it? Let's walk by the sea for a while.'

We walked eastwards towards the marina, hand in hand, the light breeze blowing our hair. He glanced at his watch. 'It's one. Shall we go for lunch in half an hour? Or are you hungry now?'

Not in the slightest. I'm much too stressed.

'I'm fine,' I replied. We crunched over the shingle, then, in a fairly quiet part of the beach, I saw an empty bench.

'David,' I said, my pulse racing. 'Can we sit down for a few minutes?'

'Of course we can.' We sat side by side, our thighs touching, our fingers entwined, listening to the shrieks of children, the plaintive squawks of the seagulls as they wheeled overhead, and the rush and suck of the breaking waves. I closed my eyes. In... Out... It sounded like a gigantic inhalation. I synchronized my own breath with it, to steady my nerves.

This is the moment. Now.

'David,' I said. 'There's something I have to tell you.'

I heard him laugh. 'Not this game again. I thought you'd given that up.'

I stared at a bit of dried seaweed by my feet. It was black and brittle.

'It *isn't* a game. There really *is* something I have to tell you. Something very serious about myself that I should have told you when we first met.' His features tightened now, as he realized, at long last, that I wasn't joking. 'But the reason why I didn't was because something completely unexpected happened. I fell in love with you. And once that had happened, I found it not just difficult, but almost impossible to tell you. I've been wrestling with it ever since.'

David shook his head in confusion. 'You look so *serious*, Miranda.'

'It *is* serious.'

He blinked. 'What is it?' I didn't reply. 'You've got a child?'

'No.' *If only it were that simple.* I stared down at the shingle, noticing the navy flints amongst the beige.

'You can't *have* children? Is that it? Because if so, it doesn't matter. There are other ways...'

I shook my head. 'That's not it either.' *If only it were—it would be far easier to say.* Behind us an ice-cream van passed by with its curiously merry-yet-melancholy jingle.

'You're ill...' David said suddenly. 'Please don't tell me you're ill, Miranda.'

'No. I'm not.'

A look of relief passed over his face. 'Then what is it? This serious thing?'

'It's something I did,' I explained quietly. 'When I was young. Something very bad.'

'Oh,' he said flatly. 'I see.' He didn't say anything else for a moment, and we just sat there, aware of the sound of the waves breaking on the beach, then withdrawing with a soft rattle of shingle. 'Was it drugs?'

'No.' I looked out to sea where a distant motor-boat was throwing up a twin wall of spray.

'You...robbed a bank? Is that it? You committed a crime? You've been in prison?'

'You're warmer now,' I said dismally, my eyes still fixed on the horizon. 'And although, no, I didn't ever go to prison, I could have done, and perhaps I *should* have done.'

'What do you mean?' I breathed in and then out, emptying the air out of my lungs. 'What do you *mean*, Miranda? What *did* you do?'

The moment has come. Here it is.

'I hurt someone,' I whispered. My heart was banging.

'You *hurt* someone? God. *Who*?'

'Well. This is the awful thing—'

'*David*?' we suddenly heard. 'David White?' David looked up, stared, and then suddenly began to smile in surprised recognition.

'I don't believe it!' he exclaimed softly. 'Mr McNaught. And Mrs McNaught. *Hello*.'

'I *thought* I recognized you,' said Bill McNaught. Their

black cocker spaniel was nose to nose with Herman now, their tails nervously twitching. 'I said to Shirley, that's young David from next door. You haven't changed much, lad.' He extended his hand. 'Nice to see you again.'

'You too. I've just been up to West Drive actually,' David explained. 'I even knocked on your door, but there was no reply.'

'We always walk along the beach on Sunday mornings,' said Mr McNaught. 'Come rain or shine.'

'Come rain or shine,' agreed his wife.

'Come rain or shine,' he said again. 'Then we go home for lunch.' Now, to my horror, he was looking at me and smiling. *Don't say it! Don't, don't say it!* 'So I see you've found your young man then.' There was a split second while David absorbed this, then I was aware, as if in slow motion, of his head turning towards me. 'Isn't that funny, Shirley?' Bill Mc-Naught went on happily. 'This is Miranda. The young lady who was looking for David just a few weeks ago.'

'Oh,' she said with pleasant surprise. 'Hello there. Nice to meet you.'

'Hello,' I replied faintly.

'So, Shirley's information obviously helped,' he went on genially. 'And it didn't take you long to track David down. I told her you were a photographer,' he explained to David, who was looking at me, dumbstruck now. 'Very glad to help her, we were. She was *most* anxious to find you, weren't you? But then, it's always nice to catch up with old college friends. And how's your mother, David? We heard she'd moved to Norfolk.'

'Yes,' he said weakly.

'To be near Michael and his family?'

'That's right.'

'Well, I'm so glad you two have got together again,' he said benignly. 'Friends Reunited and all that. Anyway, our lunch will be spoiling so we'll be on our way, but it's very nice to see you again. Do remember us kindly to your mother and Michael. So glad you two have caught up with each other again. Bye for now.'

I gave them a weak smile. 'Goodbye.'

We stood watching them retreat down the beach, the dog pulling on the lead, and then climb the steps. I felt David's eyes staring into me, with the intensity of a blowtorch. His mouth was slightly agape.

'*What* was *that* about?' he asked quietly. I didn't reply. 'I don't *understand*,' he went on. 'Who *are* you, Miranda?' *Who am I? Good question.* 'And how do you know the McNaughts? And why the *hell* did you tell them we were at university together?'

I slumped onto the bench, then looked up at him. 'Because I was trying to *find* you, that's why. I'd wanted to find you for years and years, but I was too afraid. Then, a few weeks ago, I finally plucked up the courage. So I went to West Drive, and I asked Mr McNaught where you lived now. And he didn't know, but he said he'd ask his wife, who was away; and then he asked me how I knew you. So I told him that we'd been at university together—because I couldn't possibly tell him the real reason.'

'But what *was* that reason? And how did you know that I'd once lived in West Drive?' As I stared up at him his features began to bend and blur. 'Will you please *tell* me, Miranda? I don't *understand*.'

'I knew,' I croaked, 'because I'd been there before.'

He stared at me. 'You'd been to our house *before*?' he echoed faintly. 'But *how*?' I didn't reply. Suddenly, some kind of comprehension seemed to dawn. 'Did you know Michael?'

he asked. 'Is *that* what this is all about? That you had an affair with Michael, but you didn't want to tell me?'

I shook my head. 'No. No. I've never met him.'

'Then how did you know about *me*?'

'Because…because…for the past sixteen years, you and I have had a terrible connection, of which you've been quite unaware, but I'm now going to tell you what it is.'

And so, at long last, I did.

When I finished, David was too stunned to speak. His face was as drained of colour as the chalk pebbles beneath our feet.

'It was *me*,' I said, sobbing quietly now. 'It was *me*. *I* did it. But I didn't *know* what it was. I genuinely believed it was a video—because that's what Jimmy had said. But it wasn't—it was a letter-bomb—and you opened it, and you got hurt, and I'm very, *very* sorry.'

'I…' Words still eluded him; his face was suffused with pain.

'But I just want you to know that however much you've suffered, I've suffered too. I've suffered for sixteen years because it's never, *ever* left me. I've been carrying it around like some bloody great boulder! It's weighed me down. It's *crushed* me.'

'But you should have *told* someone.'

'I *know*. But I was terrified that if I did, I'd go to jail. That's what Jimmy said. And I was sixteen, and I was *so* much under his thumb, and I was so afraid—so I kept quiet. But then, a few weeks ago, by chance, I met him again—and that was what finally broke the moral paralysis which had crippled me for so long.'

As David gazed, speechlessly, at me, I felt as though I'd been transformed into some hideous monster—a gorgon and a harpy all rolled into one.

'So it was *you*?' he whispered. He shook his head in stupefaction—and denial. *'You?'* he repeated. I nodded. *'You're* responsible for what happened that day?'

Responsible?

'Indirectly,' I wept. 'Yes. I am. And I was so...*horrified* when I found out, I overheard these women talking about it at the bus stop. That was the first I knew. So I ran to Jimmy's flat and confronted him, but he told me I'd go to Holloway if I ever said a *thing* to *anyone*. And I believed him. So I kept quiet.'

'You've kept quiet *all* these years?'

'Yes. Out of cowardice and fear. But then, six weeks ago, I decided to be brave at last, and to find you—if I could—and to tell you the truth. But it's been *so* hard, David.' I felt a hot tear snake down my cheek and seep into the corner of my mouth with a salty tang.

'Because you were still afraid?'

'Yes. But, more importantly, because of what I felt for you. It made it so much worse than it already was. And every time I tried to tell you, the words just died on my lips.'

David was no longer looking at me. He was staring out to sea, blinking slowly, as what I'd just told him began to impact. 'So it wasn't a game,' I heard him say softly.

'No.'

'You really *did* have a dreadful confession to make.'

I nodded. 'I tried to tell you so many times. But my courage kept failing, and then you began to make a joke of it, which made it even *harder.*'

He remained silent, then turned and looked at me, with an expression of ineffable sadness.

'I don't know *who* you are,' he said quietly. 'I thought I did. But I don't. I don't know you at all—I feel you're a stranger to me now.' My heart sank. 'The *lies* you've told,' he went on. 'The way you lied to the McNaughts about how you knew me. The way you contrived to meet me six weeks ago. But Lily gave it away, didn't she? Last weekend. That must have been a sticky moment for you, when she turned up at the zoo. She let slip that it was *your* idea for me to take your photo, not hers.' I nodded. 'You said it was because you'd admired that photo of mine in the *Guardian*. But that wasn't true, was it?'

'Well, it *was* true,' I protested. 'I *do* admire your photography. But no, the reason why I asked her to commission you was because I'd discovered from Bill McNaught that you'd become a photographer. So I looked you up through the Photographers' Association and tried to work out a way to meet you; then Lily presented me with an opportunity to do so.'

He shook his head again. 'Christ—I feel as though I've been *stalked*! I feel as though I've been, almost, yes…hunted. Hunted down.' I felt sick. 'No wonder you were so weird when we first met,' he went on. 'I understand it now. It was because of what you'd *done*. That's why you asked me all those strange questions about where I'd grown up and where my father had worked.'

'I didn't realize it would be *you*. Because of your accent, I'd assumed you weren't the David White I was looking for. Then you turned up and I knew at once that you *were*.'

'Because of my scars.'

'Yes,' I replied miserably. I glanced at his hands, placed firmly on his knees now, as though he was bracing himself against the hurt. 'And I was just so…shocked. But I was also behaving strangely because I realized, even then, in those first few minutes, that I was very *attracted* to you. I was in turmoil.'

'And that's why you invited me to stay for a drink?'

'That's right. Because I wanted to tell you there and then. But I didn't know how to start such a terrible conversation. So I decided that I'd call you in a short while and make some excuse to meet you again. But then, to my amazement, you phoned *me*. And we went out to dinner.'

'We went out to dinner,' he echoed and, to my shock, I saw tears standing in his eyes. 'We went out to dinner, and we had such a nice evening.'

'Yes,' I said, my throat aching. 'We did.'

'But I didn't know who you *were*…' he croaked. I saw his mouth quiver.

'No, you didn't. I intended to tell you that night, but it was impossible in the restaurant, and then I tried to tell you in the dark room, but I just…couldn't. I wanted to, but at the same time I *didn't* want to, because I liked you so much. My courage failed me. Again.'

'It's funny,' he murmured, swallowing now. 'I was so struck by your concern at what had happened to me. I found your compassion really touching. It was as though it really affected you personally. And now I know that it *did*—but not for the reasons I thought. How ironic,' he added bitterly. 'I found your tender-heartedness very endearing. But actually, it was just guilt.'

'Yes. It *was* guilt. It was awful—it *has* been awful—seeing what happened to you, knowing the part I'd played in it.'

'*Ah*,' he said, nodding. '*Now* I understand your questions about my attitude towards the person who'd done it. How *strange*,' he added, bleakly. 'I told you I'd like to meet that person. That I'd like to be face to face with them.' He turned towards me. 'But I've been face to face with them all along.' He looked at the horizon again. 'And you wanted to know whether I could ever forgive that person. Because, I now understand, you had a personal interest in knowing the answer to that.'

'Yes, it's true—I *did*. I wanted to hear you say that you could forgive me, because I already knew I was in love with you.'

'*Did* you know that, Miranda?'

'Yes.'

'Are you sure?'

'Of course I'm sure.'

'But I don't think it's true.'

'It *is*!'

'No. You've just confused love with guilt. That's why you've felt whatever it is you've felt for me these past few weeks. You were compensating for the harm you'd once done me. But I'm pretty sure it's not love.'

'It *is* love.'

'How do you know?'

'Because I do know.'

'But *how*?'

'Because, yesterday, when we were looking at that grave in Amberley churchyard, I suddenly realized that I'd like to be buried with you. That's how I know! You *have* to believe me, David.'

'No,' he sighed. 'That's where you're wrong. I don't have to believe you at all.'

'But what I'm saying is *true*.'

'How the hell do I know? You're clearly an expert in deception.'

'I'm not actually.'

'Yes you are—the subterfuge you've used!'

'Only because I *had* to, in order to find you, and to get to know you—but actually I'm not like that at all. But yes, I know it doesn't look good, and I know I *have* misled you.'

'You certainly have. What a trail of lies has led you to this point, Miranda. I almost feel sorry for you. Having to keep it up. Trying to avoid exposure. How very exhausting for you… But that leads me to another thing—which is more important than anything else—and that is, how do I know that you genuinely *didn't* know that the video wasn't just a video?'

I felt myself go cold. 'Because it's *true*. I had absolutely *no* idea. And if I had, I would never, in a million years, have delivered it, however infatuated I'd been.'

'Perhaps you've simply convinced yourself of that.'

'No. It's the *truth*. The fact is that I *believed* what Jimmy said, because I had no reason *not* to. He'd never done anything violent before.'

'But you would say that,' he said. 'Wouldn't you?' I stared at him helplessly. 'But how do I actually *know*? It's perfectly possible that you and this…Jimmy, targeted my father, together, for your own strange reasons. But now, sixteen years on, you're anxious to present yourself to me as the innocent dupe.'

'But that's exactly what I *was*! That's why Jimmy asked *me* to deliver it. Because he was too cowardly to deliver it himself.'

David stared at me, then looked out to sea again, blinking thoughtfully. 'It was put through the door in the early hours. That suggests that you were worried about being seen.'

'Of course. Because I didn't want to be hauled before the magistrates for delivering animal rights propaganda, which is what I believed it to *be*. I knew it was harassment—but I felt it was justified, because of what they were doing to laboratory animals; and I'd believed Jimmy's lies about your dad.'

'So you got up early 'specially to deliver it, did you?'

'No, I… No,' I sighed. 'I didn't. That's not how it happened. I…I…was in love with Jimmy. I've told you that. And that night in March…that night, I'd been at his flat in East Street and for the first time we'd…'

'Oh, spare me,' he groaned.

'It was a huge thing for me,' I murmured. 'I'd never been to bed with anyone before—and I was infatuated with Jimmy to the point of obsession—and to me this proved that he loved me. So that night I stayed at his flat. But I was terrified that my mother would realize that I wasn't in my room, so I knew I'd have to get home before she was up; and she was getting up very early then because of my younger sisters, so I left Jimmy's place at about a quarter to five. And as I was leaving, he picked up this parcel on the hall table—I remember having seen it lying there for quite a while, now I think about it—and he handed it to me, then told me to put it through the door of Professor White. I asked him why he wanted *me* to do it, and he said that it was because West Drive was on my way home. Which was true. So I agreed.'

'But didn't you ask what it *was*?'

'I did. And he told me it was an anti-vivisection video about monkeys, because your dad had been involved with neurological experiments.' David groaned quietly, and shook his head. 'But I believed him. And the point about Jimmy is that he'd never ever *been* violent. He was the man of peace. The hero who was an animal rights campaigner, but who had publicly *denounced* violent action—so no one had ever thought him extreme. I had *no* reason to doubt him, plus I wanted to impress him, so I said I'd deliver it for him—and I did. He did say that it would give your father a "bit of a shock". But it was only the next day, when I found out the truth, that I understood what he'd meant by that.'

'You were on a bicycle, weren't you?'

'Yes.'

'So *you* were the slight female figure seen by the milk-man?' I nodded. 'Jesus Christ,' he said quietly. 'It was you. It was *you*.' He ran his hand through his hair. 'Well, thank you for telling me at last. How long has it taken, Miranda? Six weeks? And now I want you to tell me something else.' My heart sank. 'Who is Jimmy?' He looked at me. 'Who is he? I'd like to know his full name, and what he does. You say you met him again recently, so you'll be able to tell me.'

'I can't,' I said miserably.

'You can.'

'Okay, yes, I can. I *could*. But I don't *want* to.'

'But I have the right to know.'

'That's true. But *I* also have the right *not* to tell you. And I'm very sorry about it, David. I wish I *could* tell you—but this has never been about *Jimmy*—it's about *me*. Shopping Jimmy—however awful he was—would make me feel un-derhand and wrong. Plus the fact that I know his wife, and it could destroy their marriage. And I'm sure he's done nothing horrible since, and isn't a threat to anyone.'

'So why did he do what he *did*?'

'I wish I knew! But I don't. He never explained his motive, and I only saw him once more—the following day. Then I heard not long afterwards that he'd left Brighton, and after that there was no contact at all.' We sat for a moment, listening to the sharp cries of the seagulls as they hung in the air overhead.

'How weird,' said David after a few moments. 'You and I are on different sides of the same terrible event.'

'Yes,' I murmured. 'We are. For the past sixteen years I've thought about you so much. I used to try and imagine what had happened to you and how badly you'd been hurt. All I knew was what I read in the newspaper the next day. I felt so *dreadful* about it, David—the whole thing was a terrible shock.'

'So you say.'

'Well, I say it because it's *true*. I used to write you these letters, in which I'd tell you the whole story and apologize to you. But I'd always tear them up, because I was terrified that you'd go to the police, and then my life would be ruined.'

'Poor Miranda,' he said. 'Poor Miranda…' A flicker of hope rose in my heart. 'I feel very sorry for you. I really do. And maybe what you're saying *is* true.' He shrugged. 'I don't know. All I *do* know is,' he stood up, 'that we won't be having lunch after all. Could we go to your car?'

'What for?'

'I want to get my stuff. I'll get the train back to London.'

'Oh David, *please* don't go. We can talk about it for as long as you like, but please *don't* go like this—not now.'

'But there's nothing else to say. You've finally told me the truth. I don't feel like being with you, Miranda. It's not my injuries. It's not even the effect it had on my life. It's the simple fact that that bomb was intended to kill my father. So forgive me if I don't much feel like fraternizing with the woman who put it through the door.' He picked up his jacket. 'I feel…differently about you now. I don't trust you at all. You told me when we played chess that strategic thinking isn't your strong point—but it seems to me that it *is*. I even suspect you manipulated me into falling in love with you, so that I'd forgive you. But I don't. And although, yes, I had fallen in love with you, those feelings were for someone else—the person I *thought* was you. So can we get my bags now?' he added quietly. We walked in silence to the car. I opened the boot, and he lifted out his camera bag, his holdall, and the tripod. Then he turned and walked away; and I stood there, staring at his retreating form until he was quite out of focus, no more than a dot, then a speck, and then gone.

—— CHAPTER 13 ——

'I wish he'd got *angry* with me,' I wept to Daisy when I got back to London. 'But he was too shocked.'

'Poor Miranda,' she said. 'I did think he might take it better than that.'

'Well, Christ, it's such a huge thing. I never had *any* idea how he'd react. I just hoped that he'd be able to cope with it, but he clearly couldn't.'

'So what did you do when he left?'

'I sat in the car for about an hour, just crying. Then I went to see my mum.'

'You didn't tell her, did you?'

'No. She saw I was upset, but she assumed it was about Alexander and I didn't disabuse her of that. My dad was there too.'

'*Really?*'

'They were having lunch.'

'Good God!'

'I know,' I said as my sobs subsided. 'All very civilized. But they've got this mad idea for the llamas—it's totally *nuts*.'

'What is it?'

I wiped my eyes. 'It's so crazy, I'm too embarrassed to tell you—anyway, they were busy discussing that. I stayed for about an hour then drove back to London.'

'And there was no message from David?'

'No. But I knew that there wouldn't be.'

'So what are you going to do?'

What am I going to do? 'I wish I knew, Daisy. I feel so awful.'

'What do you *want* to do?'

'I just want to convince David that I'm telling the *truth*. But that's going to be impossible, as he now believes I'm manipulative and deceitful—both of which I *have* been.'

'Only because you *had* to be.'

'I know. But he clearly thinks I'm like that all the time.'

'If he knew you well, he'd know that you're *not*.'

'But that's precisely the problem. He's known me less than two months. I *couldn't* tell him the truth before, Daisy. I tried to, but I couldn't, and now I've got myself in this terrible *mess*. He also said that he thought my feelings for him weren't genuine, that it was guilt, not love.'

I heard Daisy hesitate. 'Is there *any* truth in that?'

'No. I fell in love with him, because I fell in love with him. Love doesn't grow out of a bad conscience—resentment does.'

'That's true. And presumably he wanted to know who Jimmy was?'

'Yes. But I didn't tell him. However vile Jimmy is, it felt… *wrong*. And in any case, Jimmy is irrelevant to me in all this.'

'But he's not irrelevant to David.'

I sighed. 'I know. But there's no way round it. David also wanted to know *why* Jimmy did it—of course—and I wanted to tell him, but I couldn't, because I don't actually know *myself*.'

'Then I really think you've got to find out. Because if you could at least tell David *that* much, it would help him. He must feel so *dreadful*, Miranda.'

'He does. He feels terrible. In fact he cried, Daisy. He cried.' I felt my throat ache.

'Well…I'm not surprised. It's all been thrown up for him again, but he still doesn't have closure. So he has all the pain of revisiting it, without any resolution—plus the awful knowledge that *you* were involved. You've *got* to find out why Jimmy did it,' she reiterated.

'How am I going to do that?'

'Well…ask.'

'What? Ask *Jimmy*? Just like that?'

'Yes.'

'He'll never tell me. It's too dangerous.'

'So is *not* telling you.'

'What do you mean?'

'I mean that you could, well…threaten him. Couldn't you?'

I stared at her. '*What*?'

'Look, Miranda, Jimmy may or may not be a bad man—but sixteen years ago, he did a *very* bad thing. And as he involved you in it, he at least owes you an explanation. I suggest you demand to see him—then tell him that you've confessed to David.'

'He'll go absolutely *apeshit*.'

'He will. He's relied on your silence all this time—and now you've broken it. But tell him that you haven't actually given David his name. Then say that you won't do so—*if*—and *only* if—he agrees to explain *why* he did it.'

'But that's blackmail, Daisy.'

'*Yes!!*'

That evening I wrote a letter to David, repeating everything I'd said to him in Brighton. Then, once I'd posted it,

I decided that I *would* do as Daisy advised. I'd go and see
Jimmy—the next day. I wouldn't ring him in advance—I'd
just go to the House of Commons—the public have access—
and I'd wait in the lobby for as long as it took. Parliament
might be in summer recess, but the MPs were still working,
and Jimmy was ambitious—he wouldn't slouch. But what if
he was away? I looked at his website. It said that he would be
on holiday in Scotland for two weeks, from the sixteenth of
August, so he probably *would* be there, clearing his desk. But
what about Herman? I couldn't take him, and I couldn't leave
him for hours, so I phoned Daisy and she agreed to have him
at work.

'I'm in early tomorrow, so bring him at nine. I'm so glad
you're doing this, Miranda,' she added. 'It isn't just David
who needs to know—*you* need to know too.'

Yes, I thought miserably. I do.

The following morning I got up early, dressed smartly,
then walked over the bridge with Herman and got the tube
to Tottenham Court Road.

Daisy met me at reception.

'God you look pale. Haven't you slept?' I shook my head.
I handed Herman to her, then she gave me something.

'Put this in your bag,' she said quietly. 'I think you'll find
it handy. It's very easy to operate—and it's discreet.'

I felt my jaw slacken. 'Isn't it illegal?'

'I'm not exactly sure,' she whispered. 'But I know that
sending people letter-bombs *is*! Jimmy may refuse to see you,'
she went on. 'But if he agrees, then I just thought it would be
useful to have the conversation on record. As for persuading
him to tell you, just think of him as a difficult, domineering dog who you're going to bring to heel. Take a rolled-

up newspaper with you if necessary. Best of luck!' Then she hugged me and I left.

I got the tube to Charing Cross then walked down White-hall towards Westminster. As I saw Big Ben, and heard it chime the half hour, my heart-rate began to increase. I felt sick with fear, and I was miserable about David, but I had to do this—for him. I made my way through the knots of tour-ists to St Stephen's entrance, my knees shaking. As I expected, security was tight.

'Who are you visiting?' asked the security guard at the door.

'James Mulholland.'

'And is he expecting you?'

'Yes,' I lied.

'Please empty your pockets and put your bag on the moving belt.'

As I passed through the metal detector, I could see the tiny tape recorder quite clearly on the screen, but it didn't seem to bother anyone; they probably assumed I was a hack. Then I picked up my bag and walked down the cool, flagstone cor-ridor, past Westminster Hall, to Central Lobby.

'I'd like to see James Mulholland,' I said, as confidently as I could, though my knees were trembling.

'Do you have an appointment?' the attendant asked.

'Yes.'

'And what's your name?' I told him. 'Please wait.' He di-alled the extension, but there was no reply. 'It's on answer-phone at the moment. Please take a seat and I'll try again in a few minutes.'

After a quarter of an hour, I went up to the desk while the attendant tried Jimmy's line again, and this time he got a reply.

'His private secretary says she has no record of your meeting.'

'May I speak to her please?' He passed me the phone.

'Mr Mulholland won't be here until ten thirty,' she explained. 'But in any case, I don't have a note of you in the diary. May I ask what this is about?'

'It's about…Sussex University,' I said. 'Mr Mulholland must have forgotten to mention it to you, but if you say that Miranda Sweet would like to speak to him, urgently, about the biochemistry department at Sussex University, then I think that'll ring a few bells.'

'Well I will, but he's quite busy today. If he decides he has time to see you, I'll ring down.'

'Thank you.' I breathed a sigh of relief.

As I waited, I glanced round the octagonal lobby with its ornate vaulted ceiling. There were groups of foreign students, and workmen polishing the mosaic floor. By ten forty-five there'd been no word. Then at ten past eleven I heard my name.

'Miss Sweet,' the attendant repeated as I rushed up to the desk. 'Kindly write your name and details here, and then you'll be taken to Mr Mulholland's office.' My hand shaking slightly, I wrote my name in the register, then followed another attendant down a long green-carpeted corridor, then up three flights of steps, until I was standing outside a heavy oak door with Jimmy's name on it. I knocked and entered.

His secretary, a pleasant looking woman of about fifty, was sitting at a desk in the outer office. Just visible in the inner one was Jimmy. He was on the phone.

'Yes,' I heard him say. 'I agree it should be added to the National Curriculum. Of course.' Now, having registered my presence, he politely wound up the conversation. As he walked towards me he looked calm and self-possessed, with his slightly swaggering walk, but there was that distinct flicker of anxiety I'd seen before.

'Hello, Miranda,' he said pleasantly. 'How nice to see you. Would you like a cup of coffee?'

'Yes please.' I glanced round the room. There were files marked 'A Level', 'GCSE', 'Examination Boards', and 'Standards'. There were a couple of nice landscapes, an elegant carriage clock, and the same wedding photo I'd seen at the house.

'I'd like a coffee too please, Sarah,' he said to his secretary. 'In fact,' he added as she poured it. 'I wonder if you could possibly do me a huge favour and get me a sandwich— I missed breakfast this morning.'

'Of course,' she said as she handed me a cup. 'What would you like?'

'Anything really. I don't mind.' He handed her a ten-pound note, then invited me to sit in the deep red leather armchair which faced his desk. He waited until the door had shut, then his expression hardened. 'Right,' he said. 'What the hell's this about?' I put down the coffee. I didn't want it.

'I've told David White,' Jimmy's grey eyes widened momentarily, then his mouth hardened into a thin line. 'I've told him,' I repeated. 'He knows.'

'You. Stupid. Little. *Cow*,' he said quietly. He shook his head in shock and outrage. 'Why the *hell* did you do *that*?'

'For the simple reason that I've felt awful about it for sixteen years.'

'But you should have left it *alone*! I *told* you that at the fete!'

'I know you did, but I don't take orders from you. And I wanted to try and put it right—I always have done—so I decided to try and find David.'

'You went and *looked* for him?' he said, dumbfounded.

'Yes.'

'You mean, you've *deliberately* stirred all this up again, when it was long dead and buried?'

'It wasn't dead and buried for me.'

'But don't you realize the damage you could cause to yourself—and to *me*—if this ever gets out?'

I nodded. 'Oh yes. I realize that very well.'

He got up and walked over to the window. I could see the muscles in his jaw tense and flex as he peered through the slats in the Venetian blind. 'Do you want money, Miranda? Is that it?' he asked quietly.

'Don't be obscene.'

He turned and stared at me. 'Then what *do* you want? I mean, what is your *real* purpose in raking all this up again— *quite* unnecessarily—unless it's to try and destroy me?'

'That's not the reason at all. I just want justice for David. His life was shattered that day—thanks to you. And every time he looks at his hands, he's reminded of what happened.'

There was a moment's silence, in which I saw Jimmy swallow. 'And did you give him my name?' I just looked at him, making him wait, enjoying his anxiety. '*Did* you?' he repeated. He gave me a defiant glare, but he shifted slightly from foot to foot.

'No.' His face seemed almost to collapse with relief. 'He asked me, of course, but I decided, for *now*, not to tell him.'

'Well *don't*! Just keep your trap *shut*, like I said!'

'What I *did* tell him,' I went on quite calmly, 'was that although I delivered the video, I didn't have the faintest idea what it really was. And that's perfectly true, isn't it?' There was another silence.

'Yes,' he conceded. 'That's true.' I was aware of the vibrations of the tiny tape recorder and prayed that it was working properly.

'You tricked me into participating in a criminal act which could have resulted in the death of either David, or his father, or his mother, or brother, and I am now going to ask you *why*. And if you refuse to tell me, then I promise you I *will* tell David your real name, and *exactly* who you are. You've got about three minutes until your secretary gets back, Jimmy, so I suggest you start right now.'

'Will you *stop* calling me Jimmy—my name is *James*,' he snapped. 'And I'm going to call security and have you slung out.'

'If you do, I'll go to the press.'

'They won't be able to print it.'

'Why not?'

'Because I'll slap a libel suit on them—that's why. I can easily afford it, Miranda—and I'll win.'

'But you'll be tainted, Jimmy. Imagine the headlines. They'll stick to you for the rest of your life.'

'It'll be your word against mine. The word of a woman who was infatuated with me—and who was, moreover, *well* known to the police at that time for her little adventures on the animal rights front. No one will believe you, Miranda,' he added smoothly. 'You'll only end up destroying yourself. I've kept all your letters, by the way.'

My heart sank. 'I thought you might have done.'

'Well, I guessed—accurately, as it turns out—that you'd make trouble for me one day. Those letters prove how obsessed with me you were.'

'Yes. I was. To my shame.'

'And now that you've met me again, and discovered that I'm *very* successful, and yes, *very* happily married, you've decided to take your revenge. That's how you'll look by the time my QC's finished with you. Like a bitter, scorned woman, out to destroy a decent man.'

'I don't care how I'll look. I only care about David know-ing the truth. So I just want you to tell me. And if you don't, I'll ring him on my mobile, right now, and give him your name.' I got the phone out of my bag. 'Once he knows your identity, he'll be perfectly entitled to go to the police, and you may then find yourself at the centre of a highly publi-cized civil case. David is entitled to compensation from you for his injured hands, and he may well seek it.'

Jimmy's face had gone grey. 'You'll be tarnished too,' he muttered. 'Your TV career will be over.'

'I know. But that's the risk I've taken.'

'But I still don't *understand*,' he whined. 'Why the *hell* would you want to go and *look* for the guy?'

'I've already explained: because I no longer wanted to live with the guilt. And if you don't tell me why you targeted Derek White in the next two minutes, Jimmy, I'll ring Da-vid's number.'

'I've *told* you my name is *James*,' he hissed. 'James Mulhol-land—got that?'

'I'm sorry. But it's hard for me to remember, because when *I* knew you, you were plain Jimmy Smith. More importantly, you were the animal rights campaigner who deplored vi-olence. Although…now I think about it…I *remember* what you used to say. You used to say that violence was unaccept-able because it "attracted bad publicity for the animal rights movement"—*not*, interestingly, because it was *wrong*. Even so, I had no *idea* you were capable of what you did that day. Perhaps you'd even done it before.'

'No,' he said sullenly. He sat down again. 'I hadn't.'

'So why did you do it *then*?' I saw the muscle at the side of his mouth flex and jump. 'Why did you try to kill Derek White?'

'I *wasn't* trying to kill him,' he moaned, his head sinking slightly. 'I just...' he shrugged, '...wanted to give him a bit of a...shock. He'd been such a bastard to *me*, after all.'

'Had he?'

'*Yes*,' he said angrily. 'He *had*.'

I felt goose-bumps begin to raise themselves on my arms as I sensed the truth coming, at last. 'So what had he done then?' I asked softly, almost sympathetically.

'Oh, plenty of things,' he replied. 'Plenty,' he repeated, between clenched teeth. He shook his head again. 'If it hadn't been for him, I would have...' He stopped himself, then drew in a long breath through his nose.

'If it hadn't been for him—*what*?' There was silence for a moment, during which I was aware of the steady ticking of the clock.

'He had it in for me,' Jimmy went on sourly. 'He really had it *in* for me.' Now, he seemed almost to forget I was there, as the bitter memories came flooding back. 'White never liked me—in fact, he hated me. He made that clear from the start.'

'You were one of his students?' I asked. 'I never knew that.'

He nodded. 'I was in his microbiology set. And whatever I did was *never* good enough,' he spat. 'However *hard* I worked, I got low grades. Then, in my last year, he fucked me over. He fucked me *right* over. Why? Because he didn't like me. I should have complained. Because if it hadn't been for *that*, I would have been perfectly okay; I would have got a...' He suddenly seemed to collect himself.

'You would have got a *what*?'

'Oh, never you mind,' he muttered. 'But the point is, I didn't mean to do him any serious harm. I only wanted to make him *jump*. It was just...a firework,' he went on. 'A firework with a bit of sodium nitrate. But I'd obviously got the strength wrong. Then I heard what had happened, and, yes, it was...' he shrugged, '...regrettable.'

I laughed. 'You sound like Gerry Adams.'

'Look, I didn't *mean* for anyone to get hurt.'

'David White had to have a total of thirteen operations on his hands—five on his left one and eight on his right. He had to leave Cambridge, where he was studying medicine, early. He had flashbacks for years. He will bear the physical and emotional scars of what you did to him for the rest of his life.'

Jimmy flinched. '*Don't* tell him my name, Miranda. Please, *don't*. It's not necessary.'

I looked at him. 'All right. I won't. But if he chooses to pursue me through the civil courts—which remains a possibility—then I *will* have to say, under oath, that it was you, so you should be aware of that.'

Jimmy suddenly looked as lost and lonely as a small boy. 'I've dreaded this,' he said quietly. 'I've dreaded it for years.'

'I'm sure you have. But thanks for telling me the truth, at last.'

Suddenly the door opened, and Jimmy's secretary appeared with a paper carrier.

'I've got you egg—is that okay? Is that okay?' she repeated. 'Egg?'

He nodded absently as she handed him the bag. 'Yes,' he whispered. 'That's...fine.'

'Well, thank you very much for your time,' I said as I stood up. 'It really was a very helpful meeting. Don't worry—James—I'll see myself out.'

As I walked back down the corridor, I felt euphoric. I knew the truth at last. I'd be able to tell David, and though it might not bring him back, he would perhaps, at least, understand.

★ ★ ★

By now it was eleven forty, and by the time I got back to Daisy's it was almost half past twelve, so we were able to have a quick lunch in her office. She closed her door and, as we ate our sandwiches, I played her bits of the tape. Not only had it worked—it had come out very clearly.

'So it was student revenge then,' she said, as she passed me a bottle of water. I glanced at her files with their odd labels—'*Camel Hire*', '*Wedding Helicopters*', '*Alpine Wonderland*' and '*Moulin Rouge*'.

'Student revenge—but for what?'

'For failing microbiology obviously.'

'But that's what I don't understand. Jimmy *didn't* fail.'

'What do you mean?' She wiped her hands on her napkin.

'He got a first.'

'*Did* he?'

'Yes. In Biochemistry—so why would he go for David's father like that?' Daisy was staring at me, as confused, quite clearly, as I was—then she suddenly smiled.

'*I* know why,' she said.

'Why?'

'Because it isn't actually *true*.'

I looked at her. That thought hadn't even occurred to me. 'But I'm pretty sure it *is*. It's on his website. He'd hardly make such a claim if it were a lie.'

'Wouldn't he? I'm not sure. Lots of politicians lie.'

'But saying you got a first when you didn't would be an *enormous* risk, surely.'

Daisy shrugged. 'Politicians take risks all the time. Think of what Jeffrey Archer had to hide. And in any case, no-one ever checks what degree you got, do they, so no doubt he thought he'd get away with it.'

'Maybe you're right,' I said. 'Yes... And maybe *that's* what

Jimmy was about to say. He said that if it hadn't been for Professor White he would have got a...something. Then he stopped. He would have got a *first*. I think, maybe, *that's* what he was going to say, but he stopped himself just in time. Christ,' I laughed. 'You're right. What a turn-up! Now it all makes sense.'

'I wonder what degree he *did* get?' Daisy mused.

'I don't know.'

'What did he say when you knew him?'

'I can't remember him saying anything at all. All I knew was that he'd graduated the summer before and was staying on for a bit in Brighton while he looked for a job.'

'What did he want to do in those days?'

'He applied for all sorts of things—management consultancy, the BBC traineeship scheme. I remember he sat the foreign office exams too.'

'So top-notch career ambitions then?'

'Yes, although half the time he didn't even get interviewed.'

'Perhaps it was because of his animal rights campaigning.'

'I doubt it, as he was above-board. He was always giving local newspaper interviews saying that violence wasn't the way. He was the acceptable face of the movement, articulate and attractive, not grungy and aggressive.'

'Then it must have been because his degree was too low.'

'Quite possibly. *Yes*. And so, feeling increasingly thwarted and resentful, he blames the professor and...boom! Derek White gets it. Or rather, David does.'

'So what *did* Jimmy do for a job?'

'The profiles on the Net say he became a local radio journalist in York. He seems to have done that for at least five years.'

'So he wasn't planning to go into politics then?'

'No. If he'd been actively planning a political career, he would *never* have done what he did—*far* too risky—however much he loathed Derek White. The political career seems to have happened by chance when he interviewed Jack Straw and got offered a job as his parliamentary researcher, and then things took off from there.'

'So he went into politics knowing that he had this awful skeleton in his closet. *God*.' she breathed. 'He must have been *terrified* of it ever coming to light.'

'Yes. He admitted that just now.'

'And he must have prayed never to see *you* again.'

'He probably hoped I was *dead*.' I took the cassette out of the tiny tape recorder, labelled it, and tucked it carefully into my bag.

'Don't lose it,' said Daisy.

'I won't.'

'And are you going to play it to David?'

'I'm not...sure.'

'But it proves that you were telling the truth.'

'But my problem is that Jimmy names himself on it, so I don't want to. I'll have a think.' I handed the recorder back to her. 'Thanks. *Thanks*, Daisy—for everything.'

'It's a real pleasure.' She screwed up her sandwich wrapper and threw it into the bin. 'I'd *love* to see Jimmy brought low.'

'I guess I would too—but I feel that it's not for me to do—it's for David. We'll have to see what he does.'

'So still no word from him?'

My heart sank. 'No. But how are *you*?' I asked, as Daisy passed me a Mars Bar, then unwrapped one for herself. 'What about the llama hen party? My mum's dead keen to do it.'

'I know she is, but I'm just not sure...'

'Aren't you going to have one then?'

'I guess so,' she said absently. She still wasn't wearing her engagement ring.

'And have you decided which church?'

'Oh. No. At least…not yet,' she said vaguely. 'Nigel wants me to decide, but…I don't know…' Her voice trailed away.

'What's the matter, Daisy?' She didn't reply. 'This isn't just post-engagement stress, is it?' I said softly.

'Well, I…' She sighed, and Herman trotted up to her with a sympathetic expression on his face. 'I just feel a bit…distracted, that's all.' She picked him up and cuddled him. 'So I'm finding it hard to plan the wedding.'

'How odd, when you're so brilliant at planning other people's.'

'I know. But it's as you said—I can't quite take in the fact I'm engaged. It makes me feel strangely…flat. Plus…'

'Plus what?'

'Well, something *happened* yesterday, Miranda. Something I really didn't like. I would have mentioned it last night, but you were too upset about David.'

'And what was that?'

'Well, at lunch, Mary was there. In the pub.'

'Yes. You told me she would be. And…?'

'Someone mentioned the wedding, and she said to Nigel, "Well, you should get your Equity Partnership now." She said it in this jokey, inoffensive way, but the underlying meaning was clear. That Nigel would gain professionally by getting married.'

'That's bollocks! It makes *no* difference these days.'

'But Bloomfields is a traditional firm, so it might.'

'Yes, but they can't not promote someone just because they disapprove of their lifestyle.'

'But his new head of department is very old school. And Nige has been trying to get Equity Partnership for quite a

while now—that's why he's been working so hard. And I
suspect that if it came down to a choice between Nigel and
another similar candidate who was married with kids, then
the married one would win out. And Nigel's very ambitious,
as you know, so he's twigged this. That's what Mary was
implying.'

'I wouldn't pay the slightest attention to what she said—
she'd like to spoil things for you because Nigel was never
interested in her.'

'But when she said it, he blushed and instantly changed the
subject.'

'Look, Nigel loves you, Daisy, and that's why he wants to
marry you. I really think that's all there is to it.'

'Hmm,' she said. 'Maybe you're right. I don't know. But in
any case it isn't *just* that. It's…something bigger, actually.' She
heaved a deep, painful sigh, which caused Herman to emit a
compassionate whimper. 'Oh Christ, Miranda, I feel so *silly*
even saying it, but…'

'What?'

'Well, do you remember when we were chatting in my
garden a few weeks ago, and I said that I felt that I could tell
you anything—anything at all—and that you'd never judge
me?'

'Yes. Of course I do.'

'Well, there is something that's really bothering me, actually, and I *would* love to tell you about it, even though it'll
sound totally bananas, and I know you'll think I've *completely*
lost it…' Her voice trailed away.

'You can tell me, Daisy. What *is* it?'

'Well, I kept thinking about what you said—that day.' She
fiddled with her pen-pot. 'Recently, it's obsessed me.'

'Really? And what did I say?'

'You said that, maybe, if it didn't work out with Nigel, it was because—' Suddenly my mobile trilled out.

'Oh, *sorry*, Daisy, let me just get that. I'll tell them to go away.' I rummaged in my bag. 'Hello?'

'Is that Miranda Sweet?' said an unfamiliar female voice.

'Yes.'

'It's Karen Hall here.' *Who?* 'From the Pet Slimmer of the Year competition.'

'Oh *shit*!' I leapt to my feet. 'It's today, isn't it?'

'Yes. It is. Where *are* you?'

'I'm *so* sorry!' I gasped. I was panicking so much I thought I was going to have a heart attack.

'We've been expecting you since half past eleven. The lunch is almost over.' In the background I could hear the gentle clink of cutlery and the babble of voices.

'I'm *so* sorry,' I repeated. 'It slipped my mind.'

'We guessed that's what might have happened, but we couldn't find your mobile phone number, then someone looked it up on your website. But could you *please* make your way over as soon as possible, as you have to announce the result at two fifteen and the press are all here.' I glanced at my watch. It was twenty past one.

'I'll jump in a cab. Where is it again?'

'At the Meridien Hotel on Piccadilly,' she said, with a jus- tifiably exasperated air.

'I'm on my way.' I flipped the phone shut and tucked Herman under my arm. 'Christ, I'm just *so* distracted at the moment, Daisy—I'd forgotten I've got to announce the Pet Slimmer of the Year. I can't seem to focus on anything except my own problems at the moment.'

'I had noticed,' she said, rolling her eyes.

'I'm sorry, but it's been *such* a tricky time. And, oh God, we'll finish this conversation later on, okay—but I've got to race over there *now*.'

Thank heavens I was smartly dressed, I realized, as I ran outside and hailed a taxi. As we sped through Soho I tried to remember what I knew about the competition. They'd sent me loads of bumph about dieting Dalmatians and fat cats, but I hadn't read it. I'd just have to busk it. As we bumped down Charing Cross Road I jotted down a few notes for my speech. 'A fat pet is not a happy pet…better to be perky than porky…regular exercise…importance of sound nutrition…the many health risks of being overweight.' At last. I'd arrived. Heart pounding, I paid the driver and ran inside, where I was directed upstairs to the Edwardian Suite. I finger-combed my hair, took a couple of deep breaths, put a smile on my face, and went in.

Karen Hall saw me arrive, and stood up. I made my way over to her table, where coffee was being served.

'I'm *so* sorry,' I whispered as I sat down. My face was aflame. She handed me the press pack I'd been sent before, but had neglected to study.

'We have the five regional finalists here,' she explained. 'In your absence, I've already picked the winner, but if you could announce it, as the journalists are expecting it to be you.'

'Of course.' I couldn't have cared less which of them got it, I realized, as I quickly scanned through the blurb. There was Dixie, a dachshund from Stratford-upon-Avon, who had reduced his weight from a monstrous three stone to two. I looked at the 'before' and 'after' photos. He'd been so fat his stomach had scraped the ground, but now he looked lean and svelte. Then there was Delilah the Labrador—or rather Flabrador—who'd been a massive six stone, but who had lost twenty-one pounds. Then there was a Persian cat called

Sweetie, which had slimmed down from just over two stone to a very creditable thirteen pounds. Fourth was a vast rabbit called Fluffy, who had weighed an incredible one and a half stone and had to be pushed round the garden in a wheelbarrow before losing twelve pounds. Finally there was a mouse called Maurice, which had managed to get its weight down from a gross six ounces to a very sleek two ounces.

The press release recounted the trials and tribulations all the animals had faced in their quest to reduce. Delilah the Labrador had been making great progress when, in a moment of weakness, she stole a leg of lamb from the kitchen table and scoffed the whole thing. *That was a very bad moment*, said her owner, Brenda. *She gained two and a half pounds and got a real talking to after that!* Sweetie, the porky Persian, had gained weight when her owner's five-year-old daughter kept feeding her sardines on the sly. *It was touch and go as to whether or not she'd reach her goal in time*, said her relieved owner, Julia. *But the family are very proud of her now.*

We should applaud the willpower and determination of all our contestants, the press release concluded. *They are a shining example to us all of what can be achieved when you really try!*

I gulped down my coffee, as Karen Hall got to her feet.

'Ladies and gentlemen, the moment you've all been waiting for has now arrived.' There were a couple of excited barks from the back of the room. 'And here, to announce the 2003 PetWise Pet Slimmer of the Year, is Miranda Sweet from TV's very popular *Animal Crackers* programme!'

I got to my feet, my knees trembling. I hate public speaking.

'Thank you all for coming today,' I began. 'And I'd just like to say, before I open the gold envelope, that *all* the pets here today are winners. Their determination to diet is *very* impressive and shows what willpower can do—along with carefully controlled feeding, of course. But now, without further ado...' I ran my right thumb under the flap of the envelope, '...it is my very great pleasure to announce that the PetWise Pet Slimmer of the Year for 2003 is...Fluffy the rabbit!'

There was polite applause as Fluffy was carried up to the podium in his owner's arms. Onto the screen behind me appeared a photo of Fluffy as he was before. He was so fat you could hardly see his eyes. He looked like the Incredible Hulk.

The flashbulbs popped as I handed the slimline Fluffy and his owner their prize—a year's free insurance cover with Pet-Wise, and a year's supply of dried food.

'—This way please, Fluffy!' shouted a photographer.

'—No don't look at him, look at me.'

'—Big smile, Fluffy. Show us your teeth.'

'—Miranda—give him a kiss!'

I didn't realize that there'd be so much publicity—the paparazzi were out in some force. But now, as they snapped away, I could hear that there was a dispute developing amongst the other contestants.

'—Okay the rabbit was fat, granted,' said the owner of the Persian. 'But Sweetie got so huge her cat flap had to be widened—by *ten inches!*'

'—Well, Delilah was a right lardarse—and look at her now. Like Kate Moss!'

'—*I* don't think it's fair to make the competition interspecies.'

'—Maurice lost *four ounces*. That's sixty-six per cent of his body weight.'

'—Really? Well, maybe *he* should have won...'

I discreetly rolled my eyes—this is what I hate about competitions of this kind. The discontented losers. As I cast my eye over the room, I spotted the journalist, Tim Charlton, who'd interviewed me for the *Camden New Journal*. He was obviously doing a diary piece for the *Independent on Sunday*. He caught my eye and I smiled.

'Hello,' he said, as I stepped off the podium.

'Hi, Tim. How's it going at the Sindie?'

'It's going well, thanks. Can I get a quote from you?'

'Of course.' We concocted some story about Britain's pets being a nation of furry fatties.

'Maybe Fluffy should put out a fitness video,' I added. 'I mean, if Vanessa Feltz can, then why can't he?'

'That's perfectly reasonable,' he said seriously, as he scribbled it down. 'Actually, there was something else I wanted to ask you.'

'What's that?'

'Well, you know I want to get into political reporting?'

'Yes, I remember you saying.'

'So I've been writing one or two anonymous profiles lately for the op ed page. And I saw you at the Photographers' Gallery last month—at Arnie Noble's exhibition.'

'Did you? I didn't realize you were there.'

'Well, it was very crowded, but I was. And I couldn't help noticing that you were chatting to James Mulholland's wife, Caroline Horbury.'

'Ye-es,' I said slowly. 'That's right.'

'And this morning the editor asked me to write a profile of James Mulholland for this Sunday's paper, as he's been tipped for the Cabinet at the next reshuffle.'

'Really?' I said faintly.

'So I wondered whether you might have any interesting

little titbits that I might be able to use—it doesn't matter how trivial—just to liven the piece up.'

'Some interesting little titbits?' I echoed. I struggled with my conscience for less than a second. 'Yes,' I said. 'Actually, I *have*.'

— CHAPTER 14 —

That night I phoned Daisy, but she was at Nigel's and couldn't speak. She clearly had big problems but I'd been so distracted by my own difficulties that I'd failed to focus on hers. This realization made me feel horribly neglectful—especially as she'd been so supportive of me. And what was it she'd said—about something *I'd* said to her a few weeks back? With all my troubles I couldn't remember. So I left her a message, then went to bed, though I barely slept, drifting off just before dawn.

I awoke three hours later with the knowledge that this morning David would receive my letter. Perhaps, if his post had come early, he'd already read it. My pulse began to race at the thought. However, I knew that I couldn't, in any circumstances, call him: it was up to him to contact me. But by ten he hadn't phoned, and I knew that he wouldn't. I imagined my letter, in the bin, in fragments. I played the tape again. It was all there.

Why have you deliberately stirred it all up?…felt awful about it for sixteen years…you should have left it alone…do you want money, is that it?… Did you give him my name?… I didn't have the faintest idea what it really was… That's true… Why would you want to go and look for the guy?… I'll ring David right now… It was just a firework…regrettable.

It was explosive stuff, I thought—without irony. It was dynamite. It could blow his whole life apart. How silly of him, I thought. Manipulative though Jimmy was, it had never once crossed his mind that I might have been recording our conversation. I put the tape at the back of my drawer, then went round the corner to get a newspaper. And I was just deciding whether to get the *Guardian* or the *Independent*, when I noticed that the new September edition of *Moi!* had come in. I bought one, and, still feeling fragile after my sleepless night, I ordered a comforting *latte* in the Patisserie and then sat outside in the sunshine, reading the magazine. The 'Miss Behaviour' article was about halfway through and took up two pages. The main photograph was the one that David had printed first. I was filled with sadness as I looked at it, remembering when David had taken it— *Don't smile. A smile is concealing.* Then later, when I'd seen the image emerge— *You look slightly troubled. As though there's something very complex going on in your head.* Indeed. And now David knew what that was.

The piece was lively and well-written, and, despite India Carr's irritating probing, she'd actually said very little about my personal life—my circumspection and discretion had clearly paid off. I knew that the coverage would undoubtedly generate lots of enquiries so I decided to send Lily some flowers. I finished my *latte* and crossed over the road to the florist, and was just picking out some apricot roses when I saw Gnatalie coming up the road, on her mobile, as usual.

'No, Mummy,' I heard her say, as she passed behind me. 'I don't think he understands me *at all*. I mean…*ice-cream*? Well, exactly…he *knows* I'm lactose intolerant…Yes…I *do* think he's selfish…Hmm. But on the other hand, he's attractive and funny…and of course he's nuts about me…yes…I'm seeing him tonight.'

Why? I wondered as I selected some white gerbera. Why are you seeing him tonight? Or any night? In fact, why are you seeing him at *all*, you whiny cow? And how disloyal! Going out with him while bitching about him non-stop to her mum. That really is a case of trying to have one's gluten-free rice-cake and eat it, I thought crossly as I headed back to the house.

'Marcus is a nice guy,' I said to Herman. 'He deserves better, don't you think?' Herman heaved a sympathetic sigh.

I had an appointment in Islington at twelve, then rushed back, hoping that there might be a message from David, but there wasn't—and by three, I still hadn't heard. At half past four I saw my second client of the day—a disobedient collie cross. It wouldn't do a thing its owner said.

'He's just *so* naughty,' she kept saying as we walked onto Primrose Hill, the dog twisting and pulling on the lead. '*Heel*, will you! He's so naughty,' she said again. 'He knows perfectly *well* what I want him to do, but he just won't *do* it.'

'Dogs are not naughty,' I said. 'To say that they are, is to impute to them human motives which they're incapable of having. Dogs have no sense of "good" or "bad",' I explained. 'They don't understand "right" or "wrong". They don't have a conscience, or any concept of "guilt"—' I thought of Jimmy, '—they do only what's rewarding to *them*.'

I went through the basic principles with her; ignoring 'bad' or unwanted behaviours and positively reinforcing 'good' or desired behaviours. Then we went back to the house, where I looked up an accredited training class for her to attend. As I sat at my desk I saw that there were two messages. I was dying to play them. The emotional stress made my insides shift.

'Thank you,' I said, as she handed me her cheque. 'And good luck with him—I'm sure he'll be fine.'

I'd shown her out, and was just about to listen to the answerphone, when my mobile rang. It was my mother, sounding excited about her idiotic new llama project. She eventually got off the line, and I was just about to listen to my messages at long, long *last*, when I heard a light knock at the door. My hand stopped in mid-air. Then another one, slightly louder. It was David! I ran to the door.

'Oh!' It was like a bullet to the chest.

'Hello, Miranda.'

'Alexander,' I murmured automatically. I felt sick, and faint. I also felt angry. He smiled an apologetic little half smile, and I suddenly felt terribly sad as well.

'I'm sorry to turn up like this,' he said diffidently. 'I did leave a message for you earlier, but I thought that you might be ignoring me, so I decided I'd just…come round.'

'Oh…well, I wasn't…ignoring you. It's just that I haven't had time to listen to my messages yet. I've been too busy.' I stared at him. I'd forgotten—no, I'd suppressed—how good-looking he was.

'Can I come in?'

'Oh. Yes,' I said weakly. 'Do…'

As Alexander crossed the threshold, Herman trotted up to him, his tail wagging. 'Hello, Herman.' He crouched down to stroke him. 'Hello, little guy.' He picked him up, and Herman licked his ear. 'I've missed you.'

'Erm…would you like a cup of tea?' I asked, at a loss for anything else to say. The blood was pounding in my ears and my face felt hot.

'That would be nice. Or maybe, if you've got it, a beer?'

'Sure.' *Why are you here?* I opened the fridge. *Why?* 'Bud-weiser?'

'Thanks. I hope you're going to have one too.'

'Okay.' *Though what I really need is a valium.*

'Do you mind if I smoke?' I heard him call out.

'No,' I said weakly. 'That's fine.' He was standing in the kitchen doorway now, so tall that his head almost touched the lintel. He pulled a packet of Gitanes out of his jacket pocket, removed one, then lit it with a hand which visibly trembled. The familiar aroma filled my nostrils and I was nearly felled by a wave of nostalgic distress.

'You've done an amazing job on the house,' he said, as I handed him an ashtray. 'I remember how derelict it was when we…' he hesitated. 'When we first saw it.' *In the days when we were 'we'.* 'So the practice is going well,' he remarked nervously as he blew the smoke away. 'I saw the piece about you in *Moi!* Nice photo,' he added, as I handed him the beer. *If only you knew what lay behind it.* 'There's one of you in *The Times* today too.'

'Is there?'

'With a rabbit.'

'Oh. The animal slimming competition?'

He nodded. 'They've called it "Heavy Petting".'

'That's good. And I've seen lots of stuff about *you*.' He smiled, then looked at the floor. 'I watched the first episode of *Land Ahoy!*'

'Did you?' He seemed genuinely surprised. 'I thought you might not have wanted to.'

'Oh…no,' I protested. *Actually, you're right, I didn't—but I made myself.* 'It was very good. You looked…great. You got some terrific reviews, didn't you?'

He sat on the couch, and, still striving to project a polite detachment, I pulled up a chair about five feet away. 'Yes,' he replied, drawing deeply on the cigarette. 'I did get some nice coverage. It went very well. That was a really…' he exhaled a stream of silvery smoke, '…lucky break.' I nodded again. Then we just stared at each other, awkwardly, as we sipped our beer, like teenagers at their first party. 'So have you been okay, Miranda?' he asked softly.

'Have I been okay?' *No. I haven't. I've been in turmoil.* 'Erm…yes. Thanks. Yes. I've been…fine.'

'And what about your parents? And Daisy?' He delicately picked a shred of tobacco off his tongue.

'They're all right.' I told him about my dad's return to the UK. I even told him about my mother's lunatic new idea for the llamas. His blue eyes shone with laughter.

'Unbelievable!'

'No, honestly. She's quite serious about it. It's mad.' By now, the atmosphere had lightened. I'd even managed to smile. 'And you're off to Hollywood?'

'That's right.'

'So when are you going?'

'Tomorrow.' *Tomorrow?* I felt a sudden constriction in my throat. 'My flight's at noon. That's why I've come, actually,' he added quietly. 'You must have been wondering.'

'Well, yes. I…suppose I was.'

'It's because I didn't want to leave without seeing you again.'

'Oh.' I stared at a patch of sunlight on the floor.

'I just wanted to make sure that you were…okay.'

'Oh, I'm fine,' I murmured. 'I'm…fine.' *No, I'm not. I'm miserable! And now I'm even more miserable than I was before. Why the hell did you have to come, Alexander?*

'Because I wanted to say goodbye.' *Goodbye?*

'You make it sound so final.'

'It probably is. I'm planning to stay out there.'

'Really?'

'It's a very nice life. Lots of Brits. Lots of sunshine…'

'And lots of work too—with luck.'

He shrugged. 'I've got a few screen tests coming up. There's quite a bit of interest at the moment because *Land Ahoy!*'s just been shown in the States.'

'Reese Witherspoon,' I murmured. 'I read that you might be working with her.'

'Yes. There's a chance I might. She's brilliant.'

'I loved her in *Sweet Home Alabama*.'

'Me too.'

'Well…you'll probably become a big star, then.'

He shrugged again. 'I don't know. I just hope it'll…work out. You know,' he added with a slightly forced brightness, 'it's probably a good thing we broke up—isn't it?' He gave me a tentative smile, as though he sought my approval. 'I can't imagine you'd have liked living in L.A. very much.'

'No, I don't think I would. I saw enough of it when Dad was over there to know that.'

'Although, on the other hand, you'd have been very busy,' he pointed out. '*Lots* of neurotic pets.'

I smiled. 'Neurotic owners, rather. But you're right—L.A. isn't really for me. So, no—it probably wouldn't have worked between us long term anyway, and so it was just…as well…' *That you abandoned me.* I glanced out of the window. *And if you hadn't, we would have been married next month.* There was silence for a few moments.

'I'm sorry,' I heard him suddenly say. I looked at him, and now, to my amazement, there were tears standing in his eyes. 'I'm sorry, Miranda,' he repeated. 'That's what I've really come to say.' I was too stunned to reply, the silence between us so intense I could hear myself breathing. Then, suddenly, Alexander stood up. And I thought he was going to leave.

Instead, he pulled me to my feet, and enveloped me in an awkward hug. 'I behaved so...*badly,*' he said, his voice fracturing with feeling. 'But I couldn't bear to leave London without telling you how sorry I am. You may not believe it, but I've felt just...*terrible* these past few weeks.'

'It's okay.' I felt my own eyes now brim, and then spill over. 'It's okay, Alex...'

'I don't know what...happened that night. I guess I... panicked. And the next thing I knew you were...' his voice trailed away. *In hospital.* 'But I just hope you can...forgive me.'

'Yes. Yes, of course I can—and I *do.* I do...forgive you.' As I said that, I felt something dark and shadowy leave my soul. 'I know you didn't *mean*...' I stopped. *To desert me.*

'It all happened so fast.'

'I know.' Now we sank onto the couch, side by side, gripping each other's hands.

'But it's tormented me, Miranda. The knowledge that you got hurt. And that I should have protected you—but I... didn't. I let you down.'

'Look, I'm completely better now. It didn't take long. I've got over it—and far worse things happen to people every day.'

'But when I got the engagement ring back, I just felt so *bad*. I felt that you hated me.'

I shook my head. 'That's not true. I wasn't returning it in order to punish you. It's just that keeping it didn't feel... right.'

'I sold it,' he murmured.

'Really?'

'I gave the money to charity.'

'That was nice.'

'And I've been trying to summon up the courage to contact you, ever since I knew I was going to the States: but I thought you'd refuse to see me, which would only have made me feel worse. But then, when I got the ring, I knew that I *had* to get in touch with you. I couldn't leave this country, feeling that you despised me.'

'I don't.' *At least, not any more.*

'I knew I couldn't move forward with that hanging over me. So I just needed to come and say…what I've said.'

'It's okay,' I murmured, my throat aching. 'It's all forgotten now. And in a funny sort of *way*,' I went on, 'maybe good things have come out of it.' I thought of David and my own search for forgiveness.

'What sort of things?'

'I can't…really say. But maybe, one day, I'll tell you.'

Even as I said it, I knew that I never would.

He sighed, then stood up again. 'Well, I'd better get going, I guess. I haven't finished packing.'

'What's happening to your flat?'

'It's being let.'

'Thanks for coming, Alexander. I'm so glad you did. Will you let me know how it goes?'

'Yes,' he said. 'Of course I will. If I land anything big, I'll e-mail you. I'd like to do that.'

I handed him my card. 'I hope it all works out…really well.'

'Thanks. You too. I'm so glad I've seen you.' His deep blue eyes were shimmering again, then he leaned down and kissed my cheek.

'Can I just ask you something?' I added, as he reached for the door handle.

'Of course.'

'Which charity did you give the money to?' He paused for a moment, and I saw his face flush.

'The...Samaritans. I think they're very worthwhile.'

After Alexander had gone, I sat on the couch, staring at the floor, mentally replaying the scene, frame by frame. Then I put Herman on the lead, and we skirted Primrose Hill in the gathering dusk, then entered Regent's Park. We crossed over to the Inner Circle, and passed the theatre. There was no performance tonight. It was quiet. And now, as the residual pink of the sky turned to mauve, then cobalt, I sat on a bench, in the rose garden, the memories of my first glimpse of Alexander flooding back.

—I do beseech you—chiefly that I might set it in my prayers—what is your name?
—I'll be your patient log-man...
—Admired Miranda! Indeed the top of admiration!

I stood up, and began to walk back.

—The rarer action is in virtue, than in vengeance...

That was so, *so* true. I'd felt vengeful towards Alexander; I'd wanted to punish him—but he'd clearly been in pain, all the time. And it had been easy to forgive him—so *easy*—when I'd thought it would be impossibly hard.

As you from crimes would pardoned be,
Let your indulgence set me free!

When I got back to the house, I saw the answerphone flashing and realized I still hadn't listened to my messages. I'd been so knocked out by Alexander's visit that I'd forgotten to play them. The first message was from him, tentatively asking me to return his call. The second was from Daisy. She sounded upset. I phoned her straight back but her mobile was switched off. Maybe she was out with Nigel, or at one of her parties. I was longing to tell her about Alexander, and I wanted to know what was happening with her. What was it she'd said yesterday? She'd mentioned something that *I'd* said, when we were sitting in her garden a few weeks ago—but I couldn't for the life of me think what.

At ten I left another message for her, telling her to call me any time—day or night. But she didn't. And I didn't hear from her all the next day—or the next. She wasn't at work, and the woman on reception said they weren't sure when she was coming in—no one seemed to know where she was. I was worried by now, and was about to call Nigel or her mother when, at last, on Friday, I heard. The phone went at seven a.m. It was her.

'Miranda.' Her voice was cracking. 'It's me. I've been awake all night. Can I come over for breakfast?'

'Of *course*. I'll go and get some chocolate croissants.'

She arrived an hour later, looking pale and strained.

'I just wanted to see you. The last three days have been hell.'

I glanced at her left hand, and she saw me looking. 'I've given it back.'

'What?'

'I'm not marrying him, Miranda. I decided on Tuesday.'

'Christ,' I said quietly. 'Why? Because of the way he proposed?'

'Yes,' she sighed 'in part. It was just so *awful*. I felt…humiliated. He couldn't have made it less romantic if he'd tried. But also because I discovered that what Mary said was true. I pressed him about it on Monday night and, under duress, he virtually admitted it. But the *main* reason I'm not marrying

Nigel is because it's just plain…*wrong*—and I've known that for a very long time.'

'Then why on earth…?'

She threw up her hands. 'Because I've been such a *wimp*! Clinging to Nigel because I thought he was my best bet—and because I was afraid of starting again with someone else. I'd just got in the habit of being with him, that's all—and he seemed so suitable and safe. But what have Nige and I got in common, Miranda? *Zero!*' she went on before I could answer. '*Less* than zero actually, and you see, the point is…' Her voice trailed away. 'The point *is*…' There were tears in her eyes now, and her chin trembled with distress. And, as I reached for the box of tissues, I suddenly remembered what it was I'd said to her a few weeks earlier, as we'd sat in her garden. *If it doesn't work out with Nigel, maybe it's because it's actually your destiny to meet someone else.*

'The point *is*…' she tried again, then sank onto a chair. 'That I've…'

'Met someone else… You have, haven't you? This is what this is really about.' She nodded, then her head collapsed onto her chest. 'Oh Daisy.'

'I thought you might have guessed before,' she wept. 'It's been pretty bloody *obvious*—but you've been so wrapped up in yourself.'

'I know I have,' I said as I handed her a tissue. 'I'm sorry. I've been so distracted by my own problems. But do you think it might…work out…with this guy?'

'No! No—it *won't* work out,' she wailed.

'Why not?'

'Because he's *with* someone—but that's not the *point*. The point *is* that I've only known him just over a month, but in that time I've had *ten times* more fun with him than I've had in nearly *six years* with Nigel. And that made me finally face up to the fact that it would be *wrong* to marry Nige. Until that happened to me, I'd been happy to go along with the illusion that Nige was okay. That he'd "do" for me—but he *won't*; because he took too long to make a commitment, and then did it for the wrong reasons—and that's just not *good enough*, Miranda—I want *more!*'

'It's the guy you go microlighting with, isn't it?'

She swallowed her tears. 'Yes, it is. I did think you might have twigged before.'

'Not really, because you've been doing these things for *years*, Daisy, with all sorts of people, so I didn't attach any extra significance to him—especially as you'd just got engaged. But can't you tell him how you feel?'

'*No!*' she wept. 'It's too *embarrassing*. He's *with* someone. I've *told* you.'

'For how long?'

'About three months. But he's totally besotted with her—that's clear. But just the simple fact of meeting someone I've had such a strong feeling about, made me realize that I simply *couldn't* marry Nigel.' She wiped her eyes. 'I've returned the wedding dress, by the way. They gave me back my money—minus ten per cent for the inconvenience.'

'That was decent of them.'

'I know. They obviously felt sorry for me. But that's why I haven't been at work. I've had things like that to do—collecting the ring, and returning it to Nigel. Taking back the dress. Seeing a few people… Plus I had to get my stuff from Nigel's house—and that's another thing—there was so *little* of mine there.'

'I know. I'd always noticed that.'

'Do you know what there was? My nightdress, my washbag, my tennis kit, and a few recipe books. After five and a half years, that's *all*. He didn't really *want* to share his life with me—until he thought it would be useful to do so. But he must have known how I felt.'

'I'm sure he did. But you never pushed him into making a commitment to you.'

'I know I didn't—and what a fool! I let him get away with murder! But I was too...' she sighed, '...too scared to have it out, in case it ended. But meeting this other guy made me feel brave. So, no. I'm not going to settle for Nigel. And as for children—that can wait. I'm only thirty-three—there's still time. All I do know is I'm not going to marry someone who hasn't made me feel that I'm...' she paused, '...*essential* to his happiness. That he'd really *miss* me if I wasn't there—and I don't actually think Nigel *would*—or at least not for long. But this other guy... Oh, I've had such *fun* with him, Miranda. We've got so much in common—and he's so full of *life*.'

I suddenly noticed the short white hairs on her jumper again. And now, I realized with a jolt that they were Twiglet's. How could I have been so blind? 'It's Marcus,' I said quietly.

She rolled her eyes. 'Well done, Sherlock.'

'I'm sorry, but I didn't...think. I've been in a sort of tunnel lately—and to be fair, Daisy, you didn't *say*.'

'That's because I felt such an *idiot*. There I was, having hankered after Nigel for *so* long, and I finally get engaged to him—and *what* happens? I instantly get a massive crush on someone *else*—someone who isn't even *free*! I know we're best friends, Miranda, but I couldn't bring myself to tell you what was going on because I felt such a *fool*! And I was in a real quandary, because I did feel, for a while, that Marcus liked me—when I was doing the self-defence classes.'

'So that's why you sounded so enthusiastic about them.'

'Well, yes, it was such a lot of fun. And because you never

came, I had to work with him, as all the others were in
pairs. And I did feel then, that he…liked me. But then, to
my amazement—Nigel proposed. He proposed—just when I
didn't actually *want* him to. It was all such a mess. But now,
well, it doesn't matter. But, if you ever see Marcus again, you
won't say a thing, will you?' She put her head in her hands.
'It makes me feel utterly…*absurd.*'

'No. Of course I won't. But what has he said about his
girlfriend?'

Daisy sighed. 'Not very much. I only know her name, and
that she makes jewellery, and that she's successful and very
beautiful. Other than that he's hardly discussed her.'

'So he's never said anything negative about her, then?'

'Gosh, *no.*' Daisy looked shocked.

'What a *nice* man he is. He's very loyal. I wouldn't worry
about Natalie, Daisy.'

'What do you mean?'

'Just that. *Forget* about her, and carry on seeing Marcus.'

'But that's the problem,' she sobbed. 'I *can't.* Because the
self-defence classes are over now, and he suddenly said that he
didn't have time to take me microlighting any more.'

I suddenly remembered Marcus's odd reaction to Daisy's
engagement. He'd *liked* her. Of course. He'd been in a quandary himself. 'I think that if you tell him you're no longer
engaged—he *will.*' She looked at me curiously. 'That's all I'm
going to say, Daisy. Just…forget about Natalie. Make friends
with Marcus, as you've been doing. After all, you're free to
do whatever you like now—*with* whoever you like.'

'Yes,' she said, with a relieved sigh. 'I *am.*'

On Saturday I spent the morning dealing with my e-
mails. There was one from Lily thanking me for the flowers,
accompanied by a 'formal pawtrait' of Jennifer and Gwyneth;

then there was another one from the man with the budgie, saying that the provision of a companion had greatly improved Tweetie's mood. There was also one from the Greens, the owners of the Red setter I'd seen in late June. '*This is to let you know that a fortnight ago we had Sinead mated with a nice Irish setter called Fergus—and she's now a very happy mum-to-be.*' I smiled. '*And so,*' I read on, '*am I! When we came to see you, I had no idea that I was actually four weeks pregnant, naturally as it happens, and I've just had my three month scan.*' I e-mailed back to say how thrilled I was for them. Things often work out in quite oblique ways, I thought, as I worked through the rest of my mail.

'*Every time I try to kiss my girlfriend, her dog attacks me—please help!*' '*Do you think my Peke is a pervert? It keeps trying to make love to the cat.*' There was another e-mail from the man whose rabbit wouldn't breed. '*She's a very pretty little Angora—and we've had her introduced to three bucks now, all of them eminently suitable in our view—but absolutely nothing's happened. Do you think she's too fussy—or are we doing something wrong?*' I messaged him back, advising patience. '*Rabbits are individuals...*' I typed. And I was just going to go into some detail about the sexual psychology of the receptive doe, when the phone went. It was my mother—on her mobile.

'Darling, you've *got* to watch the early evening news. We're on!'

'Mum, I can't believe the opening of a golf club is a national news story.'

'Just *watch* it, Miranda—they've been interviewing us all morning—and, oh, sorry, can't chat—the man from *London Tonight* is waving at me.'

At five o'clock I put the TV on. We trawled through the main stories, and then it came to the 'and finally' bit.

'And finally,' said Trevor McDonald. 'A new golf club

opened in East Sussex today. Nothing particularly startling
about that, you may think. But the Lower Chalvington Golf
Club near Alfriston in East Sussex offers members an absolutely *unique* service, as our reporter, Lucy Bowles, has been
finding out.'

The film opened with a wide shot of the course and clubhouse—it did look attractive—then cut to a player teeing off.

'Lower Chalvington founder member Tom Williams tees
off...' I heard the reporter say. Now the camera pulled back
to a wide shot—and I gasped. 'With the help of a warm,
fuzzy friend.' For there, standing patiently behind the player,
his fleece rippling in the gentle breeze, was Pedro, carrying
the man's clubs. 'Meet Tom Williams's golf caddy—Pedro
the llama.' They'd actually *done* it. I hadn't really believed
they could be serious. I thought the whole thing was a joke.

'Llamas have been pack animals in the Andes for thou-
sands of years,' Lucy Bowles explained as Tom Williams led
Pedro to the next hole. 'But within the past fifteen years or
so, they've begun to attract a small but passionate following in the UK. Most llamas are kept as pets, but Pedro and
his fellow llamas like to *work*. They take walkers on treks
over the South Downs at weekends, they do hospital visits,
and the occasional advertising campaign. But from now on
they'll spend their weekdays caddying for the members of the
Lower Chalvington. The llamas belong to Alice Ingram. She
says that not only are they up to the job—they're perfect for
it.'

The camera cut to Mum, looking thrilled.

'They really *are* perfect,' she said. 'Llamas are very light-
footed—they don't have hooves—so they don't mark the
greens. They're also scrupulously clean—they only use com-
munal latrines—so they don't make a mess. They're also *very*
patient, sensitive, sweet-tempered animals. They'll stand

there, quite happily, for as long as the shot takes, just thinking nice thoughts and enjoying the view.'

Now there was a shot of Tom Williams at the third green.

'So what do you think of Pedro's caddying skills?' the reporter asked him with a smile.

'Well, he's *rather* good,' he replied. 'I've been playing with him all morning, and he's certainly better than a lot of human caddies I've had. For a start, he doesn't complain about carrying the clubs; and he doesn't make any negative comments if I don't play the shot very well. He also makes me feel curiously calm, which enables me to play better. He's not too good at club selection,' Williams added. 'But then you can't have everything, can you? C'mon, Pedro.' He gave Pedro a carrot, then led him off. Then the camera cut back to Lucy.

'The llama caddies are the brainchild of the club's general manager, Ted Sweet,' she explained. And now there was Dad, smiling broadly. 'So what gave you the idea?'

'Well, I've managed golf clubs in the States for over twenty years,' he began. 'And I knew that there was *one* club in North Carolina which had a couple of llamas on the payroll, and I happened to mention this, in passing, to Mrs Ingram about a month ago. And, to my surprise, she suggested that we tried it here. So we then had to put our plan into action—at *extremely* short notice. We placed a rush order for the specially customized golf club bags which the llamas wear. They only arrived yesterday, just in time for today's opening, and the llamas have taken to them very well. They carry two bags, one on each side, so that they're nicely balanced.'

'Isn't it just a gimmick?' the reporter suggested amiably.

'Maybe it is. But as a new club we were looking for something really show-stopping—and that's what the llamas are—

show-stoppers. On a more practical note, they also help to keep down the rough.'

'So are these the first llama golf caddies in the UK?'

'They are. In fact, we believe they're the only ones in the whole of Europe.' And now the camera pulled back for a wide shot in which you could see all the other llamas, gently tramping round the course, or standing by the holes, and then there was Trevor McDonald again.

'Whatever next?' he said with a smile. 'Llama football referees? From me and the early evening news team—goodbye.'

'Brilliant,' I breathed. 'Just *brilliant*.' So *that's* why Mum had warmed to Dad so much—she'd seen a good business opportunity there for the llamas. If the club took off she'd be quids in. And I was just trying to call her—her mobile was constantly engaged—when there was a knock at the door.

'Miss Sweet?'

'Yes?'

A man was standing there with a huge bouquet. 'These are for you. Please sign.'

I stared at the huge bouquet of roses and tiger lilies. *Who* had sent me these? As I opened the small white envelope with a shaking hand, I hoped, yes, I really hoped that they might be from David. But surely *I* should be sending flowers to *him*. I did also think they might be from Alexander, for my birthday tomorrow. But, to my surprise, they were from Tim. I read the card. *That was some 'titbit', Miranda—I'll never be able to thank you enough!*

On Sunday I was woken by Mum at half-seven.

'Happy Birthday, darling.'

'Thanks,' I croaked. 'Isn't it a bit early?'

'Sorry. I've been up since six. And did you see your dad and me last night?'

'I did. It was *great*.' I threw off the duvet, then yawned. 'I'm sorry I ever doubted you.'

'Well, we've got some wonderful coverage in the newspapers too. Go and get the *Sunday Independent*—we're on page four—it's *huge*.'

I quickly dressed and went round the corner to the newsagent. But when I saw the *Independent*, I gasped. 'MULHOLLAND'S FIRST-CLASS LIE!' it thundered, and beneath: 'EDUCATION MINISTER'S DEGREE DECEPTION.' It was labelled 'Exclusive', but the other papers had picked up on it too. 'EDUCATION MINISTER IS AN EXAM CHEAT' trumpeted the *Sunday Telegraph* above a huge photo of Jimmy. 'NOT QUALIFIED FOR THE JOB!' admonished the *Mail*. As I read the *Independent*'s front page, which had Tim Charlton's by-line on it, in huge capitals, I was so transfixed that I nearly walked out of the shop without paying. I blindly handed over the money, then, eyes still glued to the story, walked home, trying not to bump into lamp posts. Then, hands trembling, I sat at my desk.

Education Minister James Mulholland, hitherto tipped for the top, has just taken a steep career tumble. An investigation by this paper reveals that the 'first-class degree' he claims to have gained from Sussex University in Biochemistry in 1986, was, in fact, only a third. This blatant untruth—which even features on his website—has gone unchallenged for years. The Minister, on holiday in Scotland, claimed, when telephoned by us, that it was merely a 'misunderstanding', although he later corrected this to a 'mistake'. His colleagues have pronounced themselves shocked, and there's said to be 'disappointment' in his constituency, Billington. There has been no endorsement, so far, from the Prime Minister, and, far from being promoted in the autumn reshuffle, it is now predicted that the ambitious Mr Mulholland will be sent right to the back of the class.

Inside was another full-page piece, headed: *The Rise and*

Fall of James Mulholland, which also included the fact that he
had changed his name. There was an excoriating leader about
him as well. *As Minister with special responsibility for 'Lifelong
Learning', Mr Mulholland has now learned two important lessons
himself: a) that honesty is always the best policy, and b) that the
truth, invariably, will out.* His ministerial ambitions are now in
shreds, it concluded. I put the paper down, feeling a smile
spread across my face. Jimmy's political career was ruined.
And I rejoiced.

'Thank you, Daisy,' I whispered. 'Thank you for working
that one out—you clever, *clever* girl.' I called her, but there
was no reply and her mobile was turned off. Maybe she was
with her mum. Then I turned to page four of the paper,
every inch of which was devoted to the boys:

*A herd of llamas have been recruited to work as golf caddies for
a Sussex golf club...brainchild of Ted Sweet and his ex-wife, Alice
Ingram...eight llamas...special golf bag backpacks...sensitivity and
intelligence makes them suitable for the job, according to Mr Sweet.
The club, which had been struggling to attract new members, has
received hundreds of new enquiries since word began to get out last
week.*

Occupying the top half of the page was a photo of Henry
with his golf bags, captioned, *Henry Kissinger.*

'*The great thing about Henry,' said one member, Sarah Penrose,
'is that you get a kiss from him every time you play a shot—whether
or not it was any good!'*

'*But don't llamas spit?'* the reporter asked. '*No,'* Mum replied. '*Or only, occasionally, at each other—if they're arguing.'* And
why do they hum? '*That's easy,'* Dad replied. '*Llamas hum because they don't know the words.'*

'Good news, Herman,' I said. '*Very* good news. On two
fronts, at least.' He did his best to look happy. 'And today,
I'm thirty-three.' It would be a strange sort of birthday as I

wouldn't be seeing anyone. Daisy had offered to spend the day with me, but I somehow felt like being alone. I turned on London F.M. and had it on in the background while I worked—I had at least eight reports to write up.

'*Growing pressure on Mr Mulholland…*' I heard as I typed away. '*Mr Mulholland has still not issued a statement… Conspicuous lack of support from his ministerial colleagues… His admission that he has lied about his degree result has made his position as Education Minister untenable… Not a case of if he goes, but when… The Education Minister, James Mulholland, has resigned from Government,*' I heard at the top of the four o'clock bulletin. A warm glow filled my heart. Jimmy, like Trigger, had been the domineering top dog, who had had his status reduced—at *last*.

I put Herman on the lead and walked up Primrose Hill. The sun was still high, though it would soon start to sink. The joggers and kite-flyers were out in force. I sat on the bench at the top, drinking in the view, remembering my birthday last year. I'd spent it with Alexander. He'd taken me to Paris. Now here I was, alone. But worse things had happened to me than that, I thought, as I shut my eyes. Far worse…

I thought of Daisy, and how brave she'd been to leave Nigel. That leap into the void had taken more courage than fifty parachute jumps. I listened to the distant shriek of children, and the dull roar of the cars. Then I walked back down. And I was staring at the ground, lost in my thoughts, when Herman suddenly barked. I looked up, then stopped, my heart hammering against my ribs. He was coming up the hill, towards me. Was he real, or had my exhausted mind conjured an image of him? He was maybe fifty yards away. Now twenty. And now he'd drawn level.

'I thought I might find you up here.' He looked tired, and unshaven. 'So, aren't you going to say hello?'

'Hello…' I murmured.

He smiled. 'Hello, Miranda.'

'But…why have you come?'

'Can't you guess?'

'No. Not…really.'

'Well, because it's your birthday. Don't you remember? I said I'd take you out for dinner.'

'Oh…yes. I do. But you don't have to…' My voice trailed away.

'I always like to keep my word. Unless you're busy this evening?'

'No. No, I'm not busy.'

'And how have you been?'

'All right,' I replied quietly. 'And you?'

'I've been…okay too. But, do you know what? I've been in the dark room all day, and I'd really *love* a drink.'

'Would you like a beer?'

He smiled. 'Yes. I'd *love* a beer.' We walked down the hill together, in perfect step, our feet slapping against the tarmacked path. 'Now tell me, how's your birthday been?'

'Rather wonderful, actually. And it's getting better all the time.' We turned into the Mews, and now I was unlocking the door, and there on the chaise longue was the newspaper. David picked it up.

'That's quite a story, isn't it?'

'It is,' I replied feelingly. 'It's an amazing story.'

'Imagine hiding something like that.'

But he's been hiding so much more. 'Do you really want a beer?' I said. 'You could have a gin and tonic instead, or a glass of wine, or…' I opened the fridge and saw Jimmy's bottle of vintage champagne. 'We could drink *this*.' I held it up and David looked at it.

'Pol Roger *1987*? Don't you want to keep it for some special occasion?'

'This *is* a special occasion. You have no idea quite *how* special it is.' I got down two glasses and opened a carton of olives, while David twisted the cork. As the champagne foamed slightly over the rim, I saw the overflowing Jacuzzi again, and felt a sudden stab of desire for David which made my soul ache.

He raised his glass. 'To you, Miranda. Happy Birthday. It's so nice to see you again.'

'It's nice to see you too. I didn't think...you'd want to.'

'I didn't think I would either—at first. I needed...' he stopped, then shrugged. 'I needed a bit of time. That's all. To think about everything. It was a bit of a shock, to put it mildly.'

'I know...'

'I needed to process it, I suppose. To go into my dark room and develop it, until I could see it all properly. And two things happened which helped me do that. Do you want to know what they were?'

'Only if you want to tell me.'

'I got your letter—and that made me think. Then, a few days later, Daisy came to see me.'

'*Did* she? But I had no idea she'd done that.'

'I know you didn't. She got my number from my website and called me, and we met for a drink. And she told me that everything you'd said to me was absolutely, one hundred per cent true. She told me how tormented you'd been.'

'I was.'

'And she told me how much you'd liked me.'

'I did.'

'*Did?*'

I smiled. '*Do.*'

'Then she said one particular thing, which I kept thinking about afterwards, over and over. She said that the point was, that you didn't *have* to come and find me. No one made you. You could have just let it lie—especially after so long. Then I began to realize how true this was, and how awful it must have been for you. And what it had cost you—the whole sad story—and then my attitude changed.' I stared out of the window. 'I realized then how much you must have suffered.'

I felt my eyes fill. 'I *did*, David. I *did* suffer. And did Daisy tell you who was responsible for it all?'

'No. I asked her, but she said she couldn't reveal it without your permission.'

I glanced at the newspaper. 'Do you still want to know?'

'Of course I do. I've wanted to know for sixteen years.'

'And what will I do, when I tell you?'

'What will I do? Well, what *would* I do? The law doesn't allow me to go round and beat him up.'

'No. But you could sue him, if you wanted, even now. Although, he's been punished recently—in other ways.'

'Has he?'

'Oh *yes.*'

'Really? So who was it?'

'Okay, then. I'll tell you.' And so I did.

'James Mulholland,' David said wonderingly as he gazed at the newspaper. '*This* guy? You're *kidding!*'

'I'm not.'

His eyes skimmed over the page. 'It says he read Biochemistry at Sussex.'

'Yes. His name was Jimmy Smith then.'

'So he knew my dad?'

'He was in his microbiology set. That's what it was all

about. Your father failed him in two papers in his finals, as a result of which…well…he didn't do quite as well as he thought he should have done. So he decided to take revenge. He said he didn't intend any serious harm to your dad—he just wanted to give him a nasty shock. But he lied about his degree—because he wanted to be seen as a high-flyer—and couldn't bear people to know the mediocre truth. And *that's* why he's now got the sack.'

'Because he got found out?'

'Yes. With my assistance, actually.' David gave me a quizzical look. 'I knew the reporter,' I explained, 'and a few days ago, I gave him a little…hint about Jimmy's qualifications, and he clearly got digging.' I opened the drawer, and took out the tape. 'This is a recording of a meeting I had with Jimmy last week, at the House of Commons, in which, unwittingly, he virtually admitted everything. You can have it, if you like.' I handed it to him. He shrugged, then put it in his pocket. 'Don't you want to hear it?'

'Not now. Maybe later. It's okay. Good champagne this,' he added.

'Yes,' I smiled. 'And today's the *perfect* day for drinking it. Because today, you and I are both *free*. We're free of what happened.' I felt so liberated I wanted to throw back my head and laugh.

'So where shall we go, then?' said David. 'To celebrate our freedom—and your birthday?'

'I really don't know.'

'How about Odettes? Or Lemonia. Or do you want to go somewhere near me? Not the St John restaurant again, obviously. Unless you fancy pigs' testicles.'

I smiled again. 'Can't say that I do.'

'Or we could have supper on my terrace—I've got some smoked salmon in the fridge—we could get some salad and some nice bread.' He stood up. 'So what do you feel like doing?'

'Let's go to The Engineer. It's only a short walk, and they've got a nice courtyard with those umbrella gas-heaters. It's rather romantic.'

'That sounds fine to me.'

I settled Herman on his beanbag, and then we left. As we strolled out of the Mews, my mobile phone rang.

'Miranda! Happy Birthday!' It was Daisy. 'I'm sorry I didn't ring you before. But I've been so busy today, and the signal's not been great.'

'You do sound crackly—I can hardly hear you.'

'That's because I'm twelve hundred feet up!' In the background I could hear the motorbike chug of the microlight. 'I'm *soaring!*' she yelled. 'I'm on a *high!* The sunset's so gorgeous—look up!' So I did. And it was. A fiery red, promising another sunny day. And now I could hear a distinct yapping in the background.

'Is that who I think it is?'

'It is. Twiglet's up here too. He's tucked into my jacket, while Marcus pilots. He absolutely loves it—don't you, Twiggers?'

'*Yap, yap!*'

'He's got his own goggles—he looks so sweet. Thanks for your advice, Miranda,' she giggled. 'You were absolutely right. Natalie's dumped Marcus.'

'Really?' I was delighted, but hardly surprised.

'But Marcus says he doesn't mind because she's allergic to him—but I don't know what he means by that.'

'I do. I'll tell you some other time. And thank you for *your* advice,' I said with a laugh.

'Say hi to David!'

'I will. Hey—how do you know he's here?'

'Because, well, somehow, I just *do*.'

And now David took my hand in his, and we strolled down Gloucester Avenue, past the railway bridge, at the end of which we saw a green dustcart trundling slowly up the road its amber lights flashing. David suddenly walked towards it.

'What are you doing, David?' He didn't reply. Instead, he put his hand in his pocket and took out the cassette I'd given him, pulled back his arm, and threw it into the back.

'Are you sure?' I asked him.

'I'm sure.' *The rarer action is in virtue than in vengeance.* 'What's the point of trying to punish the guy? It looks like he's been punished enough—and, in any case, I've had quite a life, because of him. I would never have become a photographer if he hadn't done what he did. I would have become just another GP. Instead of which, I've been all over the world and I've seen incredible things. It did change my life, Miranda—for the worse to begin with, and then quite possibly for the better.'

And now I thought of Alexander again. Maybe the fact that I'd forgiven him had somehow brought David back to me, as though one act of reconciliation had begotten another. *As you from crimes would pardoned be*…David held my hand. *Let your indulgence set me free.*

'We'll have to do some nice things,' he said. 'I'm not going to be travelling quite as much from now on.'

'That's good.'

'We could go away at weekends.'

'Hmm.'

'We could play tennis. That would be fun, wouldn't it?'

'Yes—not that I'm much good.'

'And we could go ice-skating again. Now you'd like *that*, wouldn't you?'

'I would, but...'

'But what?'

'I'll *fall*.'

'No you won't,' David said. 'You won't fall. Because I'll hold you, Miranda. I'll hold onto you.'

I looked at him, then reached up and kissed his cheek. 'Yes,' I said quietly. 'I think you will.'

★ ★ ★ ★ ★

ACKNOWLEDGEMENTS

I am indebted, as ever, to my brilliant agent, Clare Conville, and to my wonderful editor, Lynne Drew. I would also like to thank Rachel Hore for the additional editorial guidance she provided. Without these three women, there would have been no book.

I am also very grateful to animal behaviorists Roger Mugford, Emma Magnus, Fiona Redworth, Sarah Whitehead and to Celia Haddon, whose website on pet problems, celiahaddon.co.uk, was a very useful resource. For background on life as a vet, I'd like to thank Russell Horton of the Canonbury Veterinary Practice; I'd also like to thank Meg Henry for inviting me to her puppy parties there.

Steve Waxman of The Main Event kindly gave me the lowdown on life as a party planner, and Richard Simmonds of Golf International patiently answered my questions on golf.

For my extensive research into llamas, I'm extremely grateful to Steve Young of Southdown Llama Trekking, and for their detailed explanations of the art of photography I'd like to thank Joe Cornish and David Mossman.

For political background, I owe a debt of gratitude to

George Jones, political editor of the *Daily Telegraph*, and to Patricia Constant. Any inaccuracies are entirely my own.

Geoff Finchley, A & E Consultant at Barnet Hospital, provided me with very useful information about skin grafts and burns. I'm also grateful to Ben Buttery of London Zoo, and to Joy and Martin Cummings of Amberley Castle, who would like me to point out that although they themselves are animal lovers, dogs are not actually welcome at the hotel.

As usual, I would like to thank my father, Paul, for his very helpful feedback along the way, and I am very grateful too, to Louise Clairmonte, Ellie Haworth and Katy Gardner, who all helped me in different ways.

I am *profoundly* grateful to everyone at HarperCollins for the wonderful job they do, for their friendship, for the unflagging support they give me and for their very touching enthusiasm for my books. I would like, in particular, to thank Amanda Ridout, Nick Sayers, Fiona McIntosh, Maxine Hitchcock, Sarah Walsh, John Bond, Venetia Butterfield, Jane Harris, Martin Palmer and James Prichard. For polishing my prose with such skill and sensitivity, I am indebted to Jennifer Parr.

Finally, I would like to thank Greg, who has helped and encouraged me throughout the writing of this book, which I dedicate, with much love, to him.